Another Life

JODIE CHAPMAN

PENGUIN BOOKS

PENGUIN BOOKS

UK | USA | Canada | Ireland | Australia
India | New Zealand | South Africa

Penguin Books is part of the Penguin Random House group of companies
whose addresses can be found at global.penguinrandomhouse.com

First published by Penguin Michael Joseph 2021
Published in Penguin Books 2022
001

Typeset by Jouve (UK), Milton Keynes
Printed and bound in Great Britain by Clays Ltd, Elcograf S.p.A.

The authorized representative in the EEA is Penguin Random House Ireland,
Morrison Chambers, 32 Nassau Street, Dublin D02 YH68

A CIP catalogue record for this book is available from the British Library

ISBN: 978-1-405-94632-2

For Greg
and for
Roman, Remy and Val

Has it ever struck you that life is all memory, except for the one present moment that goes by you so quick you hardly catch it going?

— Tennessee Williams

PART ONE

It didn't work the first time.

My little brother jumped from the window of his Manhattan apartment building on Christmas Eve morning. His body fell seven storeys and landed in a skip filled with four feet of freshly fallen snow. It was the snow that saved him, cushioned the blow. It had drifted down all night and not yet had the chance to solidify. The soft snow was also the reason he wasn't discovered until three hours later, when his cleaning lady walked into an empty apartment and found the window wide open. Seven storeys, four feet of snow and three hours of staring at the sky. Those are some damning odds.

I got the call as London rush hour was about to start. It had been a day of back-to-back meetings in stuffy, windowless rooms. There was little hope of catching a train home before eight, and I thought of the shit storm that would greet me when I walked through the door. But then there was a knock on the glass partition, and Jackie was waving. 'Nick, there's been an incident,' she said as I stuck my head out, and I let the door swing shut as she passed me the phone.

When I walked into the hospital room twelve hours later and saw him hooked up to monitors, a mental image appeared of us as boys: doctor and patient, tying lengths of red wool from Mum's knitting bag around our wrists and attaching them to cardboard boxes. We would recreate the sound effects – long, low beeps, the grave prognosis, a weeping wife. Almost thirty years later, we were playing again. Except the beeps were real and nobody was crying.

'You look like shit.'

I nodded. 'Where's Tilly?'

He turned to stare out the window. 'We broke up.'

He'd shattered the lower half of his spinal cord, they said. He was paralysed from the waist down and lucky to be alive. He'd never walk again. The doctor reeled them off like a shopping list.

I took each one like a bullet.

When he was finally ready to leave, I brought him back to his place and set up his new bed in the lounge. It had the best view in the apartment, which meant it didn't face a brick wall and the poky windows into other lives. I remembered how he loved to look at the sky when we were young. We'd spend summers lying in the fields behind our house, hidden in long grass, racing planes the way you do raindrops on car windows.

Here, if I angled his bed a certain way, he could look through a gap between skyscrapers and see a patch of blue. So that's what I did.

I stayed for nearly four months. Sometimes we watched TV or played cards, sometimes we sat in silence as if waiting for something to happen. I didn't leave unless his cleaning lady was there to take my place. I'd thought of cancelling her in the first few days, but Gloria quickly became my lifeline, a chance for a breath of fresh air, and to look at something other than my rapidly fading brother.

I learned to weigh everything up. I locked the windows and opened one only when standing right by it. There was the issue of fire safety, but a mental-risk assessment decided there was a smaller chance of burning alive than a repeat of the incident. I threw out my razor and grew my first beard in almost a decade. Belts were banished, knives removed, all headaches endured. I was taking no chances.

I kept his phone away, on the side or in the kitchen. He asked for it rarely, but I kept it charged in case he changed his mind.

At least once a day, his phone would vibrate with a call from Tilly. He made no attempt to answer, and after a few weeks, I switched it to silent. She'd appear, looking at me over a coquettish bare shoulder, like a waifish *ingénue* – knowing Tilly, she chose the picture – and I'd watch it and hate it and think about smashing it. But I'd just let it ring off.

One evening, after a particularly bad day in which he hadn't uttered a word, I snatched the shaking phone from the kitchen table and turned away from the door to the lounge to answer.

'What?'

'*Mon amour.* Oh, my sweet, poor Salvatore.' The sound of her accent cut deep into the silence of the past month.

'It's his brother.'

'Oh.' She paused. 'Is Salvatore there?'

'He doesn't want to speak to you, Mathilde.' I knew how she hated her name.

'Tell him I miss him.'

I thought about throwing her voice out the window. Let the snow cut her off. 'Anything else?'

'Tell him . . . tell him I am lost without him . . .' I heard the crunch of her rosary beads against the mouthpiece and imagined her cocking the phone against her shoulder as she readjusted her hair in a mirror. 'Tell him I broke it off with Chet as I could never love anyone like I love my Salvatore. Will you tell him that, darling?'

'Mathilde?'

'Hmm?'

'Please don't call again.' I threw down the phone and swore under my breath, waiting for the sound of my name, but nothing came but silence.

As the cold began to ease, the city took on a certain softness. The trees that lined the concrete avenues began to bud, and people in the streets shrugged off their coats and layers. Everyone on the outside seemed to relax into the spring. Inside, Gloria and I remained on guard.

There was a shift in conversation a few days into April. It was my fault, my stupid desire for connection.

In the used section of a bookshop on the corner of 12th and Broadway, I found a small collection of poems by Longfellow. I couldn't get back to the apartment fast enough.

'Remember this one?' I handed him the book and pointed to the title at the top of the page. *The Children's Hour.* 'How Dad would almost act it out? We could never sleep afterwards.'

Sal looked at the page and said nothing.

'Well?' My excitement was the only light in the room.

'Why do you always want to remember things?'

I made beans on toast for dinner. I'd got pretty good at cooking over the winter, using the time inside to experiment with food and bring a sort of recklessness to the endless days. There was a posh version of ratatouille – I used pre-chopped vegetables, for obvious reasons – and I mastered the art of the soufflé. But that night, just like him, I made no effort. I couldn't form my anger into words so I served it to him instead, and I set the tray down on his over-bed trolley table with a bang.

He looked up at me in surprise, and I felt a burn of self-loathing.

I woke in the night and heard him cry. I stumbled into the lounge and there he was, propped up on his elbows, staring at his dead legs and sobbing like a baby. His skin was cold and clammy in my arms, his T-shirt soaked through.

'I can't,' he said, his voice breaking like a kid's. 'I can't see her any more. She's there in my head, when I close my eyes. But she never speaks to me, and I just wish she would speak so I can hear her voice again. Where is she?'

I knew he wasn't talking about Tilly.

'I don't know, Sal.'

'Will we ever see her again?'

I shrugged. 'Perhaps. Or not. I don't know.'

Sal always wanted answers. In our early teens, our Aunt Stella got us work experience in her office. It was a company selling insurance and our first job was inputting new clients on to the computer system.

The woman training us, Mandy, had a voice best described as a dirge. She had a mass of permed hair and glasses like bottle-tops, and when she made coffee using water from the tank on the wall, scale would form frothy pools of bubbles on the surface. Sal made a vomiting sound when she made one on our first day. 'You should get that cleaned,' he said, pulling a face. 'Oh no, I love it,' she replied, smacking her lips. 'It's like a cappuccino.'

Mandy would sit and direct us between slurps as we entered information on the screen. Looking back, she can't have been more than forty, but she seemed ancient to us. She'd held her job for decades and was clearly very satisfied with it. Her hamster cheeks wobbled

6

with delight at the modicum of power she held over us. 'Enter the name, select the prefix from the dropdown, then click "next". Enter the address, put the postcode in the box marked "postcode", tick the little box, then click "next". Then—'

'But why?' said Sal.

'Why what?'

'The little box. Why do we tick that?'

Mandy frowned. We could sense the cogs turning. 'You just do.'

'Does it set something off in the background?' he said, tapping his fingers. 'What's the purpose of the tick? The box? I mean, *why* are we ticking it? And what happens if we don't?'

She squirmed in her chair, uncomfortable at being taken off-script. 'I-I don't think it really matters why. I just know that's what you do. It's never been left unticked.'

Sal was deliberately avoiding my look. He gave a long, bored sigh and spun his chair back round to face the screen, 'Fine, whatever. I just think we should know the reason.'

That was the only time Sal ever worked in an office. But the asking of the why never ceased.

'Tell me about her,' he said now, gripping the sheet. 'I'm starting to forget the details and I can't. Tell me what you remember.'

I drew back. 'I don't know what you want me to say.'

'The truth. I want the truth. Please.'

I swallowed. 'I tried to talk about Dad earlier—'

'He's not the one I want. He's not the one you want either. Why can you never talk about the things that matter?'

I looked out at yellow headlights cavorting in wild lines across the road. Neon flickered in the gloom. On the other side of locked windows, the world continued on.

Sal rubbed his eyes with the backs of his hands. 'I need to see her again. I'm done waiting.' He gestured at the shape of his legs under the sheet. 'What is there left for me now?'

'You know she loved you,' I said after a while. I sat on his bed and faced the dark city, alight with a thousand bulbs. 'And you know it wasn't your fault. These things just happen.'

Sal looked at me like I was a fool.

'Do you still not get it after all these years?' he said. 'It was all my fault. I'm the reason why.'

If I had known that would be the last time, I'd have pulled him close and hugged his cracked legs and warm heart. I'd convince him that there was much more to come, spout some shit about the future being brighter, and drill locks on every cupboard door.

But what happened is this.

I fell asleep curled up at the end of his bed, and when in the morning Gloria arrived as usual, I took a shower and decided to walk the fifteen blocks to the bakery on Spring Street to get the little cakes Sal loved. As I passed through the lounge, I could see him asleep on the bed, his hair pale in the morning sun.

Outside, New York was picking up heat. I crossed the road to walk in the shade and passed two girls of about nineteen, one laughing at something the other had said. They wore summer dresses and their shoulders were bare, and as I turned my head to look at them, I thought how life was a mixture of sad and beautiful and there was nothing you could do about it.

My phone rang as I walked back from the bakery. It was a little after 8 a.m.

A courier had buzzed the apartment with a delivery and refused to climb all seven floors for a signature. Knowing it was some urgent papers I'd been awaiting from work, Gloria had done a quick check of the windows and slipped out. She was gone no longer than six minutes, she said.

In that six minutes, my little brother threw himself off his bed, pulled his broken body along the carpeted floor to the galley kitchen, where he opened the door to the sink cupboard and unscrewed the cap and swallowed what remained of a bottle of bleach.

I've thought of that final day often. Of my foolish excitement at the book of poems and a shared memory, of his face when I gave him his tray, and then I always remember that, for his last supper, I made bloody beans on toast.

★

I know people love New York.

I know it's a place that exists within everyone, in Christmas movies from childhood, in Bob Dylan and all those dead Beat poets, in Sal who came on a holiday visa and never left, and in others who talk of returning. Even people who've never been feel like they know it. I admit that I used to think about going, of taking off for City Hall, of holding hands in the streets, of loving it because she did. When I imagined myself there, it was always with her and as if I had won somehow.

But my first visit there was a rescue mission, and when I left, it was with my brother in a box. I had failed, and it felt like the city had failed me too.

I know people love New York.

I hate it.

Anna

2003

I met her at the beginning of summer. She wore dresses with thin straps that cut into her shoulders, and I'd watch her body when she wasn't looking. It was a game I'd play in my head. I'd repeat the mantra, *don't look at her chest, don't look at her chest*, so I'd look at her lips instead. That seemed less creepy, somehow. But her body . . . the way her dress skimmed her body.

I know I should say it was the blossom. That I recall the season because of scattered blossom left over from spring. But whom do I kid. It's the dress and her body in the dress.

Fuck Keats. Every man is the same. We don't remember blossom.

Late Eighties

They say you begin to forget.

An event occurs and your brain records the details, then over the years, the picture fades until you only retain an outline. With Mum, it was the opposite. At first, when she disappeared, she went from my mind too. I guess I blocked the memories out for obvious reasons – self-preservation, perhaps – but as I grew up, there were times when they'd come flooding back. It was as if they had been locked away for safekeeping, until I was old enough to handle the pain.

Some were linked directly to my senses. I'd hear a song or walk down a certain street, and a switch would flick as it came back to me. I'd go very still and tease the memory out, and hope imagination would take care of the rest.

Mainly it's a feeling or a sound.

Let me explain.

I remember the skin on her fingers, how it was rough to the touch like a bandage. Her hands were dry from the water and soap of the endless washing-up we gave her, and there were little tufts of bitten flesh around her nails. Sometimes she would cup my face with her hands, and the sound of her skin on mine was like scratching.

Sal told me once that his strongest memory was playing with her hair.

She would sit in the pale green armchair that was covered with birds and flowers – the one she and Dad had bought from Harrods with their wedding money – and then she'd let down her golden hair. Sal and I pretended to be hairdressers, taking turns to brush and fill her curls with slides. 'Fix me up, boys,' she'd say as she settled into the chair. 'Make me look pretty tonight.' Her hair was thick and warm, and with every stroke of the brush, strands would fall to the ground. I wish I'd cut a lock and put it in an envelope, the way some parents do when they first cut a child's hair. For the future act of remembering.

And sound.

One time, she sat on a bench and watched as we played on a climbing frame in the town centre. The concrete slabs shone from the morning rain. I was doing the monkey bars, and they must have been wet because I slipped and fell and twisted my ankle. As I lay clutching my foot, she came running towards me. It's hard to describe, that particular sound of her leather shoes on the damp ground, but it was like a wet, polished knock. About five years later, I was walking out of school and a girl ran past me. She must have been wearing the same kind of shoes and it must have been raining, because her feet made the exact same sound as she ran.

I remember putting my fist to my mouth and the cold taste of blood on my tongue.

And Dad.

Dad would pile us into the car every Christmas and drive around the neighbourhood for a look at the decorations. Mum would make a flask of hot chocolate and we'd cruise slowly down the streets, enamel mug in hand, each turning to gaze and coo through our windows. There wasn't much spare money then, and Dad couldn't see the point of taking a Saturday off from golf or watching a game to untangle miles of fairy lights. 'You see them best from the street anyway,' he said once. 'What's the point in wasting time and money on a view for the neighbours, when we can tour all of theirs for free?' I guess it did make sense.

Council estates were always first class at cheese. They went over and above. 'Don't know where they get the money,' Dad would sniff, before shouting, 'Look, sons!' at a giant inflatable Santa.

We always saved the cul-de-sac until last. It was at the back of a sixties close, a long and straight run with boxy detached houses either side. At the end was a large bungalow that could be seen from the moment you turned into the street. Every year, it was the best in show. Legend was that a childless elderly couple lived there, and every December they decorated their house so kids would make a pilgrimage. They wanted to be remembered, even if only in the minds of other people's children.

'Are you ready, Sal?' Dad would call as he signalled to turn. Sal was always beside himself with joy. I don't know whether it was because we were approaching the house or because Dad had singled him out.

An enormous fir tree stretched up to the top of the telegraph poles, wrapped in fairy lights that flickered. There was the usual stable scene in the middle of the lawn, and scattered around was an audience of green and red elves wearing curled shoes. Above the garage was a giant Father Christmas aboard his sleigh, with bells and presents and a rushing Rudolph. Candy canes lined the path, a snowman stood guard by the door, and in every window were lights of all different shapes and colours. White lights were stapled along the outline of the building, around windows and doors, and if you stared long enough and shut your eyes, an imprint of the house remained. Whenever Sal or I drew a house on paper, it always took the form of the bungalow at the end of the cul-de-sac, the one with all the lights. I wonder if he ever forgot it, like I never did.

I have a memory of Mum sitting up close to Dad with his arm slung around her, the other holding the wheel. They sit on a leather bench seat, the type in fifties cars, and she rests her head on his shoulder. His collar is turned up, and he nods his head along to the sound of Christmas songs from the radio. Their skin is young.

But we never had a vintage car, and when I asked him years later, Dad said he'd never had a bench seat. Perhaps it came from an album cover, this memory, or an old movie, or a dream I once had. Still, I remember this scene in my head and could swear on a holy book that it happened, just as I can still recall the crunch of tyres on snow and the smell that would waft out when I'd open a tin of Quality Street on Christmas Day morning.

I'll always hope it happened as I remember it did.

Anna had a boyfriend when I met her. Or she did at first. Apparently he'd taken off for the summer to Australia, but the details were hazy and I never actually asked. A few of the girls talked once in the staffroom about how they'd never actually seen her with him. One said she doubted his existence. Her friend Lisa had shut them down. 'They're on a break,' she said and refused to divulge the reason. 'But he does exist.'

She wasn't someone who'd care what they thought. I noticed that straight away. I also noticed how she introduced herself to me on my first shift. Even in the unflattering cut of the cinema uniform, she was not someone your eye would pass over. Some of the girls described her looks as crooked, and there was a certain strangeness to her face, a boldness and strength in the way the bones formed behind her alabaster skin. There was nothing petite in how her features knitted together. I'd never seen another face like hers and the subject of her attractiveness would provoke great debate in the staffroom whenever she left it. I never got involved. She looked just fine to me.

We were propping open the double doors to a sold-out showing. I forget which film. As the end credits began, we each stood against a door, waiting for the audience to file out between us. 'Hi, I'm Anna,' she said, putting a hand out for me to shake. 'You're new, aren't you?'

I think I mumbled as I took her hand. Not many nineteen-year-olds were in the habit of handshakes or introductions, but like I say, she was different. I don't recall how I got her number, but life is made of small victories you forget.

The next shift, we were on a break in the staffroom together. I walked into the windowless room to find her at the table, drinking water and reading a book. She gave a brief smile and returned to the pages. A lad named Dave walked in and began describing a girl he'd just served and all the things he would do to her. When Anna didn't look up, he changed tack, declaring books a waste of time in the age of the internet. Still, Anna ignored him. What do you like in a bird? he said to me, then proceeded to list the attributes he found appealing: big tits, redheads, dirty but not slaggish. I shrugged and said I didn't really have a type, but I liked girls with a brain. Ah yeah, that sexy-librarian thing, said Dave, leaning back in his chair. Do her so hard over a pile of books that her glasses fall off. He sniggered. Yeah, not so much that, I said. More the reading of the books themselves. Anna had looked at me then.

You know she won't shag you, right? they said. We've all tried. Total virgin territory.

Anna belonged to one of those religions that look down on anything normal. Christmas, birthdays, getting drunk, sex before marriage – all off limits. Her boyfriend belonged to this club too. I suppose some might call it a cult, but I don't want to go that far. Each to their own and all that. Sometimes they put leaflets through my door. Last week, I picked one up from the doormat and looked at it hard for a moment, then crushed it into a ball. I squeezed all the air out of it and made it as small as I could before dropping it into the bin.

We didn't talk much at first. We'd be assigned to work Floor together and go into a screen at the end of a film to clear away the popcorn bags and cups. The credits would still be rolling as we cleaned up in the dark. On busy showings, there would be a few of us, sweeping away the remnants of people before others took their place. A couple of the lads would sing along to the credits or play baseball with their broom and an empty cup. They usually did this when there was a girl around. Anna didn't engage much with their efforts apart from the giving of an occasional smile. She kept herself to herself.

On the first hot weekend at the start of that summer, though, everything changed.

A few were going to spend the afternoon at the ruined church in Eastwell, hanging out and swimming in the lake. Anna would be there with Lisa, Dave said. Maybe a couple of the other girls would come too. He asked if I wanted to join them and I said I'd see what I could do.

Eastwell wasn't far, so at mid-afternoon on the Sunday, I took out the cold beers I'd bought after my previous shift and put them in a bag, then walked across the fields towards the church. The journey usually took fifteen minutes, thereabouts, but that day had a sticky heat that clung to the scalp. I took it slow. A car passed by on the way, elbows leaning from every window, a chart topper blasting through the speakers. I recognised it as Lisa's car and wondered if any of the elbows had been Anna's.

The church was a fifteenth-century ruin, abandoned and surrounded by gravestones whose inscriptions were too crumbled to read. People said it was haunted. I'd come here once as a kid. Sal and I had jumped from grave to grave, making out details of the dead.

I heard them all before I saw them.

Two cars were parked under the trees and they were all sprawled out on the grass by the lake, half naked, shrieking at some joke. The sun was high in a cloudless sky and the water shone like glass.

One of them saw me and waved, and they all turned to look. I rubbed my head and gave a sort of nod in reply. She wasn't there.

Lisa was shouting at Dave. She had an open tube of suncream in her hands and white streaks along her arms where she had yet to rub it in. He'd thrown a handful of grass over her and the blades were sticking to her skin. She was telling him off and he was drinking a Red Bull and laughing. The rest of them were laughing too. She wasn't there.

I took a can from the plastic bag and offered it around. One of the girls reached out to take it and smiled as her fingers brushed mine. She pushed out her chest and crossed and uncrossed her legs. I took my own can and went down towards the water.

I tried not to think about why she hadn't come.

It was a large lake surrounded by trees and a little bridge. The water further out looked dark and thick with weeds. Closer to the edges it was a softer blue, although it was impossible to know the depth without stepping in. There were gentle ripples on the surface of the water and the wobbling line of my own reflection.

'Jump,' said a voice.

I turned and saw Anna in the water, out of view of the grass against a pile of rocks. The bottom half of her body was obscured beneath the lake.

I smiled and raised my can. 'I would, but . . .'

'I can wait,' she said. 'Although, I am thirsty.'

She launched herself from the rocks and floated towards me, and I bent down and passed her the can. I watched her take a long sip and saw how black her hair looked when wet.

'Thanks,' she said, handing it back. 'Now drink up.'

I nodded at the water. 'Is it deep?'

She gave a smile and a quick lift of the eyebrows. 'Jump in and find out,' she said, pushing her feet against the bank so that she drifted away.

I stood and watched the lake for a while. I tried to ignore her as she floated on her back, keeping my gaze fixed somewhere in the distance, but the sun kept catching her skin. She wore a red-and-white striped bikini. Her eyes were closed.

When I'd finished my beer, I dropped it on the bank and pulled off my T-shirt and shoes. Anna watched as I put one foot in the water, then the other.

'Funny way of jumping,' she called from further out.

My smile contorted as the cold water edged up my body. I buried my instinct to scream by sinking under the surface so that I went completely under. It wasn't deep, four feet perhaps, but through the cloudy water, a jungle of weeds choked the ground.

I swam until I was close to her, then it felt right to show my face. She was treading water, her chin bobbing on the surface, a strange smile on her lips.

'Do you know what happened to the church? Why it looks like that,' she said, nodding at the broken stone walls rising up through the trees in the distance.

I turned to see, despite already knowing how it looked. I willed myself to stop burning. 'There was a fire,' I said finally.

I brushed the water from my face and smoothed my shaved head with my palm. Anna was just outside of touching distance.

'You don't talk much,' she said, looking at me.

A piercing human shriek spread out across the lake and sent a trio of geese flapping from the bank. They flew across the water over our heads. We watched them disappear above the trees on the other side.

I raised my eyebrows. 'Why speak unless you can improve the silence?'

'I never said I didn't like it,' she said, turning to float on her back.

'A-nn-a!' The long holler of a male voice carried across the lake.

She waved at the bank.

'You're needed,' shouted the voice, and she gave a thumbs-up in reply.

'Wait for me. I'll come back,' she said and swam past, brushing her foot against my leg in the invisible world beneath.

The next Monday, we all went into town after work to the local club. Everyone went out almost every night back then. Friday, Saturday, and Monday when drinks were cheap and the air reeked of karaoke. I don't know how we had the energy, how we'd work all day and go out all night, but there's no looking back at that age. All of life is ahead.

We sat on the white vinyl banquette seating, her leaning back, me leaning forward, everyone else dancing. I remember the music – some hideous garage mash-up – and the flashing lights on the dance floor, and in the darkness I took her hand. For three minutes, we looked at each other, and by the time the song had ended, we were walking up the hill towards town.

When we reached the deserted car park behind Blockbuster's, she stopped and said, I'm not going any further until you do. Once, in later years, we argued as to who made the first move. *You* kissed *me*, she insisted. I remember it perfectly.

We remember how we want to remember.

Early Nineties

After she'd gone, they packed up Mum's things. One day it was all there, and the next it wasn't. Just like her.

When we were small, Sal and I would play hide and seek around the house. I'd stand at the bottom of the stairs, cover my face with my hands and count to twenty. The house we lived in was a big old place, Victorian, with tall ceilings and dusty corners. It had been a rectory, once upon a time, then left to descend into a slow rot. Dad worked for the owner, doing odds and sods around the estate, and we lived there on a reduced rent. It felt like a mansion to us.

I'd count with long pauses to give Sal time to hide, and then I'd climb the stairs. He always went to the same place, but I'd make a big show of wondering where he'd gone, lifting the heavy flocked curtains that hung at the windows and opening every cupboard. I'd search the whole upstairs until finally I reached Mum and Dad's door. I'd push it open and bide my time circling the room, checking the surfaces to see what had moved since yesterday. A little stack of sewing on her desk, a new book open on the bedside table, a forgotten cup of water. I was fascinated by the glass pots on her dressing table, how the sun would strike through the curtains and light them up like a shrine.

After I'd finished looking, I'd walk to the heavy brown wardrobe and heave open the door. There, behind the folds of skirts and dresses, Sal would be curled into a ball, trying to disappear. I'd climb in beside him and close the door, and we'd lie at the bottom of the wardrobe, Sal running his hands through fabric while I inhaled the scent.

A few weeks after she'd gone, I suggested to Sal that we play hide and seek. I was too old for it by then, but the days were beginning to take forever and we had to do something to pass the time.

I counted and climbed, but when I opened the door, Sal was standing in front of the wardrobe with his arms fixed by his sides. I went over and looked in. The lengths of silk and polyester had been replaced with a dark and empty space. It was then I saw there was nothing. The pots, the books, the sewing. Gone.

We crawled into the wardrobe and shut the door behind us.

Anna and I spent virtually every day together that July. I remember it being hot – so hot – and we'd keep the engine running in her stopped car just to keep cool. We burned through tank-loads of fuel, not to mention a layer of skin on our lips.

You know he comes back in a month, she said once. He said he'd come back in a month.

I'd nodded and kissed her again.

After that, we fell into place. We'd meet up before work, or when one finished a shift, the other took a break and we'd head out to the wall behind the bins. I remember the mix of the scent of her perfume – jasmine, the bottle said – with the stale whiff of rotting chips. Looking back, I wonder why we didn't change location, but we were horny, hungry, young. The bins were close – we'd have wasted time travelling further – and they were private. We just wanted to get on with wanting each other.

Laura and I never kiss like that. Maybe we did in the early days, but not any more. I don't expect it, though. There's a hunger in youth for every experience. Kissing is a new activity and it's free. You couldn't keep up with that hunger, not with twinges in your back and joints that click. I don't expect it now.

There was a heatwave across Europe that summer. One of the warmest for up to five hundred years, they said. The water level of the Danube fell so low that Second World War bombs and tanks were revealed on the riverbed. They'd been there all the time, buried deep under the surface, unexploded, deadly, just waiting to be discovered. Closer to home, parts of the motorway melted away.

The heat always reminds me.

In the beginning, we found every excuse to touch each other. Anna would reach across and open the glove box in her car, leaning on my knee as she searched for a CD. I'd brush an invisible strand of hair from her cheek. Or we'd lie in the park and she'd put an earphone to my ear and press play on her iPod.

We spent two nights together. I knew she had a curfew, so it must have been something she'd arranged in advance, probably said she was staying with a friend. I suppose we were just friends. I've spent years working it out.

We were on my bed. An episode of *Fawlty Towers* played on the black-and-white TV across the room, the picture fuzzy from the Sellotaped aerial. She could recite every line, and I leant my head against the pillow and watched her as she laughed.

This moment I remember. She must have realised I was looking, because she smoothed her hair and crawled across the bed and kissed me.

'What do you want from your life?' she said.

I brushed the hair from her face. 'Nobody's ever asked me that.'

'You're kidding.'

'My mum probably did.' I paused. 'I wrote stories as a kid. She liked me to read them out loud, and after I finished she'd always clap and say I had a gift. Mums are biased, though.'

Anna smiled. 'I bet you'd make a wonderful writer.'

This expression of faith was surprising. I had never told anyone about my writing, especially not Daz and the lads who would file it away for future taking-the-piss. 'How about you?' I said. 'What do you want?'

She leant her head on my chest. 'I love to paint,' she said. 'And I'd love to go back to New York one day. I spent three months there last year on a school exchange thing and it's such an incredible place. Let's live in the East Village and be a couple of creative bums together.' She kissed my skin.

I ran downstairs to smoke out front. Are you really going to leave me alone in your room? she'd said, with a conspiratorial widening of her eyes. I did. I left her there, lying on my bed, despite knowing the nicotine kick would do little to quell the buzz. I liked the idea of her being in a space that was solely mine. When I glanced up mid-smoke, she was at the window, looking down. From the way she was leaning, her hand under her chin and her elbows out wide, I could tell her bare knees were on my pillow, and something about this gave me a strange sort of thrill. I smiled and she waved, then drew back. As I stood there and finished, I imagined her looking at my things, taking me in. When I opened the door, she was right where I'd left her.

The first night she spent there, in my room, in my bed, we did nothing. We kissed and spoke and slept. When darkness came, we spent it folded together in my bed for one, her body dressed in my favourite T-shirt.

'How many girls have slept in this bed?' she asked when the sun appeared at an ungodly hour.

I shrugged. 'Does it matter?'

I went on to tell her of a time at uni the previous summer, when a girl had knocked on the door looking for my roommate. He was out but due back later, so I invited her in to wait. Ten minutes later, she was in my bed. The lads had laughed so hard when I'd recounted it in the pub, and they'd slapped my back and bought my next round.

When I finished, she shook her head and turned over to face the wall.

I should not have told her that story.

The second night is much more lucid. I have remembered it many times.

'Where's your dad?' Anna asked as we walked upstairs. 'I've not met him yet.'

'Out,' I said. 'He's always out.'

We lay on my bed, the duvet thrown off. The window was open, but there was nothing in the air but thick July.

'I think I want to cut my hair,' she said.

'Why?'

'And go blonde. Like a Hitchcock heroine.'

'You're crazy,' I said, stroking her leg, pale against my olive skin.

'Would you not want me any more?'

'You have beautiful hair. Why would you do a thing like that to your beautiful hair?'

She placed her palm against mine. 'It grows back. Hair's dead anyway.'

I don't remember peeling off her clothes, but I remember how she looked and how she wasn't shy. She wasn't bare like most girls, and this fascinated me. Even now, I can close my eyes and see her there. Memory is a dangerous game.

At times, there was her and there was me and there was nothing in between.

As we neared the final act, I looked at her and said, 'Are you sure?'

She closed her eyes and nodded, but I knew and stopped.

'You know it's not black?' she said afterwards, draped across my stomach. 'My hair, I mean.'

It must have been about 2 a.m. What had felt like half an hour of touching had actually been three hours. Even now, we couldn't let each other go. I stroked her back with the tips of my fingers, tracing circles on the surface of her skin.

'It looks black,' I said. In the darkness, her hair blended with the shadows.

'Look at it up close in sunshine and you'll see it's dark brown.'

I pulled her up the bed so I could put my arms around her. 'I love it, whatever you want to call it.'

'Have you always shaved yours?' she said, resting on my chest. I imagined the raging beat of my heart against her ear.

I ran a hand across my head. 'I get it cut whenever I'm nervous. It makes me feel better, somehow. Cutting my hair.'

I felt her hands on the backs of my shoulders, her fingers clinging to my skin, and she tensed her grip in reply.

I kissed her hot, wet mouth.

For what felt like months afterwards, I found strands of her long, black hair in my bed.

There's a town like Ashford in every county, I'm sure. Roundabouts leading to roundabouts. The concrete jungle of a town centre, with its high street that eventually curves down a hill towards traffic, some incarnation of a pound shop in the space where Woolworth's used to be, an indoor parade of shops with a glass roof that was touted as 'the face of the future' when its ribbon was cut in the late eighties.

On paper, it's a hot ticket. Grammar schools, a John Lewis, two cinemas, a brewery, the designer outlet, and outskirt villages like Wye where house prices are kept steep by legions of 4x4s and yoga on the green. There's even an international station to take you to Europe. Get on a train and your next stop is Paris.

In reality, I think some people move here and scratch their heads. With its three McDonald's and Champneys spa, it could be called a town still figuring itself out. The new parts thrive while the sixties blocks slump, desperate for interest, even for the wrecking ball of the town planner. The designer outlet draws a crowd, but at the expense of the high street lying half a mile away, choked by a four-lane ring road.

On this ring road is a tiny graveyard, a sliver of land wedged between a square patch of grass and a car park. It's not really a graveyard, though. A few years back, I read that the jam-packed headstones were taken from the adjacent Town Centre Burial Ground when it was redeveloped into an area for relaxation. The council put down a few benches and flower beds and moved the headstones a few feet away into the corner. So now they sit tight up together, out of the way, facing the nineties façade of a bowling alley across lines of traffic while empty benches sit six feet above the anonymous bodies. I sat on a bench once, smoking, listening to the hum of cars and watching the collective smog of exhaust fumes. Everything felt disjointed.

Speaking of graveyards, Anna once took me to Bybrook cemetery to hunt for the grave of a dead philosopher called Simone Weil. It took our whole lunch hour to find a simple square slab of granite on the ground, a name and dates etched into the stone. We stood in front of it, silent, the multiplex where we worked rising a few metres away on the other side of the fence. 'She didn't know whether to believe in God,' Anna said, staring at the grave, 'because she said nothing could be known either way.' I just nodded. I didn't reply that I only recognised her name because it was the same as the four-lane A-road that led to Sainsbury's.

As kids, we lived in a village on the edge of town. It was quiet and rural with trees lining the roads and a village green where they played cricket at weekends. But nobody from out of town ever knew the name of the village, so whenever people asked where I was from, I always just said Ashford.

I moved away once to university, up north, where I made tea wrong and got labelled a southern softie. *There's no 'r' in bath, y' know.* They were right, I suppose. I do make shit tea.

I toyed with the idea of not returning. Manchester was cheap and there seemed to be an acceptance of the different ways that people chose to live, and I thought about getting a lackey job at a paper and working my way up. But there was Sal, back in Ashford, and even after three years, I never knew where I was. The rain got to me, too.

That's the thing about Ashford. People moan about it and some do leave and begin anew, but for those that stay, there's a comfort in knowing the street names and short cuts and the faces in the pub.

Some of us aren't made to start again.

It all had a fairly unremarkable beginning.

I say 'it' like our family was an object. Deliberately made. To be handled with kid gloves. But families aren't really like that, are they? They grow, one at a time, and not always on purpose. Someone settles, a condom splits, and life jerks off down a new path. Or maybe it fixes a thread around the torso and drags you, and you kick and fight, but few have the strength to change their stars.

But families should be handled with care. Because, as I know, they have a tendency to break. Perhaps if we mummified ourselves with that postal tape they wrap round cardboard boxes, transparent with FRAGILE writ red in screaming letters, perhaps then people would have no excuse to say *You take things to heart too much* or *I didn't know how you felt*. They'd have no excuse because it would, quite literally, be written all over your face.

Stop talking in riddles, says Dad in my head. Start making sense.

Late Eighties

Every fortnight, when Arsenal were at home, Dad would drive us up to London in whatever rusty car he'd got his hands on. Sal and I sat in the back with our Walkman headphones fixed to our ears, constantly adjusting our music volume so it couldn't be heard above the sports commentary on the radio. You know the bass of your music gives your father a headache, Mum would say before Dad got in the car. Keep it down low and we'll all have a peaceful trip. Musical bass and the opening of car windows always set him off. *The vibrations!*

Nana and Grandpa lived in a council house in Stoke Newington. It was a sixties box, wedged between other sixties boxes with concrete front gardens and bars on the windows. Grandpa had been mugged countless times on his way back from the casino – he never put up a fight, and if anything would try to engage them in a chat. Somehow he never learned to wear a more modest watch or keep the wearing of jewellery to a minimum. It was there to be enjoyed, he'd say with a raucous laugh. Let them have fun with it.

The pattern of those Saturdays always stayed the same. We arrived late morning to the smell of Nana cooking a roast. Mum would grab an apron and start stirring a pot while Dad kissed Nana and decamped to the lounge with the paper. Sal and I sat at the kitchen table and looked through the Argos catalogue, making mental lists of what we'd like for our next five birthdays. Sal pined for a Scalextric set; he would stare at the picture of the boy playing with the deluxe edition that did figures of eight across the floor. At times, I wondered whether he was looking at the cars and track or if it was the face of the boy that had caught his gaze. What it would be like to be the kid who wanted something and got it.

Sometimes, when no one was looking, we'd sneak a peek at the bra pages.

At midday, Grandpa arrived home in a plume of cigar smoke after a round of cards at the club. Even before he'd shaken off his sheepskin coat and fedora hat, he'd swoop down and envelop Sal and me in an almighty hug, bestowing wet kisses on our hungry cheeks. His scratchy white moustache always left red marks on our skin, and I'd miss the soreness when they faded.

Seed of McCoy, he'd say with a triumphant air. I took this to mean that he was proud of his grandsons.

Stella and Bill often came by on these afternoons. Our uncle was a quiet man with small half-moon glasses permanently fixed to the end of his nose. He said very little and had this strange habit of walking backwards out of the room, slightly bowing, like a butler. He was an odd match for our glamorous Aunty Stel, who whooshed through in her leopard coat with her dyed red hair piled high on her head. It sounds awful, but when Bill died of cancer a few years later, we hardly noticed he'd gone.

After dinner, the men would head off to Highbury. They stood in the kitchen and piled on their layers, Grandpa dominating the scene in his enormous sheepskin and feathered winter hat, and a cigar to his mouth, ready. Dad would be there in his flat cap and leather jacket, the only nod to Arsenal coming from his red-and-white striped scarf. Uncle Bill, though, always went for it. He wore the long-sleeved top from the double winning kit of '71, the red beanie, a candy-cane scarf, and a red padded coat with the club's shield proudly sewn on the pocket. He even had the bumbag. On the rare occasion Dad took me to a game, I'd stand mesmerised each time Arsenal were fouled by the opposition, and my timid uncle would transform into a madman who'd rage at the ref and spend ninety minutes curling his hands into fists.

While the men were at the game, Mum, Nana and Stella sat round the kitchen table, preparing the evening's tea. They sipped gold-label Coke, and Mum and Stella took turns to sit on the counter and lean out the window for a cigarette. Whenever I think of those women together, they always exist in a kitchen. All these years on, I can close my eyes and there they are, peeling spuds and laughing at a filthy joke.

'How's tricks, Sal?' Stella called from the kitchen one time.

'Fine thanks, Aunty Stel,' he replied from where we were out-stretched on the sofa watching *Indiana Jones*. One of our favourite things about Nana and Grandpa was their satellite dish.

'I've told you, less of the aunty. I'm too young for that. Stella's my name and it's the same to you boys.'

'Paul won't have it, Stel,' said Mum.

'You tell my brother I don't give—'

'Stella,' said Nana sharply.

I peeled myself off the sofa and went into the kitchen for a drink.

'Fine,' said Stella, perched on the counter. She was scratching her leg and inspecting a ladder in her tights from her ankle to her knee. 'As always, I'll defer to my elder brother. But honestly, Mum, I think I should be able to choose my own bloody name.' She jammed the end of her cigarette into the ashtray and jumped down. 'And how about you, Nicko? Got a girl pregnant yet?'

'Stella!' Mum this time.

I smiled as my face burned. 'No,' I whispered.

She laughed. 'There's a guilty look if ever I saw one. Mark my words, Lou, this one's going to be keeping secrets. He'll have all the girls running.'

'Yeah,' called Sal from the lounge, ''cept they'll be going the other way.'

'All right, all right,' said Mum. 'Let's leave it there before it starts something.'

'I'm only nearly ten, Aunty Stel,' I said. 'Girls don't know I exist anyway.'

'Just wait,' she said with a confiding wink. 'A few years from now, you'll fall in love and it'll be hell on earth. Best ones always are.'

'Isn't love meant to be a good thing?' I said.

'Sometimes. But when it gets under your skin, that's when you know it's real. When it makes you dizzy and hungry and you can't eat a thing.'

Mum snorted. 'Bill's clearly not having that effect on you.'

'Who said I was talking about Bill?' They screamed with laughter, then Stella turned back. 'Like your mum and dad. I introduced them – did you know that? Your mum and I went to a disco down the precinct.

We got dolled up at her house – remember, Lou? That silver flamenco dress you saved a whole month's wage to get?'

Mum's face shone. 'I loved that dress. And I did my hair like Farrah Fawcett that night.' She slipped an arm around Sal, who'd appeared at the door, and hugged him tight.

'And there were no blokes at the disco. Well, none worth having. A few Mariannes, maybe, but they were hardly going to be interested in us.'

'Mariannes?' I said.

'Never you mind,' said Nana.

'Mariannes, y'know, gays,' said Stella. 'They were fun to dance with, knew all the moves, but they're hardly going to know how to grope for trout in a peculiar river.'

Mum covered her face with her hands. 'Stick to the story, Stella.'

'I knew your mum would be right up your dad's street, so we checked out early and popped into The Red Lion on the way home. I called him over, your ma fluttered her blue eyelids at him, and I knew right away they were meant to be. He didn't even care that she asked him for a Cinzano and lemonade. A right goner, was your dad. Happy for the barman to think him a prat.'

I loved these stories. Stella had the knack of making each time sound like the first time she'd told it, and although we'd heard this one before, Sal and I listened in silent hope for a new detail. Something we could turn over in our minds on the long journey home.

'Tell them about that time with Paul and the jukebox,' said Mum, resting her chin on her hand. I could see she loved listening too.

Sal and I leant in.

'You mean New Year's?' said Stella, lighting another smoke. 'Oh, God almighty. Remember—'

Then came the sound of a key in a lock. The men came in, the women got up, and that was the end of that.

I was in Stoke Newington recently and took a walk down Arundel Grove. The boxy houses still cluster together with TV aerials waving from flat roofs, billowing net curtains, rubbish bins out front. But the bars at the doors have been taken down, and as I walked to the bus stop, I passed café after café with trendy tables out front. A bloke sat with a tiny coffee and laptop, hammering away at keys with no fear of a mugger taking a shine.

Nana and Grandpa and that life are long gone. But the memories never stop playing.

July 2003

'My God, look.'

I was already halfway up the path, key at the ready, hoping Dad was still at work or had stopped off at the pub. When she'd suggested mine as a destination, I assumed Anna was joking, but my nervous laugh was stared down. Now she paused at the gate, realising she'd made a mistake in coming.

'You can head, off, if you like,' I said, looking down at the key in my hand.

'Eh?'

'Have you got somewhere to be? It's fine, if so.'

Her face was creased in my direction, and I sensed the impatience that would flare whenever she didn't get my meaning.

'What are you on about?' she said. 'Where am I meant to be going?'

'I just thought . . .'

'I was talking about those.' She pointed to the three sunflowers at the edge of the driveway. They waved gently in the breeze, all five feet of them, knowing they were being admired.

I nodded as if I'd understood all along. 'Yeah, they're part of the furniture now.'

She waited.

'My Aunty Stella planted them the first summer after Mum went.' My voice caught on the final word. I rushed on. 'She said we needed something to greet us when we arrived home from school, something bright. It was either flowers or painting the front door bright yellow, and I don't think our dad would have taken to that.'

'They're beautiful,' said Anna, looking from me to them and back again. 'Do they work?'

'Work?'

'Do you smile when you see them?'

I stared at the backs of the flowers. They were strong this year.

Already fully blooming, their stalks staunch and proud, their leaves almost touched each other. It was the first time this summer I'd noticed them.

'I guess. Stella replants them each year. It's a tradition she always keeps.' I moved next to Anna and touched the dark centre of one. 'See the middle? When the plant dies at the end of the season, these all dry out and turn to seed. Stella saves a few to go into the ground in spring.'

'So these growing now are descended from the first she ever planted.'

I thought about this. 'There must be good light in this spot.'

'I've never been sure about sunflowers,' said Anna, reaching out to stroke the petals. 'I've only seen them in a vase, or a supermarket, surrounded by plastic. There was something freakish about them. But they look different here. They look right.'

'Only three tend to grow, somehow.'

'*Only* three?'

'She always plants four, but one never makes it. We used to take bets on which it would be.'

I sensed Anna glance up at me.

'I like the sound of your Aunty Stella,' she said, and pushed me gently towards the house.

'How about you?' I said. 'How many have been in your bed?'

It was after the first night. I woke mid-morning when the outside world was heading to desks and climbed over her sleeping body to go down and make a bacon sandwich. When I returned with a plate and a cup of tea, I opened the door and saw her lying there, a bare leg entwined around my duvet. She was awake, her black hair splayed out across my pillow, her eyes studying my room. All these years later, I remember the feel of that bedroom so clearly, and it's because of this picture of her in my head.

Anna didn't answer straight away, but handed me the empty plate and took a sip of murky tea. I sat on the edge of the bed and watched her propped up on an elbow, still wrapped in my sheets.

'You know there's never been any in my actual bed,' she said, licking a spot of ketchup from her wrist. 'You know my situation.'

I nodded. I pretended I knew it all.

'And I don't want to talk about the broken hearts.' She picked at the hem of my Tupac top. She'd casually slipped it on before we finally went to sleep, as I watched the outline of her shadow on my bedroom wall. 'Can we focus on the now?'

'Let me ask you a question.'

She raised an eyebrow.

'What would happen if you were caught in my bed?'

She looked at her hands. 'It wouldn't be an option.'

'Even though nothing happened?'

Anna sat up. 'To you, nothing happened. In my world, this,' she nodded at the crumpled sheets, 'is a shit storm.'

I wish my twenty-two-year-old self had understood what those words meant. That the risk she was running was a declaration of feeling in itself. If I could go back and make him listen, perhaps none of those years would be wasted. They say actions speak louder than words, but don't they also say that youth is wasted on the young? These stupid mottos have all come from someone's regret.

Early Nineties

The three occasions I went to the Arsenal as a boy are etched deep into my mind. I know it was only because someone had dropped out and it was too late to sell the ticket, and it was always someone rubbish like Norwich or Sheffield Wednesday, but when we'd get close to the stadium and the crowds began to thicken, Dad would take my hand and pull me through.

He'd buy the *Gooner* fanzine from the bloke on the corner, and when he disappeared at half-time with the men for a pint at the bar, I'd sit in my seat and read it from cover to cover. On the walk back, we'd share a portion of chips and I'd throw out lines like *Wright's on a losing streak* or *Campbell's useless, just another one of Graham's blue-eyed boys*. Things like that. I don't know whether they were on the money or not, but sometimes Dad would give me a shrug or a sort of smile.

When we turned the corner into Arundel Grove, Sal's face would be there at the net curtains, pushed against the glass. He'd be gone by the time we reached the house, and I'd walk in, laughing with the men. I'd ruffle his hair, he'd mutter *piss off*, and I'd launch into a minute-by-minute recap of the past three hours. It was like living it all over again.

Sal never let on how desperate he was to go. And Dad didn't once offer him a ticket.

Summer 2003

We were very different. I don't really know what it was that drew us together. She hated my music, and I wasn't hugely into the underground guitar scene that she liked. Greasy bands that wore beat-up Converse and shoelaces tied round their wrists. We clearly had different taste in films too, and working at a cinema, there was a lot of that.

I took a part-time post in Projection sometime during that summer, lacing up the reels and starting the films. Not many people wanted to be up there – it was noisy and dark, and many of the staff were teenagers who saw work as another social fix. There was no messing about like you could do behind the concession stand or when cleaning screens. There was an exactness to the job, a skill, and you needed good attention to detail.

'I went up there for a while,' said Anna when I told her I was considering it. 'I spliced together *The Importance of Being Earnest* in the wrong order, and it played for almost a week before anyone noticed. "That's not how it should be," someone said afterwards. "Either they've bastardised Wilde or you've messed up." ' She laughed. 'They kicked me out after that. I didn't care. I felt like a vampire, spending eight hours in darkness.'

I loved the dark. The little flickers of light coming from the windows into the screens, where I would watch the backs of people's heads as they munched popcorn and zoned out. They gave no conscious thought to my existence, but their enjoyment depended hugely on me. There is power in invisibility.

Before it could be shown to the public, every film had to be watched in its entirety; a box ticked on a clipboard when a cigarette burn appeared to show the switch to the next spliced reel. These previews took place late at night, after other films had finished playing and, with teenagers being fairly nocturnal, the screen would be filled with off-shift members of staff.

Anna would often watch them too. If it was a big event movie, there would be loads in there, but the more art-house films weren't much of a draw. Then it was just us.

There was one, *Far From Heaven*, a film set in fifties suburban America about a housewife and her closeted-gay husband. Suppressed emotion, forbidden love. It was too melodramatic for my tastes, and when the lights came up, I made a *pfft* noise and said, 'Well, that's two hours I'll never get back.' Anna had turned to me with a pained expression. 'What are you talking about?' she said. 'It was wonderful.'

Like I said, we were different. We bickered a lot of the time, like an old married couple. She had a teasing side and we would spar, parry, back and forth, until our fingers poked the other's skin and our lips found each other. I liked that we didn't share many interests. It felt more instinctive, our attraction, like it couldn't be explained on paper or matched up by an algorithm. It was something in the air, a feeling, a knowledge. A blue moon.

One week, there was a special Classic Wednesday screening of *Cinema Paradiso*. Anna switched her shift so she could preview it with me on the Tuesday, and, as expected, we were the only ones there.

In the film, an old projectionist works in an Italian cinema and is helped by a small boy from the village. The Catholic priest insists that all scenes featuring nudity and even kissing are cut from the reels before the films are shown to the public. Often they don't then make sense. At the end, after the projectionist has died, the small boy – now a man – returns to the village and is given a reel left for him by the projectionist. He watches it and cries. It is all the censored love scenes spliced together. A memento from another life.

During this scene, Anna reached across the seat between us and took my hand. I looked at her, and in the flickering light, saw her wet cheeks.

It was a beautiful film. The boy's name was Salvatore. I loved it.

The day after *Cinema Paradiso* had played to the public, I took the reels apart and packed them up into their canisters. Before I did, I placed the love scene in the splicer and cut a couple of frames from the print. I wanted one from every kiss, but knowing this could draw attention, I contented myself with two. I cut them carefully, taping the film back together, and slipped the stolen kisses into my pocket.

After my shift, she drove me home and we spent a while curled up on the back seat. When I went to leave, I reached into my pocket and pulled out the frames. She put out her hand when asked and as I gave them to her, I took a mental snapshot of her face and walked quickly past the sunflowers to my door.

I took her to meet the lads a couple of weeks in. It was the typical Sunday afternoon at the usual pub with the regular crowd, and the heat had pushed everyone out to the beer garden.

Part of me had been dreading this moment. I'd thought about it happening, how the conversation might go, the looks exchanged, how the boys would take her, how she'd view them, and in turn, how she'd view me. Perhaps it won't happen, I told myself. Perhaps I can somehow get to the end of my life without this ever happening.

But one night when she dropped me home after a shared shift, when I was getting out of her car after twenty minutes of kissing her, she looked up from the driver's seat and said, 'I want to meet your friends. Make it happen.' And then she sped off.

So two days later, I did.

We walked into the pub in our usual way. Her first, then me ten seconds later. There may be someone passing by, she'd say. Give me time to scan the room, just in case. She'd give me a nod through the window and I'd know it was safe to walk in and stand beside her.

We collected our drinks and she followed me through the double doors to the beer garden. Everyone was there, laughing and smoking, their faces a middling shade of heatwave pink. As we stepped out, a few lads raised their pints in hello.

'Everyone, this is Anna,' I said, taking a seat at the end of a long run of picnic tables. 'Anna, this is everyone.'

She gave a shy smile and sat next to me, tucking her legs in neatly next to mine.

'So this is the famous Anna,' said a voice from behind, and then a hand came between us. 'Delighted to make your acquaintance. Daz.'

Anna took it with an eyebrow raised. 'Oh, I've heard all about you. Pleasure.' She caught sight of the tattoo on his hand: IBIZA spelt out, a letter on each knuckle. 'I'm guessing that was quite a trip.'

'Hope so,' he said. 'It's not 'til November.'

Her eyes widened. 'You've not been but you've had the tattoo? What if it's shit?'

He shrugged. 'We won't let that happen, will we, lads?' He held up his beer and they all gave a cheer.

I filled her in. 'Daz got hammered on New Year's Eve, and in a moment of drunken self-reflection, thought tattooing an upcoming trip on to his hand would mean he entered the millennium in the right spirit. You know, *carpe diem*.'

'Classic,' said Anna, chinking his glass with her own.

'Except Daz broke his leg a week before the trip and everyone had to go without him.' I winked at Daz. 'They're all going again this year, just so the tattoo can mean something.'

Anna laughed then looked at him, embarrassed. 'Sorry. Am I not meant to find it funny?'

'You're fine,' I said, lighting a cigarette. 'We all took the mick, but don't worry, Daz. I have faith you'll make it a good trip.'

'You not going?' said Anna to me.

Daz put down his drink and squeezed my shoulders. I could tell he was trying to bruise the skin. 'Poor Nick's a nervous flyer, aren't you, son? Rather piss himself than go on a plane.'

Then she did something I've never forgotten. Above the table, she reached out and held my hand. We had kissed in the private space of her car, or hidden in dark car parks or shadowy corners. But this was the first time she'd ever touched me in public, and that's how it felt. Public. For everyone to see.

'Careful, Nicolai,' said Daz, waving his cigarette at us. 'Slippery slope.'

'I take it you've not got a girlfriend?'

Something about her use of the word 'girlfriend' made my hand tighten on hers.

'Me?' Daz snorted. 'Men are like bees. Why stick with one flower when there's an entire garden? The goal is to make the honey. You won't make honey if you stick to one flower.'

'I think mosquitoes are a more fitting analogy,' said Anna.

'Eh?' said Daz.

Anna clapped her hands mid-air and wiped a dead insect against the side of the table.

'Sorry,' she said. 'Go on.'

A wedge of ash fell from Daz's fag into his beer, but he was too busy staring at Anna to notice. His mouth hung open like a dumb dog's and she looked up with a smile.

'Rather you than me, lad,' said Daz, patting my back, and headed inside to the fruit machine.

I could tell the lads didn't get her. She could match them in a swear jar, but she had a shyness in certain company that could come across as snobbish. On some days, she'd hold forth in conversation, steering the topic and talking with expert social ease. On others, she sat in silence, listening and offering only a smile. I don't think she knew this about herself, these two conflicting sides she offered the world, or perhaps she did and didn't care. Anyway, who's to say my perception of her was any truer than her own.

But when you watch someone in the company of others, you see them in a whole new way. She could be the girl dancing on tables one night, and the next she'd be hiding in the shadows. Just when I thought I understood her, she would melt away and become a completely new person, and I'd have to start all over again.

That's how it was with Anna.

I've relied on Stella to fill in the gaps over the years.

After it happened, she continued Mum's tradition of taking us for a Happy Meal on our birthdays. We'd outgrown it by then, of course, but Stella insisted. Sal and I would sit in a pink-and-beige booth and wait for her to bring over the tray brimming with Coke and fries, and we'd munch our way through as she told the stories.

One I especially loved was when Mum was turned away from an over-21s night at a bar in the East End. She'd made plans with Dad to meet there a week after that first night, and she and Stella had turned up, all of their nineteen years, only to be turned away by the bouncer. At first, Stella attempted to charm her way past the velvet rope, but when that failed, she turned the air a raging blue. Mum dragged her away round the corner, and when Stella had recovered her poise, Mum calmly pointed to a hole in the chain fence that surrounded the beer garden. Stella refused to enter via any means other than the front door, but Mum picked up her skirt and burrowed her way through the hole. After that, Stella said, there was no stopping her.

I loved this idea of her finding a way. Happy to risk the breaking of rules to get what she wanted. I wish I had some of that.

Summer 2003

'Your friend Daz is quite something.'

We were on my bed. We'd got back from the pub and were watching an old episode of *Only Fools and Horses*. She had her head on my lap as I leant against the wall, and I was acting like it was the most normal thing in the world.

'He doesn't mean it like that.'

'No, that's the kicker,' she said. 'None of you set out to be arseholes. It just comes naturally.'

'Play nicely.'

'What if I don't?' She stroked the hairs on my leg.

'I know it doesn't seem like it, but he's a good bloke. It's just when he's around a girl that he goes into funny dick mode.'

She laughed. 'Maybe it's because all that goes into his mouth are pasties and lager. The guy looks like he's never consumed a vegetable.'

I thought about it. 'You know, I'm not sure he has, unless pasta sauce counts as a vegetable. See, this is why he needs a woman.'

'Eh?'

'To look after him and sort him out.'

She sat up. 'Because that's what a woman's for? To take care of someone who can't take care of himself?'

'That's not what I mean.' I could feel things moving in the wrong direction and I didn't want to go there. 'He just needs the love of a good woman.' Now I sounded like Motown.

'What you mean is he needs a mother.' She flicked her hair over her shoulder.

'No, I don't mean that either.'

'"Male, twenty-two",' she began, mimicking the voice of a Wanted ad. '"Eats shit, drinks shit, talks shit, looking for a hot woman to service all his needs, whether it's good home cooking or daily blow jobs." Sign me up, baby.'

53

I said nothing.

'Maybe women don't want to spend their lives looking after men,' she went on. 'Perhaps they'd like to meet someone who has their shit together. Is that too much to ask? Someone who isn't walking around with a sign that says, "Fix me. I'm a twat. It's because I don't have a woman that I'm a twat. Nothing to do with the fact that the reason I don't have a woman is *because* I'm a twat." '

'That's a pretty long sign. You might convey the message better if you edit it down.'

She turned to look at me, and I wondered if she could see under my skin how fast my heart was beating.

'You're laughing at me.'

'No, I'm not. I'm just trying to defuse this ridiculous situation.'

She stood. 'By laughing at me.'

I put my hands up in surrender. 'Look, I really think this conversation has gone down a crazy road. Let's bring it back somewhere sensible.'

She snatched her bag from where she'd thrown it when we'd walked in half an hour before, when we'd been grabbing and kissing each other.

'You're all the same. You're just looking for another mother. Isn't one enough?' Her face burned as she finished her sentence.

I let the words sit there in the air for a while. 'Yes,' I said. 'Yes, it is.'

She fumbled in her bag for her keys. 'I don't feel great. I shouldn't have come.'

'I'll see you out.'

'Don't bother.' She couldn't get out the door fast enough.

After a minute or so, I heard the slamming of her car door. There was a pause, then she started the engine and was gone.

Two days later, we were working the same shift. We'd not spoken since, and I walked into the building with my headphones on and my eyes to the ground. I knew from the rota that she was on Box Office for the week, and as I walked across the foyer, I sensed her gaze following me.

When I exited the locker room, an arm reached out and pulled me into the adjacent stock cupboard. She shut the door and pushed me against the wall, pressing her body to mine.

'I'm sorry,' she said as she kissed my mouth. 'I'm sorry I said that thing I said. You know.'

I knew.

'You're just so calm all the time,' she said. 'Even when I'm a bitch to you, you're so fucking calm and passive that I can't take it. You make my blood boil.'

I felt the heat of her against me, and something inside just broke. I pushed her backwards on to the sacks of unpopped corn and sensed her body crumple under my weight. It felt good. Her teeth tore at my tongue and I tasted blood as I pulled at her top, feeling my way up her skin.

'Wait,' she breathed in my ear, and my hands went still. I let myself slump against her as I caught my breath and allowed the madness in my body to subside.

When I drew myself up and extended a hand, she took it with a firm grip. We stood there for a few moments, apart, watching the other catch their breath. Then we tucked ourselves in and she smoothed her hair and felt her cheeks with the back of her hands.

'Look what you do to me,' she said, half to herself. 'I'm a stranger when I'm with you.'

You'll be the end of me, I replied in my head.

Late Eighties

There were only two occasions when I heard Mum and Dad fight.

The first was when Dad grew a beard. He'd been clean-shaven all my life, always at the mirror piling on cream with the smooth wooden-handled brush with bristles that went blonde at the tips. Sometimes I'd perch on the corner of the bath and watch as he made himself up like Father Christmas before running his cut-throat razor over his face with expert precision. He'd talk me through the steps, throwing out an occasional question to check I was listening.

Then one day, I noticed his skin beginning to disappear from his face. I went into the bathroom and saw a thin layer of dust covering the brush. It became part of my routine to glance at it each morning and see whether it had been touched. Each time it was in exactly the same place, and I'd imagine what his face looked like that day and how long it would take for it to grow past his shoulders. At dinnertime, I'd study him between mouthfuls. It's funny how the face of someone you know can transform into that of a completely different person when you stare long enough.

Mum began to make little comments in the light-hearted way she did. *Something wrong with your razor?* or *I'd best start bringing your tea earlier in the mornings so you have time to shave.* Dad would just grunt.

After a couple of weeks, she changed tack. Rather than hanging it up, she'd leave his coat dumped on the chair by the door where he left it. The tin of polish would be left by his shoes for him to clean them himself. Food was deposited on his plate with a forceful thwack of the spoon. He had to get his own beer.

Finally, one day she lost it. Sal and I got off the school bus and walked in to find them screaming at each other, our mother throwing plates against the wall. We stood on the mat and looked from one to the other.

When she saw us, Mum covered her face with her hands and ran upstairs. Dad rolled his eyes before disappearing into the living room with the paper. I dropped my bag and went slowly up the stairs, leaving Sal to stare at the pieces of best china all over the floor.

Outside her room, I leant my ear against the door and heard her crying. It wasn't the short, staccato yelps that Sal or I made when we fell off our bikes, but a long, guttural moan.

I knew that if I stepped away, the floorboards would creak and she'd think I had listened and left, so I pushed against the door and went inside.

She sat on the side of the bed, her back to the door, her body facing the window. I could see her face reflected in the dressing-table mirror, and when she looked up and saw me, she clamped her hand to her mouth as if to seal off the sound inside her.

I walked round the bed to be close to her. The hollows of her eyes were red raw and her skin looked like it was hurting. She wouldn't look at me. I could see she was working to stop herself from crying, and the thought of her trying to be someone she wasn't made my throat start to ache. My hands reached out to touch her, and I leant down and pressed my lips against the top of her head.

At this, she grabbed my arm and pulled me close, burying her face in my chest and sobbing without sound into my cheap polyester blazer she'd bought from the market a few months before. It was one size too big, but she said I'd start growing into a man soon enough.

Downstairs, Sal had picked up all the broken pieces and sealed them in a little cardboard box. He took the black marker from his pen pot and wrote TAKE CARE on the top, then left it on the mat by the door so Mum could choose what to do with it.

The only other time I saw them fight was when Dad invited Nigel over to watch the game.

Nigel would come with us to London sometimes. He'd sit at Nana's table, eating her roast potatoes, calling her by her first name and acting part of the family. 'This is blinding, Rose,' he'd say as she served him dessert. 'Don't suppose you've got any custard to go with that cream?'

His head was smooth as an egg, and he seemed to be trying to compensate by growing the longest handlebar moustache. Tomato soup was the funniest. When he lifted the bowl to his mouth for the dregs, the ends of his 'tache would drop in and soak up any remnants. Sal and I kicked each other under the table and laughed into our sleeves.

Nigel was a user. He only took an interest in Dad when there was a game on, when he could scrounge a spare ticket or watch the away games from our sofa. Not many people had the sports channels back then.

Dad had terrible judgement. He was suspicious of almost everyone, but if you paid him a compliment, he was like a dog at your feet. And Nigel was highly skilled in the art of flattery. He'd play dumb when it came to news of transfers and signings, allowing Dad the pleasure of being the first to enlighten him.

Sometimes he'd involve me in these charades, pulling my cheek and saying things like, 'You're a lucky boy, Nick. What son wouldn't want a dad that lived and breathed football like Paul Mendoza? Cut him open and he'd bleed Arsenal, wouldn't you, Paul?' And Dad would just smile, completely taken in.

Mum was on to him.

'I don't like that man,' she said to Dad once. 'I don't like how he makes you look.'

'You don't have to like him,' he replied. 'Two teas, one sugar.'

That was the end of it.

But one day, Nigel knocked on the door and Mum hadn't known he was coming. She took him through to the living room without saying a word, then slammed the door behind her.

Dad thundered into the kitchen. Sal and I were on the landing, hanging over the banister to hear every word.

'I don't exist,' she was saying, slamming washed pots on the metal draining board. 'Little woman, here to serve.'

'Calm down,' he said. 'You're embarrassing yourself.'

'Don't I get a say in who I spend my evening with? Is it too much to ask for me to be consulted?'

'Next time I'll warn you he's coming so you can compose yourself.'

'Next time? Maybe there won't be a next time. Maybe you'll come home to find me gone. Off for a better life.' Her voice quivered on the final word.

'A one-bedder in the town centre? Try it. I'm sure I'll manage.'

It was his turn to slam the door. We watched as he walked down the hall, a six-pack of beers tucked under his arm.

Sal didn't get why she wouldn't put up a fight. 'Why doesn't she tell him to go fuck himself?' Even at a tender age, he was well versed in profanity.

I shrugged. 'Maybe she doesn't know how. Or maybe she loves him.'

'Love? He's an arsehole. And if that's how you love someone, no thank you.'

'Do you think this is what every family's like?' I said.

'Dunno. But sod getting married and having kids if it is.'

I nodded.

Dad would sometimes get up from the dinner table without saying a word. He'd wipe his mouth with his napkin, push back his chair and walk out while the rest of us were still eating. This was usually when Arsenal lost.

Mum would sit and not say anything. I'd pretend not to notice. But Sal would lean back on his chair and bellow, 'You're welcome,' as loud as he could. There was never any comeback from Dad as he walked down the hall. It was almost like he refused to acknowledge Sal's existence.

'Why do you let him do that to you?' Sal would say to Mum, and she'd just shrug and start scraping the plates into the bin.

Once, when Mum was at the supermarket, Sal and I were doing homework at the kitchen table when Dad walked in.

'Hello, sons.'

Arsenal had just won.

'Need something?' I said.

'Your mother not back yet?'

'Not yet,' said Sal. 'Do you need help finding the kettle?'

Dad caught sight of the sink piled high with the soup things from lunch.

'Mum said she'd do it when she got back,' I said quickly, but Dad began to roll up his sleeves.

'No need,' he said.

Sal and I looked at each other.

'You know, boys, when I was in the army, we had to polish our boots so the captain could see his face shine in them. My boots always got nicked because I kept them in better condition than anyone else.'

Sal stuck his fingers in his ears.

'Know what I was also an expert at?' He pointed with a flourish at the sink. 'I could wash the breakfast things of the entire platoon within six minutes flat. Here.' He turned on the tap and passed me his watch. 'When I say GO, start the timer.'

He got the temperature right and shut off the tap. 'Go!'

Never before had we seen our father wash up. It was always Mum's back that faced us in that corner of the room, her hands in the Marigolds, her that smelled of suds. Yet here was Paul Mendoza, our dad, who didn't know where the cutlery was kept: a whole new man.

'Stop!' He slammed down the final pot.

'One minute and forty-three seconds!'

He bowed. 'And that was just a handful of plates and a soup pot. Imagine an entire squadron.'

'Fantastic,' said Sal, slipping down from his stool and heading out of the room. 'Now you have no excuse not to do it every day.'

Mum's key turned in the lock, and moments later she appeared in the doorway, loaded down with bags.

'All right, darling?' said Dad, stepping back to let her through. 'You were a while.'

'The crowds,' Mum said as she heaved the bags on to the counter. 'I must have queued for half an hour at the checkout.' She rested herself against the shopping and closed her eyes.

'I could murder a cup of tea,' said Dad.

'What?' She opened her eyes. 'Oh, right. Yes.'

'No hurry,' he said, taking the paper from one of the bags and moving towards the door. 'It can wait until you've put everything away.'

He whistled a tune as he walked down the hall.

We never understood why she didn't stick up for herself. Or why it took Nigel and a beard to break her.

2003

We were sitting in a shady corner of the memorial gardens, kissing and talking shit. The sun was blazing and she loved the heat, but thought it safer in the shade. Less chance of being seen. It was late morning and already busy. A mix of gangs of teens, old people on benches, lovers entwined.

It was just us in our corner. We were surrounded by lush, tropical plants, and when we lay down and looked at the palms against the blue sky, the heat from the earth warmed our backs and it felt like we were on some distant island. The monotonous sound of ring-road traffic was really the soothing lull of a tide.

'If you could go anywhere, where would it be?'

'Italy,' I said without hesitation.

'Me too!' She propped herself up on her elbow and faced me. 'You'd find so much inspiration for your writing there. Whereabouts?'

I shrugged. 'I'm pretty sure even the rough areas are beautiful. But maybe Venice.' I turned to face her. 'Wait. Surely you've been to Italy.'

Anna blushed. 'I've never been to Venice.'

'I'd have thought you'd say Venice is a cliché.'

She made a face. 'But how do you avoid cliché? Surely trying to escape and live life free from it is cliché in itself? We're fucked which-ever way.'

'You swear more than anyone I know.'

She laughed as she picked at the grass. 'A girl rebels against her religious upbringing by dropping f-bombs at every turn. Classic cliché. Would you prefer it if I didn't?'

I shook my head. 'You're fine as you are.'

'Good,' she said, lying back to face the sky. 'Because I wouldn't give a shit if you did.'

★

I needed to buy summer shoes so we walked further into town, Anna slightly ahead the whole time and scanning faces when we entered a shop.

'It's like you're my bodyguard,' I whispered in her ear, and she looked at me and smiled.

'Are you the one that needs protecting then?' she said, riffling through a rack of clothes. She pulled out a dark blue T-shirt. 'This would look great on you. I love a guy in navy.' She seemed to change her mind and put it back. 'Shoes, remember?'

I picked some canvas slip-ons and went to pay as she wandered off towards the back. As I passed the rail, I threw a glance over my shoulder to check her position, found a navy T-shirt in my size and handed it to the girl on the desk.

Later, we walked back to her car. I could feel the heat radiating through the concrete beneath my shoes. The air smelled of hot tarmac, like petrol about to explode.

'Wait,' she said, pulling at my arm. 'What if we did it? What if we went to Italy?'

I stopped. 'Together?'

'Yes.' She tightened her grip. 'Let's do it. Let's go.'

'When?'

'I've heard Venice is beautiful in winter. Quieter.' She smiled. 'Less cliché.'

I didn't know how to reply. How I could say yes without first checking if she was sure, if she'd thought through the logistics, the parents, the sneaking around. How would we get away with it? I didn't know how to answer, so I didn't.

'Come on,' she said, dragging me back towards town. 'What are you so afraid of?'

We went into a travel agency and came out with an armload of brochures, glossy pages of gondolas and café tables and skylines at sunset. All the Italian tropes, Anna said, not bothering to walk the usual three feet in front of me. She didn't seem to care who saw.

'Oh.' I felt the familiar crush of disappointment as I came to a stop. 'I don't have a passport.'

She looked at me like I'd said the stupidest thing.

'I've not been abroad in over ten years,' I said, trying to explain. My fingers closed around my lighter in my pocket.

She thought about this, then turned and began walking the other way, I assumed to return the brochures.

'Where are you going?' I said.

'Post office,' she said over her shoulder. 'Will you stop finding excuses?'

At the counter, we collected the application form and stopped at the photo booth. I peered at my reflection in the skinny mirror and ran a hand across my shaven head.

She pushed me inside on to the stool. 'Don't smile, remember?' she said as she fed coins into the slot.

'Stop,' I said as she stepped back and drew the curtain. 'I have change.' There was a white pop of light as I spoke.

'That's one wasted,' she said from outside. 'Three left.'

I settled my features and kept them still, despite the chaos raging inside. Out the corner of my eye, I could see her tanned legs from beneath the curtain. Her red-painted toes. I tried not to smile and the screen flashed again.

That day I remember as fragments. Lying on the grass in the Mems, walking to her car, the post office, then back at mine, where we flicked through brochures on my bed and discussed where to go. It exists in my mind like a movie montage. Not quite real, a little cliché, all the best bits. Maybe the words weren't spoken exactly like I remember, but you get a sense of it, and what really do we ever possess of another human being but a sense of them? They're a smudge at the end of a sentence. A foggy mirror through which we try to make sense of ourselves.

The two usable pictures went off with the paperwork, and the other of me – unfit for purpose – she tore off and slipped in her purse. I kept the final one. It's of her leaning in through the curtain, her side profile as she stuck her tongue in my ear. And my mouth is laughing, in surprise, in shock, in terror. My eyes are squeezed shut and my skin is red, as if all the blood has rushed to the surface, as if I can't quite believe it, as if I am happy.

Early Nineties

When something traumatic happens to a child, memories divide into two camps: the before and the after. If childhood is a pie, the something traumatic is the knife slicing through. It's the writing of a word and crossing it out. A young brain can't understand the heinous. It makes sense through metaphor.

This is how it was for me.

A girl at primary school sent me a love letter just after it happened. Her name was Tammy and she wore tiny star-shaped studs in her ears that had to be taped for PE. She wrote me a note on pink paper that smelled of strawberries, and she dotted her 'i's with flowers. *Tammy loves Nick. Does Nick love Tammy? Don't break my heart.* And then she'd drawn a heart with a crack to show it breaking.

Joanne Butler handed me the note in the playground and walked off to stand with Tammy and the other girls. They watched me slowly open the folded paper and read the words, and I remember getting to the drawing of the heart and staring at it for several seconds longer than I should have. Something about that lightning strike down the middle, wrenching it in two. After a minute or so, I looked up and saw the girls laughing, all except Tammy, and although I didn't love Tammy, I gave her a smile as if I did, and she smiled back and looked happy. It felt like I did a nice thing. Then the bell rang, and I crumpled the note into a tiny ball and let it drop to the ground.

I have a memory that belongs in both camps.

My childhood obsession with the circus stemmed from repeat viewings of *Bronco Billy*, in which Clint Eastwood threw knives at his girlfriend as she lay strapped to a spinning wheel. The toy I chose for my ninth birthday was a Playmobil circus act of performing monkeys, and I spent hours organising them on their little bench and swing, attaching their hands to the trapeze and spinning them over and over. I can't tell you what it was I loved about the circus. I just did.

I would daydream about us all going together, but we weren't the kind of family who went on days out. You know the type – the ones with annual passes to Thorpe Park or Legoland, who make arrangements to go with other families, who don't take a packed lunch but eat in the on-site restaurant and choose whatever they want from a laminated menu. They get together often at these expensive places of fun, to laugh together, or make regular pilgrimages to Disney, go for a Sunday roast or kick a ball around the local park. We were not one of those families.

Dad once drove down to Devon to collect a golf club he'd purchased from a dealer. Apparently it was very rare, with the pound signs to go with it, and Dad didn't trust the dealer or had suspicions about the postal service so drove the two hundred miles to get it himself. Somehow, Mum convinced him to take me and we spent eight hours in the car together. I rode up front next to him, and at one point on the journey home, he even let me put on a cassette of my own. I was telling him about the group and what I'd read about how they wrote the song, and he actually seemed to be listening. The golf club rested on the back seat – apparently it was very, very good – and he was smiling and in that mood where he'd ruffle my hair.

At a set of traffic lights, I looked out the window at a huge poster pasted on to a wooden billboard. I don't know where I found the courage, but I said, 'Will you take me to the circus, Dad?'

'Eh?'

I pointed at the sign, at the lion with its mouth wide open, at the ringmaster and his curled, exaggerated moustache. He had his arms outstretched, inviting us in. 'Will you take me?'

Dad said nothing for a minute. He did the grimace that he makes when he's thinking of what to say and stalling for time. 'Would you like that then? The circus?'

I nodded. 'I've always wanted to go.'

'Have you?' He stroked his chin. 'Okay, son. Tell you what. When a circus comes to town, I'll take you.'

I was so happy that I couldn't even say thank you.

Six months later, everything happened.

The crack through the heart.

One day, about nine months after that, I ran in from school and threw down my bag.

'Dad!'

He was in the lounge with his feet on the footstool, his nose deep in the sports pages.

'It's coming next month, Dad,' I said, out of breath, feeling like I was going to die.

'Hmm?'

'The circus. Remember? There's one coming to town next month.'

He half put down the paper, confused. 'Remind me.'

'Remember when we went to Devon last year to get your golf club? We saw the poster? You said you'd take me?' I couldn't hide my frustration.

I watched his face change. Sal was half in the room, holding the door, his expression one of pity at the way I was falling over myself. He always knew more than me. But he said he'd take me, I'd insisted in the car. He always says that he never goes back on his word. Right, Aunty Stel?

She had gripped the steering wheel and kept her eyes fixed ahead.

Now I waited for Dad to confirm what I knew, that he'd simply forgotten. He scratched his chin and finally said, 'Of course I remember. Leave it with me, son. I'll talk it over with Stella and get the tickets.' And he went back behind the paper.

I threw Sal a triumphant smile. *See*, it said. *Told you.*

He just rolled his eyes and disappeared through the door.

Every day for the next few weeks, I'd come home and search through the pile of papers living on the desk, waiting for the evidence to appear. Finally, one afternoon, atop a stack of bills, three tickets poked out from a white envelope. The Saturday-afternoon show. Cheap seats, but who the hell cared. The rich red-and-gold foil border looked a million dollars to me.

Saturday arrived. Sal and I got up an hour early, dressed and went down to the kitchen, where Stella was at the hob stirring the porridge.

'Hello, Aunty Stel,' I said, taking a seat and grabbing a spoon. 'What are you doing here on a weekend?'

She turned slowly towards our confused faces, then swore under her breath. 'He didn't tell you, did he?' She said it like she already knew.

'Tell us what?' said Sal as Dad walked in, cradling a golf club.

'All right, Stel,' he said. 'I'll see you later.'

I began to understand.

'You've got some nerve, Paul.' She took off her apron and waved it in my direction. 'Look at his face.'

'But Dad, you're taking me.'

He grimaced. 'I've got a tournament, son. Been arranged for months. They asked me to organise it and I don't like to go back on my word. You don't mind, do you? Besides, you'll have much more fun with your Aunty Stella.' He ruffled my hair.

I couldn't look at him. I couldn't look at Stella or Sal. My face began to burn and I rubbed my sleeve across my eyes. The chair made a scraping sound on the lino.

'Nick,' said Stella, but I ducked under her arm and ran to my room.

I pushed my hot face into the cold pillow, into the familiar place where everything went black.

There are less than two years between Sal and me, so even in my earliest memories, we formed a sort of trio with Mum. But I remember one time when I was eight or so, we went out for the day, just Mum and I. She did that sometimes. She'd ask one of us – the 'chosen one', we'd call it – to stick our tongue out and she'd frown and say, *Hmm, looks a bit ropey in there. I think you're too ill for school. How about it?* And then we'd hang out at home watching a video or eat chips in the park or go to Whitstable and throw stones in the sea. I don't know why she did it. I guess she missed us when we weren't there.

We dropped Sal off at school and went to the cinema, where they were showing *Back to the Future II*. She'd made peanut-butter-and-cucumber sandwiches cut into quarters, and I unwrapped the foil and ate them while she took sips from a hip flask of the home-made cocktail she'd smuggled in. The sandwiches tasted good as we smiled at each other in the dark, and we sat and watched Marty McFly as he tried to prevent everything from falling apart, as he defended his mum against Biff and as he travelled through time to save his family and stop his future from unravelling.

Fuck. I wish I had a time machine.

Summer 2003

'Is it a spaceship?' said Anna, her eyes bright.

We were standing in the corner of my garden. Before us was a silver dome, like a giant Christmas bauble, set on top of a circular brick base. A small, low door led inside. In the garden of a Victorian rectory, it did indeed look like something from another world.

'It's an observatory,' I said, 'for looking at the stars. A scientist lived here before and would sit out at night with a telescope. The roof opens and spins. I haven't been inside since I was a kid.'

'Will you show me?'

'It's probably full of cobwebs.'

She reached up and pulled her hair on top of her head, fastening it with the elastic she'd been wearing on her wrist. 'I'm game if you are.'

I gave the door a slight push and the hinges made a jarring noise as the rotten wood splintered open. I bent down and peered into the darkness.

'It's a portal into another dimension,' Anna said, crouching down next to me. Her bare arm brushed mine and I noticed on her wrist the imprint of the band now in her hair.

'Wait.' I jogged up the garden to the veranda stretching along the back of the house. I threw open the lid to a tatty wooden chest and took out the cushions and seat pads, giving them a whack against the box to release several years of dust.

Anna had crawled inside by the time I returned. I slid the cushions through the door and followed them in on my knees.

I stood next to her in the dark. The crack of light coming through the door cast an eerie brightness on her face.

'They'd better not be for a mattress, Nicolas,' she said, looking down at the cushions.

Her saying my name did strange things to me.

The space inside the observatory was cramped, with just enough headroom for two people. Something about the darkness made me brave, and I leant in a few inches and kissed her.

She drew back so our noses were touching. 'I love it when you put your teeth around my tongue.'

I pulled her close.

'Stop,' she said, pushing me off. 'The roof, remember?'

I took the lighter from my pocket and a flick of ignition bathed the inside in an orange glow. I waved it around until I found the bolt that slid across, and pushed with all my strength until it gave way. The light poured in.

'If this is a time machine, is there room for me?'

We looked down at a pair of skinny legs and flip-flops outside the door. Anna turned.

'My brother,' I said.

Sal was already ducking through the door and Anna pressed herself against me to make room for him.

'You must be Sal,' she said, extending a hand. 'I'm Anna.'

Sal's face was one huge smile. 'Oh, I know who you are.'

She looked at me and I looked at him. *Don't you dare*, I said in my head.

'Listen up, Anna,' said Sal, sitting back on a cushion against the wall. 'I've just scored some spectacular weed from a mate and it would be my absolute pleasure to share it with you.'

We followed his lead and sat down to form the three points of a triangle. She stretched out her legs and let her feet rest on my lap. I lit a cigarette.

'I'm good, but you go right ahead.'

'You're missing out,' said Sal. 'It's quality stuff. Pure.'

'Anna doesn't like smoking,' I said, taking a drag of my own.

'It's not really smoking,' Sal said, taking out his Rizlas and a bag of green weed. 'That shit'll kill you.' He nods at my hand. 'This is just like cracking open a beer at the end of the day.'

'Sal's a walking contradiction,' I said to her. 'He's anti-smoking, won't touch processed food and plays football twice a week, but he takes every drug going and sees zero conflict in any of that.'

'Not heroin, though, surely?' said Anna.

Sal licked the paper and shook his head. 'I'm not brave enough for needles.'

'What's it like?' said Anna. 'I mean, when you smoke it. What does it do?'

He lit the end of the spliff and took a long drag. The end pulsed bright.

'It makes the world beautiful.'

He blew the smoke upwards and we watched it pass through the roof towards the sky.

'Pass it over,' she said, extending a hand.

I raised my eyebrows as Sal gave it to her and she put it to her lips. She coughed and laughed as she handed it back.

'Well, look at you,' I said.

She smiled at me. 'Have I shocked you, old man?'

'I never know which Anna I'm going to get when I'm with you.'

'I never know which Anna I'm going to be.'

She gestured to Sal and leant forward for another drag, a deeper one. It must have been good stuff because it already seemed to be working. She kicked off her sandals and nudged me with her toes.

'I don't know how you got here,' said Sal, 'but you won't be able to drive after this.'

She shrugged and closed her eyes. 'Then I'll just have to stay the night.'

Sal gave me a wink. 'You're welcome.'

There was a long, low rumble in the distance and we looked at each other, then through the open roof. The sky was a pale blue, but the sound was unmistakable. 'They did say rain,' said Sal.

We listened, and a few seconds later, it came again. 'A few miles off yet,' he said.

Anna, still looking at the sky:

' "You will hear thunder and remember me,
And think: she wanted storms." '

'Did you just make that up?' said Sal, spliff in mid-air.

'God, no,' she said. 'It's by a Russian poet, Anna Akhmatova. I've always loved it.'

Sal exhaled towards the sky. 'Always been more of a maths bod, myself.'

Anna made a face. 'Words are so much more flexible. The answer can be whatever you like as long as you argue it well enough. Numbers are so cold and exact. There's no bending their truth.'

'That's why they're beautiful,' I said. 'They're unchanging.'

'You have something in common then,' Anna said as she crawled across to sit next to me. 'I've never met two brothers more different. Are you really related?'

'How do you mean?' I said.

She picked up my arm and draped it around her. 'Look at you both. Even your names are night and day.'

'Our dad picked mine,' I said, ignoring the thud in my chest. 'He wanted us to have typically British names, but Mum insisted with Sal. She wanted to work in Dad's Italian heritage. I think they agreed a different name at first, but Mum went alone to register the birth and changed it to Salvatore. Brave, really.'

'I doubt he even noticed,' said Sal.

'It's a beautiful name,' said Anna. 'Salvatore. Saviour.'

'The irony, eh,' said Sal, stubbing out the joint and sealing it away in the plastic bag. 'Right. I'll love you and leave you.'

Anna slid her hand into my pocket and the hairs on my arm stood up.

'Anna,' said Sal, putting out his fist for her to bump. 'Pleasure.'

'I like Salvatore already,' she said when he'd gone.

'He's a beauty.'

'Why does he do all that?' she said, stroking the flesh on the underside of my arm. 'The drugs.'

'He's done it for years,' I said, tapping my leg to distract the fire in my body. 'I think it started as a way of getting away from himself, not being alone with his thoughts. Some people are like that, I guess. They want to crowd out the noise in their heads. Now it's just habit.'

'Maybe I'll take it up.'

'Don't you dare.'

Anna turned and straddled me, pulling her top over her head. I reached up and unclipped her hair and it fell over her shoulders, brushing my cheek as she cradled my face and pushed down on my body. I slid my hand up her bare leg and pushed hard against her through her shorts. She was shaking.

'Do you know how much I want you?' she said in my ear.

It sounded like something she thought she should say, and I took hold of her wrists and said, 'No.'

'You make me so wet,' she whispered.

'No, Anna. Stop.'

'What do you mean?' she said, and I saw the high in her eyes.

I stroked her cheek. 'I don't want you this way.'

'Oh, I get it.' She climbed off my lap and bent over away from me. She looked at me over her shoulder. 'You want it like this?'

I took hold of her pocket and pulled her on to my lap. 'Just kiss me.'

She pulled back. 'Are you gay or something?'

'What? No. I think that was clear when you were on top of me.'

'So what's the problem?'

I sighed. 'Come on. You're high.'

'Don't be a prick.'

'I don't mean to patronise you,' I said, remembering from past experience how this would go. 'I don't want you that way, that's all.'

She laughed and tried to edge off my lap. 'Right,' she said. 'I forgot about these games you like to play. Of course, you have to be in control. Never mind what *I* want or when *I* want it.'

I let go and she moved away. 'There are no games,' I said. 'There's just you and me.'

She sat back and pulled her top on, then put her hands to her face and made a sound between a laugh and sob. 'God, what an idiot.'

'Listen, I'm sorry,' I said, trying to touch her. 'It's got nothing to do with you. Actually, it's got everything to do with you.'

Another laugh.

'You think I don't want you?' I said, swallowing hard. 'I'm a bloke, aren't I? But it matters to me that you're here too, in this room, in your head, right with me. You're hot as hell even when you're high, but I want you awake when I touch you. To know I'm touching you. Not lost out of your fucking mind.'

She bit her lip. 'How do you do that?' she said.

'Do what?'

'Put me straight without losing your shit.'

I lit another cigarette. 'I'm screaming at you on the inside.'

We sat in silence for a while. The sun had gone, and the rain must have passed us over. The sky was that deep blue it goes between sunset and darkness. The gloaming, Mum called it once. We'd been sitting on the chalk crown at the top of Wye Downs, watching the houses below turn on their lights.

'I'd like to ask you something,' Anna said. 'If you'll let me.'

I waited.

'Your mum. Where is she?'

I heard the birds singing in the trees. Calling each other home, to bed, to rest until tomorrow. The air was very still.

I didn't answer at first. I continued with my cigarette, feeling it flood my lungs and mind with its deadly peace, then stubbed it out. And then I sat back in the shadows, away from her, and for the first time in my life, I told the story of my mother.

After I had finished, she put her hands over her face and cried.

Early Nineties

Stella was around a lot after it happened. She would do the school run on days Dad was working or when we couldn't get a lift with another mum. When we needed new uniform, it was her that took us to Marks & Spencer to be fitted, and when there was a cake sale at school, it was Stella who bought one from the shop.

After she drove us home from the circus, we ate our Happy Meals at the table and then Sal and I went to bed. For a while, I sat in my pyjamas on the landing and listened to her do the washing-up. I squeezed my temples between the spindles, closed my eyes, and imagined it was Mum.

She went into the living room to say goodbye when she'd finished, and then she was by the front door, slipping her arms into her coat.

Dad appeared in the doorway with his hands in his pockets. I watched from the landing, the lack of upstairs window light keeping me hidden from view.

'It went okay then?'

'Fine,' she said, doing up the buttons. 'It went fine. We had candy-floss and I let them have a go on the arcades. I think I succeeded in making him forget you weren't there.'

Dad nodded, not listening, clinking the change in his pocket. 'I wondered . . .' He scratched his head. 'What if you moved in? I could make up the spare room nice. It would be easier for you, not having to drive here and back each day.'

Stella put her hands in her coat pockets and sighed. 'No, Paul.'

He straightened his back. 'They need you, Stella.'

She gave a laugh, a sad one, and shook her head. 'No, they need their dad.'

'What am I supposed to do? I need to work and put food on the table. I can't be washing clothes and changing beds too.'

She sucked in air through her teeth. 'You spend enough time at that working man's club of yours. And you realise I have a job?'

'Pulling pints at a pub.' He gave a sarcastic grunt.

'Yeah, I don't think tinkering with filthy cars for thirty quid a day is much better, so watch your lip.' Stella leant down and picked up her bag. 'I'm happy to help out now and again, Paul, but I do have a life of my own.'

'It's not as if you've got a family to be dealing with.'

She threw him a sharp look. 'If I'd wanted kids, I'd have had them,' she said.

'Oh, they'd be glad to hear that,' he said. 'They think the world of you. Turns out you'd rather be playing bingo and hobnobbing with Jack the lads than caring for your own nephews.'

Stella took out her keys and gave them a little shake. 'I love those boys more than you can ever imagine, but it's not me they need. Don't think I've forgotten how it was between you and Dad when we were young. Do you want your boys having the same experience with you?'

Dad looked at the floor.

'Get yourself a housekeeper,' said Stella, opening the door. 'I'll be by on Monday with a casserole.'

Sal had a way with girls.

At school, he was accompanied almost everywhere by a circle of them. Fashionable girls. You know the ones. They spent half their lives in front of mirrors ironing their hair, puckering lips at their reflections, turning and examining themselves from every conceivable angle. They screamed from the sidelines at football matches and hugged each other when Sal scored. I watched a group of them once get out of a car and wait for the adult to drive away before rolling up their skirts to resemble a belt. They loosened their ties and unbuttoned their shirts. Adjusted each other's hair. Then they hooked arms and strode into school.

These were the girls we all wanted. They knew their best assets and put them out for us to see. Teenage boys have no imagination. I mean, if you go to buy a sofa and have a choice between the blue on display or a little swatch of green, you choose the blue. Job done. It's easier to visualise and so the simpler choice. I do know I shouldn't compare girls to sofas.

Boys are like that, though. They need things spelled out.

But Sal didn't want any of those girls. I think he liked the chase as much as the reward. It always did seem to me he picked the harder way for everything. But maybe he thought there was nothing left to discover.

His type was small, dark and passionate. The kind who did Theatre Studies and would ring their eyes in black pencil like a petrified raccoon. They always wore black, their hair short and messy or long and wild, and if it wasn't brunette then they dyed it to be so. Nobody was quite sure where they came in the pecking order of coolness, and this held a kind of allure in itself.

Stacey was the first girl I remember. She'd left our school the year before and got a part-time job in a menswear shop in town. Daz and

I would go in and pretend to be interested in the clothes, which were designer and far too pricey for our paper-round wages. The bell would chime as we entered and she'd signal for us to follow her towards the back. I've got something that would look perfect on you, she'd say, and she'd make us try on a coat or jumper and stand behind us in front of the mirror, adjusting a sleeve or the fit on our horny teenage bodies. Daz spent an entire term's wages on a Boxfresh jumper she said made his arms look buff. She must have worked on commission. Daz also didn't talk to Sal for weeks when we saw him snogging her outside Woolworth's at the end of summer.

He messed around with a few, but Sal's first proper girlfriend was Cleo. Her real name was Chloe, but she didn't think it was interesting enough so she rearranged the letters. He met her at the video store when his stoner manager asked him to interview applicants for a part-time job. Cleo was the first and last through the door.

They spent her first shift arguing over *Forrest Gump*. It's shit, she said. Corny as hell. How many world events can they pack into one person's life? Sal wouldn't have it: Well, millions of people disagree. I couldn't care less, she replied. I think it's shit and so it's shit. It went back and forth like this until closing time when Sal locked the door and they screwed up against the shelves behind the till where the videos were kept.

That's how he told it anyway.

They didn't last long. She was into weird stuff, Sal said after it ended. She'd make him call her by the name of her best friend when they were in bed, and at first he had been into it, but then she began to insist on it every time. She hated being touched, he said, unless he pretended she was someone else. They broke up the following summer when she moved away to study Biomechanical Engineering. She'd changed her name back to Chloe by then.

Tess came next. I liked Tess. She seemed relatively normal after Chloe. She still fitted the mould of dark and petite, but there wasn't the complexity of the others. Or perhaps I didn't know her well enough. It was clear though that Tess adored Sal, and she would rest her chin on her hands whenever he spoke and cock her head to one side as if she was really listening. I liked that.

'Tess seems great,' I said to him once over a pint.

'Hmm? Yeah, I guess.' He was frowning at a message that had appeared on his phone.

'Better than the one you had before. Chloe, I mean. She seems like her head's screwed on.'

He put down his phone. 'No, you're right. Tess is great. I can't see it lasting, to be honest.'

'But you seem so great together? Happy, even.'

'No, we are,' he said. 'We are happy.'

'Is that a bad thing?'

He sighed. 'I guess some people like the idea of today being the same as yesterday. That they know how tomorrow will be.'

'There's a safety in it, I suppose.'

'Yeah. It would be easier that way.' He downed his pint.

Sal and Tess were together five years. They were one of those couples that other people wanted to be. The couple spending evenings entwined on the sofa watching old movies. The couple with the same taste in wall colours and which gig to see or which dessert to split. When they shared a curry, Sal dipped his poppadoms in the onions and mango chutney while Tess preferred the yoghurt and lime.

They discussed getting married, having kids or at least a puppy. Sal would bring up the subject of moving away, of buying a round-the-world ticket and seeing which country fitted best, at which Tess would smile and say that a year in France would be quite doable.

Then, one day, Tess arrived home early to find Sal in bed with someone else. She started destroying the apartment, clawing at the curtains and ripping the wallpaper they'd chosen together off in big clumps. Sal tried to calm her, holding tightly to her thin wrists and leaving purple bruises on her skin. He was trying to stop her hurting herself, he said to me on the phone afterwards. He didn't know his own strength.

They weren't even screwing, Tess told me later. Their clothes were in a tangle on the floor and the room stank of sex, but it wasn't that that made her break. It was the way the woman held him, cradling his head as he slept against her chest, his hands tucked peacefully under his chin. He never let me hold him like that, she said. I always wanted to hold him and he always pulled away.

When Tess found them, the woman stretched out her arms and yawned like it was the most normal thing. She threw off their covers and lay naked on their bed, watching and smiling as they screamed at each other.

That was the beginning of Mathilde.

Summer 2003

'Come in.'

Anna's house was one of six identical houses on a close in the good part of town. One of those executive detached houses that beams from the front of a brochure or accompanies an article in the Money or Property section. *You've arrived*, it says with its perfect red bricks and white weatherboarding. Aspirational.

She stood in the vaulted front entrance, barefoot, leaning against the door frame. I'd changed my clothes twice, taken two buses to get here, and she said *Come in* like it was the most casual thing in the world. Like I was her boyfriend.

I closed the door and slipped off my shoes, partly from habit, but also because the polished white marble floor didn't look like it would take kindly to foreign contaminants. The cold tiles stuck to my sweaty skin.

'Did you find it okay?' she said, hands on hips.

'It was fine.'

'It's so out of the way up here. I always wonder if it's too far for people to come.'

'It's fine.'

'It's so hot today.' She pressed the back of her wrist to her forehead. 'Drink?'

'Sure.'

I followed her down the hall towards a sunny window at the end. Glass doors led off each side to ever larger rooms, all pale carpets and shiny surfaces. It felt like a stage set of heaven. Bright, white, nowhere to hide.

I watched her walk. Her body looked just as good in denim cut-offs as it had in my bed.

'Coke?' she said as we entered the kitchen.

The word echoed around the room. Acres of countertop encircled a giant island in the middle and I gave the stone surface a light tap. Definitely not the cheap stuff.

'Sure.'

As she opened the American fridge, I glimpsed a reflection of what looked like a shifting ghost in the polished silver door, something uneasy in this picture of calm. It took a moment to realise it was me.

Anna passed me a can and put hers against her forehead, closing her eyes in relief. Her lips parted slightly.

'Nice place,' I said, moving my weight from one foot to the other.

'You think?' She opened her eyes and gave a bored shrug. 'If you like that sort of thing.'

'Don't you, then?'

She snapped the ring-pull. 'Who needs two dishwashers?'

That's when I saw there were multiples of everything. Two ovens, two dishwashers, two sinks, two wine fridges. Above the kitchen island hung three fuchsia-pink pendants, identical, positioned exactly above three bar stools. And then I noticed there was nothing on the countertops. Where is the toaster, I thought. Where's the kettle and pots of utensils, and the toppling pile of bills?

I looked at Anna, leaning on her elbows against the marble-topped island, and it occurred to me how she also looked out of place, with her chipped nails and warm touch. The only thing that seemed to match was the vibrancy of her red lips against the pendants. And then I noticed she was wearing lipstick.

'Are you hungry?' she asked.

I shrugged. 'Are you?'

She went to the fridge. 'I'll make a sandwich,' she said, taking out the butter, chopped deli ham and a jar of pickles.

I watched as she buttered the bread. She dug the knife deep into the tub and carved out thick wedges that she spread in generous stripes across each slice. There was no stealing butter from one to use on another, of rationing one wedge across two or even three slices like Dad. If she'd been making toast, it would have sat in round, expensive pools on top, refusing to melt. It would have run gloriously down our chins. I buttered bread like Dad, and I wondered how it would be if Anna and I ever lived together. Whether either of us would change our habits to be more like the other, or if we'd argue over how the other person buttered bread.

The sandwich tasted knockout. When we finished, she picked a dishwasher and loaded it with our plates.

'Grand tour?' she said, pushing it shut.

'When do they get back?'

'Tonight. Their plane lands in an hour.'

She led me through a series of rooms, pointing out random things and referring to her parents as Mother and Father throughout. 'Inside this are first editions of every Bond book,' she said, patting the huge safe in the corner of the study. 'Father's pride and joy.' And in the dining room, 'Where Mother sits each morning with her peppermint tea and Bible study before brunch and a manicure.'

The only photo on display was a large studio portrait in the lounge of the four of them. Mother and Father perched on chairs with their children either side, one hand resting on a parent's shoulder and another holding the parent's hand. Their pastel clothes stood out against the dark, mottled background, their faces gleaming with middle-class respectability. It was about five years ago, going by the look of Anna. She was dressed in a purple dress with puffy sleeves and smiled with all the gawk of an early teen. Father was bald with glasses. Mother tanned and hot in that older-woman way. Her brother looked like one of the boys at school who took the piss when I walked in the room. Nike trainers and perfect hair.

'Revolting, isn't it?' said Anna from behind.

'It's certainly something.' I pushed my hands further into my pockets.

'We look like the family of a serial killer. Mother in her twinset and pearls. She spent a month laying out different outfits on the bed, coordinating us into her idea of the perfect family.' She sucked air through her teeth. 'Look how she had me immortalised. In fucking lilac.'

'I think you look super hot.'

'I'm fourteen there, you perv.'

I shrugged. 'That would have made me seventeen. Only slightly dodge.'

'Come.' She took my hand and pulled me towards the door.

It was a house where every room was adorned with a word or catchphrase. EAT in heavily scrolled letters on the dining room sideboard, COOK above the kitchen oven, a cross stitch of RELAX in the lounge. In the bathroom, BATHE floated above the door in complementary hues of blue. A bowl of pebbles sat on the windowsill. 'Mother collects a stone from every beach.' Anna turned one over to reveal an inscription in black marker pen. *Barbados, '98.*

I wondered if she had a swimming pool. It seemed like the type of house that would. On the walk over, I stopped to buy a cold beer at a newsagent with a billboard outside: *Zoo Animals Given Sun Cream & Ice Lollies.* We need the rain, I overheard an old lady telling the cashier. My lettuces are dying.

I followed her upstairs, tracing my fingers over hers as she slid a hand along the banister. The feel of her skin against the cold metal felt dangerous, and I boldly reached out to touch her bare waist with my other hand. When she paused at the top, I pulled her back against me and kissed the curve of her neck. I felt powerful, feeling her go soft in my arms. I knew she wanted me, just as I wanted her.

'Wait,' she said, pulling away. 'The tour, remember?'

She pushed open the nearest door. 'Dear brother's room.' I caught sight of a perfectly made bed and a row of what looked like expensive guitars in a staggered display on the walls. It looked uncluttered and unlived in. 'He's abroad,' said Anna. 'Serving where the need is great.'

'What?'

She closed the door. 'Never mind.'

At the next door, she paused to look at me. 'My room.'

It was five times the size of mine. There was the same pale carpet that hugged the rest of the house, but here the walls were a bright scarlet that shocked you on entering. 'Mother hates it,' she said with satisfaction. A single bed jutted out into the middle. Stuck to the dressing-table mirror were Polaroids from nights out. Anna with her friends, Anna with her hands flung wide on a dance floor, Anna in front of her car with keys aloft in one hand and a champagne flute in the other. Pots of make-up lay strewn across the table, alongside jewellery and a stack of books. A brush lay on its side, the bristles tangled with long strands of black like the ones she'd left in my bed.

A girl's bedroom has always felt like a foreign country. They do things differently there.

I sat on the edge of the bed that no man had ever slept in. She crawled over and climbed on to my lap, cupping my face with her hands and bringing her mouth to mine.

It felt like I'd passed some kind of test and I returned the urgency of her kiss. Then she stopped. 'One more room.'

She led me down the hall to a door at the end. Through it was a master suite, a cavernous room with vaulted ceiling and mirrored wardrobes along one side. A door in the corner led into what I presumed to be a bathroom, but here the tour seemed to end. She pulled me over to the bed, a giant divan covered in peach satin.

'What are you doing?'

She kneeled on the floor and came close to my ear. 'Quiet,' she whispered, and I felt her tongue inside. She began to undo my jeans and pushed me back until I lay on the bed.

My heart began to pound and pleasure shot through my entire body. I fixed my gaze on the sign above the bed, a wooden board with LOVE carved out in deep, thick letters.

I gave in.

I didn't like Mathilde from the beginning.

She was exactly Sal's type, all dark hair and pale face like moonlight. Her beauty was obvious, but didn't she know it. Laura described her as 'impossibly chic', and she did have that thing that certain French women have, where they know how to look good without revealing how they got there. Effortless.

Her wardrobe consisted of black skinny jeans, biker boots, and fuzzy oversized jumpers with open backs that she'd casually pull down to reveal a naked shoulder. 'Cover up, you'll catch a chill,' I'd say like a concerned uncle. I knew it was a dickish thing to say. She'd just arch an eyebrow in reply.

Mathilde had zero sense of humour. The room would be dying from a joke Sal made and she'd just sit with her bare ankles pulled up beneath her, looking bored and superior. It was maddening how someone obsessed with the empty surface of things could take herself so seriously.

We were the only smokers in the group. You'd think this would have bonded us somehow, the private conversations we'd share in our outdoor exile, but even in this, she found a way to act out of my league.

'Eurgh, the smell,' she'd say as I lit up, waving her arms as if under attack. 'You English with your factory filth. *Merde*. Killing the rest of us.'

She'd begin to roll a cigarette.

'You know rollies give off just as much smoke, Mathilde?'

'*Oui, oui*, Nicolas,' she'd say in a bored voice.

We always called each other by our full names, although she'd say mine in French and drop the 's' so it sounded incomplete. She always found a way to go one better.

Mathilde wore an antique rosary around her neck despite not being remotely religious. The beads were coloured different shades of brown and reminded me of those old camel seat covers, like Grandpa had in his car when we were kids. The cross was heavy ornate silver, and she'd sit there, her face full of disdain as she stroked her dead Jesus. I saw a film once where a nun was strangled to death with her own rosary. It made me think of Mathilde.

'I wish you'd make an effort with Tilly,' Sal said to me. 'She really likes you, you know. She doesn't get why you act so weird around her.'

She had this way with Sal that put him in a helpless state. Everything he did was about pacifying her and maintaining the impossible standards she demanded. I thought perhaps she was an expert in hypnosis, and at times wondered if there was any truth to the idea of black magic. I'd find myself watching to see if she cast some kind of spell. Laura said I was paranoid.

'But what does he see in her?' I said. 'Apart from the obvious aesthetic appeal, I mean.'

'But isn't that ninety per cent of the reason why men like women?' said Laura. 'Besides, Sal seems so much better lately. Did you see his pupils last night? He's clearly not on the pills so she must be doing something right.'

It was true that Sal was partying less and consuming fewer drugs. I knew that was a good thing. But I also knew that the reason for this change was that Mathilde wanted him by her side, adoring her and making her meals that she'd later puke up in the bathroom. The positive effect had a negative cause, and I couldn't bring myself to accept it.

I tried talking to him.

'But I love her,' Sal said. He stared at his pint. 'Shit, I really do. I've never said that before. I've never meant it, anyway.'

I could tell from his face he was too far in.

'It just seems like she dominates you,' I said. 'Maybe you shouldn't make it so obvious how you feel about her.'

Sal looked confused. 'Why would I do that?'

'Just don't put yourself out there as much,' I said, taking a deep drag of my cigarette. 'I don't want you to get hurt. That's all.'

'You're saying I'm a different person when I'm around her,' he said, 'and you're right. She makes me want to be a better man and whatever she needs me to be. Isn't that a good thing, though? Trying to be better? Isn't that what love should be?'

I shrugged. We finished our pints.

That night, I looked at Laura as she slept beside me. Her blonde hair looked almost black against the pillow. She was turned away on her side and the shape of her back silhouetted against the window as her body rose and fell. I knew her movements like the ticking of a familiar clock. I lay there and thought about her for a while. I thought about someone else too, and then I closed my eyes.

Summer 2003

'Tell me what you believe,' I said.

'Why?'

'I want to know what's real to you.'

We were sitting on the stones at Dungeness, the sky white with humidity. We were together virtually every day at this point, as if we somehow knew the end was coming. At work, though, we avoided each other. The gossip was wildfire that needed just a little wind to make it spread, and this I wanted for myself. There was the added bonus of what it did to us when we were finally alone. The feel of her skin took on an intensity when I held her, like a fever I didn't want cured.

Nobody knew us at Dungeness.

'What's real to me?' She plunged her fingers into the stones. 'It's been nineteen years and I'm still working that out.'

'What happens when you die?'

She shifted. I could sense her discomfort and part of me wanted to change the subject, but I'll admit that most of me wanted to make her uncomfortable.

'The Bible says . . .' She took a deep breath. 'The Bible calls death a deep sleep. One day, there will be a great war on earth called Armageddon, and everyone who's died will come back to life on a Paradise earth.'

I nodded as if I understood. 'So, when's Armageddon coming?'

'The Bible says we're living in the Last Days, so any day.'

'You mean it could come tomorrow?'

She nodded with an embarrassed smile. 'When I was little, the adults told me I'd never finish school because The End will have come. They said I'd never get married or have kids, because by then we'd be in the New World.'

I raised my eyebrows. 'Wow.'

'That must sound so strange to you.'

'You said everyone that's died will come back to life, but what then?'

Anna took a moment to answer. 'They live forever in Paradise. Life without end.'

'Well, that sounds nice,' I said. 'I'll have some of that. But what happens in this war? This . . . Armageddon?'

'It's a battle between good and evil,' she said, avoiding eye contact. 'Those in the truth and judged as good will survive into Paradise, and those deemed wicked will be destroyed.'

I stroked my chin thoughtfully. 'Define "good".'

She covered her blushing face with her hands. 'What are you trying to do to me? Do you want a bloody Bible study?'

'Isn't this what you do when you knock on people's doors?'

'Yes, strangers' doors. I do my hour and then I'm done. Don't make me do it on my days off.'

'I thought it was important to you.'

'It is.' She picked up a stone and closed her hand around it. 'But I've spent my whole life being different from everyone else in the room. I don't want to think about that stuff when I'm with you.'

Across the beach was a wooden hut with its stable doors open for business. I left Anna on the stones and trudged across to get us a drink. An old man sat inside on a moulded plastic chair, his face hidden behind the garish front page of a tabloid. He wore a fedora hat pushed back on his head that made me think of my grandpa.

I cleared my throat. He looked up and threw down his paper. Sensing he wasn't in the mood for small talk, I turned to look at the sea as he poured two teas into Styrofoam cups.

Anna was watching as I walked back across the beach. The sun had found a break between the clouds and shone a spotlight on the little patch of stones where she sat. I thought how strange it was that she'd never know what it was like to be her through my eyes.

We sipped from our cups and watched the flat sea.

'Do you know what you are?' she said after a while.

I looked at her.

'You're worldly.'

'Worldly?'

'*The world is passing away and so is its desire . . . but the one who does the will of God remains forever.* You're "of the world", and you bring nothing but destruction.'

I finished the dregs of my tea. 'So I'm guessing I die at this Armageddon?'

She didn't seem to find this funny.

'How do I not be a "worldly"?' I said.

'You become one of them . . . one of us.'

'So it's like the Catholics,' I said, remembering church visits at school. 'Drink Christ's blood and blot out your sins? I can work with that.'

'No, don't go there with the blood. No transfusions, remember? Blood is sacred. It represents life and nobody has the right to give or take it except God.'

I lit a cigarette. 'It all sounds very interesting. Another world. Maybe you can be my teacher.'

'Me?' Anna laughed. 'I'm not even qualified to be the student.'

I moved my cigarette to my other hand, away from her. 'You make it sound very controlling,' I said.

'I suppose it is. There are a lot of rules.'

'But you seem to have a lot of freedom. You're not kept on a tight leash.'

'Am I a dog?'

'No,' I said, laughing. 'I mean, you're here with me. You work with a load of us – what did you call it – *worldlies*?'

'I have a curfew, remember.'

'Yes, but so do a lot of people.'

'We can't avoid living in the world, and I have to earn money. But I'm meant to work and then go home, only hang out with people who are also in the truth.'

'*The Truth?*'

She blushed. 'It's what we call the faith. Sorry, that must sound strange if you're not used to it. I forget when I'm with you that we're not the same.'

It did sound strange. Mean. Arrogant. 'It's fascinating,' I said, taking a drag.

'They don't know I'm here with you,' she said, her skin still burning. 'Teenagers are meant to rebel, right?'

'So I'm a secret.'

'Lisa's a secret. They don't know she exists. I have a fake friend, Susie, who apparently is part of a congregation on the coast. They think I'm with her.'

'Isn't there an irony in calling it *The Truth* and then lying to your parents by living a double life?'

Anna pulled her knees up to her chest, closing herself off. 'I don't know why you ask me questions and then criticise. I'm not expecting you to understand. I don't myself at times. But it's as natural to me as my arm or foot. I don't know how to separate from it.'

I reached out and grabbed her arm. 'Hey,' I said. 'Sorry for being a dick. I'm just trying to understand and it's hard, because just as it's completely natural to you, it's completely unnatural to me.'

I watched her fingers play with the hot stones.

'It's like I'm two Annas,' she said. 'Split down the middle, each incomplete. I wish I didn't find it fun to do the bad things, but I do.'

'Well, I can be a dick,' I said, sitting up. 'But I wouldn't call myself a bad thing.'

Her face burned again. 'Now it's my turn to say sorry.'

I smiled to absolve her of any guilt. It was becoming clear to me that she had enough shame being loaded on to her back by others. I wanted no part of that. Perhaps I could be her refuge. God, how stupid I was.

'I'm meant to serve because I want to,' she said, 'not because I'm forced. If they put me in chains, they know I'd break free. It has to be my decision.'

'And it is something you want?'

Her face was edged with sadness. 'It's all I've ever known, Nick. I don't know any different. Any time I've tried another path, it's never gone well. This feels like a safe place where I won't get hurt.'

We fell silent and I concentrated on my smoke. Lately I was charging through a pack a day, partly for the soothing rush of nicotine, but also because the act of holding a cigarette felt like a weapon or shield against the power of what I felt for her. I also knew she hated me smoking, and some twisted thing in my psyche loved to bait her.

'Do you ever feel like there's something inside of you too big to understand?' she said. 'An ache for something deeper?' She gripped a fistful of stones. 'Sometimes I just want to go a little mad. See where it takes me.'

I reached out and grabbed a handful of her dress and pulled her on to my mouth. She tasted me right back.

'That lighthouse,' she said, nodding at the needle rising up from the shingles behind the tea shack. 'Walk with me there.'

We walked across without speaking, the only sounds coming from the crushing of the stones beneath our feet and the long grass thrown about in the wind. In the distance, the power station loomed large against the bleakness of the sky, the white smoke plumes rising and disappearing into the day.

The green double doors at the foot of the lighthouse were open, and the windowless interior looked inviting and cool.

'Shall we?' I said, as if inviting her to dance.

I brushed her arm as we entered and felt a pang of electric shock.

We paid the entrance fee and paused at the foot of the stairs to look up at the long spiral ahead. It went round and around and round and around, and although the balcony and view from the top were hidden, we told ourselves it was worth it. The heat was beginning to crawl down my back, but I took her hand in mine and we began to climb.

A third of the way up, she let go of my fingers and leant against the rail. 'Whose idea was this again?' Her face was pink with rushing blood.

'Yours.'

'Well, you should have said no.'

'Because you'd have loved that, wouldn't you?'

'Shut up.' She wiped the back of her arm across her forehead and continued to climb.

I rolled up my sleeves, and this act reminded me of something. 'If my dad was here, he'd be taking these two at a time. *Come on, boy. Pick up your feet.*'

'I'm yet to meet your dad, but from what you say, I imagine him as the dad from an eighties film that threatens to send his kid to military school.'

I stopped and laughed, at both the joke and disbelief at how many more steps there were to go.

'A perfect comparison.' I climbed another. 'He's just one of many reasons I'm never getting married or having kids.'

I felt Anna pause behind me, but I carried on.

My momentum gave way ten steps later. I felt my knee buckle and I crouched down on the step, laughing as I caught my breath.

'Smoker's lungs,' said Anna, marching past. 'Serves you right.'

A harshness to her tone made me look up as she passed. She wore a face of intense concentration, as if in a single-minded race to the finish line. I considered calling surrender and going back down, but we were now closer to the top than the bottom.

She reached there first and didn't wait. When I arrived a few moments later, she'd disappeared around the platform to the other side of the lamp, out of sight.

From: ANNA
To: NICK
Subject:

You asked me today what was real to me.

I did my best to explain, but my best will never be enough.

How can I tell you that when I was eight, I would go with my family every Tuesday night to a little old lady's flat to study the Revelation book. Her name was May and she lived alone. The wallpaper was cream and textured, with raised patterns that I would trace with my fingers as I slipped off my shoes. The living room furniture was pushed to the edges and a circle of chairs laid out. If it was full, the children sat on the floor. One of the older sisters that came was Beryl. She had a purple leg, a husband out of the truth, and after the study was over, she'd pass a paper bag of sweets around the kids. Beryl always had an answer ready, even for the hardest questions in the book. Her faith was strong.

The Revelation book was a heavy red hardback with gold writing across the front. Inside were vivid descriptions of how the world as we know it will be destroyed at Armageddon. Buildings will topple, the earth will quake, God's anger will spill across the entire earth. The pictures in this book have never left me: piles of dead people, a woman screaming as she carries her dead child, the faces of all those who did not listen contorted in pain, terror, grief. But there were also pictures of peace. After the war, after families have been annihilated, we will stand on green hills and smile.

There was no question which side I was on. And there was no question about my school friends, with their birthday parties and their trick-or-treating and their glittery, evil Christmas. In my head, they were the ones whose mothers would be screaming. They were the ones who would be limp in their mothers' arms.

How can I tell you that? How can I tell you that my salvation can only come with the destruction of others?

By the front door was a small table of china figurines, trinket boxes, snow globes, little toys, and all these useless ornaments had price stickers – 10p, 20p, 50p. Every Sunday, May dropped every penny she made from these sales into the contribution box at the back of the hall. When the book study ended, I'd browse the items on offer before begging my mum to let me spend my pocket money on a china dog, or a dented brass pot, or a glass guitar filled with multi-coloured sand. The answer was usually no, but I felt bad not buying May's items, especially as no one else ever did. *But the money goes to the congregation*, I would plead as my mother silenced me with her eyes. How can she say no, I thought, when it would make May so happy if I gave her twenty pence, and it would make God happy too. Why could my mother not see that I was trying to make others happy? Isn't that what I was meant to do?

I tried to leave this life before, but something pulled me back. It does even now. How can I leave the only world I've ever known? How can I break those neurons in my head, the ones that call this *Truth*, the ones that began to form as I learned to walk and talk? How can I turn my back on Beryl and May and God? If they are so certain that this is true, who am I to say it's not? How can I make my mother the woman in the picture, the one carrying her dead, wicked child? How can I risk finding out that she wouldn't pick me up when I fell?

I'm asking questions you can never answer.

Do you see? Do you see now?

Of course you don't. Who the fuck could.

Summer 2003

After the Second Night

'I hope you're making a bacon sandwich again,' Anna whispered in my ear when I woke that morning.

I rubbed my eyes and looked at her. Her make-up had smudged overnight to give what I've heard described as a smoky eye. She was smiling, her hands tucked neatly under her cheek on the pillow. What the fuck was I doing with a girl like this in my bed?

'I'll make you anything you want,' I said.

Sal was at the kitchen table, and he blinked and gave a sleepy wave as we entered. He wore the proof of several pints on his face.

'Rough night?' I said.

He covered his face with his hands. 'You've no idea.'

'Tea?' said Anna, picking up the kettle. She had pulled on my T-shirt and her denim shorts before coming downstairs barefoot. I'd slipped on a clean top, but Sal wore nothing but boxers.

I started on the bacon as Anna asked Sal about his evening. As he talked of drunken fights outside the club, I thought of my own night – how I'd lain with her on my bed, talking and not talking, feeling our way around each other's bodies. I turned and leant against the counter, and she caught my eye and smiled.

'This'll help,' she said, when the tea was poured. She placed a chipped mug on the table in front of him and stroked his head. 'Or I can make a Bloody Mary if that's more your thing. Hair of the dog?'

Sal looked up at her adoringly. 'Marry me and have my children,' he said in a serious voice.

Anna laughed. 'One day, perhaps.'

'You do want kids then?'

'Of course. Who doesn't?'

Sal glanced over and gave a long whistle like a falling bomb. Anna blushed as she stared at her feet, and there was a heavy silence until the bacon began to spit.

'I thought you wanted to run off to New York and be a painter?' I said at last.

'I do.'

'Hard to be bohemian when you're married and saddled with kids, though.'

Finally she looked at me and it was my turn to look away. 'We can have it all these days, or haven't you heard? You just have to use your imagination.'

We went out one night with the work crowd.

I walked into the pub to find them huddled around a few tables at the front. She was in the corner with Lisa, deep in conversation. I raised a hand in greeting to the group and she saw and continued talking. No wave, no smile, no acknowledgement. I went to the bar.

When we stumbled down the hill to the club a few drinks later, she marched on ahead with her arm linked through Lisa's. I followed further back, smoking and laughing at a crude joke. She'd still hardly looked in my direction.

I found myself next to her at the bar. The music was so loud that I had to lean into her ear to make myself heard. 'You going to say hi then?'

She glanced at the dance floor and smiled. 'You haven't said hello either.'

'Hello.'

She looked at me. 'Hi.'

'Come here often?'

She laughed and flicked her hair over her shoulder. 'You'll have to do better than that.'

'Careful, Nick,' shouted one of the lads from behind. 'Her fella will be back soon. Or are you still "on a break"?' He mimicked quotation marks with his fingers.

Anna made a face. 'Mind your own business, yeah?'

He put both hands up in mock defeat and moved off through the crowd, leaving us in the cold shade of his words. There was a heavy silence despite the music and we turned away from each other.

'Drink?' I said finally, and she nodded and folded her arms.

I watched her dance for a while. I kept to the edges, talking with the others and a few of the old school gang who were also out. Every now and again, she threw me a glance, and each time, I'd sip my beer and look elsewhere.

A couple of drinks in, she left the dance floor in the direction of the toilets. Lisa followed close behind, stopping when she saw me. I gave a friendly smile and looked away, but she was already striding over.

'I need to talk to you,' she said, taking my arm and leading me into a quieter corner where we didn't need to shout. She did it quickly, looking over her shoulder, I assume to check Anna hadn't seen.

'You good?'

Lisa put her hands on her hips. 'What are you doing?'

I frowned. 'In life, or . . . ?'

She shook her head and I knew comedy wouldn't cut it. 'You like her, right?'

I took a sip of my beer.

Lisa gave a sarcastic smile, like she'd already figured what type of man I was going to be. 'Let me tell you a story,' she said, folding her arms. 'It's about a girl called Anna, who fell in love when she was seventeen. Fell in love with a prize prick, that is. She worshipped the dickhead, so much so that she did things she wasn't meant to do.' Lisa raised her eyebrows as if I knew what she was talking about. 'Her parents kicked her out when she refused to break it off. Called it *tough love*. Yeah, right. She came to live with me because none of her family wanted anything to do with her. I was there when she cried herself to sleep because she loved and missed them, and I was there when she cried because that bastard went and broke her heart.'

I looked down at my glass.

'Are you going to be another bastard, Nick?' said Lisa. 'Because I don't know you that well, but I think you have the potential to be a decent guy. And I can tell she likes you far more than she should.'

I knew she was waiting for me to speak and I turned towards the dance floor.

'She's not like us,' Lisa said. 'You know her shit. What we think is normal in a relationship she's only meant to do if married. And she's only meant to be with someone of the same faith. Personally, I think her family are vile for what they did, but it's all she's ever known. She doesn't want to lose them again.'

Anna came back in and looked about the room. She seemed to be searching for someone.

I glanced back at Lisa. 'I know what you're saying.'

She studied my face and gave a slow nod. 'Don't mess her around. I swear you'll regret it.'

I didn't reply and watched her disappear through the club towards Anna. I waited in the corner for a while, finishing my drink, trying not to look across to where she stood.

I thought about slipping out and going home. I knew that was what I should do.

Just after midnight, Anna brushed past and took hold of my fingers. 'Fancy getting out of here?'

I looked at her and nodded.

We met outside. I was smoking in the road, and she put on her denim jacket and stood a few feet away with her arms folded.

'Where do we go?' I said.

She glanced up the hill towards town. 'I'm pretty hungry.'

We began towards the bright lights. When we were out of sight of the club, she stepped close and put her arm through mine. Neither of us spoke.

Near the top of the hill, she led me off into a side street behind some old Victorian buildings. It was more like an alley, dark and secluded and away from the road. It stank of piss.

She pushed me against the wall and kissed me.

'So when is he back?' I don't know why I said it. I didn't want to know.

She stopped. 'Does it matter?'

'Doesn't it?'

'You tell me.'

'Why are you with me right now?'

She gave a sharp intake of breath and looked down, leaning her head slightly against my chest. 'I don't know. You're like a drug to me. A fix I shouldn't have.'

'What are we doing here?' I said, stroking her hair. She was looking up at me and searching my face for something. 'Are we mad?'

'I'll probably marry him,' she said, looking at my mouth. 'You won't understand, I know. But that's probably what I'll do.'

And then she pressed herself against me and her mouth was on mine, and I knew I was playing with fire, but sometimes we crave the heat. She reached her hands under my shirt and touched my skin. The electric jolt of some unknown thing flooded my veins.

'I have to let you go,' she said, but she didn't pull away and I drowned out her words with my tongue.

There was a difference in Anna after I told her about Mum.

It's hard to pinpoint exactly what changed, and really, nothing much did. We still teased each other, we still argued, we still feverishly made up, but there was a newness to the way she looked at me. I'd notice her watching from the sidelines, when the telly was on or sitting in traffic. Her fingertips would brush along the back of my neck, she'd break away during a kiss to press her lips against the tip of my nose, or she'd insist on me having the last mouthful of the food we were sharing. It was as if the shape of whatever was between us had shifted into something softer. The change was slight, but potent.

She was the first girl I'd ever told. Part of me regretted telling. I knew how to deal with other people's tears – soothe their backs, calming words, suggest a pot of tea – I was used to those. But I didn't want pity, and I especially didn't want pity from her.

She held me longer than before. When we embraced, it had always been her pulling away first, but now she lingered. Now it was me that drew back.

One time, on my bed, she made me take off my T-shirt and lie on my front, then traced her fingers softly over the skin of my back, not even stopping when I opened my eyes and saw that an hour had passed.

'I can't describe how good that feels,' I said. 'But stop if you like.'

'Close your eyes.'

I didn't fight. I couldn't.

'I read once that a person's touch can mend a broken heart,' said Anna. 'I hope that's true.'

I didn't stop to ask whose heart she meant.

September 1991

Its name is Maison de la Cascade, and we practise saying it in exaggerated French accents on the journey down from Calais – Mum, Stella, Sal and I. Dad is driving, mainly in silence, although he occasionally switches on the radio to search for a transatlantic sports channel. This is code for *shut up now*, and we retreat into our worlds, turning our faces to the flashes of countryside rolling by. I nudge Sal whenever I see a chateau in the distance and he does the same to me. Mum has secretly given us each a tub of legit Pringles to last the journey, and we suck each crisp against the roofs of our mouths so as to prevent the driver from hearing the crunch. Greasy fingers on leather seats is apparently a problem, even when the seats are second-hand and have had ten years of arses farting into their crevices.

The roads are mainly clear, it being the end of summer and everyone back at school. Holidays are cheaper at the start of term. Sal and I rarely got our pick of the classroom desks, but it was that or no trip at all.

We reach the house at dinnertime. It's set down a little lane, away from the main drag of the village. There is a sweeping driveway made from crazy paving, bright red shutters fanning every window, and terracotta pots of red flowers – geraniums are my favourite, says Mum – sitting in the sun.

Mum opens a can of beer from the cool box in the boot and hands it to Dad, and he takes it without a word and heads inside, likely for the nearest sofa. Stella and Mum begin unpacking the car, and Sal and I run off to explore.

To the right of the garage is a path of steps that snakes down around the fig trees. We run with the energy that comes from being confined to a car for several hours, and as we descend, the trickling water heard at the top gets louder and stronger, so that when we leap off the final step, the sound is a screaming crescendo of a waterfall gushing into a pool. *Maison de la Cascade*.

We stop and stare, our mouths agape. As an eleven-year-old boy, I'm sure the words *that is beautiful* do not appear in my head, but I'm transfixed by the sight and sound of the pool, by how the drops of water look like diamonds, by how it rushes in and out and never stops. We have never seen anything like it and it feels like a dream. I don't know what Sal is thinking, but I sense he knows this too.

I hear a splash and then Sal is in the pool. It's more of a large pond, not wide but deep, surrounded by layers of natural stone and long tufts of reeded grass. Sal's clothes lie in a pile beside my feet, and as he turns in the water and floats on his back, his lean torso gleams in the sunlight. I kick off my shorts and jump in, and we float around together like fallen leaves. The sun weaves in and out of the spiky plants surrounding the top of the waterfall, and when I close my eyes, an imprint of the scene remains.

'Let's do this every day,' I say to Sal, but the only reply is the sound of rushing water.

The first few days pass in a blur. It is much like when we are at home, with Mum in the kitchen and Dad sitting and watching something. Sal and I spend most of the time in the pool. We go inside only to use the toilet or sleep, and even then we would do both outside if we could get away with it.

We swim and play football in the sun. We paddle our feet in the stream that leads to the waterfall, making dams and bridges with twigs and leaves. Mum brings us little bottles of Panaché and we kick back and pretend to be men. We climb the steep banks that surround the house, or at least I do until we spot a thick, dark snake uncurling itself in the sun on a ridge halfway up. After that, I keep to the grass and the water, but Sal still climbs. I think now he is looking for snakes.

We don't really do much. It feels great.

From the pool, we hear Mum and Stella laughing as they prepare the meals. The radio is permanently blaring, and they sing along to 'Joe le Taxi' and chain-smoke out the open window.

The day before we're due to leave, we're all out at the pool – Sal and I swimming, Mum and Stella sitting further out on sun loungers – when Dad comes down the steps, jingling the loose change in his pocket.

'You all right, love?' Mum asks, starting to sit up. 'Want me to make you something?'

'Why would I need you to make me something?' he says. 'Am I not allowed to come down and see my own family?'

Mum gives a small, strained smile and leans slowly back.

'Hello, boys,' he says, bending down to ruffle our hair. 'Enjoying the holiday, are you?'

Sal flinches at his touch.

'You know, lads,' says Dad, kicking off his clothes. 'I used to be on the swimming team in the army. Best bomber in the air and best bomber in the water.'

'No, Paul,' says Stella from under a big floppy hat. 'We don't want to be soaked just so you can prove yourself.'

He stands back to take a running leap and launches himself, expertly moulding his body into a ball that hits the exact middle of the pool. A plume of water rains down around the grass. Moments later, he appears at the surface and puts his hands up in anticipation of an adoring audience.

Mum and I are the only ones clapping.

Sal climbs out of the water and shakes himself dry. He grabs a towel from the lounger and rubs hard at his hair. 'I'm going inside. Anyone want anything?'

'A lolly, please,' I call out from the pool.

Mum is drying the pages of her book against her skirt. 'Bring out the box, Sal.'

He nods and runs up the steps.

'You having a good time, son?' asks Dad as he gets out. I nod as he stands there in the sunshine for a moment, his hands on his hips and his eyes closed against the sun. He looks like one of those Greek statues in the British Museum. He flicks back his hair and walks to the loungers, where he sits down behind Mum, who is still drying herself with a towel.

'Make the most of it,' he says, pulling her towards him and doing something to make her squeal. 'You'll be back to reality soon enough.'

I watch as he whispers in Mum's ear and she laughs and gives me a wink. Sinking back into the water, I turn and float on my back. In the distant blue sky, an aeroplane is passing and I think of the people in their seats, eating rubbery food in little trays with their suitcases stowed underneath them. I imagine a bomb exploding and them raining down in pieces.

'Hands up!'

And then Stella is screaming. It's a sound that goes on for years and years.

Later, I discover that on his way out with the box from the freezer, Sal had noticed the garage door ajar. The farmer who owned the house was often popping by to collect things from the garage, which he usually kept locked by way of a thick padlock. But today he'd left it open, and Sal, being Sal, had gone inside.

Propped up in the corner, he'd found a rifle.

I don't know what kind of rifle it was. Those kinds of details don't really matter. Or do they? Whenever there's a school shooting, people want to know what kind of gun was used, how many rounds of bullets it took, what the shooter said to the crying students, where they hid, which video games he played, the colour of his skin. People love the details.

So I'll do my best.

They were those spiral lollipops that looked like helter-skelters, lime flavoured with some exotic-sounding French word emblazoned across the front of the box. The box itself was slightly soggy from the deep ice that clung to the sides of the freezer.

I think the rifle was for killing birds.

Sal had wedged the box under the same arm that held the gun.

He said he'd only meant to scare us. Actually, he said he didn't even mean to do that. He thought we'd laugh, he said. He thought we'd all say, *wow, Sal, that's cool* and then he'd hand out the lollies.

He was so excited that he took the steps two at a time. As he reached the bottom and called out, the box began to slip from his grip and his arm tensed to stop it falling. But what his brain also did was send a message to his finger to tense the rifle, and so his finger did exactly that, pressing the trigger and firing the gun. When they investigated the scene afterwards, they found a chipped section of stone behind the waterfall, where the bullet had hit and ricocheted across the pond towards the loungers, where it hit our mother in the left temple and didn't come out the other side.

Nothing that could be done, they said.

Died instantly, they said.

PART TWO

Summer 2003

Near the End

The day was hot.

Each day that summer started out the same, but this one I remember differently. I remember the beads of sweat crawling through my hair – what there was of it – how they slipped like snakes along my scalp to my neck, or the back of my ear, before sliding down the rest of my body. The days when we were together, I didn't care about the heat. It stuck me to her, and her to me, and that was quite all right.

'Let's go to Eastwell,' Anna had said when she reached mine. 'Everyone's at the beach today. It's safe. Let's go back to the lake.'

We were walking along a country lane. The hedgerows were short and forced us into the brunt of the heat, our shadows stretched before us. What we did, they did too. When I took her hand, the figure in front reached out to grasp its lover, and when I pulled her in for a kiss, I looked sideways at the mirror as two became one.

'I've just realised something,' she said, drawing back. 'I've never seen you dance.'

'There's a reason for that.'

She raised an eyebrow in expectation.

'I don't dance.'

'Rubbish. Everybody dances. Even if it's alone in their bedroom.'

I shook my head. 'Not even then.'

She stopped and raised her arms in protest, as if what I had just said was a statement of seismic proportion. There was a light sheen of sweat on her forehead and I imagined it tasting of salt.

'Well then,' she said. 'I'll have to be the girl to show you how.' And she grabbed my arm and pulled me close so our stomachs were touching. She placed my hand on her shoulder, her own on my waist, and our other hands joined together towards the road.

'Aren't I meant to lead?' I said as she lurched us forward.

'Says who?' she said, pushing us on to do the tango. 'Just having a penis doesn't give you rights.'

I slid my arm down around her waist and gripped her tight, then picked her up and spun us around and around until we collapsed dizzy in the road and laughing.

'You're a shite dancer, you know that,' she said, laughing and wiping her wrist against her forehead. 'But I'm pleased to be your first.'

We smiled at each other and began to lean in for the kiss when there was a rustling behind and a fox pushed through the hedge. Something dangled from its jaws. The fox stopped when it saw us, then dropped whatever was in its mouth and darted off up the lane.

'Oh, look,' said Anna, gesturing at the tiny brown creature panting on the ground.

We scrambled to our feet and ran over. It was a baby rabbit, its stomach split open, bloody entrails oozing through the wound. It lay on the road with its eyes half open and stared into the dry beat of the sun. There were humble fights for breath.

'No,' said Anna and dropped to her knees. 'No, poor thing. Poor, poor thing. Its life was just beginning.' Her hands reached out instinctively to touch it, and I leant down and stopped her.

'Don't,' I said, taking her wrist. 'It might be diseased. Look at it. There's nothing we can do.'

She looked up and her eyes were wet. 'But we can't leave it like this.'

I searched the lane and returned with large torn leaves that I used to scoop up the rabbit – *Gentle*, Anna kept saying. *Don't hurt it* – and carefully deposited its barely alive body on the shady side of the road.

A few hours later, when we returned this way home, we would find the creature dead and Anna would claw at a patch of baked earth to make room for a shallow grave. But now, she gripped my arm as we walked on, throwing the occasional glance over her shoulder. We were quiet until we reached the lake.

There it was, shimmering, how water does in memory. We stood on the bridge and watched a while, then walked along to the ruined church and lay on the bank in the shadows.

I turned my head to her. 'That's why I struggle to believe in a god.'

Her eyes were fixed on the tree canopy overhead.

'Your belief that everyone will live forever,' I went on. 'I struggle with that, because death is an entirely natural part of life. These trees are already starting to drop their leaves, and soon, everything will be dead. Then life starts again in spring. It's a cycle. It's the natural order of things.'

'Trees don't die in winter,' she said. 'They rest. And that's how death is described in the Bible – a deep sleep. One day, the dead will wake up. Imagine if the trees didn't pulse with new life in spring. You *know* it's going to happen. Why should it seem so magical for the same thing to happen to us?'

'But that's my point. It's new life. Not the one that came before.'

'How do you mean?'

'Those sunflowers by my house,' I said. 'They bloom and fade before they die and are cut down. Next year, Stella will plant more. But *those* sunflowers have one chance. There will be others like them, but never one the same.'

'Are you a gardener now?'

'Listen to me. The sunflower accepts that this is it. It doesn't ask why. It doesn't spend the short time it has to bloom wondering if now is when it should be blooming.'

Her silence told me she was listening. I wish I had too.

'You're talking about trees, though,' she said quietly. 'About flowers. They're not living things like us. They don't have a heart pumping blood.'

'But the rabbit did. It had a heart like us, and a home like us, and a family, like us. But it also had a predator. If God made the animal kingdom, then surely death was part of that. Life ends, and the carcass becomes food for the earth to grow new life. Nothing lasts forever.'

'I know what you're saying,' Anna said after a while. 'But how can this be it? Think of what our minds are capable of and how our bodies work, how a baby starts from nothing. How can that all be down to chance? That's terrifying.'

'Living forever seems terrifying. Each day the same as the next.'

She smiled. 'The Bible says God will satisfy the desire of every living thing, so you don't need to worry.'

'He didn't quite do that with Eve, though.'

'What?'

'Adam and Eve?'

'I know who Eve is, thank you.'

'He didn't satisfy her desire. She went looking for forbidden fruit.'

'Well, yes.' She was surprised, I could tell. I hadn't said about my recent visit to the library.

'Eve wouldn't have gone looking for an apple if she had everything she needed, would she?'

'She was wilful,' Anna said, after a beat.

'But he made her that way?'

'He gave her free will, yes,' she said slowly. 'But she chose to use it poorly.'

'So you have the right to choose, but if you choose a path he doesn't like, then you're condemned to certain death or hell or whatever you call it. Does that sound fair?' I tried to keep my tone light.

'For someone with no belief in God, you certainly know your Bible stories.'

I riffled around in my pocket and brought out my smokes. 'Maybe I've read enough to know I don't believe it.'

'It's fun being lectured on the fundamentals of Christianity by a heathen,' Anna said, putting her hands behind her head. 'Please continue.'

'I just take issue with that concept of free will.' I lit my cigarette and let it rest in my hand furthest from her. 'Because it seems that God's putting a gun to your head. Serve me and live. Don't and die. Funny kind of free will.'

She stared up at the trees. 'I guess it depends how you look at it.'

'Well, he failed with Eve. He had the chance to create his best work and he ballsed it up, first try. If they were perfect and yet chose the fruit, what hope do the rest of us have?'

'I've never seen you so passionate about a subject as you are about this.'

I turned towards her, propped up on one elbow. 'Hear me out. They took the fruit from the tree of the knowledge of good and bad, right? That's the one tree in the garden God said they couldn't touch, because . . . what would happen?'

'Their eyes would be opened so that they knew good and bad, and then they would die.' She reeled off the script, word perfect.

'So until they ate the fruit, they didn't know what good or bad meant. How then could they know eating the fruit was *bad* if they didn't know what badness was?' I made little stabs in the air with my cigarette to make my point.

'But they disobeyed God.'

'But he didn't arm them with knowledge. He deliberately made them naïve, then planted a tree as a test and allowed an evil snake to deceive them. Why didn't he protect them from the predator? And how would they even recognise a dishonest snake if they had no concept of dishonesty?' I lay back down. 'God's the one up to the tricks.'

'Blasphemer.' Her hand shot out and gripped my arm, and I couldn't tell if she was joking.

'There's no way he's satisfying every desire. If he's even real, then he's the one that created desire in the first place, the good and the bad.'

'It's the future desires he'll satisfy. In the New World. When we're perfect.'

'We?'

I took a drag and our eyes met. Anna bit her lip as if regretting her words, and looked down to where our hands were touching.

'All I know is what I feel in here,' I touched my fist to my heart, 'and here,' to my brain. 'That's true. That's real. Everything else is unknowable.'

There was the long, mounting drone of a plane in the sky, the sound of thunder, or the end of the world. She let go of my arm and drew her hand up to rest on her waist, and we lay there for what felt like ages. She bit her nails while I finished my cigarette.

Then she stood and went down to the water, and I watched her kick off her shoes as a strap from her red dress fell from her shoulder. She didn't turn to look at me or shake off the rest of her clothes. There was one step forward, another, and then she walked fully clothed into the lake.

She sank under the surface and came up a moment later. The water lapped gently as she floated on her back, facing the sky.

I sat up and watched her for a while. She drifted between the light and shade, her hands and feet pushing back and forth against the current. Her red dress billowed around her like a pool of blood. Finally she straightened and turned, submerged up to her neck. 'Come in with me,' she said softly, and I left my fags and phone with my shoes and walked down to the edge.

I dived in.

I saw her legs above a tangle of weeds underwater, and when I reached her, I put my hands through the green mist and felt my way up her body. When I broke through the surface, she pushed herself against me and wrapped her legs around my waist, kissing my mouth.

This is the moment, I thought to myself. This is exactly the moment.

We went for each other with a strange, carnal hunger. Our clothes were no match for the fury from our hands and our fingers. We found a way.

Then came that old familiar 'Wait'.

God no, I thought. Whatever you want, but please God no.

She stopped and looked at me, the water dripping from her face, her expression wild, my body breathless.

She broke away and pulled me towards the bank. We swam to shore and climbed out, remnants of the lake trickling from our bodies. Here is where she began to peel off her clothes, and watching her, I did the same. We stood naked in front of each other in the midday sun, then she took my hand and led me further in towards the church. There, hidden from the lane and beneath the bracken, she pulled me down on top of her.

Still, I could not catch my breath. All I could do was look at her, this girl I had wanted all summer, who now took my hands and pressed them to her skin and was completely sure. This girl, who brought my ear to her lips and whispered, 'Promise you'll tell no one.'

This girl, to whom I said, 'I promise.'

Late Eighties

We go down to the Isle of Wight for the October half-term in the year of an Indian summer. The two hot days are spent on the beach, building sandcastles with a found pink bucket and burying Mum in the sand. Sal digs a moat around a city of sandcastles, and Mum runs back and forth to the sea, filling the bucket with water that she pours carefully into the moat. We watch as the water seeps through the sand and disappears, then she turns and jogs back to the shore to repeat the process. We never fill the moat and she never stops trying.

Dad doesn't figure in this part of the memory. He is absent, probably behind a newspaper or asleep after too many beers. It's always Mum there with us.

The rest of the week is a washout, and we spend it cooped up in a tiny chalet, with rain lashing windows as we play endless games of Snakes and Ladders. There is nowhere to hang our dripping coats and the place smells like wet dog.

On the ferry home, Sal loses Elephant. It's a small blue cuddly toy that he began to carry everywhere from the age of about three. Dad would comment that six-year-old boys shouldn't be hugging teddy bears, and Sal would clinch it to his chest and insist that it wasn't a bear. Mum and I would just look away.

It's about an hour after we get off the Portsmouth ferry that Sal cries out. Mum and I look around us, in the footwells, in bags, but there is no sign of Elephant.

'You must have left him where you sat in the window on the ferry, watching the boats,' says Mum, and Sal begins to cry.

'We have to go back,' he says.

Dad snorts. 'Of course we're not going back. We're nearly halfway home.'

Sal rubs the tears from his cheeks. 'But I can't leave him there. What will he do?'

'I'm sure it'll be fine,' says Dad. 'Creatures with stuffing for brains don't usually feel things.'

'What will I do? No, we *have* to go back.'

'This is exactly what you need. You're far too old to be attached to a grubby toy.' Dad tightens his grip on the steering wheel.

Sal's face turns a hot red. He balls his bony hands into fists and pushes down on his legs, trying to bruise his own skin. His eyes are squeezed shut to hold back the dam, and I watch as his body starts to shake.

Mum has turned around in the front. She reaches round the seat to hold his leg and tries to grab his hand. 'Darling, darling, it's okay. I'll ring the ferry people when we get home and I'll get them to search for Elephant. We'll get him back, sweetheart.'

'You're giving him false hope,' Dad says, staring straight ahead. 'They'll never find it and you know it.'

Mum throws him a look I've never seen before. She turns back to Sal, who is making low, growling noises like a hurt animal. He has been doing this lately. Getting angry in an effort not to cry.

'Paul,' says Mum, turning back to face the front. 'Please pull over. He needs me.'

'We're on the motorway, Louise.'

'There's a service station coming up.' Her voice is calm and distant. 'You can pull in there for two minutes. That's all I ask you for.'

Dad sighs and swerves off into the slip road. Someone honks their horn and he makes a face at the rear-view mirror. I can't see the car behind so it looks like he's scowling at me.

When the car stops, Mum jumps out to open the door and Sal falls into her arms. He buries his face in the folds of her cotton jacket and I watch as his skinny body shudders without making a sound. Mum is rubbing his back and making soothing noises in his ear. She puts a hand on the back of his head and holds him tight against her, the vibration of her heart seeming to soften the violence of Sal's grief.

I turn to stare out the window.

Finally, he stops crying. He hangs limp in her arms, exhausted by his own rage, and she rocks him from side to side like he is her baby again. The only sounds are the rushing of the motorway and the slow tapping of Dad's fingers on the steering wheel.

A week later, we come home from school and propped against Sal's pillow sits Elephant. He arrived that morning, Mum says, fresh off the boat, where he'd been found tucked behind a chair. She'd rung the ferry office every day until they took her seriously, and now here he is, sent through the postal system in brown paper.

Sal sits on his bed and stares at Elephant for what seems like hours. He picks him up and inspects every inch of him, looking for the faded label and the discoloured foot that prove he's not a replacement.

'But will he remember?' he says to Mum.

She frowns. 'Remember?'

'That we left him.' Sal looks sideways at Elephant.

She sits down on the bed and puts her arm around him. 'We'll just have to give him lots of cuddles, won't we, Nick? Explain it was an accident, that's all. Nobody's fault. The important thing is we got him back.'

Sal doesn't look convinced. He pulls Mum towards him and leans in. 'But an elephant never forgets,' he whispers.

She thinks about this for a moment then runs a hand through Sal's hair. 'These things happen, sweetheart. We'll make him feel loved. That'll fix it.' She kisses him. 'Now how about I make us some pancakes?'

A couple of weeks later it is Sal's birthday, and Mum takes us to the toy shop for the annual tradition of choosing our own gift. He walks past the aisles of cars and trucks where he usually lingers and goes instead to the cuddly toys. There, he picks up a big fluffy scarlet elephant that's within budget and hugs it tightly to his chest.

'Are you sure?' says Mum, slightly confused.

He nods and braces his arms as if preparing for a fight.

'Well, okay then.'

Back home, he goes to our room and shuts the door, and from that moment, Old Elephant lives in the box of toys along with everything else and it is New Elephant that is loved.

Late August 2003

Those days with Anna come back to me in fragments, the pieces of a cracked mirror; jagged, broken hints of a man I could have been. As the years go by, I lose pieces here and there, until I am left now with an incomplete picture, only the moments I have thought about most. Those synapses are well trodden. And who knows which parts I have edged with metal to make them catch the sun.

Another evening, sometime in the midst of that heat, Anna and I were messing about on my bed. We hung out a lot in my room over the course of that summer. There weren't many places we could go without risk of discovery, and my legs were too long for hours in her Ford Fiesta.

I was lying on the bed with my T-shirt off. A soft breeze blew in through the window. She was on my lap, her dress hitched up around her waist, one leg either side of me. I tried to concentrate.

'Have you got anything other than shitty rap music?' she'd said a few minutes earlier, riffling through my CD rack.

'Check Sal's room. He likes blaring guitars, like you do.' Sal was between rentals and had no choice but to move home for the summer.

'I can't go into your brother's room. What if he's in there with a girl, like you?' She tickled me. 'No, you go. Bring me back a stack. That's an order.'

When I returned, Anna made her choice and pressed play on the stereo before climbing on to my lap. For the next four minutes, she kissed me between the bars of 'Karma Police', stopping to sing every word.

Still lying there, I lit a fag and smoked it, one hand behind my head and the other resting on the ashtray by the window. I rarely smoked in my room – if I did, it was always leaning out into the street – but there was no way I was volunteering her to move.

'I'll have a go,' she said, and I wondered what she meant. She waved to me to put the cigarette to her lips.

'You sure?' I said, surprised. 'I don't want to be responsible for turning you into an addict.'

I held it to her lips and she breathed in too quickly, flooding her lungs and violently coughing.

'Eurgh,' she said, when she'd whacked her chest enough and found her voice. 'How can you do that all the time? No wonder you taste like you do.'

I narrowed my eyes as I took another drag, and when I breathed out, the smoke came out in rings. 'You don't like my smoky kick?'

She closed her eyes and inhaled as she leant down, as if she secretly adored the smell. Our faces were close, and she kissed me.

'Hate it,' she whispered, and made a face before kissing me again. 'Disgusting.' – Kiss. – 'Vile.' – Kiss. – 'You're the filthiest thing I've ever tasted.'

We must have spent a while just lazing about, kissing each other. This was often the pattern of our days. I've imagined Daz and the lads and their reactions if I'd told them we did nothing most times but this. They would never have believed it. Their method was to slip a hand under the top, a greedy thrust, see how far they could get. By now, Anna and I had already been to the lake, but we acted like we knew it wouldn't happen again. We never spoke of it afterwards, as if it was too sacred a thing to pull apart and dissect with words.

She always seemed so strong to me, but what the hell do I know about women?

There was no talk of this boyfriend since he'd arrived back, and I heard a rumour at work that the break was still going. That he'd wanted to get back together and she wasn't sure. But then sometimes she didn't respond to my texts for hours, and in those endless minutes I fantasised about them together: had they gone too far in the back of her car, was he the type to slip a palm down the front of her jeans and would she let him do as he liked? The scenes went on and on in my head.

I should have fought. I should have had it out with her, probed deeper, used the information to prepare my own case. But the reality was that I didn't want to pollute the time we had together, to let that other life she had get its claws on us too. There I go, talking of reality. When that entire summer felt like a dream, one from which I never wanted to wake.

'What is it about him?' I asked during a lull. She was still on my lap, and so far I had done a professional job of ignoring the incessant throbbing in my shorts.

She knew who I meant. 'Why do you want to know?' she said, with a slight shake of her head.

Because I fucking want you, I wanted to say. *Because I don't want anyone else to have you. Because surely you're exhausted by all this feeling too.*

'I'm trying to understand your position,' I said. 'We come from two different worlds.'

She stroked my stomach and gave a sad smile. 'It feels good to make other people happy,' she said softly, and I remembered what Lisa had told me in the club about her family. *Tough love.* 'And I have to get married, remember?'

'You talk about following the rules, but then you're here . . . and you're not. Do you even believe it?'

She leant back. 'We've spoken about this before. I don't expect you to understand.'

'Listen,' I said gently, sitting up slightly and taking her hand. 'I'm just trying to get it, that's all. Because it's important to you, and . . .'

. . . because you're important to me.

'. . . because I'm pretending to be good when I'm really a slut?'

'What? No, stop.' I could feel where this was going and wished I had never opened my mouth. 'Anna, please. I don't think that way.'

She looked startled at the sound of her name.

'Why do you have to get married?' I said. 'Why is living or even just being with someone so dreadful?'

'It's not an option for me,' she said, her face reddening. 'I'd lose everyone I know. That was made clear the last time . . . Like I said, you won't get it and that's fine. You're not a person that even likes the concept of marriage. And why is that, by the way?'

'It's not true that you'd lose everyone. Lisa wouldn't leave you.'

She sighed. 'I'm not even meant to be friends with Lisa,' she said. 'She's worldly, remember? I'm not meant to go to clubs, or get drunk, or hang out with work friends, wear short skirts, go to uni, or sit in worldly boys' bedrooms. If I got found out . . .' She shook her head.

'Why can't you go to university? Is it because they teach you to think for yourself?' I tried to keep my voice level. 'A person who gets A-grades in every subject should go to university.'

Her shoulders shrugged, but her face suggested she was listening.

'Why don't you like the idea of marriage?' she said again.

I'd clearly not deflected it well enough, and there was no beer or fag to prevent me from answering. 'I just think that if people want to end a relationship, they should be free to. They shouldn't have to seek permission from the government, to meet rules and criteria before it's allowed.'

She frowned. 'So you're planning on every relationship ending?'

'No, but I'm not sure there's a need for marriage any more. Now that women have freedom and it's not a business transaction. People should have the right to move on if they're unhappy.'

'So there's no conversation to be had? That's it. Closed book?'

I thought about this. 'I don't get why it even has to be an issue. I'm twenty-two. Who on earth thinks about marriage at our age?'

She looked up at the ceiling and gave a long exhale. 'You're right. I don't even know why we're talking about it.'

'Hey.' I put my hand on her leg and she softened at my touch. 'My experience of marriage growing up is probably very different to yours. Perhaps your parents were better at it, but it seemed like people stopped trying once they'd said "I do". That one person could treat the other however they liked, because they knew that person would stay. They were institutionalised and it was too hard to leave. I don't want that.'

'Maybe your future doesn't have to be like your past.'

'But look, even your rules are different – aren't you only meant to marry someone from your faith?'

She played with the end of her dress. 'Officially, yes. But you can get away with marrying an unbeliever. It's frowned upon, but it isn't something that would get you kicked out. It's the getting married that matters.'

'It seems like they want you to be someone you're not.'

There was a long silence. We heard the cars speed down the street.

'I do believe it,' she said finally. 'Everyone seems to get it in a way I don't, but that doesn't mean it's not true. There's something there. I'm just feeling my way through, and hopefully the fog will shift and it will make sense. I don't talk about it because it's a reminder that I shouldn't be with you.' She looked at me. 'I shouldn't be with you.' She repeated it almost as if in a trance.

No, I thought. *No no no no no.*

'So you're going to go off and marry a good boy because it will make your parents happy? Is that the life you want?'

She touched her cheek as if I had slapped her. 'Don't,' she said, and then her tone hardened: 'I told you he'd be back by the end of summer. You knew how it was all along.'

'Sowing your wild oats with me, then?'

She shook her head and climbed off. Her phone fell on the floor with a thud, and she reached down and threw it in her bag. 'Because this has been all about my pleasure, right? You've not done too badly out of it.'

I watched from my bed as she pulled on her shoes and slung her bag over her shoulder. This was my chance to tell her, to open my mouth and declare the words charging through my head. That the day by the lake had been anything but ordinary. That I was not that kind of bloke. But then Lisa had said she had fallen for a bastard, so maybe it was the bastards she loved.

She grabbed her keys and paused at the door, turning, flicking her hair and lifting her chin. 'You expect me to know who I am, to have it all figured out, because the possibility that I'm still finding out is just too confusing for you. What about you? Who the hell is Nick Mendoza?' She slammed the door.

I listened for the familiar sound of her car, then lit the first of many cigarettes.

Later that week, Dad took me for a drink at his club. We sat at the bar and watched the boxing on the fuzzy TV in the corner. The only other person in there was old Harry, who was pissed and shouting at the screen.

'They're all the same, women, the lot of them,' said Dad as he finished his pint.

I checked my phone constantly.

How stupid humans are.

Sal never went to university. When we were kids, this was always how he planned to escape.

The way it worked at the time, you applied for a loan to pay the one grand a year tuition. You could then apply for an extra loan to cover living expenses, or else try for a maintenance grant. Of course, if you had rich parents, none of this mattered. Yours was a golden ticket.

But we didn't have rich parents. We had Dad, who'd spent his life doing bits for cash. This worked well in my first year away at uni. I got a loan for my tuition and, thanks to Dad's lack of official income, I qualified for a maintenance grant. This I deposited immediately into a high-interest savings account and got a part-time bar job to pay for my expenses. I've always been good at keeping to a budget.

The beginning of my third year coincided with what would have been Sal's first. By then, Dad had landed a proper job running a local garage, doing a bit on the tools as well as running the office and dealing with customers. For the first time in our lives, he received a monthly salary in a bank account. It was a tidy sum. This meant I no longer qualified for maintenance grants and neither would Sal.

'Can't you get them to pay you cash for a year?' said Sal, a few weeks before the deadline. 'I'll do what Nick did and save the grant. I'll get a job on the side and make extra to see me through the other two years.'

It was Sunday morning and Dad was making a fry-up. I'd laid the table and was making tea as Sal stood in the doorway, gripping the frame.

'Let's not pretend you'd save anything,' said Dad, cracking an egg. 'You'd probably smoke it within the first month. And what would they think if I asked them for cash in an envelope? It's not that kind of job. You want me to go back to living hand to mouth?'

Sal raked a hand through his hair. 'There must be a way.'

'You can get a loan to cover expenses,' I said, pouring the milk.

'I'll already have a loan to cover tuition. I'll end up with a mountain of debt.'

'There's nothing to stop you going somewhere local,' said Dad. 'Carry on at the video shop in the evenings and weekends. Your child benefit will be ending this year when you turn eighteen, but I won't charge you rent. Take it or leave it.'

Sal looked at me. As in all these conversations, I assumed the role of a silent referee. I raised my eyebrows to suggest it was a good offer, but it was clear from how he folded his arms that he didn't agree.

'Hardly the real uni experience.'

'No, you're right,' said Dad, ripping the plastic film off a tray of mushrooms. 'I'd say it's a far more valuable lesson. It'll teach you that life doesn't hand you everything on a plate. Cause and effect.'

'What's hilarious is I don't qualify for a grant because they assume you'll support me,' said Sal. 'The irony.'

'What's ironic is you going to university when you seem to know everything already. Just like your mother.'

'What?' we said together.

'She was just the same. Always with this plan or that plan, and no thought for anyone else. Revolutionaries.' He snorted as he sliced a tomato clean through. 'Well, you're not the first and you won't be the last.'

'Don't worry,' said Sal. 'I want nothing from you. I don't even want your name on the form. I'll take a gap year and save. I won't give you the satisfaction of having any control over my life.'

Dad laughed, but I could see the colour of his neck beginning to darken. 'Your problem is you've been brought up all wrong,' he said.

Sal pushed his hands against the door frame and his body began to tremble. 'And whose fault would that be?' he said. 'You're my fucking father!'

The floorboards shook as he stomped his skinny frame down the hall and up the stairs. His door slammed. The bacon started smoking and Dad grabbed the pan.

When I walked in, Sal was leaning on his palms against the

yellowing walls. He faced the floor and his body was heaving, fighting for breath.

'Sal?' I touched his shoulder. 'Hey.'

'Even now,' he said, 'I can't bear how he talks about her. Like he knew her. Like he really knew who she was.' And he curled his hand into a fist and punched the wall. He cried out in pain and did it again.

'Sal!' I grabbed his arm.

'I didn't come from him,' he said. 'I didn't come from that piece of shit. I don't look anything like him, do I? So there's a chance.'

It was true. Sal looked nothing like Dad. He had Mum's wild, blonde hair – like a burst mattress, said Stella – and his frame was wiry. He had none of Dad's olive colouring, not the piercing eyes or stocky frame that I had inherited. But he had the anger. It came through in flashes, in different ways to Paul Mendoza and with none of the sullenness, but it was there all the same. Under the surface of the knuckles. A scab just waiting to be picked.

I started to speak.

'It's a good offer. It costs me hundreds a month just to eat and sleep. And you could carry on with everything as it is now. Football, your mates. You could even save for a car. Nothing would have to change.'

'No thank you, consigliere.'

'Don't be melodramatic.'

Sal stared at me. 'You don't get it, do you? It can't stay the same. Wake up. I need to get the hell out of here.'

He moved out as soon as he could, taking just the essentials like in an emergency evacuation. He got a flat with a football mate whose name I forget. It was above a chip shop, damp and with mice, but they got free portions from the chippy in exchange for not reporting the rodents. When exams were over, he took on extra hours at the video store to pay the rent. I think he knew he was digging himself into a hole, but once the bills were paid, he had enough left over for a bit of weed and a pub crawl once a week, and he seemed happy with that. I texted him now and then to check whether he needed anything, and he always replied that he was fine. He seemed happy with that.

September 2003

I'd been ready nearly forty minutes when her text came through: *Just coming down your road now.x*

I took a final look in the mirror and ran a hand over my freshly shaven head, before giving the tie knot a little shake to check it was still secure. I hadn't worn a suit since Mum's funeral, but here I was, a decade later, dressed up in a week's wages' worth of navy.

A car was slowing down outside. Shiny. New.

I left my cigarettes on the bed. I'd broken the cellophane seal before I even took a morning piss, and somehow half the pack was now jammed into the ashtray. I opened the box of nicotine patches from my pocket and stuck one on my arm beneath my shirt.

As I walked to the waiting car, I folded the navy suit jacket over my arm and spied Anna's face in the back. She was looking at me through the window, and I smoothed my tie and watched the ground as it disappeared under my feet.

I opened the rear door and climbed in next to her. Her friends in the front introduced themselves with affable ease – *Hi! I'm Pete and this is Jen* – as she watched from the sidelines.

She kept her hands very much to herself as I leant back and fastened my seat belt. She wore an appropriately modest outfit, a dress that fell just below her knees and covered her shoulders. It made little difference. Even in our Sunday best, the air felt rife with danger.

'Well, look at you,' she said finally.

Anna had agreed to take me a few days before.

It had been a month since she'd driven off from my house, and we'd avoided each other until now. Perhaps I was waiting for her to make a move, to test what was left of her feelings. Every evening when she didn't text, every morning when my phone screen shouted the absence of her name, my head would say *See, she's with him*. This head of mine knew impossible things, but doubt and fear invent their own answers. I'd be damned if I was going to message her first. Society said that pride mattered, so I should cling to the shred I had left.

At work, I learned to keep my eyes and ears alert at all times, so that by the time I saw her, I'd already clocked her position. If she was walking towards me down a corridor, I'd become engrossed in whatever I was carrying, or perhaps adjust a 3D stand in apparent danger of toppling over. I'd be so lost in my activity that we'd pass seemingly without notice, or else our eyes would meet at the final moment and I'd contort my face into an eyebrows-raised-kind-of-smile, the type you hope suggests brevity and casualness, but could also be construed as needing the loo.

Finally, we were assigned to work Bar together. I knew it would happen eventually. Usually there are rules about working the same areas as partners or exes, but when nobody knows the history, neither do they know the present.

My shift started an hour after hers. I pushed open the door and she was standing in the empty bar, polishing glasses. She looked up as the door swished shut.

'Hi,' I said.

She did the eyebrows-raised-kind-of-smile.

'Want a hand?'

'Sure.' She picked up a tea towel and threw it at my face. 'Here.'

'Okay.' I leant across and picked up a glass. 'How are things?' I said after we'd each polished a glass in silence. 'Been a while.'

'Great. Really great.'

From the furious effort she was making, I half expected the champagne glass to smash.

It did.

'Shit.'

'I've got it,' I said, moving behind the bar.

She muttered something I couldn't hear as she opened the cupboard doors and slammed each of them shut. And then, 'Where's the bloody dustpan and brush?'

'Calm down. I said I've got it.' I put my hands on her arms and guided her to one side. The dustpan and brush were in the first cupboard she'd opened.

Anna sat on a bar stool and watched as I cleared the tiny shards of glass from the counter. The phone on the side began to ring and she jumped, then leant across and picked it up.

'Hello? Yes, I broke a glass.' She looked up at the security camera as she spoke, the one pointing at us at the bar. 'Well, if you'd been watching, which you clearly were, you'd have seen it was an accident . . . I am working, I'm polishing glasses . . . So I have to stand, do I . . . Tell you what, why not come and carve out my pound of flesh right now, or else just dock the 20p from my pay . . . No, I know . . . Fine, bye.'

She picked up another glass. I was still wiping down the side and pretended not to have heard the conversation.

'I hate working here,' she said.

'No, you don't,' I said, sweeping the floor near her feet.

'Yes, I do.'

'So leave.'

'My God, you men,' she said, laughing. 'You sound like him on the phone. Stop telling me what I am, or what to do.'

'Careful,' I said, giving a slight nod to the camera. 'They're probably reading your pretty lips right now.'

She turned her face away and picked up another glass. 'Don't be giving me the pretty lips. You've not spoken to me in a month and avoided me at every turn, so you don't get to pay me compliments.'

I tipped the broken glass into an empty cardboard box. 'Stop acting like you don't want it. It's written all over your face.'

She looked at me with a mixture of fury and surprise. *I've done it*, I thought. *She's speechless.*

'Because you don't want it, do you?' she said, her eyes narrowing. 'You're above all that. So calm, so chilled, so in control. But perhaps you're just incapable of feeling anything. Or unable to voice what you want, like, really want. You give everything up without a fight.'

Anna threw down the towel and walked through the swinging doors to the galley kitchen out back, where she took the oven trays from the shelves and slammed them down on the metal counter.

I slowly untied the apron and pulled it over my head. I bundled it into a ball and threw it on the side, then I too went into the kitchen and into the view of another camera.

'What do you want from me?' I asked.

She dropped another pot.

'Tell me what you want.'

Anna walked to the freezer at the far end and took out a bag of baguettes that she tore open and spilled on to a tray. 'You always want to be told,' she said. 'That's the problem right there. You never do the telling.'

I walked past and slipped my hand into her trouser pocket, pulling her gently along with me. When we were out of sight of the camera, I became more forceful, taking her elbows and dragging her closer.

'What do you want?' I said again. 'My blood?'

She looked at me. 'Yes. I want your blood.'

And then she shivered, and I stepped forward to hold her, but something in her expression told me she was scared. It was as if this was what she'd been waiting for, what I had been waiting for, and we were on the cusp of something new that could begin. A different fate, another life, if just one of us spoke up. But right now she looked like she might cry, and this was not what I wanted.

'Wait,' I said, letting go. I grabbed a bag of chips from the freezer and dashed into the camera's view to throw them into one of the pots. As I jogged back, she started to laugh.

I knew the moment had gone.

I've become skilled over the years at playing the fool in times of need. It defuses countless situations, even those that in hindsight would benefit me greatly if I just let them play out.

'Here,' I said, pulling her towards me. I held her close and she relaxed against my body and pressed her face against my chest.

We stood there for a minute, not speaking, not moving, even when the phone outside began to ring.

Anna dropped me home. It was a busy shift and extra staff came in to help. We didn't talk for the rest of the night, but at the end, we were left alone to clear up.

'I'll give you a lift home, if you like,' she said, scanning the floor for any rubbish. 'If you haven't got plans, that is.'

'No,' I said, switching off the lights, and she looked at me in the dark. 'I mean, I haven't got plans.'

Anna met me in the KFC car park, like she'd done throughout the summer. Her car still smelled of jasmine, as if the air and cheap upholstery had absorbed her essence.

We didn't say much on the journey. Outside my house, she seemed to hesitate and I cleared my throat. 'Why don't you pull up for a bit?'

She turned off the engine and it felt like the silence would break through the windscreen.

'God, that was a knackering shift,' she said finally, closing her eyes and leaning against the window. 'My feet are killing me.'

'Give them here.'

'Eh?'

I slapped my leg with my hand. 'Get those shoes off and let me rub them for you.'

'Don't be ridiculous. I've been running around for eight hours. They'll be sweaty as hell.'

'It's a good thing you have nice feet then. Come on.'

She looked amused. 'You actually want my feet?'

'It's a good offer.'

Anna thought about it for a moment, then leant down to slip off her shoes. 'You asked for it. Even if they stink, you can't reject me now.' She rolled back her chair and swung her legs across the gearbox, resting her bare feet on my lap. 'You're crazy, you know that.'

I picked up her foot and began to rub it gently.

'I didn't know you were left-handed,' she said, watching me. 'You're even rarer than I thought.'

I smiled at her in the dark. 'My dad tried hard to make me switch. He refused to give me anything unless I took it with my right hand. Said life would be harder otherwise.'

'Harsh.'

'He was right,' I said, looking at the house. 'I couldn't use a fountain pen at school because I always smudged the ink. The teacher made me sit at the front so he could keep an eye. He said I couldn't be trusted not to ruin my work and so gave me a pencil. Did wonders for my confidence, as you can imagine.'

'Your teacher sounds like a knob.'

There was a solace in the rhythm as I confessed my truth while my fingers kneaded her skin. I could feel the bones of her toes deep down under the flesh, where the blood and muscle lay hidden from view. She did indeed have beautiful feet.

'I've never been much of a foot man,' I said. 'But I think I could develop a fetish for yours.'

'How romantic,' she said, her eyes closed.

I remembered something she once said in my bed, and I bent down and slid my mouth over her big toe. She instinctively gasped and I had to tense my grip on her foot to stop her kicking my face.

'What are you doing?'

'I remember you like that.'

'I do.' She bit her lip. 'That's why you have to stop.'

I ignored her. It had been weeks since we'd touched each other, and there was something about my mouth on an unexpected part of her body that felt dangerously intimate. She gave a soft gasp and pulled her foot away.

'I mean it. Stop.'

I picked up her other foot to rub. 'That little moan was all I wanted.'

She gave a shiver, as if I was still sucking her. 'I can't help that it feels so good.'

'What we all want to know is who was the first to suck Anna's toe?'

Two boy racers flew by, leaning on their horns as they tried to out-rev each other in their garish, souped-up motors. The sounds faded away. The silence came back louder.

'I'd better go.' Anna shifted in her seat and I released my hold.

'When are you next working?' I said, knowing her rota by heart.

'Monday,' she said, looking at the keys in her hand.

'A whole weekend off?'

She turned away to face my house. 'Yeah. I have this thing.'

I allowed the silence to grow.

She drummed her fingers on the steering wheel. 'An assembly.

Bible stuff. Two days sitting in a hall listening to suited men give talks.' She yawned. 'Can't wait.'

'Talks?'

She picked at a loose thread on her trouser leg. 'How to be a better Christian, how to live, how to dress, how to be. You name it, there's a rule.'

'You have to go both days?'

She nodded. 'Aren't I the lucky one?'

'Is it just for people of your religion?'

'Pretty much.'

'How about you take me?'

Anna looked at me, frowning. She laughed. 'You're joking.'

'I've never been more serious in my life,' I said, and in my head, this made total sense. 'Go on. Let me come along one of the days.'

'No, no . . . You don't get it. It's incredibly boring. I'm only going because I have to go. You don't *choose* to go.'

'Don't you knock on people's doors to try and convert them? Well, here you are. Jackpot.'

'But you don't believe in God?'

I rubbed my chin. 'I'm open to new things, and this is something important to you. I guess a part of me is intrigued.'

She looked embarrassed and terrified, and I knew it was within my power to make her feel better, to laugh and say *Relax, I'm joking* and return everything to normal. But the truth was, I wasn't joking. I had to know more about the mountain that stood between us. The huge, powerful, shadowy mass that seemed to dominate every part of her life. I needed to know what I was up against, and whether it was even possible for me to climb.

So I watched and waited for her blushes to fade, for her to think it over as she pulled on her socks and shoes, and I didn't say a word as she folded and unfolded her arms. But then she turned and looked at me and nodded, and I'm sure I saw something in her face that was happy.

We got there early as Anna's friend Pete was volunteering to run something. The venue was a rectangular box in the middle of the countryside, immaculately white with walls of glass. An attempt had been made to soften its edges by planting trees throughout the grounds, but the overall effect was startling and unexpected, as if it had been dropped overnight from outer space.

There were no crosses or icons anywhere and it felt nothing like the churches I'd visited on school trips. Everything was shiny and new, with limestone floors, brilliant white walls and artful accents of wood. All along one side of the entrance lobby were tall glass windows, through which light poured down in shafts. It had a vacant feel.

The only aspect that marked it as a religious building was a collection of pictures hanging at regular intervals along the white lobby walls: scenes of war and devastation, of fire raining down from heaven upon screaming hordes of people. As we passed, the pictures gradually changed to scenes of peace, of happy families eating picnics on rolling fields of green, gathering water from a glistening stream that stretched far into the horizon and up to heaven. One picture showed a girl cuddling a lion. Her trusting face was buried in its golden mane as it rested its paws in her small hands. The people in these peaceful pictures, with their placid and undisturbed faces, were clothed in pastel polo shirts, cotton dresses and different types of national dress. They all held baskets of fruit.

It was like an art gallery, but without the little signs that explain the meaning. I suppose if you were here, you already knew.

Anna turned as we passed and gave an embarrassed shrug.

The auditorium itself was like a theatre, with different levels arranged around a long stage. A thousand identical seats patiently waited to be filled. At the end of the stage was a small square pool with a banner hanging overhead: *You will know the truth, and the truth will set you free.* It could be seen from every seat.

'There are my parents,' Anna said, nodding at two distant figures on the other side of the hall. 'Let's sit here.' And she put her things down on the seats nearest to where we were standing.

She'd arranged for Pete and Jen to sit with us. Apparently it wouldn't do to sit alone – tongues would wag – but I found out much later that my being there was already breeding talk, the kind that would follow her for months and possibly years to come. Someone of the world is to be welcomed, but the arms only open so much.

As the hall began to fill, I noticed how alike everyone was. They were dressed in smart attire, men in suits and women in dresses or skirts, and the children looked like miniature replicas of their parents. Everyone looked clean and presentable with shiny faces, as if they were all interviewing for the same job.

When the orchestral music began and people sat down, it struck me how little difference there was between a thousand empty seats and a thousand filled ones. You lose sight of the individual when everyone is the same. Later, I'd realise that's the point.

Pete handed me a bible as the first talk began, and Anna shifted in her seat.

'Friendship with the world is enmity with God,' said the smart man on stage. He held a black bible aloft as if every word came from God himself. 'We must remember that Satan is a lion seeking to devour us. He is catching us with traps designed to appeal to our flesh, our desire, the hidden cravings of our hearts, and it is only by marking a line in the sand and stepping on the side of our Father that will result in Life.'

At one point, when looking around at the passive faces, some of which occasionally glanced our way, I remembered how I'd held her in my bed. How she'd fallen asleep in my arms and nobody here knew a damn thing about it.

'So guard your hearts, brothers and sisters,' the speaker went on. 'Do not be tempted by the ways of the world, with their offers of momentary pleasure. Remember that we are awaiting another life, a perfect life, when all will be made new and death will never touch us. Hold fast to this. Hold fast to what is true.'

A couple of hours in, Anna slipped me a note: *You asked for it.* I wrote: *Stop distracting me.* Then an elbow in my ribs.

Halfway through a talk, a group of people stood up in front of the stage. The speaker asked questions to which they answered a solemn 'Yes'. As orchestral music began to play again from the speakers, they filed out through a side door. 'This is the baptism,' Anna whispered. I nodded like I understood.

A few minutes later, two men in white T-shirts entered the pool at the end of the stage. One by one, they took hold of each of the 'baptismal candidates' and lowered them gently into the water. The audience gave a solemn clap each time. When they lifted the person back up, each baptiser turned to a window at the side of the pool, where a man gave a nod.

'Who's that?' I whispered.

'He makes sure the person goes completely under. If even a finger is out the water, they have to do it again. Total submersion. There can't be any doubt.'

I raised an eyebrow and she bit the tip of her finger.

At midday, we sat in dining rooms to eat the meal deals we'd grabbed from the service station. Pete poured tea from a Thermos Jen had made him.

'How you finding it, Nick? Following along okay?'

'He does have a degree,' said Anna. 'So you don't need to talk to him like he's a moron.'

Pete put up his hands. 'Hope I didn't cause offence there, Nick.'

I shook my head. 'You're fine. There is a lot to take in.'

Anna looked at me with a sad smile, then her gaze went to the window behind. Her expression clouded over. 'Back in a sec,' she said, giving my shoulder a light nudge as she went out.

Pete and Jen turned to look through the window and exchanged knowing looks. 'Young love,' said Pete to me in a hushed voice, although he can't himself have been older than twenty-five.

It seemed right for me to turn and look. On the other side of the glass, Anna was talking intently with someone who I assumed was her (ex?) boyfriend. The first thing I noticed was how good-looking he was. I'm talking straight from a magazine: sandy hair that fell exactly where planned, expensive clothes, white teeth. Anna had her back to me, but she stood with her arms folded as he talked, his hands on his hips and an occasional flick of his Robert Redford hair. He seemed upset, and I recognised the look of desire that plagued his face.

I turned away, craving a cigarette.

The door opened, then Anna was by my side.

'Trouble in paradise?' said Pete.

'Ready?' Anna said to me.

'Where are we going?'

'Anywhere but here.'

Anywhere meant walking around the grounds.

When we were out of view of the crowd milling about outside, I took the nicotine patches from my pocket. I rolled up my sleeve and removed the old one, screwing it up into the packet before slapping a fresh one on my skin.

'Your willpower is impressive,' said Anna, watching.

'Give me a few hours and I'll throw you under a bus,' I said, fixing my sleeve.

'I bet you're regretting the trade-off now.'

'Will you stop? I'm glad to be here. I'm glad I came.'

We walked around the car park, a respectable distance apart.

'That thing they did,' I said after a while. 'The baptism. What does it mean? I listened to the talk, but being a newbie, I couldn't follow it all.'

She was quiet for a moment and folded her arms. 'It's a dedication that you make as an individual. You promise yourself to God forever and swear to do his will.'

'Like a christening?'

'Yes, except we don't baptise babies. You have to be of an age where you can make such a huge decision, because really, it's the biggest decision of your life. To commit yourself to the faith.'

'Have you done it?'

She looked past me into the distance. 'When I was twelve.'

'Twelve?' It came out shriller than I had intended. 'So they do practise child baptism.'

'Very funny.'

'Twelve's hardly an age you know your own mind.'

She gave a sort of shrug and avoided my eye. 'I would have had to do it eventually. What's the difference between twelve and twenty-one?'

'Nine physical years and probably twenty mental ones.'

Anna frowned and went to punch my arm, but thought better of it. 'You're right,' she said. 'Twelve is young, and I've felt nothing but guilt ever since. It feels at times like it wants more than I'm able to give.'

I knew how this felt. 'It does seem a huge commitment.'

'Sorry about Pete,' she said after a while. 'I'm not his biggest fan, as you can probably tell.'

'You've met Daz?'

She laughed and played with her hair as we walked.

'To be honest,' I said, 'I'm surprised you're friends. He's not someone I would put you with.'

'I'm not, really. Jen and I were close once. Same age, same congregation. Then she married Pete and we've drifted apart. He doesn't like me either – apparently I'm a bad influence – so there's no love lost.'

'Why are you a bad influence?'

'I'm *a sister with opinions*.' She made quotation marks with her fingers and smiled, but her laughter sounded sad. 'I'm meant to toe the line. Do what I'm told.'

'You are indeed bursting with your point of view.'

Anna looked surprised. 'Have you got a problem with it too?'

I shook my head. 'I like it.'

'Yes, well, I have to pick and choose who I'm open with. I can indulge that side of myself with you.'

'What a compliment.'

A blush spread across her face. 'It is.'

'Your friend seems super young to get married.'

'She was seventeen. I know, I know. It must seem insane. But if you want to be with someone, you have no other option.' She kicked at the ground with her heel. 'Welcome to my world.'

She looked so lovely standing there. Strong and vulnerable, hard and soft. I thought of the hunger I had seen in his eyes. I knew the damnation.

When I returned from the gents, I found her surrounded by an animated throng of people. Her friends. Redford was there, standing with a group of lads. He gave me a sideways look and made no move towards a handshake or introduction. Anna was laughing at something being

148

whispered in her ear, and she seemed perfectly at ease in their company. I wanted to stand and watch her look so alive, but then one of them saw me and tapped her arm.

Anna's expression immediately changed. Her eyes shifted towards the floor, her fingers pulled at the ends of her hair. She was embarrassed of me. God, Nick, you idiot. She didn't want you here. My skin began to itch. This would be a moment I would bookmark for years to come.

She gestured for me to walk over. 'Everyone, this is Nick.'

'Hi Nick,' the girls chanted, looking me up and down. I was a specimen in a jar. Other.

Friendship with the world is enmity with God. They said this a lot throughout the day. Those outside the faith seemed to be lumped together into a body called *The World*. This was painted as a cruel and terrifying place, where non-believers prowled and looked to bite, and where true love did not exist. She had described me at Dungeness as *worldly*, and now that I thought of it, even in the moments when I held her close, there was something in her eyes that was fearful.

Birds and fishes aren't meant to mix, my Nana used to say. One is hunter and the other is prey.

I'd not been home two minutes when her text came through: *You survived. Let me make it up to you. Pick you up in an hour?x*

I took a deep drag on my cigarette and felt the sweetness of the high coursing through my veins. *Sure*, I replied.

We went back to Dungeness.

The sun was beginning to set as we drove, the clouds stretching out like fingers, the light spilling through. Everything was golden. At times it was hard to see the road ahead, but she didn't open her visor.

'God, look at that,' she said, leaning forward in her seat.

I nodded. 'It's nice.'

'Nice is a cup of tea with a slice of cake, or opening an average present. How can something as majestic as that sunset, which you'll never see again, be "nice"?'

'You like the sunset, I like the sunset. What does it matter which word I use?'

Anna sank back and fixed her hands at ten-and-two on the wheel. The sun soon set and took our voices with it.

When we reached the beach I got out and put my hands in my pockets against the sharp wind coming off the sea. She stood on the other side of the car, facing the coastline, not speaking. I didn't know what I was doing there. It felt like everything was unravelling.

I followed as she walked across the stones.

When we reached the sea, she stopped and shivered, and I took off my jacket and put it around her shoulders.

'I don't want your jacket.'

'You're cold and I'm not. Take it.'

'I don't want your jacket,' she said again.

'Will you stop being so proud? I'm trying to help and my jacket fixes the problem. I don't need it.'

'It's not the jacket I want, Nick.' Her voice was quiet now. She made no move to shrug it off from her shoulders but turned her face away.

My name sounded foreign on her tongue. I'd rarely heard her say it, and there was something unsettling in her use of a word so familiar to me. It is strange how in the most intimate relationships, a name becomes pointless and redundant. It's replaced with another word – Mum, Darling, Dear – formations of letters imbued with something stronger. Few have permission to use these words. Our names are labels for strangers.

But Anna and I had no word for each other. We transcended letters, those man-made things. There was a feeling and an instinct, and it was through this that we connected. But stuff gets missed this way. Loves, lifetimes, ghosts of what could have been. We should mark in bold the important things.

My name on her lips sounded like an ending, and in that moment, I hated it.

'Sorry if I made you uncomfortable today,' I said. I'd thought about it all the way home.

'Why would you think that?'

I shrugged. 'Maybe coming along was a stupid thing to do.'

I felt Anna look at me, the wind whipping up her hair. Time seemed to lengthen, and I steeled my body for the rejection that was sure to come.

'I was thirteen the first time I went to a school friend's house,' she said. 'We bunked off and walked back to hers to watch telly. But I spent the whole time staring at the things in her house, the photos on the wall, and I kept thinking, *this is what a worldly house looks like.* It looked exactly like every other house, but in my mind, it was different.' She took a deep breath. 'I've learned to do that my whole life. Divide everything into two camps. I know the behaviour expected of me in each one. Today there was a fuzzing of the edges, an overlap, and I didn't know how to be.'

'I'm sorry.'

'I did want you there.'

'I pushed you into it.' I threw a stone into the water.

'I'm glad you came. I am.' She looked away. 'And I thought maybe . . .'

I threw another and it skimmed the surface of the water before sinking. 'Maybe?'

Anna pulled my jacket tight around her. 'Why don't you finish the sentence?'

'But I don't know what you're trying to say.'

She threw back her head. 'I took you, didn't I? If I stuck my tongue down your throat, I bet you'd get it then.'

'Now you're talking,' I said, but she didn't laugh.

'Maybe that is why people stick their tongues down each other's throats,' she said, half to herself. 'They're trying to get inside.'

'I did just have a mint, by the way.'

She looked at me like I was a fucking idiot.

'I don't understand you men,' she said, turning to face the sea. 'You're hungry so you eat. You're thirsty so you drink. When you're horny, you screw, and when your ears are tired of listening, they close up.'

'We're simple creatures.'

'You're damned simple. Dinosaurs. All you care about is satisfying your craving and lust, and when you've had your fill, you throw what remains away. It's such an archaic way to be. Fleshly. Like cavemen.'

I remembered Lisa's words in the club, how Anna had been hurt before, and a warning: *If you hurt her, you'll regret it.* My hands pushed deeper into my pockets. I wanted to speak, but the memory of her embarrassment at my presence had jammed itself in my throat. 'I don't know what you mean.'

Anna turned and looked at me. That dark, wild stare.

'You don't? Truly?'

She walked closer and stopped a foot away, the moon illuminating her edges. All I could get was a sense of her.

'When you see a sunset,' she said, 'it doesn't make you ache. When you see the fading light, golden, the way it hits the trees, it doesn't make you feel alive, or present, or root you to the ground. Men are obsessed with the physical. They measure strength by their biceps, and when they feel desire, it's just a stirring in the trousers. You rise and fall, like a traffic signal. Nothing seems to linger.'

'We're not all like that.'

'No?' She took a breath and looked out towards the lighthouse. 'So tell me what you are, then. Tell me how you feel. Say it now.'

I watched her.

I wanted to say many things, of how when she brushes my arm, it stuns me, so that I cannot find the words. When she gets up from my bed, I turn and inhale the pillow, and the smell of her pores and skin and hair drug me so that I'm light-headed. When she sits on my lap and drops her head to kiss me and her hair falls down around us, I'm covered with darkness and can no longer see, and I want to stay there forever. These are the things I wanted to tell her. These are the things I would have liked to say.

I shrugged and she looked away.

I was halfway through my shift and the only one in the booth. The projectors were on their final run of the night, and it would soon be time to lace them up again, ready for tomorrow.

I waited beside the first projector scheduled to finish. The screen was packed with people. I loved it up here, controlling things. Playing God.

The sound of the projection room in a multiplex is hard to describe. The air is thick with the noise of machines, whirring with life as film is pulled through the projector so fast that you cannot see it. Now, of course, everything is done by downloads and hard drives. These days, it must be almost silent in the booth, those learned hours of skill replaced by the flick of a switch. Play. Repeat. But that's not how it used to be. It used to be that you could hardly hear yourself think.

The door to the booth swung open and shut as the film ended. It made no sound in this jungle of mechanical noise.

I watched Anna look up and down the long length of the room before noticing me. I pulled at the cloth tucked into my back pocket and got busy cleaning the machine.

Her silent footsteps were quick.

'Hey,' I called from behind the projector. 'Didn't know you were on tonight.'

She stopped on the other side of the platters, a frown etched into her face. 'I've just heard . . .' She put her fingers in her ears. 'I've just heard you've handed in your notice?'

I took my time coming round to her side. It had been a week since her assembly, since I'd realised she was embarrassed of me. I handed the duty manager a resignation letter on my following shift.

'Why? Why have you done that?'

'It just feels like the right time.'

'For what?'

'I never meant this to be long-term. The job. It was just a transitional thing while I looked for something else. You know, the first rung of the ladder I want to climb.'

'So where are you going?'

I hadn't even got that far, but said, 'I've got a mate who works for a company in town doing market research – running polls, phoning people for their views, that sort of thing. He says there's a job going.'

'So you – someone who never talks – are getting a job that requires you to find out what people really think? That's a joke, right?'

I smiled as I ran the cloth around the edge of a platter. 'That's very good.'

'But, I . . .' She looked down at her hands. 'I'd get it if you were taking a step up, but market research? Come on. You're swapping one minimum wage for another.'

'I like learning new things.'

'Yes,' she said. 'It seems you like to collect new experiences. Like religious assemblies. Is it that thing they say writers do, try stuff out for fun because *everything is copy*? Will that turn up in a book one day?' She folded her arms.

'Why does it matter if I've handed in my notice?'

'Give me a reason for doing it.'

'Tell me why you care.'

Anna made a frustrated sound through her teeth. 'Are you ever going to talk? Is this why you took the job up here, to surround yourself with noise and have an excuse not to open your mouth?'

'Why am I the one who has to talk?'

'You want it to be me? You want a girl to throw herself at you?' She shook her head. 'Well, I can't do that.'

I could tell she was hurt. I'd known her long enough to recognise her defence mechanisms, how she'd cut with words or make jokes to hide her sadness. She didn't want the world to see her broken. We were alike in that way.

But we were a lost cause. I knew now I could never share her faith, and I didn't believe she could ever leave. *It's as natural to me as my arm or foot*, she'd said at Dungeness. *I don't know how to separate from it.* Lisa's words still reverberated around my head. What would be the point of saying something now, when there could be no resolution? What would be the point in hurting her more?

I told myself I had thought it through.

'I think it's time,' I said. 'Don't you?'

She stiffened, and then a smile broke out across her face. 'How's that for a Hollywood ending,' she said, and turned to walk away.

I stood rooted to the floor.

'Don't worry, I won't fight you for top billing,' she called over her shoulder. 'You're welcome to it.'

She walked out, and then came the click of a projector shutting down.

I worked methodically for the rest of the night, lacing each of the twelve projectors so they were ready to go again. I checked the rollers. I fed the film through, getting the tension just so, and used a brush to wipe off the fine layer of purple dust that fell from the print as it played. This is the nature of 35 mm, the emulsion wearing away. For a print's first few runs, it leaves behind a smattering of purple dust. Fragments of its skin. Eventually, a print will toughen up and last for thousands of showings, but a new film cannot be enjoyed without hurtling at great speed, without darkness, without light, without giving a little of itself each time. Its disintegration is the normal order of things.

In the days to come when I worked out my notice, when she would avoid me every shared shift, I began to resent these films with their neat little endings, and their artifice, and their lies.

But now, years later, I miss that job. I miss that purple dust.

Date: 01/10/2003

From: ANNA
To: NICK
Subject:

I worked your street today. When we came towards the village, Jen said, 'Isn't this where that guy lives?' and when we drove by, she pointed and said *there*. And I looked up at your window and thought: *there*.

I hid round the corner when she knocked on your door. No one answered, but I couldn't risk your dad or even you finding me on your step, in my modest dress and shoes, offering a brochure about saving your soul.

Because if it is all true, this is what will happen: If you don't listen to the message, if you don't read the leaflet she stuffed through your door, then you'll be annihilated at Armageddon and that will be the end of you. This is what I've been taught. I know you and the world think this is crazy, but this is what I've been told my whole life by the people I love.

Here's the madness of the entire thing . . . The end of you would be the end of me too.

1993

Once he'd started to look at us again, a year or so after it happened, Dad wouldn't leave us alone. *Get your feet off my sofa,* he'd say, rapping our toes with a rolled-up paper. *You think this is your own private room?* Or he'd pause as he walked along the landing and push open our door. *What a dump,* with dramatic beats between each word. *There'll be no TV or gallivanting on bikes until it's immaculate.* Meanwhile, the dishes piled up until Stella or I got busy.

He's just morphing his pain into discipline, I said to Sal. He doesn't know what to do with it. Sal said he couldn't give a fuck. Stop always looking for the good, he said. Some people are just bastards. It so happens we've ended up with one for a dad. No, I said. No. He's masking his true self. It's a generational thing, it's what men did. Sal shook his head. *What should I do?* I wanted to scream. *Face a reality that involves a dead mum and a fucker of a dad?* Hope keeps you going.

One day, we went to the golf course. I think Stella had dangled a carrot, trading a clean of the entire house if he took us out.

I'd caught the tail end of this barter as I came down the stairs.

'But where would I take them?' Dad was looking around the hall, perhaps finally noticing the dust and cobwebs choking the space. He ran a hand through his hair.

'They're your sons, Paul. Use your imagination.'

His imagination took us to his second home.

Sal and I had never tried golf. All our mates played football and so we did too, exchanging FIFA stickers or playing Subbuteo, studying the league table every Monday before school. Sal was the star of the football team – nimble and quick, a natural athlete, and the praise and adoration were like a drug. He practised penalty kicks whenever he could. I enjoyed playing, but I was slower and, with my bigger build, was generally put in goal.

But we didn't do golf. None of our friends did golf. Golf was a grown-up thing.

I saw a boy from primary school in the car park when we arrived. The eleven-plus exam had been just after France, and despite being predicted to pass with flying colours, I didn't get anywhere close. I'd been pretty friendly with this boy before school ended and he went off to the grammar. It had been two years since, and when he looked over, I smiled and waved. He turned away.

'Here. I borrowed a junior size from the clubhouse,' said Dad on the first hole, pulling a club from his bag. 'You can share. I'll tee off first. Show you how it's done.'

We watched him walk across and place a tee in the ground, then balance a ball on top. He then took the pose that he often did at home in the living room, although this time there was an actual golf club in his hand rather than air. He placed his feet slightly apart, stretched his fingers before gripping the club, rocked his weight between his feet, then swung back and struck the ball. We watched it disappear against the blue sky before dropping on to the green.

He looked happy with that.

'Right, next.'

Sal nodded at me to go first, so I did, doing my best to mimic Dad's pose.

Dad gave a good-natured laugh. 'No, son,' he said. 'That's not how it's done. Here.' He moved me to one side with both hands then took the club, turning and getting into position. 'Now, straighten your legs like this and hold the club out in front, letting your upper arms rest on your chest.' He turned to make sure I was watching before continuing with the lesson, placing emphasis on words like *control* and adding *like so* at the end of every sentence. 'Tip forward from your hips like so, then let your legs soften like so, and you'll notice that the club is about a hand-span away from the inside of my left thigh. Like so. See, Nick? You see, Sal?'

'Yeah,' said Sal, looking away down the course. 'Tip, soften, a hand-span. Got it.'

'Now you try, son,' said Dad, handing me the club and stepping back. 'Remember – posture, posture, posture.' He was beaming now, pleased to have an audience. We could not compete with his years of experience, and this delighted him.

I struck the ball and it flew through the air, dropping into the longer grass a few metres from the green.

'Good effort, son,' said Dad, folding his arms. 'You can't expect to hit the green like I did on your first try. We'll fish the ball out the rough when we walk down there. Next.'

I raised the club towards Sal and he strolled over, hands in his pockets. He got in position and did the little rocking that Dad does right before a shot. He stood like Dad, swung the club like Dad, and it sailed through the air and landed on the green, just like Dad's.

'Wow, Sal,' I said, whistling. 'Look at that. You're a natural.'

A huge grin splashed across Sal's face. He was as surprised as me.

We both turned towards Dad, whose mouth had settled into a firm line. 'Right,' he said, picking up his bag and slinging it over his shoulder. 'Next hole.' He began walking towards the green.

I walked up behind him. 'Nice one, Salvatore,' I said, slapping his back.

He gave a brief smile and looked away.

Sal was indeed a natural. He hit the green with every shot, sometimes coming within metres of the hole. Dad's silence grew louder with every cheer I gave.

I deliberately didn't get better. Each of mine hit the rough, and this gave ample opportunity for Dad to instruct me on how to improve. If my shots had also started reaching the green, Dad wouldn't have known what to do with himself.

On the sixth hole, it all came to pieces.

Four women were in front of us. They'd been there from the start, always one hole ahead, and there wasn't much waiting around before they moved on. But there were four of them and three of us, and so by the sixth hole, time had caught us up.

Dad was always an impatient type, but there was something about waiting for a group of women to vacate a hole on a golf course that he found especially stressful. It started with huffing and sighing, the folding of arms and jutting out of the chin. The pantomime villain was a role he knew by heart.

Sal and I faced away. Even at that tender age, our radar for knowing what was socially appropriate was more finely tuned than Dad's. We didn't care about waiting. We'd have waited forever to avoid what was to come.

One of the women noticed Dad's puffing and whispered to the others so that they all turned to look. There was laughter and hushed voices and they continued with their shots. Dad's face was now almost scarlet.

He began clearing his throat.

When that didn't work, he threw up his hands in mock wonder and said, 'Can you believe this?'

'They'll be done in a minute,' muttered Sal.

'Eh?'

'Just wait for them to finish.'

'This is preposterous,' said Dad, his hands still frozen in mid-air. 'I knew it was a mistake, letting women into the club. I knew it would be its undoing.'

'What exactly is the matter?' one of them called, her hand on her hip.

'What's the matter?' he said, shaking his head. 'You women are gassing instead of golfing, and I'm waiting with my sons to take the next shot. That's the matter, love.'

I died a little inside.

'We'll be done in a minute, sweetheart,' called the woman, walking towards the tee. She shook her head at her friends.

'Not playing like that you won't,' he replied, cupping a hand round his mouth for extra volume. 'Bring your arms into your chest.'

'Oh my God,' I said under my breath.

'Leave them alone,' said Sal in a low voice.

'I'll leave them alone when they start listening,' he replied, still staring at the women. 'Come on. Haven't you got dinners to make?' He smiled at his own joke.

They finished their shots and one of the women stuck a finger up at Dad as they walked towards the green.

He gave a brusque wave as he strode towards the tee. 'Yes, yes, move on.'

I began to follow, aware that Sal was not.

Dad set down his ball and stood back to wait for the women to clear the green. I sensed Sal thundering towards us. He held the club that I needed, but I could tell from his face that he had no intention of giving it up.

'Why do you have to be like that?' he shouted at Dad.

'Like what?'

'Putting on a fucking show all the time,' said Sal. 'Making people feel like shit. Is there something missing in you?'

'Watch your language and watch your tone,' said Dad, his voice dangerous.

'Why? *You* say whatever you want. Maybe I'll make you feel as small as you make everyone else feel. Taste your own fucking medicine.'

'Do not talk to me like that, Salvatore, or you will regret it.'

'Fine,' said Sal. 'Nothing gets through your skull anyway. I don't think even a bullet would have done any damage. You're stone. You're fucking stone.'

Dad's eyes narrowed. He looked at Sal with what seemed like pure, white hate. I opened my mouth, but nothing came out.

'Even today, taking us out, you could have asked what we'd like to do, but instead you bring us here because it's what *you* like and it's what *you're* good at, and you'll take any opportunity to show yourself off. Do you want to know what I think of your beloved golf?'

'No, actually,' said Dad. 'I don't.'

'Sal . . .'

'Here's what I think,' he said, holding up the club. He placed both hands over the grip as if about to take a shot, then he raised it high above his head and brought it down hard against the ground, gouging out the soil. 'Posture,' he spat, and beat the ground again. 'It's all in the posture.'

Dad turned towards the group of women, who were now still, watching from the green. He trembled with embarrassed rage.

Sal threw down the club and contorted his hands into fists. 'Why wasn't it you?' he shouted at Dad, his voice breaking. 'Why couldn't it have been you?'

And then he ran. He ran and he ran and he ran.

October 2003

The club pulsated with bodies, all jerking and writhing to a techno tune. I kept to the edges and worked my way round, scanning faces in the dark, in hope and fear of finding what I came for.

Daz ordered drinks. I lit a cigarette and leant back against the bar. It didn't take long.

She was in the middle of the dance floor, moving and singing along with the rest of the work crowd. They held their bottles high as they circled each other, sipping occasionally from straws and laughing as they shouted in each other's ears. The ceiling dripped with sweat.

I watched her for a while, enjoying the advantage of not being seen. She wore tight jeans and a top that looked like a handkerchief. It tied in knots around her neck and bare back. The coloured lights threw shapes on her skin.

A couple of blokes were grinding against her in the dark. I watched one put his hand on her bare waist, then the other said something and they both laughed.

I downed my pint and ordered another. I didn't give a damn about a thing.

Halfway through the next one, I changed my mind. I nudged Daz, who was chatting to a girl, and was about to shout goodbye when she saw me.

She stopped. For a moment it looked as if she was going to turn away, but then she was pushing through the crowd. I picked up my pint.

'So he's alive,' she said when she reached me. Hands on hips.

'Sorry I've not replied to your texts,' I said, taking a drag. 'Been mad busy. New job and that.'

'Yes, telesales must be extremely taxing.' She flicked her hair over her shoulder and her eyes had that dangerous, drunk look.

'It's not telesales, remember. It's—'

'Here you go, Anna,' came a male voice from the side. I recognised one of the men who'd been dancing with her as he handed her a drink.

'Enjoy your evening,' she said, allowing herself to be led back into the thick of it.

I turned away to face the bar. In the mirrored splashback, I could see her between the two men, laughing and throwing her arms in the air. Their hands were hidden in the shadows. I raised the glass to my lips.

Beside me was a fairly attractive blonde. She seemed to be with the girl talking to Daz, and like me she looked a little lost, so I said, 'Fancy a drink?' She smiled.

One beer later, I had my hand on her waist and she was feeling my hair. Girls were always doing that. 'It's so soft,' she shouted. 'You should grow it.' I had no intention of kissing her, but I didn't pull away when she put her mouth on mine.

Moments later, Anna's voice was in my ear. 'You bastard. You selfish, selfish bastard.'

And then the girl screamed and pulled away, and I felt cold liquid on my skin through my shirt. I turned and there was Anna, an upside-down glass in her hand. She was looking at me and crying.

'Why did you have to do that?' she shouted. 'Why couldn't you just let me be?'

Her friends were looking over, their confused expressions revealing what I'd always known: she'd never said a thing about us.

I took Anna by the shoulders and steered her towards the entrance, away from curious eyes. She allowed herself to be guided at first, but as it got quieter, she realised what I was doing and began to fight back.

'Get off. I don't want you touching me.'

'Come on. You're drunk.'

She pulled away and spun round. Her eyes were fiery coals. 'Here we go. Always condescending, acting like my dad. You're three years older than me, for God's sake.'

'Here.' I tried to take her hand but she pushed my arm away.

'Go back to your blonde.'

'You weren't being too subtle yourself.'

A bouncer approached us with the regulation arms folded. 'Calm this down or take it outside.'

'She's fine,' I said, holding up my hands. 'Give us a minute and she'll be fine. Promise.'

'Oh, will I now?' said Anna. 'Don't talk like I'm not here. And you . . .' She jabbed a finger into his hard chest. 'Take your acorn of power and shove it up your—'

'OUT!'

I grabbed her hand and pulled her through the double doors, out into the cold October night. The sound of the bass pumped through the Victorian bricks of the old mill. We stood apart.

'Shit,' she said.

'Couldn't you have at least behaved for the bouncer?'

'Oh, he was desperate to pump his load,' she said, watching the crowd through the window. 'Besides, it was me thrown out. You can go back if you haven't finished sucking that girl's face off.'

'Let's get you home.'

'Are you insane? Look at me. I'm staying at Lisa's.'

'Where is she?'

'Off with someone in there.' She stumbled over to the edge of the kerb and sat down in the road.

'Ring her,' I said.

'She won't hear it.'

I took her phone and found Lisa's number. It rang and rang.

'Who was that girl, anyway?' she said, shivering and hugging her knees.

'Where's your coat?'

She nodded at the car park. 'Lisa's car.'

I sat and put my arms around her, rubbing her skin to get the blood rushing. She leant her forehead against her knees and gave a light moan. 'Why's the world spinning?' she said. 'Make it stop.'

'We should get you some water.'

'Answer my question,' she said. 'Who was the girl? I've no right to ask, but—'

'Who were the men?'

Anna's face was inches from mine. 'If you expect me to push away every bloke trying to dance, I may as well never leave the house.'

'Listen, it's not my business. You can do whatever you want.'

For a wild instant, I thought she was going to say something, and my heart turned. But then she leant in and I was kissed for the second time that night. She tasted of synthetic cherry.

'Stop, Anna,' I said, pulling away.

'I know I'm drunk. But I want this.'

'You ask about some random girl kissing me in a club, but maybe you should be the one explaining. Is he your ex or not?'

At this, she pulled away and I bit my lip. She struggled to her feet, then walked in zigzags across the road. It was too early for the line of taxis that would soon form, and the lane was quiet.

I followed a safe distance behind and stopped when she did. Her bare back looked orange in the glow of the streetlight, and I remembered being pressed up against her as we fell asleep in my bed.

'You'd never marry me, would you?' she said, facing the opposite direction. 'Ever.'

She'd come out and said it. Just like that. After a summer of hints and talking in circles, shrugs and subject changing, it took several alcopops and a kiss from a stranger for her to break first.

'Don't take it personally,' I said.

'So this is how it ends,' she said, her arms hugged to her body. 'You refusing my hypothetical, future proposal outside a shitty nightclub in Ashford town centre. Aim high, Anna. Aim high.'

'Can't we just see what happens? Why slap a label on something that is already doing okay?'

She half turned towards me, the left side of her face obscured in shadow. Her expression was mocking, or sad, or perhaps she understood what I never could.

'You still don't get it,' she said, before stopping her mouth with a hand. 'No, that's not fair. You're fine as you are. It's me that didn't see.'

'See what?'

'I never do until it's too late.'

'What didn't we get? What didn't you see?' I shifted my weight to the other foot. Why didn't I reach out and touch her?

She turned so her entire face was visible. 'Why do I keep doing this to myself? Trying to make both worlds work, as if I could be the first to step outside and still keep hold of everyone around me? Why can't I be someone who just accepts her lot?'

Then she began to sway and it looked as if she'd faint. I stepped forward to catch her, but she wrenched away towards the pavement, where she fell on to a low wall and vomited into the grass.

I held her hair and soothed her back as she was sick again.

She stayed leaning on the wall for a moment, groaning quietly, then turned her head to me. 'I'm so sorry.'

'What was in that drink?'

She stood and looked down at herself. There were lumps of sick on her jeans, and I broke a large leaf from a tree and brushed them off.

'I just don't care any more,' she said to the air.

'You'll never get a taxi now. Not like that. Here.' I gave her my arm. 'We'll go back to mine.'

'What? No, I can't.'

'I'm down the road, remember? I'll sleep downstairs. You've got nowhere else to go.'

Anna held my arm and we turned for home. When she stumbled in her heels, I put my arm around her waist to keep her steady.

It took us almost an hour to get to mine. We kept stopping for her to regain her balance, and I knew there had been something in that drink. I'd seen her drunk before, but this was something else. I thought of those men and their smiles as they watched her, and imagined their faces smashed to a pulp.

When we turned into my road, I saw from my watch it was closing time. I considered ringing Lisa, but I knew it would unleash a tsunami of shit. I tried to think of what Anna would want.

I was unlocking the door when she went limp against me. The door swung open and banged the wall as I caught her, and I swore as the upstairs light came on. When I carried her across the threshold, Dad appeared and I braced myself as he came downstairs.

'Her drink was spiked. She passed out as we got back and I couldn't stop the door because I was trying not to let her fall. Sorry for waking you. Go back to bed.'

'Here,' he said, reaching out to pick her up, taking care where he put his hands. He nodded towards the lounge. 'Open the door.'

We walked in and I cleared the sofa. He laid her down and stood next to me.

'I thought I'd put her in my bed and sleep down here, but I'm worried she might be sick and choke.' I gave him a sideways look.

Dad nodded. 'Bring your stuff down and sleep on the floor. I'll get a blanket.'

When I came back downstairs, I took a bowl from the kitchen cupboard and set it down next to her. Dad handed me a freshly made up duvet and pillow, and I eased the pillow underneath her head and tucked the duvet around her legs.

Dad passed me a glass of water. 'You should get her to drink this.'

I knelt down and touched her arm. 'Anna,' I whispered, squeezing her skin. 'Anna, wake up.'

She was dead to the world.

'Keep an eye on her,' Dad said. 'Make sure she doesn't sleep on her back.'

He looked at me and went out of the room.

I took her phone out and texted Lisa: *I'm fine. Don't worry. Call you tomorrow.*

Then I made my bed on the floor beside her, turning to face her so I could hear her breathe.

I woke the next morning to find her sitting cross-legged on the sofa, watching me.

'Hey,' I said, sitting up.

She raised the mug in her hand. 'Your dad made me tea.' An embarrassed smile.

I rubbed my eyes. 'Oh. Right.'

'He's nice, your dad.' She took a sip from the mug. There were black smudges under her eyes. I looked at the pillow and saw they were on there too.

'How you feeling?' I said.

'Dreadful. I can't remember a thing from last night, other than being in the club. I'm really sorry.'

'For what?'

She shrugged. 'Shouting at you? Obviously I've been sick, so that's nice. Sorry you saw me that way. I've never felt like that before.'

'Do me a favour?'

She looked at me.

'Don't take drinks from strangers, please. You're too trusting.'

She smiled. 'I've always had a problem saying no.'

I wanted to reach out and touch her.

'I wouldn't have thought that of you,' I said.

'Yeah, well . . .' She set the empty cup down on the side and picked up her phone. 'How you think of me isn't necessarily how I am.'

That was the final night we spent together.

From: ANNA
To: NICK
Subject:

All these emails I keep writing. I know I'll never send a single one.

November 2003

I didn't notice Stella at the end of the driveway until I'd closed the front door. I pulled my jacket tight against the autumn air and was putting in my second earphone when I heard her usual *hello, love*.

She wore leopard print as always, her red hair bundled under a patterned scarf, and in her hand was a pair of secateurs. I shuffled towards her, kicking the yellow leaves and listening to the sounds of my feet as they dragged along the path.

'Where you off to, sunshine?' she said, grabbing a bucket and balancing it on the fence against her body.

I pulled a cigarette from my pack. 'Daz is coming by,' I said, cupping my hand and lighting up. 'It's Saturday, so . . . you know.'

'And how is young Darren? Still scaring the girls?'

'He's good. Daz is good.'

She studied my face with a frown, doing the motherly thing. 'You look tired, Nick.'

I gave a customary shrug as I shifted my feet. 'Yeah, well . . . Life.'

'You're much too young to be giving that answer.'

I exhaled towards the sunflowers that now hung drooped and faded. 'I'm the oldest I've ever been.'

Stella arched an eyebrow in reply as she began scraping seeds into the bucket. She pulled at the centre of a sunflower with her fingers and there was a soft skid as the seeds fell against hollow metal. 'What about that girl you've been seeing, the one Sal told me about? Is she the cause of this fatigue? Too much heart-thumping to get any sleep?'

I looked for Daz. No sign. My watch said he was late and I glanced down the road again. 'Something like that.'

'You enjoy it, Nicko,' she said, moving on to the next flower. 'Nothing like a first flush of love. Salvatore says she's a good one too. Says you're hooked. You'd best watch out or I think he may give you some competition.'

I smoked my cigarette.

'And how am I, you ask?'

I gave a sheepish smile. 'Sorry, Aunty Stel,' I said. 'So how about you? Anyone on the horizon?'

She snorted. 'Lord, no. Pickings are slim at my age. They're either divorced – and for good reason – or they're prowlers, or they just want a woman to bring them dinner while they watch the evening game. No, thanks.'

'You quite happy on your own then?'

She moved on to the final flower. 'Well, I wouldn't say no to a bit of fun. But they always want more of me than I'm keen to give, Nick. You get fussy at my age. Health problems start creeping in, and you have to look at a bloke and decide whether you'd be happy seeing him without his teeth in, or listening as he prattles on beside you in the care home.'

'You're quite a way off that.'

She nodded. 'That I am. But life flies after twenty-five. You'll see.'

I heard the familiar turbo growl of Daz's exhaust and watched as it charged down the road towards me.

'You enjoy this girl, Nick. Treat each other right. I envy you the madness.' Stella set down the bucket and opened the secateurs. 'Ah well, here we go again. Another year gone. What did I say about time speeding up?'

Daz leant on the horn as he skidded to a halt, and I mumbled a goodbye to Stella and dropped my cigarette. When I shut the door, Daz waved and sped off in hope that my middle-aged aunt would be impressed by his bright blue – 0–60 in less than six seconds – Subaru with oversized spoiler at the rear.

I looked back in the mirror as Stella leant down to cut the stems of the sunflowers that had offered something bright for the summer of 2003.

Date: 20/02/2004

From: ANNA
To: NICK
Subject:

Hey. It's been months. I thought you'd text or call. Did it mean nothing to you? Was I just another notch, like that time at uni with that girl? I remember you telling me on that first night in your bed, laughing, like shagging a stranger was an everyday thing.

I tried on wedding dresses today. I went with Jen and my mum to a bridal shop and they pulled out meringues and bias-cut and floaty chiffon and I looked like a fraud in every one. I stood as everyone adjusted my hair and made cooing noises, and when they spun me around and I saw my reflection, I thought of you. Bloody you.

I've thought about texting but what's the point. I'm not sure I could take the rejection again. Anyway, it would seem I've chosen another path.

Here I am, trying to be good.

That boyfriend she had when I first met her.
  She married him.

PART THREE

Life went back to normal afterwards. It wasn't that hard. After all, we'd only hung out over the course of a summer. One summer. That's maybe ninety days out of the eight thousand or so I'd been alive. Ninety days was one per cent of my life. Ninety days should hardly register.

But I'd get a weird vibration in my chest on the streets we'd walked together, or at the cinema, and in the pub where I once took her to meet the boys. My shoulders tensed whenever I saw a red Ford Fiesta. But I never saw her again. Not until years later.

I didn't talk about her. Girls would ask on maybe a second or third date, 'So, ever been in love?' And I'd shrug or screw up my face and say, 'You know . . .'

You know.

But sometimes she'd appear there in my head, when I'd be looking out a window at the rain, or photocopying my passport, or in summer when sunshine bathed my skin. Especially then. She'd come out of my pores in my sweat and I'd wipe her away from my top lip or she'd hang in the thick humidity like a blanket.

I tried to make sense of it. I bought a notebook and scribbled lines down as they came, hoping to trap the ghost of her in the pages so she'd vacate my head. I went a little crazy when Lisa told Sal she'd got married, filling the pages with indecipherable shit.

She was like those film reels I had spliced together. For a few weeks, they had their moment, the audience believing it was real, but eventually, they were taken apart and sent back. They had a beginning, middle and an end. Just like everything.

Summer 2013

'New York?'

'Yeah.'

Sal and I were in my garden at the barbecue, drinking beer. I occasionally picked up a utensil and gave the burgers a prod. Laura had asked me to keep an eye on them. I was not a man who considered my barbecue skills to be symbolic of my ability to survive in a wilderness, but I thought I should do my best not to burn them.

'How? When?' I had many questions.

'Tilly's been offered a job on a new show at MTV. Hosting. It's a huge opportunity. She can't turn it down.'

I could feel the sun burning my neck. 'But what about you?'

'I'm going too,' said Sal, sipping his beer. 'So we'll be fine.'

'No. I mean what are you going to do out there?'

Sal shrugged. 'I have some money saved, believe it or not. And I've a mate out there who says he can get me a job to start with. Bike courier or something. Unofficial, obviously.'

I jabbed the end of a kebab. 'I'm not sure a bike messenger's salary will get you far in a place like Manhattan.'

Sal sighed. 'Like I said, it's a start. Tilly and I can share an apartment, obviously. MTV's taking care of all that. God, Nick. Change the script for once.'

I took a swig of my beer. 'I'm just not sure you've thought it through.'

'No, you're never sure of anything,' said Sal. 'That's the difference between us. I didn't need to think it through. As soon as Tilly told me, I knew it was right. We've even talked about one day ending up in San Francisco.'

I couldn't look at him. I turned a kebab that didn't need turning.

'Besides,' he went on. 'I'm hardly setting the world alight as the manager of a video store. When did you last go out and rent a film? My job's a dinosaur.'

'So manage something else.'

Sal threw his bottle in the bin and it smashed upon impact. 'Some of us don't want to rot away in middle management.'

'What about Dad?' I said.

'What about him?'

These six words summed us up.

Laura came through the patio doors holding a plate of sliced burger buns. 'I've just heard the news,' she said, kissing Sal on the cheek. 'How exciting.'

Sal smiled. 'Do you need any help?'

Laura slid her arm around my waist and I gave her a quick kiss on the head. 'Grab the ketchup? Then I think we're good to go.'

Sal edged past Mathilde, who was adjusting her hair using her reflection on the patio door. She was blonde now. I wondered what Sal thought of that and I knew he wouldn't care.

'So where will you live?' said Laura, working her fingers into my jean pocket.

I pulled away to pick up the tongs.

'Hmm?' said Mathilde, as she twirled her hair around her fingers. 'Oh, my producers have sorted me a beautiful, bijou apartment, right in *le coeur* of the West Village. And Salvatore says he has a friend who has a room he can rent. So we're all set.'

I stabbed the chicken legs with a thermometer and watched the dial inch round.

'Mmm,' said Mathilde, leaning in to smell the flowers growing on the wall. 'That scent . . . *c'est beau*. It's jasmine, yes?'

Laura nodded as she took the ketchup from Sal. 'We went to the garden centre when we moved in. That was Nick's choice. It's taken a couple of years to settle, but now it flowers beautifully. Personally, I find the scent a little overpowering.'

'What happened there?' said Sal, nodding at the end fence that separated the garden from the alley behind. We turned to look. There was a round gaping hole between the posts, as if something had smashed its way through.

'Some drunk kicked it in last summer,' said Laura, handing Sal a plate. 'Still waiting for your brother to fix it.' She winked at me.

'Meat's ready,' I said, dropping the tongs.

We helped ourselves to food and sat in the patio chairs in the sun. Sal had moved Mathilde's chair into the shade by the wall of the house, and she sat there with her legs tucked underneath her, separate from the rest of us. She picked at her salad leaves and looked around in disgust.

'You really should get rid of this hideous concrete and put down some grass, no?'

Laura wrinkled her nose. 'Yes, I suppose so. But there are things we want to do on the inside first.'

'Well, with four bedrooms, it's certainly big enough for the two of you. A nursery next, perhaps.' The bitch gave me a smile.

Laura coughed. 'Drink, anyone?'

Afterwards, I took in the empty dishes. I filled the dishwasher, enjoying the precision and logic required to make everything fit. This was something I did take pride in, my ability to stack a dishwasher. It's a rare skill. You have to put the cups in the right section and ensure that everything is within range of the jets. Of course, the jets only work when the door is closed, so you have to have foresight. Laura would roll her eyes, but there's a comfort to thinking of the worst possible outcome and adjusting things to avoid it.

I shut the door and heard a playful scream outside. Through the open window, I could see Mathilde sitting on Sal's lap, screaming with pleasure and fear as he tickled her. 'Don't pretend you don't love it,' he was saying softly, and she was slapping him as he burrowed his fingers under her top.

Mathilde straddled him. She whispered in his ear and they looked at each other for a moment before kissing passionately. Sal held her face in his hands.

'Excuse me,' said Laura, waiting for me to step aside before taking a cloth from the drawer. She turned her back to the garden and wiped down the side. I opened the fridge and took out another beer.

'Well done,' I said. 'That was nice.'

She said nothing as she wiped the crumbs into the sink. I watched her rinse round and wring out the cloth, then fold it in half and drape it over the tap. We could hear Mathilde still laughing.

'Good.' She coughed. 'Shame the burgers were burned.'

Laura and I rarely argued, but we did that night.

'Sorry if I'm being weird,' I said as we undressed. 'It's just her. I wish Sal would see it.'

She laughed. 'See what? He's happy. If I didn't know you better, I'd think you were in love with her.'

My mouth dropped open. 'Don't be ridiculous.'

'Don't worry, we all know who you're really in love with.' She kicked off her jeans into the corner of the room.

'I don't know what you're talking about.'

'For all Tilly's rudeness, I actually quite like her. It's refreshing being around someone who says what they think and isn't scared of what might happen. Perhaps that's why you hate her so much. She's too brave for you.'

Laura pulled the sheet up to her chin, reached out to the lamp and the room went dark.

I stood there for a minute, my arms folded. The music from a house party down the street drifted in through the open window.

I picked up my pillow and went downstairs.

2010

The Wedding

I was two days past thirty when I next saw Anna.

It was at the wedding of a childhood friend. Dan was a boy from school who morphed into a drinking mate down the pub and would later become a friendly face on the football circuit. He became good friends with Sal.

Sal and I headed up to the wedding together. It was at a small, dark registry office in North London, with tatty red chairs and heavy curtains. I'd spent the morning deciding which suit to wear. Grey with a faint red check or a navy. When Sal arrived, he took one look at them laid out on the bed and said, 'Grey.'

I looked at him. 'Is that seriously what you're wearing?'

He glanced down at his clothes — a Hawaiian shirt, blue trousers and a pale pink jacket. 'What's wrong with it?'

I picked the navy.

We arrived as a white hackney cab was pulling up. Taking our seats in the ceremony room — packed with grey suits and colourful hats — I tried to ignore the call of the Marlboros from my jacket pocket.

When the music started, we stood and turned to face the entrance, and that's when I saw her. Across the room in a red dress. Staring straight at me.

I don't know whether she smiled or waved, because I instantly put my hands in my pockets and looked at the bride. I don't remember anything about the ceremony. I was just conscious of the back of my head and that I was glad I'd worn the navy.

They vowed and kissed and walked back out, and I could finally have my cigarette.

The procession outside didn't seem to be moving, so I took the side entrance and slipped out into summer.

I lit up and took a deep drag. There. Instant release between the shoulders. I walked along and stood at the corner where I could watch the crowd milling around the registry steps. There she was, at the back. Alone.

After the confetti throw, there were happy whoops and the crowd began to disperse. Someone shouted 'Anna' and she turned, smiling, and caught sight of me in the background. I didn't look away this time. The power of a cigarette.

When she reached me, she folded her arms and said, 'Hello, stranger.'

I leant in and gave her a hug, holding the cigarette away. 'Hi.'

'Still killing yourself,' she said with a friendly smile.

I took a final drag, threw it on the ground and immediately regretted it. What a waste.

'Bride or groom?' I said, playing with my collar which refused to sit over my tie.

'Jess and I were at art school together,' she said, watching me fumble. 'I'm a painter now.'

I acted like this was a surprise. 'What do you paint?'

'Theatre and film sets, mainly. But I paint my own work too. Here, let me.' She reached out and smoothed my collar with a steady hand. 'You here alone?'

I nodded in the direction of the crowd as Sal came towards us. 'You remember my brother?'

'Of course.' She smiled as he reached us. 'Hello, Sal.'

I watched the recognition cloud over Sal's face, and he looked from her to me and back again. 'Anna! Look at you. Still gorgeous, I see.' He gave her a long hug. 'It must be, what, five years?'

'Seven,' I said.

'You always were a charmer, Salvatore,' said Anna, laughing. She smoothed her hair and I saw the flash of gold on her finger.

'I hate to be the one to break up the party,' said Sal, casually draping an arm around her shoulders, 'but as is the custom with modern nuptials, we're being herded on to a red double-decker and shipped off to the reception. I don't know about you kids, but I'm dying for a drink. Shall we?'

Sal swung Anna around and began walking with her towards the bus, his finger looped through his pink jacket over his shoulder. I took another look at the cigarette on the ground – definitely not salvageable – and began to follow. Anna was laughing as he whispered in her ear. Sal had always been the one who could talk.

The reception was near Tufnell Park at a twenty-first-century incarnation of a pub, with farmhouse tables and walls in fashionable grey. The food was served on chopping boards, and trays were filled with jam jars of Pimms with polka-dotted straws.

When we arrived, Sal immediately disappeared in a crowd of footballers watching the match on someone's phone. I fetched Anna and myself a drink and nodded towards an obliging wall outside.

'So where's your plus-one?' I said.

She hitched up her dress and carefully inched on to the wall. 'Not his vibe. I knew they were tight with numbers, so I said I'd come alone.' She smoothed her lap. 'You know I got married?'

'I did.' I lit another cigarette. It would be a day I'd regret not bringing a second pack. 'Why's it not his vibe?'

She sipped her wine. 'He wouldn't know anyone. Some people are like that, I guess.'

'Not much fun going to a wedding on your own, though.'

'I can take care of myself.'

I smiled. 'Oh, I know you can.'

Across the road, the photographer was arranging a family line-up, and the bride's grandparents were loudly complaining that the backdrop was of a laundrette.

'If I did it all again, it would be like this,' said Anna.

'Swearing grannies?'

She smiled. 'Pub lunch, laundrette, sirens raging. It's more real, somehow.'

I couldn't bring myself to ask, but she went on anyway.

'Mine was all the trimmings. Stately home, fancy car, second cousins. My mother-in-law wouldn't have had it any other way.' She made a face and drained her glass.

'I can't imagine you taking orders from a mother-in-law.'

Anna shrugged. 'How many twenty-year-olds can afford a wedding? I wasn't footing the bill so I went along with it. And everything went to plan. The sun shone, my bridesmaids looked perfect, everybody danced. Then just before we left, I hugged someone and said, "I can't believe it's over." And they replied, "Over? It's only just begun."'

We looked at each other.

'Drink?' I said.

When I took my seat for the meal, I found myself between Sal and a nice-looking blonde. I introduced myself and decided that for the next two hours, I would be the attentive and interesting Nick. I'd clocked Anna's location when we sat down, and throughout all three courses, I didn't look at her once.

The pavement outside was packed with smokers and the drinks were kicking in. Sal held forth, loudly recalling a winning goal. I got a drink from the bar and went towards the staircase at the back. Tables were being pushed to the edges of the room as the band tuned up for the first dance. I climbed the stairs and moved towards the open window, and there was Anna on the balcony, watching the crowd, alone.

I cleared my throat. She turned.

'Room for one more?' I said, stepping through. I passed her my glass to hold as I cupped my hands and lit my final cigarette.

'There's something incredibly arrogant about a person who lights up next to a non-smoker.'

I exhaled into the sky above her head. 'Sorry.'

'No, you're not,' she said, handing me back my drink.

'I wish I could stop.'

'But you're addicted.'

I looked at her. 'I'm addicted.'

She glanced over the balcony. Her skin was backlit from the fading sun between the buildings. 'You're a man, aren't you?'

I coughed. 'I guess so.'

'Explain something to me.' She gestured towards the crowd below. 'Their conversation is all *we thrashed you, you dived, we're above you*. It's relentless. Why do men talk like that?'

I leant next to her on the balcony and our arms touched. 'About football? Something to talk about, I guess. A language. It means we don't have to talk about anything real.'

'But it's out of your control. None of them scored any goals. Some millionaire did. Why talk with such passion about a result you have no involvement in?'

My eyes fixed on Sal, chatting animatedly and passing around a joint. 'I call it healthy competition. Which would you rather – they talk about football or kick each other's heads in?'

She nudged me with her elbow. 'Stop making sense.'

There was a pause, and I wished I could have leant across and kissed her. Instead, I said, 'So really, how are you?'

She pulled at the end of a ribbon tied to the balcony and gave a wry smile. 'How long have you got?'

'How are you getting home?'

She didn't reply straight away, curling the ribbon between her fingers. 'I'm at a hotel. You?'

'Same.'

There was a shout from below, and the drunken beginning of a football chant.

'There's something I've wanted to say to you for years,' she said, turning her body to face me. The strap of her dress had slipped from her shoulder, and she was so close I could pick up her scent. Jasmine.

'Those nights when I stayed at your house . . . You never pushed me into doing stuff. I want to acknowledge that.'

I reached out and lifted her strap on to her shoulder. Seven years since I'd touched her skin. 'No problem.'

She looked at me, long and hard. That's the only way to describe it.

'That day at the lake . . .' she said, and then a loud voice announced the first dance.

The crowd began moving in. We waited until the pub door slammed, the howling subsided, then we climbed back through the window.

After the bride and groom had performed their choreographed dance, the party began. I stood by Sal and watched Anna dance.

She threw up her arms as she spun round and I couldn't take my eyes off her.

Later, I went outside for a bummed smoke. It was dark except for a lone streetlight and the warm glow through the windows. I watched Anna move through the room in her red dress and hug the couple. Then she was at my side.

'Listen,' she said, taking my arm. 'If you're not busy tomorrow, let's meet up? Unless you have plans. It just feels like there's more to say.'

'Where shall we meet?'

She smiled. 'Your number's still the same? I'll call you.' She put her hand out for a passing black cab, then she jumped in and was gone.

Anna said to meet her at eleven at the Sir John Soane's Museum in Lincoln's Inn Fields. It was raining.

At a quarter to eleven, I got out of the cab and ran up the entrance steps. It was the kind of rain that soaked within seconds, and I was glad of the umbrella I had swiped from the hotel.

Of course she was late.

I saw her rushing down the square on the side of the park towards the museum. The rain was fierce by now, and she held a thin jacket over her head as she ran. She wore a white summer dress, drenched. I jogged down to meet her with my umbrella, and she smiled when she saw me.

'Quick, quick,' she said as we ran through the puddles.

We stood in the doorway, laughing, her wet dress clinging to her skin.

'Bloody hell,' she said. 'What a state I am.'

When she came out of the restroom a few minutes later, her hair hung long and black around her face, and I thought to myself, *This is what she looks like wet, this is what she looks like.* A familiar picture appeared in my mind of her in a bikini, swimming in a lake. And then there was a sinking feeling in my stomach, hard and heavy. I didn't know what to say, so I stood there with my hands in my pockets and looked at the floor.

The museum was the home of some dead architect who'd bought

three townhouses and knocked them together. It was just like Anna to meet me here. She could talk me through the rooms, point out facts, feel satisfied that I was completely out of my depth.

We walked silently through the rooms. A narrow winding staircase led downstairs and my hand followed hers down the banister. We stepped into the crypt — a series of dark, cave-like rooms crammed with ancient artefacts, pots, friezes and a sarcophagus covered in ancient Egyptian hieroglyphics. Light streamed through the domed window in the ceiling two storeys up and bathed it in a churchy glow.

'I'm trying to understand why you've brought me to a tomb,' I said, peering inside the bath-like structure.

'My first kiss was in a graveyard.' She smiled. 'I was twelve and he was fifteen. We leant up against a headstone and smoked a joint, then he kissed me and put his hand up my top.'

'Did you slap him?'

She looked at me with stars in her eyes. 'I loved it.'

We stepped out into the sun. The rain had moved on but the sky was black, and the rays streaming through made everything seem unreal. Ever since that day, I've noticed that after it rains, there's often the most glorious light.

We stood on the pavement, a few feet apart. Her dress was almost dry and no longer clung to her legs, but I looked at them anyway.

'So,' she said — and I'm sure she caught me looking — 'Where do we go from here?'

From there, we went to Hoxton Square.

Scattered about the park were groups of people, enjoying lunch in the midday sun. The cloud must have missed the square, because the grass crunched beneath our feet.

We chose an empty corner under a leafy tree. I thought about offering my jacket as a blanket, and although you never know which way that'll go, I did it anyway. She accepted. I unscrewed the cap on the bottle of rosé we'd bought from the corner shop and handed it to her for the first swig. I made a joke about being like teenagers. She laughed and a blush crept up my neck.

'So what happened to Nick the writer?'

I took a long sip. 'What happens to all of us.'

'Which is . . . ?'

'Life?'

She tutted. 'Pathetic excuse.'

I nodded in agreement. 'And hardly true of you. The girl who said she wanted to be a painter has gone on to be exactly that.'

Anna pushed her palm out further on the grass so it almost touched my elbow. 'I sometimes write too.'

I raised my eyebrows, although nothing about her surprised me. 'I imagine you're very good at it. Far better than me, no doubt.'

'So you don't write at all any more?'

'Sal gave me a notebook for my birthday a few years ago and I write pages if I'm in the mood. Something tells me I'll write a few tonight.'

I brushed her fingers as I passed the bottle.

'I find writing so cathartic,' said Anna. 'It feels similar to painting, except you hold a pen instead of a brush, and it's easier crossing out words than scraping paint off canvas.'

'I'd like to find a way of saying my stuff out loud and poetry seems to help.'

'We should do a swap,' she said, raising the wine to her lips. 'Send me some words and I'll do the same.'

I shook my head. 'No chance.'

She pulled at the grass and the blades fell through her fingers. 'I saw you looking yesterday.'

I took a sip from the bottle and said nothing.

'At my hand.'

I shrugged.

'Some people never take it off,' she said, playing with the ring on her finger. 'From the second it goes on, they keep it there all their lives. Superstition. Isn't that funny?'

'And you?'

She took the bottle and smiled. There was sadness to it. 'It's just a ring.'

We passed the wine between us and watched the park thicken with hot, suited bodies and plastic-wrapped food. The air hummed with the easy laughter of the Friday crowd, and I noticed a young couple nearby, out of earshot, lying next to each other in a tangled embrace. The way they lay, parallel to the earth, eyes only for each other. It brought to mind memories I couldn't forget.

'I was a mess after that summer,' I said, turning the empty bottle over in my hands. 'I thought you'd come back to me. Give her space, I thought, and she'll come back.' I looked at her. 'And you never did.'

She gave a quiet shrug. 'I made it clear I had to get married. You made it clear you never would.'

'We were so sure of everything back then. How we wanted our lives to be.'

'Were we?' She stared at me until I turned away. 'I remember differently.'

'I should have stopped you from going. I thought I was doing the right thing, letting you go back to that life.'

'So I was more than a summer fling?' She closed her eyes for a second. 'You never said.'

'Neither did you.'

She bit her lip. 'A girl wants to be told.'

'So much for feminism.'

'Don't do that,' she said, shaking her head.

'What?'

'Expect us to be one way. You don't realise it's not clear-cut – that we're human beings just like you, with shades of grey, with differences.' She sat up and hugged her legs. 'Three months before my wedding, I sat in our new car outside our new house and told him I didn't want to work any more. I wanted to be a housewife and have children, be a wife and mother, just like all the women around me growing up.'

'Did you really want that?'

'Course not. But if I was going to surrender myself to that life, it felt like I should do it completely.' She paused. 'It's impossible for you as a man to understand how it was, growing up in my religion. Women are meant to be meek and submissive, qualities that don't come naturally to me. I've spent my life battling that thinking, and also desperately wishing I could fall in line.'

'Why did you marry him?' I love what wine can do.

She rested her chin on her knees, her arms still hugging her legs. 'I was in love with the idea of him. All those wild years were spent kicking at everything I'd been taught. Looking, testing, feeling. But all along, I knew I'd go back. The choice was presented to me as life or death, and who wouldn't choose life? There was a moment when I wondered . . .' She looked up. 'I don't expect you to understand. He was my way back into the fold, and it felt like the only thing to do.'

'What would he think about you being here with me right now?'

She glanced down at her hands. 'Is it wrong then, seeing an old friend? I suppose maybe it depends on the friend.'

We listened to the noise of other people's conversations. The sun beat down, bathing our skin in warmth, as it has done every summer of our lives. As it always will. The way it feels never changes.

'That time I came to your assembly at that hall,' I said. 'Remember?'

Her cheeks grew pink. 'Of course I remember.'

'When I came outside at lunch, you were surrounded by all your friends and looked so embarrassed when you saw me. Like you wished I wasn't there.'

She blinked. 'Yeah, I was embarrassed,' she said, frowning, 'of how I must look to you, pretending to be this good Christian girl when you'd known me in a way they hadn't. I was afraid you'd see right through me.'

My stomach turned. 'Oh.'

It wasn't me she'd been embarrassed about. It was herself. It was about her, of what I would think of *her*. Not me. Not me. Not fucking me.

'But it went deeper than that,' she continued. 'I learned to split myself in two back then. It was a way of avoiding the guilt over my friendship with Lisa, and the huge love I felt for certain people who came into my life. *Worldly* people. I wasn't meant to get close, remember? But I loved how I could let my guard down around you, be someone who just felt things instead of analysing every urge for its sinfulness. Then on Sundays I'd put on my best dress and go to the Kingdom Hall and be who they wanted me to be. That day you came to the assembly was the first time my two worlds collided. I didn't know which Anna was the real one.'

To hear that she had felt a safety in my presence that summer confirmed a knowledge that I couldn't explain. The words could not travel past the tightness of my throat, so I reached out and touched her wrist. I had to.

She let me hold her for a moment, then carefully pulled her arm away.

'The older I get . . .' she said. 'Shouldn't I know the answers by now?'

'Meaning of life? I thought you had that.'

She made a strange sound in her throat, half laugh and half sob. 'So did I.'

Then she said: 'It's like being in a room where everyone's dancing. They sway and clap and stamp their feet, but you can't hear the music. You *want* to, my God, you want to. They're smiling and having the time of their lives, and they slap your back like you feel it too. And in that moment, you have a choice. You can start to dance and hope you'll hear it, because maybe the music really is playing and it's you that's the problem. Or you refuse to pretend and you shake your head and say *I don't hear it*.' Her eyes glazed over as she looked ahead. 'I've always danced along . . .'

'Maybe you need to sing your own song.'

She shook her head and held her cheeks. 'Blaze my own trail and forge my own path? I'm done with riddles. I want to live.'

Later, when I'm in bed and thinking through the day, I remember how she looked in her white summer dress, with her legs tucked underneath and her hair slightly frizzy from the rain. I wanted to kiss her and know her and feel her skin.

But there are rules about married people, and I try to obey those rules. Even so, when I'm lying in bed, I scan my mind for clues and sense that she felt it too. The strange and heavy weight of the air between us, thick with danger and something unknown. A ring is no match for that.

*

When I met Sal at the pub the following week, he bought the first round and went, 'So what happened the next day with Anna?'

'We talked, then said goodbye.'

'Same as what always happens then.'

'What can I do?' I said. 'She's married. I'm not the one who can say anything.'

Sal shook his head. 'Do you ever think about how it must be for her? Growing up in some weird religion where she's not an equal or allowed a point of view? Where she's ordered to obey something other than her own feelings? Maybe she's waiting for you to speak. And what's the worst that can happen? You put your hand out and she turns away. Who cares? Isn't it worth the risk?'

I sipped my pint. 'I nearly did.'

Sal groaned into his hands. 'Fucking hell,' he said. 'That's a life, is it? You know, one day, we'll all be standing round at your funeral with you laid out in a box. Here lies Nicolas Mendoza, the priest will say. He nearly did.'

Lemon meringue pie / by Anna

I am eight years old at my mother's table
I take a fork and push it
down the middle
Through the white yellow brown of home-made delight
Look how it wobbles
They say the way to a heart is through the stomach
I love my mother
But she does not know this
We do not talk of such things

The baked puff of cloud is sweet on my tongue
Like the one when I was fourteen
When all I wanted were kisses and letters
Or the one who said he loved me before I'd even looked in the mirror
There you are
The tartness of your skin
you, the one who fucked me 'til my heart bled
Or the one I liked when we spun the bottle
Who pulled me by the hair and spat on
Hot tarmac
Your bitter tangs I took as tokens
You were all yellow
Thinking you were looking at the stars
Being men

And now we come to the good one
Safe as the colour of biscuit in tea
Encasing the rest and holding it together
Look how solid it is, secure.
I have to push a little harder here
But my fork still cuts through
See how the watchtower crumbles
The fluted edges fall

Then there is the one who is a mouthful of everything together
The one my buds can't easily discern
I close my eyes and hold him a moment
On my tongue
At the back of my throat
As he slides down my body into my stomach
Glorious

Why did my mother not teach me to eat a pie nicely?
How to not leave a trail of crumbs on my lips
On the floor for others to clean
Or how one should always end on something sweet
I know
She was too busy making one for herself
Eat it all up like a good little girl
Don't make a fuss
Don't make a fuss

They say the way to a heart is through the stomach
I cannot cook

     but perhaps there's still time

The Wedding, Continued

'Why don't you go for it?' said a voice to my left, and I recognised it as belonging to the blonde I'd sat next to at dinner.

'Sorry?' I drew my eyes away from the dance floor and turned to look. Laura, her name was. She had a nice face. Sensible-looking. We'd made pleasant enough chit-chat throughout the meal and I remembered she did something in admin at a university.

'The woman you've been staring at. In the red dress.'

I gave an uneasy laugh. 'Have I? I don't know about that.' Like a reflex, I looked at the dance floor, then away again. 'She's an old friend,' I said, picking up my beer. 'Haven't seen her in a while, that's all.'

'She's pretty,' she said, nodding. 'What's stopping you?'

I shook my head as if to suggest she'd got it completely wrong. 'She's married.'

Laura raised an eyebrow. 'Didn't get in there fast enough, then.'

I took a mouthful of warm beer. 'Something like that.'

We said nothing for a moment. The music went on around us, and those dancing stamped their feet on the floorboards and threw their arms out in a type of Highland fling. I stood there, next to her, this woman who was half stranger and half acquaintance, and despite the noise, I had a sudden urge to fill the silence.

'It's been a nice wedding,' I said, raising my voice so it could be heard.

She had her arms folded in an awkward pose. I noticed little black blobs in the inner corners of her eyes and looked away so she wouldn't know I'd seen them. I didn't want her to feel embarrassed later when she glanced at herself in a mirror and saw they were there.

'Yes,' she said, and I knew she was watching Anna. 'I love weddings.'

I didn't reply. I looked everywhere except the dance floor.

Sal came in from outside and waved as he walked towards the bar. He made a drinking motion and I put my finger up to say *wait*. 'Would you like a drink?' I asked Laura.

She smiled and raised her empty glass. 'White wine would be nice, thanks.'

I indicated to Sal and pointed to Laura's wine glass. White, I mouthed, and he gave a thumbs-up.

I nodded along in time to the music as I waited for our drinks. She kept her arms folded and tapped her finger on her elbow, and every now and again she'd look down at her feet.

'Whereabouts do you work in London?' she said after a minute, cupping her mouth with a hand to make herself heard.

I did a mental scan of our conversation at dinner, when we'd swapped basic rundowns of our lives. 'Near St Pancras,' I shouted back.

'Remind me what you do?'

'I calculate pensions for local government,' I said. 'And it's as boring as it sounds.'

Laura shook her head. 'Good, solid job. That's important in times like these.'

'Actually, I've just been promoted. I manage the department now.'

She looked at me, impressed. Those I'd told hadn't shown much interest beyond a faint lifting of the eyebrows. Dad had sniffed, and when I'd mentioned it to Anna on the bus from the ceremony, she gave a slight frown and asked how long I'd wanted to work in management.

Sal arrived with the drinks and handed Laura a glass of red wine.

I looked at him. 'I said white.'

He looked confused. 'I thought you said *wine*.' He shrugged as he gave me my pint. 'I've never been able to lip-read.'

'Is red okay?' I said to Laura, unsure. 'Here, let me change it.'

'No,' she said, moving the glass out of my reach. 'It's fine, honestly. Thank you,' she said to Sal.

He gave a brief smile then turned to watch the dance floor. 'Anna's going for it,' he said, nudging me.

I didn't know where to look. 'Yeah.'

'I'm going to keep her company,' said Sal, and he patted the back of my head. 'Don't worry, I won't fall in love with her too.' He took his pint with him and tapped Anna on the shoulder. She turned and hugged him and they danced *Pulp Fiction*-style to the music.

Laura's eyes were on me. After a moment, she turned her attention back to the dancing and took a sip of her drink, then gave it a stare before setting it down on the nearest table.

Anna looked up and our eyes met. She glanced at Laura, then me, then back at Laura.

'So do you enjoy working at a university?' I said, turning to Laura.

She unfolded her arms and smoothed the back of her hair. 'Yes, it's hilarious,' she said, then put her hand to her mouth.

'Really?'

She blushed and covered her face with her hands. 'Sorry,' she said, laughing. 'I don't know why I just said that. It's not hilarious at all. I think I've had too much wine.'

I smiled at her. She was nervous. For some reason, this made me feel better and I necked a long gulp of beer. I could sense Anna throwing us looks, and I turned instinctively to Laura. 'Nice dress,' I said. This was a half-truth. It was nice, nothing about it offensive, but then nothing particularly special either. I just wanted to say something to make her feel good.

She tugged at the hem. The dress was covered in tiny yellow flowers. 'Do you think?' she said. 'I ordered loads and didn't really like any of them. This was the best of a bad bunch.'

I didn't know what to say to this, so I nodded and downed the rest of my beer.

The song ended and the dancers clapped themselves and leant on each other for a breather. Attention was again turned our way.

'Listen,' I said into her ear. 'I don't normally do this, but can I take your number? You know, in case I'm ever in Canterbury and need to visit a uni.'

She looked down at her hands and smiled. 'That would be nice,' she said, and I took out my phone to add a new contact.

1991

Sal and I began sharing a bed not long after France.

The bad dreams came thick and fast, and I'd wake in the night to see him sitting up outside the covers, thrashing his arms and screaming. I didn't know what to do at first. He wouldn't stop so I crept along to Dad's room and tapped on the door, but there was no answer. When I looked in, I saw his bed was empty and assumed he was downstairs in front of the telly. I went back to bed and Sal eventually calmed down, but Dad still didn't come.

The next time, I woke to find Sal standing on the windowsill, his face and hands pressed against the glass. The moon cast a shadow on the wall of a caged boy fighting to get out. He wouldn't respond when I tried to talk him down, and I knew you should never wake a sleepwalker. Again, Dad's bed was untouched, and when I went downstairs, the TV and lights were off too.

But Dad was there the next morning at breakfast. Sitting at the table, his head in his hands, staring at a cup of black coffee. We poured our own cereal and I got the milk from the fridge, and when he stood and gave a long sigh, I smelt the whisky on his breath.

It was easier to push our beds together. That way, I could stop him lashing out, put my arms around him and hold tight. On good nights when nothing happened, I imagined it was my presence that calmed him, that the warm lump of my body kept the nightmares at bay.

Stella was impressed when she discovered I knew how to use the washing machine. 'Stone the crows,' she said, and gave me a long look, as if trying to figure me out. 'Not your father's son, then.'

I just shrugged. I didn't tell her about Sal's new thing of wetting the bed. She couldn't have done anything about it so there didn't seem much point.

Dad came to New York to visit Sal about a month after it happened.

'There's no point me coming out yet,' he said on the phone a few days into my stay. 'You're there, and he's being cared for by doctors. Much better if I come when he's discharged. I can only afford to fly out once, anyway.'

I hadn't argued. I knew Sal would rather he kept to his side of the Atlantic.

He arrived a few days after we'd left hospital. He took a bus from the airport to Penn Station – the cheapest way – and then walked the dozen or so blocks to the apartment. I left Gloria with Sal while I went down to help carry his case up.

'What's wrong with the lift?' was the first thing he said.

'Broken. They're getting someone in.'

He rolled his eyes and walked ahead up the stairs, stopping at each floor to wait for me to signal if we'd arrived.

When I opened the door, he strode in and wrinkled his nose at the stale air. He began a tour of the rooms, looking them over without saying a word. I introduced him to Gloria, who was just leaving, and he shouted to her slowly, as if *she* was the tourist. In the living room, Sal was lying on the trolley bed, his head towards the window. A talk show was on the TV, but nobody was watching.

Dad went over to Sal. 'Hello, son,' he said, and gave Sal's leg a light pat.

Sal slowly turned his head to look at Dad, then down at the hand on his dead leg that had no feeling. 'Hi,' he said finally.

Dad put his hands behind his back. 'And how are you?' he asked, in that grave, attentive voice he used sometimes.

'Paralysed.'

Dad coughed. 'Well, yes, I know that. But how are you in yourself?'

'I don't know, Dad. I'll probably need help every time I go for a shit for the rest of my life. How would you be?'

Dad pursed his lips.

'Coffee?' I said.

'Now you're talking,' said Dad, dropping into the armchair and taking the sports section from the table. 'You remember. Black, one sugar.'

I put a new paper in the filter machine and measured out the correct amount of coffee, then filled a jug with water and poured it into the back compartment before pressing the switch. Every sound echoed through the silent apartment.

'Arsenal playing rubbish,' I heard Dad say.

No answer.

'Wenger has to go,' he continued. 'They may as well take an axe to that trophy cabinet and chop it into firewood if they keep renewing his contract.' He tutted and shook the paper.

'Here you go,' I said a moment later, handing him his coffee. He raised an eyebrow in thanks.

'So where's Tally?' He slurped the tar-like liquid.

'Tilly,' I said, looking at Sal.

'Shouldn't she be here, nursing him?'

I cleared my throat. 'She's not around any more.'

'Oh, shame,' he said, looking back down at the paper. 'Pretty little thing, that one.'

Sal gave a slow exhale through his teeth and started to shuffle on the bed. The steel frame creaked and I made a mental note to go to the hardware store tomorrow and get something to fix it. A kind of spray, perhaps. Anything to quell the noisy reminder that his feet no longer touched the ground.

I went over and began pulling at his pillow. 'Here,' I said, trying to ease it out. 'Let me. Do you want to turn on your side? Is your pillow comfortable?'

He wrenched the pillow back. 'Leave it.'

'Just tell me what you're trying to do.'

'I'm trying to turn over on my fucking own. Is that okay?' Sal used his elbows to support his upper body and grimaced as he twisted towards the window, then punched the pillow into the crook of his neck.

I stared at the line of his back for a minute, picked up the TV remote and changed the channel.

'Good idea. See if the game's on,' said Dad, throwing down the paper and gesturing for the remote.

That night, I suggested we get Chinese takeout. I thought Dad would enjoy the quintessential American experience of eating from origami-style boxes, but when it came, he turned it out on to a plate and ignored the chopsticks. 'Cutlery?' he said, folding the corner of a napkin into his collar.

We watched a *Seinfeld* repeat. Nobody laughed. Sal just picked at his food.

Outside, Saturday night was starting up. Sirens wailed at regular intervals, and people shouted in the streets. When he'd finished his food, Dad put his tray on the coffee table and walked to the window, his napkin still tucked under his chin. He stood with his hands behind his back.

'New York is the greatest city in the world,' he said, shaking his head. 'I only wish I knew it better.'

I glanced at Sal and did a comical rolling of the eyes, and he looked away without smiling.

'You know, son,' said Dad, half turning to Sal. 'You should get yourself an American wife. Green card. That's the ticket.' His eyes flicked to Sal's legs. 'Too late for that, obviously.'

'Yeah,' said Sal, staring at the wall. 'Who'd want me now, eh?'

'Dad doesn't mean that,' I said, willing him to hear.

'Mm?' Dad turned to Sal. 'Well, they're sure to be sending you home, now they know of your existence.'

Sal looked at me. 'What?'

'We don't know anything yet,' I said, shaking my head at Sal and slightly raising a hand to pacify him. 'They weren't really sure what would happen. The doctors, that is.'

Dad snorted. 'He doesn't have medical insurance, does he? Do you really think they'll give him a free pass to stay in the country if he owes hundreds of thousands in healthcare? Besides, who'd pay for a full-time carer? He's a liability. Stop giving him false hope. Of course he's going home.'

There was a heavy silence, punctuated by an occasional car horn and the shriek of a pedestrian. House music pumped out of a car stereo. Sal stared at his feet, his eyes glazed as his mind raced through an imaginary future. It was true that I had already spent a small fortune kitting out the apartment to accommodate his new way of life, and what I had left would hardly make a dent in the hospital bill.

'And they'll never let you back again,' said Dad, frowning with authority. 'Not now you've outstayed by several years. Burned your bridges there, my boy.'

I covered my face with my hands.

Hey. So we're here. Sorry it's taken a while for me to get back to you. It's been a crazy few weeks getting set up. Tilly's apartment is in the west village area and is amazing. It's on a street with loads of trees and feels exactly like a village. It's pretty small though so we're not sure whether there will be room for me. I'm staying with my mate ben who lives out here. You remember him from football? He says I can stay as long as I want. In fact he might be moving to Chicago for work next year for a bit and says I can live here while hes gone. His place has two bedrooms and a cleaning lady and he's minted so he doesn't care about me paying much rent. ive got my first shift next week so it will be good to start earning though. im fine, don't worry, but I can see how quickly the savings will go. Its weird being somewhere you've seen all your life in films. It looks the same but different. Ive got to see quite a lot of it since we arrived as tills has had lots of events to go to, you know the networking thing, and she says id just be bored. So ive spent hours just walking around and seeing where it takes me. This city smells like nowhere else, and people seem angry a lot of the time. But I guess they've just got somewhere to be. I like it though. There's a kind of freedom to it or maybe it just feels like that because im used to ashford. I went to a party with Tilly the other day in some fancy penthouse and it was so funny watching these people talk. They all call each other darling and act like they're best friends but then they kiss the air and never actually touch each other. And everyone says they're working on something big. i wonder if any of them actually are. okay. Gotta go. Going out tonight as Tilly has rehearsals. peace. ps. They sell baked beans in a shop round the corner. The proper stuff. im never coming back.

Autumn 2010

For our first date, Laura and I went to a Mexican restaurant in Canterbury.

I'd messaged her a few months after the wedding to ask if she wanted to meet for a drink the following Friday. How about dinner? she replied immediately. There's a place near my work that's amazing. Sure, I typed. Ten minutes later, she sent me confirmation of the booking.

She was already there when I walked through the door, sitting with her hands clasped in front as if waiting for an interview. When she saw me walking over, she took a sip from her cocktail and smoothed her hair.

'Hi,' she said with a nervous laugh as I leant in to kiss her cheek. She wore a low-cut dress and as I sat down, I thought to myself how she looked better than I remembered.

'They asked if I wanted something while I waited,' she said, gesturing to her glass. 'I said I'd try a margarita and they brought me a glass the size of a bucket. I'm afraid it may have already gone to my head.' She laughed again.

'Good idea,' I said, nodding to the waiter. 'Take the edge off. I think I'll join you.'

Two buckets in, she asked what I was doing for Christmas.

'The usual,' I said, pinching the corner of the napkin. 'Overdone turkey cooked by my dad, the oven getting the blame, all of us getting gradually pissed until we pass out on the sofa. If my brother's still in the same room by early evening, I consider that a successful Christmas Day.'

'Why doesn't your mum cook the turkey?'

'Because she's dead.'

Laura choked on her drink and turned to splutter towards the wall. 'Oh God,' she said, her face scarlet. 'Oh God. I'm so sorry.'

My attempt at making a joke about what is always a conversation-killer had clearly backfired, so instead I fell back on an old faithful: pulling a daft face as if it was a boring little life detail that wasn't remotely upsetting. 'Don't be. It happened a long time ago.'

There was the start of an awkward silence and instinctively I turned towards the kitchen for sign of our food. 'How about you?' I said. 'What delights does the season have in store for you?'

Laura coughed into her hand, still pink with embarrassment. 'Oh, you know. The usual.' She grew redder, 'I mean . . . maybe "usual" isn't the right word. I guess everyone's idea of that is different.'

'Hey,' I said, picking up my glass. 'Let's start afresh. I'm sorry if I made you feel awkward. There isn't much of a way of softening that detail in conversation.'

We clinked glasses and she gave a grateful smile.

'My siblings and I usually stay over at my parents' on Christmas Eve, then we get up in the morning all together and open the first round of presents. My sisters and I make French toast for breakfast – it's a Foster family tradition – then it's round two of gifts before a cocktail, and afterwards we make a start on dinner.'

'How many siblings do you have?'

'There's five of us. Three girls, two boys. I'm slap-bang in the middle.'

I raised my eyebrows. 'It must be pretty cramped if you all stay overnight.'

'Oh, Mum and Dad have never moved. We still all have our rooms made up how we left them. My grandparents live in an annexe next door. Dad had the old stables converted for them to live in once they were too old to care for themselves. So yes, it is quite full-on.'

As she talked, my mind scrapped the mental image of her family in a suburban semi and replaced it with a historic country pile, a giant tree in the hallway, flagstone flooring, bulging stockings on the fireplace. They probably played board games in the evening. So this was her normal.

'I love Christmas, though,' she said. 'I always become such a kid, and I love the passing on of traditions from one generation to the other. My mum says this year she'll teach me the recipe for the cake she makes for Christmas Day evening. Grandma taught it to her, and hers before her. It always passes down through the female line.'

Our food arrived and I changed the subject.

I'd been wondering all week what to do about the bill. This is why I suggested drinks, I said to Daz. Much easier taking turns to buy a round. But it's the twenty-first century, said Daz. She works, don't she? Then split it. You don't want to hook a bird that cries women's lib only when it suits her. Yeah, I said, but maybe she likes the gentleman thing so at least I should *offer*.

I needn't have worried. The waiter set the tray down in the middle and I was the only one to reach for it.

'Thanks so much,' she said as we stood and put on our coats. 'That was delicious. Didn't I say this place was good?'

'Here,' I said, 'don't forget your . . .'

We both leant across the table to get her glove at the same time and our hands touched. She snatched her arm away like she'd had an electric shock.

'Thanks,' she said, taking the glove and trying to hide the blush on her face.

Outside the restaurant, we stood a metre apart and looked about at passing traffic.

'We could go for a drink if you like,' I said, unsure of what to say.

'I'd better not,' she said, looking down at my shoes. 'Those margaritas have quite done me in.' And then she leant in to kiss my mouth, and I put my arms around her to steady her footing and stop her falling in front of a passing car.

She stepped back and laughed into her hand. 'God, that was brave of me. Sorry.'

'That's okay,' I said.

'Really?' She smiled to herself. 'I had a really nice time. Let me know if you'd like to do it again.'

She was attractive, kind, she asked questions about my life, and there was a level-headedness to her that was appealing. Perhaps that was the key to it all, this whole business of meeting someone and settling down. Not fireworks or a tight knot of fear in the stomach, but rationality and, maybe, being wanted more by the other person. I'd never tried it that way. Maybe I should.

'Sure,' I said, pulling out a cigarette. 'Why not?'

'Great.' Laura gave a drunk, happy smile. 'Text me an idea of what we could do?' She slung her bag over her shoulder and turned to walk towards the station. 'I really did have a lovely time, Nick Mendoza,' she called over her shoulder. The words had a studied air, as if planned in front of a mirror.

I watched her walk away.

2003

I remember words from a lost conversation. I don't know how we got there or where we went next. This is all I've got.

We're in the back seat of her car, it's raining and the windows are slick with damp. I stroke the skin of her leg that rests on my lap.

Do you think we'll be friends? I say, feeling the light hairs on her knee. You know, in the future. Will we still be talking to each other?

Anna looks at me with long, slow blinks. A slight shake of her head.

Too many sparks, she says. I don't fancy catching on fire.

Mid-Eighties

It was a Saturday morning and Dad went off to a tournament. He left first thing that morning, a packed lunch from Mum tucked under his arm, his clubs in the boot, allowing plenty of time to drive to Hertfordshire. We had Mum to ourselves.

These were always fun days. She'd let us spend them in our pyjamas, watching back-to-back films, even if the sun was blazing. Dad would never let us turn on the telly when the sun was out. He'd shoo us outside with some line about how lucky we were to be alive, then he'd settle back in his armchair and put on whatever he liked.

Mum, though, she let us do as we wanted. Looking back, it was as if she knew she didn't have time to waste.

We watched from the window as Dad drove off, then came the sound of footsteps on the stairs and we dived back under the covers. Mum opened the door and stuck her head in. 'Come on,' she whispered, and we jumped up and ran down the landing to her room, where we leapt into her bed.

This was another forbidden thing. If we had nightmares, Mum would come into our room and squeeze into one of our beds. If we really cried, she stayed all night.

'Let's make a tent,' said Sal, burrowing under the covers.

'You'll need pillows,' Mum said, and passed them down the bed. He stood them up vertically to make two tentpoles and we shimmied down the mattress into the camp.

Sal sat cross-legged in the middle and looked about. There was a small smile on his lips, and he clasped his hands in his lap and twiddled his thumbs. 'There's only just enough room for three,' he said. 'Nobody else. Nobody else allowed.'

'What about Dad?' said Mum.

Sal shook his head.

'Where would he go?' I said to Mum.

She looked about the confined space. It was hot from our breath. 'Maybe we could shrink him down a bit. But there won't be room for either of you soon. You're only going to get bigger and then you'll be men too.'

'What about you?' I said. 'Are you going to get bigger?'

She smiled and shook her head. 'You stop growing when you become an adult. You start shrinking instead.'

Sal found this hilarious. He pulled up the top of his dinosaur pyjamas and started beating his belly.

'You know what doesn't start shrinking, though?' she said, looking at us both. 'Your heart.'

I wrinkled my nose. 'Actually?'

'Truth.'

'So the rest of you gets smaller and smaller, but your heart stays exactly the same?' Sal put his hands up to his neck and did a mad laugh. 'That's crazy.'

'I'll tell you a secret, though,' Mum whispered, and we leant in so our heads were almost touching. 'If you want to be really happy, your heart needs to grow even more.'

Sal started tickling my feet. 'Stop,' I said, slapping his hand away.

'Did you hear me, boys?'

'Yeah,' said Sal and he screamed as I tickled him back. 'Your heart gets bigger. Yeah, we heard.'

'But you have to let it.'

Time and date: 16/09/2014 10:47

From: Anna <anna.not.hannah03@gmail.com>
To: Nick <nick.mendoza.2003@gmail.com>
Subject: Re: Hey
Status: Sent

Hey!

So good to hear from you. It's been too long. How are things?
Couldn't glean much from your email . . . Man of many words, as
always. Are you still writing? Hope so.

All is well with me, thanks. Work has been insane (which is
wonderful, obviously) but means I have less time for reading and
general staring out of windows, and you know how I love that.
Maybe one day I'll figure out that work/life balance.

I do have some news. I'm pregnant. Not sure if it's weird or not for
me to tell you that. Something inside said I should. I had wondered
whether to email, but then you messaged to say hi and it was like
you'd read my mind. So, yeah . . . *with child*. Feeling great, though.
First time in possibly forever that I have a sense of inner peace and
calm. Everything is out of my hands for once, and it feels sort of
liberating.

Hope all is well with you. Did Sal ever make it to New York? I miss
it so much. Can't wait to go back one day.

Hope you're well.

A.x

I loved her. God, how I loved her.
There. I have said it.

'Tell me again why we're doing this,' I said as we crossed the road towards town. There was a sharp chill to the wind and I pulled up my collar in self-defence.

'It was your idea, remember, making an effort with Tilly, so don't blame me if it's a horrendous night.' Laura faked a jab in my ribs.

'Yeah, but I was banking on Sal saying no.'

Laura laughed and stepped closer, putting her arm through mine as we walked. I glanced at her and saw she'd done something different with her hair. She saw me looking and smiled.

'You look really nice,' I said.

She squeezed my arm and her eyes wandered down from my face. 'I wish you had let me iron your shirt.'

We arrived at the restaurant at exactly 8.30 p.m., the time of the reservation. There was no sign yet of Sal and Mathilde, and we allowed the waiter to lead us to the table, which was slap bang in the middle of the room. The tables around the edges were filled and a low hum of voices pulsed above the faint sound of inoffensive jazz.

'Should we be facing or next to each other?' Laura said, unsure.

'Here,' I said, pulling out two chairs on the same side. I helped take off her jacket.

I'd picked a newish restaurant in town that proclaimed itself 'modern dining', smallish and family run. It was probably the most sophisticated of all of Ashford's culinary offerings, and I knew if I'd suggested a chain, Mathilde would only have rolled her eyes.

'Should we order drinks?' Laura said after a few minutes of waiting. She picked up the menu.

My reply was drowned out by the sound of Mathilde, who appeared in the doorway with Sal close behind, his hand in hers. He must have cracked a joke because Mathilde found whatever he'd said hilarious, which seemed uncharacteristic of her. The entire room stopped their conversations and turned to watch her flick her hair.

Mathilde shrugged off her leather jacket and dropped into the chair opposite. She was still laughing to herself and didn't bother with much of a hello other than a quick flirt of the eyebrows. Sal leant down to kiss Laura on the cheek.

'Sorry we're late,' he said, rubbing his lips and smiling. 'We, uh, got held up.'

'It's warm in here, no?' said Mathilde, fanning herself with a menu.

'Really? I think it's quite cool,' I said, and turned to Laura. 'What do you think? Warm or cool?'

Laura gave a sideways look. *Stop it.* ' "You say potato and I say potahto." '

'You look different, Laura,' said Mathilde, resting a hand beneath her chin and narrowing her eyes. 'Your hair. It's normally poker straight.'

Laura blushed and pulled at the wavy ends. 'I'm not sure it suits me.'

'You look great,' I said, nudging her elbow with my own.

'Not really,' she said and moved her knife an inch. 'I thought I'd try it out, but . . .' She made a face.

I hoped the others would back me up, but Sal was too busy looking at Mathilde, who was too busy being noticed by Sal.

We ordered drinks and engaged in the usual chit-chat. Sal's job would soon be extinct, he said. Nobody wanted to go out and rent films any more when they could download them instead. He was probably going to have to get out, but what else he'd do, he didn't know. He spent most of the time talking about Mathilde and her role at MTV. Apparently some big shot thought she had potential as a presenter and they were going to test her on a new show. Mathilde sat back and let Sal talk. There was no embarrassment as he gushed and no attempt to play down the compliments he paid her. She knew her worth.

'Any plans this weekend?' said Laura, filling the first silence.

Sal and Mathilde exchanged glances.

'We've been roped into seeing Tilly's friend's new baby. Guess what they've named her,' said Sal, leaning in for dramatic effect. 'Moon.'

Laura put a hand to her mouth. 'For goodness' sake.'

'What do you think?' I asked Mathilde.

She raised an eyebrow. 'It's certainly memorable.'

'I read once that a New Zealand court blocked someone from naming their twins "Benson and Hedges".'

'*Oui!*' said Mathilde, clapping her hands. 'I saw that. And another tried to name their daughter "Talula does the hula in Hawaii."'

I shook my head. 'No, you're making that up.'

'It's true!' She slapped the table and laughed. 'I refused to believe it too.'

For a second, we smiled at each other and Laura squeezed my knee. I could see Sal out the corner of my eye, looking between us with a strange, joyful look on his face. He was begging for scraps. It was within my power to give him a banquet.

'Tilly,' I said, passing her the drinks menu, 'this may be extremely stereotypical on my part, but can you recommend us a bottle of wine?'

A smile teased across her features as she took it. 'We must choose our food first. Salmon for me. Laura?'

'The chicken pasta,' she said, having decided as soon as we'd sat down.

Mathilde waved to the waiter and ordered a bottle of the Pinot Noir, which she said would pair well with our chicken and fish. I raised an eyebrow at Sal, who'd picked steak, and he shook his head and said he preferred a beer anyway.

Mathilde stood and swung her leather jacket around her shoulders. 'I'm going for a smoke.'

'I'll join you,' I said.

I held the door open and we went outside into a quiet Saturday night. Bright light spilled out from a kebab shop across the street, and there was the distant pulse of cars on the ring road. Mathilde sat on a low windowsill to roll her cigarette. I turned away to shield my flame from the wind and saw Sal and Laura talking intently through the glass.

'It's cold tonight,' I said, rolling back my shoulders.

Mathilde licked and pressed the paper, then put the tip between her teeth as she rooted around in her bag for a lighter. Having mine still in my hand, I reached out and flicked it into life. She stared at it for a moment, then leant in to kiss the flame. Her blouse fell open slightly to reveal an inch of black lace. I quickly looked away.

'So how does it feel?' she said, sitting up and leaning back against the window.

I blinked. 'What?'

She paused to take a drag. 'This *making an effort*. Isn't that what you called it?'

I gave a wry smile. Of course he'd tell her.

'Salvatore and I don't have secrets.'

'Clearly.'

She cocked her head to one side and glanced up at me. I wasn't looking but I could feel her eyes on my face, then my shoulders, before she travelled down my body to my feet and back again. It was a full body scan. I wondered what she'd found.

'You don't like me, do you, Nicolas?'

I kicked lightly at a loose cobble, then gave a slow exhale and looked at her through the smoke. 'Would you care if I didn't?'

She looked impressed. 'Of course not.'

'It's not part of my plan to hate on my brother's girlfriend.'

'Ah, so you do have some kind of plan.' She crossed her legs. 'I was beginning to wonder.'

'Wonder?'

'It seems you let life just happen to you.'

I shifted my weight to the other foot. 'Does it.'

She gave a light shrug. 'It's just my opinion, Nicolas. Don't get mad. Although Salvatore does agree with me. He says you've always been like that.'

I was quiet for a moment, focusing on the feeling of my smoke on the back of my throat. 'I'm pleased to amuse you both.'

Mathilde frowned. 'I wouldn't call wasting your life amusing.'

'Wasting my li— Is this because you think I don't like you?'

She gave me a long stare, continuing to take little puffs throughout, and then looked away with a small smile. 'I didn't mean to upset you. *Pardon*. I'll be quiet now.' She locked her lips and threw away the key.

We spent a minute or two in silence, and I watched as a man in the kebab shop carved strips of congealed meat into a polystyrene tray. A woman leant on the counter, waiting, her eyelids hanging heavy in a drunken state.

'I don't dislike you,' I said finally. 'Sometimes I struggle with how you treat Sal, but that's just being an older brother. You get used to putting others first.'

She hugged an arm across her waist and rested the point of her other elbow on her wrist. This made it easier to ferry the cigarette to her lips. 'Salvatore knows how I feel about him,' she said. 'I don't care about making sure you know it too. What's the point in putting on a show?'

Mathilde's dad left when she was five years old, Sal told me once. He walked out of their Parisian apartment one morning and never went back, moving instead to Cannes to live with his teenage assistant. Mathilde and her dad had been close, going for ice creams in the park while her mother spent long lunches with friends, and at first he rang every week to ask how she was doing at school. But gradually, as he built more of a life on the Med, the calls became sporadic and out of the blue, until it became just another Christmas and birthday tradition.

When in her company, I have tried to remember this.

'I'm glad he knows,' I said. 'That's what matters.'

'Does Laura know?'

'Excuse me?'

She looked at me. 'Does Laura know how you feel about *her*?'

I knew she was baiting me, and I threw my fag end on the ground and pushed both hands in my pockets. 'Our food's probably ready.'

Mathilde didn't move. 'Sometimes, Nicolas, I think you and I are quite alike.'

I couldn't help but laugh. 'And how do you figure that?'

She stood on her spiked heels and smoothed down her skirt. 'I've seen you watching Salvatore with me, and I recognise the look in your eyes.' She dropped the end of her cigarette. 'You and I both have thunder in our hearts. The difference is, I listen to mine. I don't try to squash it like a bug.'

She turned and walked back through the door. I followed. Laura poured me a glass of water from the carafe. Her mouth formed a sentence, but the words were drowned out by the noise in my head.

In all my previous conversations with Mathilde, I'd assumed I was the one doing the studying, but she had lasered through my bullshit and got straight to the heart. It was difficult now to simply dislike her, or dismiss her as empty, because everything she'd said was true.

When our food arrived, the conversation dwelt on lighter things: a new film at the cinema, Sal's team's performance in the local league, an upcoming holiday they were taking. I contributed the odd comment, but mainly I let them talk. Everyone murmured positively about the food, including Mathilde, who – according to her – was hard to please, but mine was dry and tasteless on my tongue, as if my senses had lost their colour. The wine, I could tell, was excellent.

Mathilde left the table after we'd finished, and I watched Laura follow her through to the back.

'Tell me,' I said, leaning forward in my chair. 'Isn't there some kind of brotherly code for not telling our girlfriends everything?'

Sal tore off a chunk of bread and frowned. 'Translation?'

'You told Mathilde this whole night was for me to make an effort to like her.'

He looked confused. 'But that *is* the reason?'

I sighed. 'Am I the only one who knows a civilised society cannot run on people saying what they think all the time? There'd be chaos. Ever heard of tact?'

Sal looked at me, amused. 'How's that working out for you?'

'Try it sometime.'

He chewed mouthfuls of bread, watching me with an easy smile on his face. The way he sat, slouched with an arm extended over the back of Mathilde's chair, oozed with the lazy confidence I'd always wished for myself.

'And how *are* you and Laura, by the way?'

'I'm not sure Laura and I are the ones that need examining.'

Sal shrugged. 'It's hard to tell, that's all. There never seem to be any ups and downs. Always an even plateau.'

I paused. 'I thought you liked Laura?'

'I do. I'm just wondering if *you* like Laura. But maybe still waters run deep.'

I rubbed my chin. 'Am I meant to perform a song and dance to convince you that I care for my girlfriend? Be something I'm not?' As I finished the sentence, I heard Mathilde's voice in my head: *What's the point in putting on a show?*

Sal finished his beer and gestured to the waiter for another.

'So,' I said, leaning back in my chair, 'tell me about this surprise party I'm not supposed to know about.'

He shook his head. 'Nope. I'm not one for pissing off your girlfriend. Although I'm curious as to why thirty-two requires a party.'

'I think she's trying to make up for the fact you never threw one two years ago. You know how I love surprises.'

'I did try telling her, but she seems to think she knows you better.' He smiled. 'I look forward to finding out.'

'What I like about Laura,' I said, staring into my wine glass, 'in case you're wondering, is that she's always looking to improve the little things. It's not about fireworks or grand gestures, or moving mountains. It's about creating an easy life that doesn't . . .' I paused to find the right word.

'Rock your boat?'

I was quiet for a moment, Mathilde's words still in my head. 'She makes me feel calm,' I said. 'No drama. That's something, right?'

Sal began to reply, but a bell tinkled on the front door and I looked up to see his ex, Tess, walk in. She stopped when she saw us, her mouth dropping open, then turned to a man behind and whispered in his ear. Sal was still talking, his back to her. The waiter indicated to them to follow him to the room at the back, and as they passed, Tess smiled at me and paused by the table. It was then I saw her stomach between her coat, large and round, as if she'd stuffed a basketball up her top.

Sal looked up and saw her. He stayed exactly where he was, sprawled open in the chair, but his face cracked a large smile. 'Tess, hey.'

Tess looked between us both, her cheeks red and her voice stumbling. 'You look well.' She put an instinctive hand on her bump.

Sal twigged. 'Congratulations,' he said warmly.

'When are you due?' I asked, noticing her gaze drink in Sal. It must have been five years since they'd broken up, but it was clear he was no distant memory.

'Oh . . . a couple of months,' she said, glancing awkwardly at the man behind. 'On the home stretch.'

I murmured another congratulatory statement as Sal looked about for a sign of his beer. 'That's really great, Tess,' I said, hoping to make up for his lack of interest.

'Well, enjoy your meal,' she said, taking hold of the man's hand. 'Good to see you.'

'Best of luck,' I said, kicking Sal under the table.

He frowned at me, then realised. 'Oh, bye. Good luck.'

As she moved slowly away behind Sal, I saw Mathilde and Laura coming through from the back. Mathilde had obviously seen her at the table, and as they passed, she looked down at Tess's stomach and gave her a thunderous look.

Sal gave a brief nod behind him. 'That was *my* safe option,' he said. 'Dodged a bullet there.'

When Mathilde pulled the chair out a little too forcefully, he turned with an adoring smile. The sight of his ex seemed to have evaporated from his consciousness, but evidently not from Mathilde's.

'Hey,' said Laura, kissing me. I could smell the wine on her breath and her eyes had that soft look that comes at that sweet spot of tipsy. She leant into my ear. 'I love you, you know.'

I took her hand and pressed it against my lips. We smiled at each other.

Across the table, Sal was leaning towards Mathilde. 'What's wrong?' he asked, and I could tell he was trying to be quiet. 'What have I done?'

Mathilde drained her wine glass and folded her arms.

'Shall we get dessert?' said Laura, taking the menu that had been left.

'Not for me,' said Mathilde, and she gave a forced smile. 'But don't let that stop you.'

'Okay,' said Laura, a little unsure. She was wising up to the vibe from across the table. 'Sal?' But he wasn't paying attention.

'I'll have a look,' I said, leaning in. 'What do you fancy? Shall we share something?'

'Tills, please,' said Sal in her ear, but she brushed him away.

'Maybe we should just get the bill,' Laura said, looking at me. We tried to communicate without words or facial expressions. We were doing a shit job.

'No, no,' said Mathilde, reaching across and taking the menu. 'You want dessert so you must have dessert. Let's see.' She pursed her lips as she scanned the menu. 'The cheesecake. A little sickly after pasta, maybe. Or bread and butter pudding? Such a strange concept, that one. Why have bread with butter to start and then sprinkle it with sugar for dessert? You British are very bizarre with your choices. I've never understood it. But then there's no – how do you say – accounting for taste?'

Sal watched her with a hand over his mouth. He looked still and composed, except for the frequent swallowing action he made in his throat. I remembered it from when we were kids, this reflex, how he'd almost be swallowing deep breaths of air to suffocate the emotion boiling up inside.

'No dessert for me,' I said to Laura. 'I've had enough this evening.'

She nodded and folded her hands in her lap.

I signalled for the bill and we endured a silence as we waited. Mathilde sat with her arms crossed, but then she stood and without a word, took her jacket and went out through the front door. Sal sat still for a moment, lost in thought, before jumping up and following her. They stood on the other side of the window, arguing with wild gestures of their arms.

When the waiter arrived, I gave a quick scan of the bill and handed him my card. Laura looked at me and I shrugged and said, 'Well, it was my idea.'

Outside in the cold night, they were going at full pelt.

'I saw how you were looking at her,' Mathilde hissed, jabbing a finger into his chest.

Laura and I stood to one side, our hands in pockets or folded against our chests like parents at Sunday football. We looked from one to the other.

'How I looked at her?' said Sal, his hands on his head. 'Are you kidding? Tills, I had my back to you for a start.'

'So I'm a liar?' Her face was outraged, as she twisted her arms into her jacket.

'What am I supposed to do when she stops by the table? I haven't seen her in, what, seven years. All I said was "hi" and "congrats". And have you forgotten that the reason we broke up was so I could be with you? Christ, Tilly, she even found us in her own bed.'

Laura gave a small gasp and I remembered leaving out this detail when I told her the story.

Mathilde laughed and nodded as if what she was about to say was absolute truth. 'And I bet you're hugely regretting that decision. Now she's bursting with babies.'

'This is crazy,' said Sal, shaking his head. 'I don't want Tess. You're the only one that I want. You know that because I tell you every single fucking day.'

Mathilde stood there for a minute, staring at the ground. The pavements were busy with bodies stumbling out through pub doors. They either passed by towards the club down the hill, or into the kebab shop on the other side of the road. A small crowd was now looking over, enjoying the entertainment between mouthfuls of burger loaded with special sauce.

Finally, Mathilde looked up. She drew her jacket tight and tucked her bag into the crook of her arm. 'You know,' she said to Sal, 'I think this has gone far enough. We had something exquisite, you and I, and we burned brighter than most. But the fire went out a long time ago, and we're too dumb to know it.'

Sal's expression switched from disbelief to fear. 'Tilly, don't.'

'Come on, Salvatore,' she said. 'Admit it. We had a good time.'

'Why don't we just go home?' I said, stepping forward. The curious faces were multiplying. 'Sleep off the wine, take stock and pick this up tomorrow.'

Mathilde arched an eyebrow, but her voice was soft: 'That's your motto, isn't it, Nicolas. Shut off the feeling? Avoid it? Never say what you really feel? Yes, Salvatore told me all about her. Your one that got away.'

I clenched my fist in my jeans pocket.

'I think we're done here,' she said, turning to go.

'Tilly, please,' said Sal. He was crying. 'I'm sorry, okay? I'm sorry I spoke to her. I don't fucking want her. I never did. It was always you. You. Fucking you.'

She began to walk off and he started to follow, calling her name. When it was clear that she wasn't going to stop or turn, he drew his foot back and kicked hard at a lamp post, shouting her name for every drunk to hear.

Laura covered her face with her hands.

My feet pounded the pavement and then my arms were around him. 'Don't, Sal. She's not worth it,' I said as he sobbed against me, but it was no use. He heard nothing but the violence of his heart.

The next day was Sunday and we let him sleep late. Shortly after ten, I carried a mug of tea upstairs and tapped my fingers lightly against the spare-room door.

After we'd got him into bed the previous night, Laura and I had stood in the kitchen and talked through the evening, piecing together the clues.

'How was she when you left the table together?' I said. 'What did you talk about?'

Laura frowned as she thought back. 'The usual. Me asking questions. The brand of her lipstick, her job, if she missed Paris. She didn't even use the loo – just stood by the mirror and played with her hair.'

I shook my head. 'She's something else.'

Laura didn't say anything, and I looked up at her leaning back against the counter. The only light in the room came from the alley streetlights at the end of the garden, their soft glow edging her profile with orange trim. The side of her nearest me was in deep shadow.

'Yeah, she is . . .' she started. 'This will sound odd to you, but I'm kind of jealous.'

'Of Mathilde?'

She nodded. 'Everything happens so easily for her.'

'She's spoilt.'

'Perhaps. But she gets up in the morning and already looks great. You know she doesn't take her eye make-up off before bed? See, you shrug, but that's a cardinal sin. If I did that, I'd be a panda, but she gets up and looks like . . .' she waved a hand in the air, '. . . *that.*'

I pulled at the corner of a pile of utility bills on the counter, there to be filed away. 'I like how you look,' I said, 'and there are more important things.'

'Yeah,' she said, drily. 'She aces those too. Gets an unpaid job at MTV as an intern, is spotted by a producer who wants to make her a TV presenter, and just like that, with no qualifications, she'll hit the big time. I, however, forego any fun to study and get good results, leave uni with a decent degree and will spend the rest of my life in a desk job that has zero impact on anyone else.'

'I thought you liked working in education?'

'It's hardly that, is it? You say you work in education and people assume you're Robin Williams in *Dead Poets Society*. I ensure stocks of whiteboard pens and paper never run low.'

'You're the one that keeps things steady. O captain, my captain?' I smiled, but Laura just stared through the window at our untended garden. 'I don't get why you would want Mathilde's life.'

She sighed. 'I'm not saying I do. I just know that even if I did, I'd never get it. She's just one of those girls.'

'What girls?'

'The rule breakers. They do what they like and it still works out fine.'

Sal mumbled and I nudged open the door. He was awake under the covers, staring out the window, I assume at the tree hanging over from next door. This was the room with the best view; the fields in the distance above the rest of the estate. Just enough room for a double bed and a few small items of furniture. Cosy. I'd suggested it as our room when we moved in, but Laura had preferred the spacious master bed in the loft with the triple wardrobe, en suite and no view.

'Morning,' I said, setting the tea on the mirrored bedside table. I saw my reflection and it shocked me for a moment, the sight of my chin and neck from an angle I'd never known. It was me, but not the me I knew.

Sal looked like newly awoken shit.

'What time is it?' he said, rubbing his eyes.

'Ten-ish,' I said, leaning against the closed door.

His eyes widened and he leapt up, scrambling about for his phone. 'Fuck, why didn't you wake me?' He grabbed his jeans from the floor and rooted through his pockets. The screen lit up when he touched it, and his shoulders slumped at the sight of no messages. He immediately began drafting one as he sank back on the bed.

I sat on the chair in the corner, the one Laura had chosen from IKEA as a place for guests to drape their clothes. It was hard and wooden and the spindles pressed against my spine.

Sal threw the phone on the bed with the screen facing upwards. He adjusted the pillow to lean against the wall and picked up his tea, rubbing his face with his other hand.

'Has she messaged?' I asked, forgetting my plan to talk of anything but her.

Sal didn't reply. His face had a nervous energy, a raw mix of exhaustion and alertness that when he was younger would manifest as a craving for a spliff. He didn't bother asking if I had anything he could smoke. He just tapped the mug with his fingernails in a frantic, repetitive beat.

'Well, I guess that's that,' I said, with a sympathetic smile. 'You know you can stay here as long as you like, right?'

The tapping stopped and he looked at me. 'What?'

'While you get yourself sorted. We can take my car to get your things from the flat, maybe when Mathilde's at work. When's best?'

He frowned, but his face looked amused, like he was trying not to smile. 'You don't mean . . . Oh, Nick. No.'

'What?' I felt a cold sweat prickle on the back of my neck.

'We haven't broken up. No, see, this happens all the time.'

'Last night?'

'Yeah.' He sipped his tea.

'Last night happens all the time? Rows in the street? She tells you it's over and you break down in front of the whole of Ashford, hyperventilating and beating your chest. This is normal behaviour, is it?'

'Last night was perhaps especially full-on, but we row, yes.'

I shook my head. 'Oh, Sal.'

Sal cleared his throat, his smile swapped for pure irritation. 'Save the big-brother routine for another day. I'm not in the mood.'

I couldn't decide whether to start laughing, or punch a fist into my palm. 'I don't get why you're happy for her to treat you like this.'

'You don't know her.'

'I know she hates her dad because he walked out on her when she was a kid. You told me that. Doesn't that explain it? She's making you suffer because you're a man, and a woman's view of men is often shaped by her relationship with her father.'

Sal laughed. 'What is this, *Freud for Dummies*? Seriously, Nick. Bloody hell. Stop trying to analyse everyone all the damn time.'

I wanted to shake him. 'Laugh if you like, but it's true. A person's ability to relate to the world is moulded by their interaction with their parents as a child.'

'Well then, we're fucked,' said Sal, snorting. He took a long swig of tea and checked his phone.

'I'm just trying to understand,' I said, slowly realising that this was never going to end.

'No, you're not,' he said. 'You're trying to take care of me because that's what you've always done. And I get that, Nick. I do. Maybe if I was the older one, I'd do the same. But listen to me when I say you don't know a damn thing about her.'

'I tried, Sal. I arranged last night—'

'Oh, come on. Like when she walked into the restaurant and said it was warm and you disagreed? Or when you kept throwing her looks every time she mentioned herself? You think people don't notice but you're clear as fucking day.'

'She does talk about herself a lot.'

'She likes herself!' he almost shouted. 'What's wrong with that?

You want us all to hate ourselves and be miserable and make sure everyone else knows it?'

I ran through the night in my head; the hair flicking, the confident way she ordered wine – no asking the waiter for his recommendation or canvassing the table for their preferences – the cool and calm acceptance of every nice thing said about her. She liked who she was. She wasn't afraid of herself. I knew I found that threatening.

'I don't know her like you do,' I said. 'But all I have to go on is how she acts in my presence around my little brother. And maybe it's because of our own useless dad that I feel like I have to be one to you.' My voice struggled on the final word.

Sal didn't reply for a minute. He ran a finger round the rim of the cup resting in his lap and the silence grew between us. This was not familiar territory.

Finally, he spoke. 'Tilly's relationship with her dad is partly why I fell in love with her. She knows how it feels not to be wanted. To be abandoned by someone who should love you. Few people know that.'

I couldn't leave it. 'He loves you,' I said. 'In his own way.'

Sal gave a grim smile. 'Still fighting Paul Mendoza's corner then?'

'Don't you remember the times when we were kids when he tried, when he really tried. The Arsenal games—'

'—that you went to and I never did.'

'Or when he'd take us round town to see the Christmas lights, how he'd call out to you before we reached your favourite house—'

'Yeah,' said Sal, 'I remember the lights. How one year in all the excitement I spilled my hot chocolate on the seat so he refused to take us again. Yeah, I remember.'

I bit my lip. He was right. I remembered differently. The visits to Highbury, Dad reading the match programme aloud as we waited for the game to start, the soggy chips in newspaper on the walk home. Those days had meant so much to me. And yet Sal hadn't been there once. But how could I help that? Should I throw out the good memories I have of our dad, the ones I can count on one hand, do I pretend they never happened? How do we think of another human being if not based on our own experience of them? We are not fixed or permanent statues, we are ever-changing mists, clouds that are seen as dogs or cats depending on the person looking up. The thought of this is hopeful and so lonely.

'You were always the favoured one,' said Sal. 'The firstborn. But you also weren't the one who destroyed his life, who fired the gun that shot the bullet. I blew pieces of her brain across his suntanned limbs. I took away the only person who adored him. Why would he still love me after that?'

The words blistered my gut. They tripped off his tongue, happy-go-lucky, as if he had turned them over in his mind so often that they no longer held any power. They were as familiar as a finger or a toe.

I had thought them too, but only within the beat of my own head.

'You look at Tilly and you see drama,' he said. 'But that's what I need. Like a drug. Every day is different, every day has something new to make me feel alive, to stop me dwelling on the pain that drips through me like a fucking tap.'

I looked at the carpet and nodded.

There was a light knock at the door, and Laura's face appeared in the gap she opened up.

'Hey,' she said, giving Sal a shy smile. 'How are you feeling?'

'You know. Waiting for a word.'

'I'm making a fry-up, if you want one. Soak up all that beer?'

He gave a thumbs-up, and she glanced at me as she closed the door. Apart from our conversation in the kitchen, Laura had been oddly quiet since last night. I wondered if Mathilde's words had come back with the sober face of morning. *Yes, Salvatore told me all about her. Your one that got away.*

Sal was typing another message.

'Has she texted?'

No reply, and I knew the answer.

When he put down his phone, I said: 'So tell me this. Why did the sight of Tess set her off?'

Sal sighed. He raked a hand through his hair and kept it there. 'We were chatting a few weeks ago, and in an offhand, three-beer kind of way, I said I'd love us to have a kid. It was a casual comment. I don't think I even meant it.'

'It's good to make sure you're in agreement about these things.'

'Yeah, well, Tilly and I don't work like that. Spreadsheet-Nick might not get it, but we take each day as it comes, live in the moment, the future doesn't exist.'

'What happened?'

'She said she'd make a terrible mother. She refuses to pass her shit on to someone else.' He put down the mug. 'I think seeing Tess made her worry that I'd regret not having kids. You think Tills is hard as nails, right? Yeah. That's what she wants you to think.'

Despite myself, I felt a twinge of admiration for Mathilde, or perhaps relief at discovering a common ground. We knew our weaknesses.

Sal's phone beeped and he grabbed it. He began typing furiously, his forehead creasing like the spine of a loved book. 'Gotta go,' he said, pulling on his jeans. 'The fry-up,' I said, but he was through the door and running down the stairs, the cracks appearing in his bravado. Clearly this row was anything but ordinary. 'Tell Laura I'm sorry,' and then the slam of the front door.

I thought of Mathilde, her recognition of herself and the way she lived without seeking the approval of others. Like a magnet, I was attracted and repelled by her. Both charges are potent. And just as a magnet has the power to control or cause chaos, depending on how an object yields to its force, Mathilde had the potential to alter my world, for better or for worse. She was a fire that could not be contained, and I was the spectator. Fascinated. Terrified.

Someone else once made me feel that way.

From: ANNA
To: NICK
Subject:

I have done everything I was meant to.

I have sold off pieces of myself that I forgot existed. Not an arm or leg or something obvious, but little gouges from my wrist or ankle, scratches that go deep, scoops of flesh from my inner thigh or the underside of my foot, small enough not to notice until one day I can no longer stand. The tiny chips over time are hard to spot, but they're there. No one sees you giving away these cuts of yourself. Not until you no longer have anything left to give, and by then, your worth is gone.

You sabotage yourself for everyone else, and for what?

I have done everything I was told.

And I am broken.

PART FOUR

2018

The funeral was held on a Thursday.

Dad insisted on a burial. It was double the price of cremation and more paperwork, but he was adamant no son of his would be burned in an oven with nothing to show for it. I think this is a commonly held view among the older generation. An obsession with leaving a stake in the ground, like scratching *I woz ere* into a desk on the last day of school. This was also typical of Dad. Nothing for months and then a grand, sweeping gesture.

I remember a conversation Sal and I once had about being buried alive. As boys, we had a constant fascination with the macabre. He read once in a *Reader's Digest* how they dug up old graves to reuse the ground, and on opening coffins they sometimes found scratch marks under the lid. Buried alive. *Imagine knowing you were going to die,* he said. *Like, a second time. All the bugs crawling over you and up your bum and knowing there's nothing you can do about it.* He shivered from a mix of fear and delight. *I definitely want to be buried.* All the savings I had left were spent on flying his body home.

I try not to dwell on the idea of bugs crawling over my brother's body. But on dark nights or when it's raining, it is all I can think about.

I paid for the local priest to speak at the graveside. Sal wasn't religious, none of us were, but the event seemed to require someone to manage it, or at least string a few words together. The thought of it made my mouth dry. It seemed worth the expense.

We made a lonely procession. A few handfuls of us in black coats and umbrellas, picking up mud on our best shoes. Dad and I stood at the front and carried Sal's feet on our shoulders, but when we made the final turn to the open grave, I stumbled and someone else took over.

Stella arranged for flowers to be put on the other grave. We'd tried to get Sal as close as we could. After it was over, Stella and Dad went to pay their respects and I waited by the car.

It was open invite at the pub afterwards and it was clear he'd been loved. Standing room only. We stood in groups holding paper plates of sausage rolls and sandwiches cut into triangles. Dad took root at the bar.

'I'm so sorry, Nick,' everyone murmured in my ear. Sal's ex-girlfriends – Tess couldn't face it – threw their arms around my neck and left wet smudges on my jacket. The lads patted my back and hid their mouths with their beers.

A few of his New York acquaintances had made the trip. Good of them, really. They shook my hand and between mouthfuls of fruit-cake said things like, 'He was always the life and soul of the party. Who would have known? Was he depressed?' Those who really knew him didn't ask stupid questions. I thanked them for coming and bought them each a drink.

Mathilde couldn't make it. Apparently she'd moved to LA and it clashed with auditions for pilot season. She sent flowers instead. White fucking lilies.

Maybe she couldn't face it either, said Laura. You wouldn't want her there anyway. Be grateful.

Be grateful.

Oh, and Anna was there. Maybe I should have said.

I'd left Dad and Stella by the graves and begun walking back towards the road. The rain had softened to drizzle and I turned up my coat collar and lit a cigarette.

Ahead by the gate, I saw a figure waiting underneath an umbrella. I knew her instantly. There was something in the way she held her-self, even in the rain, as if she would not be defeated. I took a deep drag.

I looked up when I reached her. Her face looked the same, a little older, lovelier. It had been several years since I'd seen her at the wed-ding. She wore a black dress and pearls and looked at me with sad eyes, and although I had wondered if she'd come, if the endless online tributes to Sal would find their way to her, I found myself wishing she hadn't.

She leant in and I felt the cool touch of her leather glove on my neck. Neither of us spoke. I wondered how long was appropriate to hold her and which of us would pull away first.

'I wish I knew what to say,' she said into my coat.

'Just don't tell me you're sorry,' I said, holding the cigarette behind my back. 'Everyone's sorry, and I'm not sure I could take it from you.'

She let go.

'Good of you to come.'

She looked at the ground. 'I wasn't sure, but . . .' Her eyes were on me. 'I loved Sal. You know that.'

'I do.'

'I wish it was the right time to say it's good to see you,' she said. 'It's been so long.'

I turned my face away to exhale the smoke and nodded. 'It must have been a trek to get here from Scotland.'

She blinked. 'Oh. No, I moved out a few months ago. I'm back in Ashford now.'

'Oh.'

'It's complicated,' she said, and tucked her hair behind her ear.

I cleared my throat to speak, but nothing came out.

'I thought Sal was better,' she said, looking down at her gloved hands. 'I know something like that will never leave you, but when I knew him back then, I thought he'd found a way.'

I shrugged as if the thought was a new one, as if it hadn't repeated in glorious Technicolor through my brain each day since I'd flown across the Atlantic. 'His girlfriend had just ended it.'

Anna gave a slow nod. 'The French one you told me about years ago? He adored her, didn't he?'

'She had this strange power over him,' I said with a grim smile. 'I could never understand it, but then maybe it was him I never understood.'

'We can't control who we love, though.'

I listened to the rain as it dripped down the leathery evergreen leaves on the bush beside us. The iron railings gleamed black.

Everything looked sharp, senses heightened, the way it does when death comes to visit and there's a brief glimpse into deeper things.

'You coming to the pub?' I said. 'There'll be a few you know. Plus the chance to have awkward conversations and watch my dad get hammered.'

She looked down the road. 'I think it's better I give it a miss. Don't want to cause you any trouble, especially today.'

I followed her look in the direction of my car several metres away, and two eyes inside pretending not to watch us.

'Oh, right. Yeah.'

'I am sorry, though, Nick.' She leant in again and kissed my cheek. 'Sorry for being sorry, but that's just the way it has to be.'

She stepped away.

I put my hands in my pockets. 'Sal had these nightmares when he was a kid. Some nights, I had to help him down from the window. I've wondered if that's how it happened, the first time when he fell – that he had a nightmare and there was nobody to pull him back. And then he just knew there was no future lying in a bed. Never getting up again. Because you have to be desperate to drink bleach, right? You have to really want it to end.'

Anna was quiet. She watched me kick the ground. The rain stopped and she closed her umbrella.

'I know what it's like to have no home,' she said, 'and feel like a stranger with your own family. You just want someone to love you. It makes you do desperate things.'

She straightened her back as if to say goodbye and stayed right where she stood.

'Maybe we can do that drink sometime?' she said, pressing fingers to her wet cheeks.

'I'd like that.'

She began to walk in the opposite direction. I breathed in my dying cigarette and listened to the fading sound of her leather shoes on the wet pavement.

Look back, I said inside. And when she reached the end of the road, hidden from the waiting cars, she did.

★

Anna messaged soon after and asked if I still read much. Not really, I typed back. But you always wanted to be a writer, she said. How can you write if you don't read? I waited a while then said, yeah, I don't really write any more. She didn't reply to that.

It was a few days later when she messaged again: I've just finished a book I think you'd like. Raymond Carver's *What We Talk About When We Talk About Love*. Try it. I think it's you.

I didn't reply, but the following lunch break, I went out and bought it.

It was a thin volume of short stories about older men and women still figuring things out. Characters who'd failed somehow at life, whether a marriage or a job or a friendship. They were all broken in some way. Someone would ask a question and a character would respond with a comment about the weather or else say nothing at all. I read a story each day on my morning commute to the sound of a classical playlist I downloaded to drown out other people.

After the final page of the final story, I stared out the train window and tried to work out what she was telling me.

We went back and forth like that for a while. Sending each other the name of a film the other should watch, or books, or a song they should hear. We didn't have permission to say what we wanted to say, and even if we did, there was no guarantee we would have done so. We kept to pop culture and the words of other people to speak for us. There was a permanence to it that way. You could revisit that book or that song, and it would be like hearing each other say it all over again, even though neither of us had ever actually said it. We could shape the words and meaning to what we needed in that moment.

It was a type of invention and fantasy, I think we both knew that, but that was fine. Perhaps it was more real that way.

Desire / by Anna

You should know my fear
If you have me, no longer will you want me
You won't write pages
The nib of your pen will run dry
You would be like every man
Or every person
Who wanted something so much they burned themselves up with
  wanting
Like Henry who craved his Anne
Divorced Rome for her
Then cut off her head and said
She bewitched him

There is a scene that repeats in my head. It's almost a part of me now.

We go to Venice at the end of November.

The hotel is on the Grand Canal, a pink square building with whitewashed walls. Our room is small and absent of things, apart from a bed and a rickety wardrobe. Through the double doors is a narrow stone balcony on the water.

We spend most of the weekend fucking.

I want you to make love to me, she says on the first night, so I do, going slow and stroking her hair like I know she wants. Then we fuck against the wall. She tells me to pick her up and I wrap her legs around my body. When she puts her hands on the back of my shoulders, I tense my arms against her touch. I make love to her in other ways too, but we always face each other. She says she wants to see me, to know it's me that's there.

After we're done, we throw open the doors at the end of the bed and watch the white curtains float in the breeze. Outside are rooftops and red sunsets, but we lie naked on top of the sheets and I don't really notice the view.

We order room service and take long showers.

On the second day, she drags me from the bed and we go for a walk. We stumble across a square with a church in one corner and children playing on the cobbles. The sun bounces off the peeling coloured walls. Outside every door and window are boxes filled with red geraniums, and I close my eyes and inhale the scent.

She wears a white summer dress and a straw hat. In the middle of the square, a band of old men with leathered faces give her appreciative looks and talk to her as if she's one of their own. She smiles and shrugs and takes hold of my hand, and when they see me, their mouths drop open.

We sit and drink beer at a café table. I pay the bill and she leads me by the hand into the little church. I lean against a pew and watch as she exclaims at painted frescoes and the beauty of the light. After a while, the sight of the gold makes her feel ill, and we walk back out into the sunshine, my hand on her waist.

We find another table at another café. They bring us a carafe of the house wine and we sit close together, sipping and staining our lips. After the first glass, she turns and gives me a long kiss. She doesn't care who sees us.

When we come apart, I turn to pour more wine and see the first line of a web has been cast from my glass to hers. A tiny spider works away, spinning our present into the past. I break its web and close my fist around it.

On our final night, we have run out of money. We share the cheapest meal from the menu and wash it down with red wine.

We spend another hour in bed and then I step on to the balcony for a smoke. The sun is setting in the distance, and there is the sound of laughter and lapping water as the gondolas float past.

She rises from the bed and comes to me. Nothing is said as she leans against my back, moulding herself to my form. As she presses her body into the line of mine, I feel the quick, strong beat of her heart, like a siren, and it occurs to me that she is a human being, just like me.

Spring 1997

We should have been at school that day.

We'd got on the bus that morning, Sal and I, and made our way to the back, where Daz lay sprawled across the seats. He moved his feet and we dropped down as if carrying lead weights in our pockets.

'You both look like shit,' he said, throwing his tie over his shoulder.

I leant my head against the window and shut my eyes. I'd hardly slept that night and hoped he'd get the hint that I wasn't in the mood for banter.

'You good, Salvatore?' said Daz, ruffling Sal's hair.

Sal ducked away. 'Piss off, Darren,' he said, resting his leg in a triangular shape on the adjacent seat to build a wall between them.

The bus came to a halt at the next stop and Daz gave a long whistle as a girl got on. She wore the grammar school uniform and looked terrified every morning when she had to find a seat.

'All right, darlin'?' Daz called. 'Come back here and sit on my face if you like.'

'You know she's, like, twelve,' I said. 'That's pretty sick, Daz.'

He threw up his hands. 'How's it my fault if Year Sevens look older these days? She's a butterface, but Christ, that body.'

There were two grammar schools in Ashford, the girls' and the boys'. If you passed your eleven-plus, you went to a grammar and from there it was plain sailing to uni and a decent job. Kids that didn't pass went to the comprehensive, where the majority left at sixteen for a supermarket job or to sign on. Some slipped through the cracks, going on to good things, but it was a harder fight. I've never understood it, judging kids by the rep of a school formed years before they got there, but anyway. We all went to the comp.

'You and grammar school girls,' said Sal, rolling a cigarette.

'You know they're at it full-on lesbo in the cupboards,' said Daz, closing his eyes with a sigh. 'It's not right, keeping horny girls cooped up. They need a guy to sort them out.'

'And I bet you're the guy,' I said, watching the revolving doors of an office building spin around with suits. All going in, none coming out.

'Bloody hell,' said Daz. 'I wouldn't know where to start.'

'I won't be on the bus home,' said Sal, slipping the smoke into his pocket.

'Hot date?' said Daz.

'Why?' I said, looking past him at Sal.

'I haven't done my maths. Bellend's already given me an extension and said that if I missed it again, I'd get detention.'

'I had him last year,' said Daz, sniffing. 'What a cock.'

'Yeah,' said Sal. 'He hates me.'

'It may have something to do with you once crawling under the table and Tipp-Exing "twat" all over his patent leather shoes,' I said.

'That was quality,' said Daz, swaying with laughter. 'Can't believe you didn't get expelled.'

Sal shrugged. 'They said I would have if it hadn't been so soon after . . .' He paused and looked out the window. 'I think it demonstrated creativity, personally.'

'Know what?' said Daz. 'Sod this. Let's not give them power over us. Why don't we have a day to ourselves? Your dad's at work, right?' He reached into his bag and pulled out a VHS. 'I nicked my brother's new porno and it's blinding.'

Sal leant forward. 'I'm up for it.'

'How 'bout it, Nicolas?' said Daz, slapping my back.

'We've got exams soon, Daz. It's a pretty big year.'

'Mate, too late for that now. It's either up here,' he pointed two fingers at his brain, 'or it's not. Come on. We won't have many days left for this. Now or never.'

They cheered as I put a hand up in surrender and Daz hit the red STOP button. We bounced along the aisle to the front and Daz blew a kiss to the girl as I pushed him off the bus.

'Don't do that,' I said.

'Defending her honour?' He offered me a fag.

'Just let her ride the bus.' I cupped my hands and flicked the lighter.

'Oh, don't worry, she can ride whatever she wants,' said Daz, and he did a thrusting action at the bus as it pulled away. 'I'm just a taster of what she can expect in the real world.'

We walked together on the pavement, Daz spinning his record bag by its straps. Cars and vans sped past and the air was thick with rush-hour fumes. We had to almost shout to be heard.

'I like grammar school girls,' said Sal, pulling his rucksack on his back.

Daz found this hilarious. 'How the hell would you know? You even fingered someone yet?'

'I'm not a virgin,' said Sal, taking out his smoke.

I stopped and stared at my fourteen-year-old brother. 'What?'

'Shut up,' said Daz. 'You've had sex with a bird? Pull the other one.'

Sal smiled as he lit up. 'Don't believe me then.'

'Who?' I said.

'You don't know her.'

Daz rolled his eyes. 'No trail. How convenient.'

'I don't care if you believe me,' said Sal, walking on. 'I'm hardly going to tell you her name, am I? You'd probably write "slut" across her locker or something stupid.'

'Where'd you do it?' I said, catching him up.

'Her house after school. That time I helped set up for House Drama. We finished early and she asked if I wanted to go back to hers and watch something.'

'Aha,' said Daz, walking slightly behind us. 'So she does Drama.'

Sal spun round. 'Seriously, Darren, piss off. I'm not telling you her name and you're not working it out. If you do and tell her or anyone else, I'll cut your throat.' His hands were tight fists.

Daz took a step back. 'Easy, Sal. Jeez.'

We walked on in silence for a while, letting the traffic fall behind. Gradually the houses started widening out. The view became greener as the pavement narrowed, forcing us into single file. Sal went in front, Daz at the back. I had a million questions.

'So give us a rundown,' said Daz. 'I mean, course I've shagged birds. But every one's different, innit.'

Daz brimmed with self-confidence. At nearly sixteen, we were both desperate to lose it. Daz prowled school discos with a hip flask of vodka that he'd sneak into plastic cups of orange juice. He'd offer one to a girl, upfront about the contents, and she'd usually drink it to show how cool she was about alcohol. They always got off with him, but it never got further than a hand up the top. He would never have shut up if he'd made it further.

'If you've shagged loads, then you already know, don't you?' said Sal.

Daz put on the porno when we got back to ours. I grabbed a six-pack of crisps from the kitchen and the cans of Dr Pepper we'd bought from the newsagent on the way home. We sat in the living room, eating and drinking and jeering at the screen as a repairman screwed a housewife over her husband's desk. The postman knocked on the door and he joined in, then a pretty young neighbour popped round for a cup of sugar. Before too long, the husband arrived home from his office job and it became an almighty gang bang.

Afterwards, we took it in turns to visit the bathroom.

Daz belched and stretched his arms towards the ceiling. 'How's that for skiving off?'

Sal appeared in the doorway, dressed in casual clothes. 'I'm going out on my bike,' he said, putting on his bucket hat.

'I'm up for that,' Daz said, getting up.

'But you haven't got your bike?' I said, ejecting the video and handing it to Daz. I picked up the crisp packets and hugged the empty cans to my chest.

'He could ride Dad's,' said Sal as he opened the back door.

'What? No.'

'He never rides it,' said Sal, sitting on the step and pulling on his trainers.

'It'll be safe as houses, Nicolas,' Daz said, doing a Scout's honour sign.

I continued shaking my head. 'No way. Definitely not. Now wait while I put this stuff in the bin.'

The living room was empty when I returned. I pushed my feet half into my trainers so my heels hung out the back, and ran round the side to find Sal and Daz pulling the bikes out of the garage.

'Is anyone going to listen to me?' I said, blocking the entrance. My larger frame had to count for something.

Sal pushed past with his bike. 'Here,' he said, tipping the handlebars towards Daz. 'You ride mine. I'll ride Paul's.'

'No,' I said, putting my hand out against Sal's chest. He looked at me with a bored expression. 'I'll ride Dad's. You take mine.'

Daz climbed on to the saddle and cleared his throat. 'If we've finished Pass the Parcel, can we get the hell on with it?'

I remember '97 as a hot summer. It was only early spring, that day we skipped school, but there was already a sweat in the air and down our backs. Daz and Sal stripped off their tops as we rode, Daz swinging his like a lasso as he cycled with no hands. This was the year he bleached his hair, and he'd gelled it into spikes so it resembled a pineapple.

Our BMXs were second-hand when we got them, and the frames and wheels bore the marks of a full and active life. There were scratches from the wheelies in nearby country lanes, hours of practising and whooping each other, and races to see who could go longest. There were times we'd sped downhill and hit potholes that took us over the handlebars, the wounds on our bodies healing but leaving dents on the chassis to tell the tale. When we fell, we got up and climbed back on. Bike rides and stolen pornos were how we spent those days.

Sal and Daz did bunny hops and endo turns while I followed further back. I was taking no risks on Dad's bike. His had been brand new, the one awarded top marks in all the magazines, and he'd hardly ridden it in the ten years since. Any mark would show.

'Fuck, I'm roasting,' said Daz, wiping the sweat from his chin.

We were approaching a built-up part of the country lane, with houses of all eras spread out either side. They had generous gaps between boundaries and long gardens out back. Being in the countryside, Sal and I were used to these kinds of roads, but for Daz, who lived on a council estate, these were 'posh houses'. They had driveways for more than one car and you could shout inside without disturbing the neighbours.

We slowed down to let a van pass, and as it did, the driver gave us a hard look. We were used to this look. It was something only adults did, where they found us guilty of the crime of being young and not giving a damn. Daz stared back, and as it sped off, he stuck up his finger for the rear-view mirror.

Sal grabbed his arm.

'He didn't see,' said Daz.

'No, look,' Sal said, pointing at the house next to us. He edged his bike forward so he was hidden from view by a clipped privet hedge along the front. 'In the garden, through that gate.'

Daz and I leant forward on our bikes for a better view. Between the house and garage was an open gate and through it we could see much of the back garden. A long line of bushes divided it from next door, and facing this was an expensive-looking wooden deckchair. What caught Sal's attention were the two bottles of beer in the fancy cup holders of the fancy deckchair.

'God, yes,' said Daz.

'Don't be daft,' I said. 'If you want to get pissed, let's go home and raid the drinks cabinet.'

'Who wants whisky on a day like this?' said Sal.

'But you can't see the whole garden,' I said, hearing my whining desperation. 'They might be round the corner.'

'He's probably inside having a dump,' said Daz, rubbing his hands together as if this was a master plan of his making. 'He's clearly coming back, though, so we'd better move fast. Go on, Salvatore. Make our day.'

I shook my head, but didn't say anything. I was tired of playing the dad. And a cold beer was a tempting prospect.

Sal propped his bike against the hedge and leant round into the drive. He looked at the windows, then strode across the brick paving, his feet silent beneath his skinny frame. He ducked down along the side of the house and peered round to look in the garden. It must have been clear, because he crept across the lawn and picked up the beers. Then he looked up at the hedges and stopped.

'What's he doing?' I said. 'Why isn't he coming back?'

Daz shrugged but I could tell he was nervous. He moved from side to side on his toes and tapped his hands on the handlebar. Finally he gave a low whistle. 'Sal,' he hissed. 'Move.'

Sal looked at us, his mouth open, then turned back to the hedge.

Daz leant his bike against Sal's and crossed the drive like a secret assassin, but when he reached Sal, he too stopped and stared.

Seconds passed like hours. I looked about at the quiet road, but the only sounds were birds in the trees and the distant pulse of a radio. I leant Dad's bike against the hedge and tiptoed across the drive and down the side. I was concentrating so hard on not being seen that I didn't notice a large metal wind-chime hanging from the garage roof. Sal and Daz jumped at the noise and my hands flew up to stop the bars banging together, but this just made it worse. I ran across the grass and pulled at Sal's arm.

'Are you crazy?' I said under my breath. 'Let's go.'

'Fuck me,' said Daz in a trance. 'Look at that.'

I turned and looked.

The hedge was thick apart from a patch in the middle. Here, the twigs had been newly cut or snapped off, and provided a near-perfect view to the other side. Through the branches, we could make out a girl of about seventeen or eighteen on a sun lounger. She wore nothing but sunglasses and the bottom half of a bikini, and lay sprawled out on the lounger for the sun's rays to penetrate her skin.

Perhaps it was the porno we'd watched, or the crazy heat, or the fact we were teenage boys who'd never seen a naked girl in real life, but we stood there frozen and forgetful about this view not being ours.

I was first to look away, and that's when I saw the deckchair positioned up against the hedge and the beers in Sal's hands, dripping with cold dew.

Before I could speak, there came the sound of a door being thrown open and hitting a wall.

'What the—'

We spun round to see a half-naked bloke in shorts and flip-flops coming out on to the patio. I half recognised his face. A pair of binoculars swung round his neck and the swell of a middle-aged gut leered over the tight band of his shorts.

Daz was fastest. He was across the lawn and back on his bike before the guy had found something to pick up. Being closest to the road, I wasn't far behind, but Sal had been on the wrong side of the deck-chair, and this added precious seconds that left him in direct fire when the man rained a garden rake down on his head. Sal shouted as the rusty teeth sank into his shoulder. He dropped a bottle and it smashed to pieces on the slabs.

Sal stumbled through the gate. The man followed behind, still waving the rake and shouting something I couldn't make out.

Sal began pushing his bike down the road, then jumped on and pedalled away. Daz had taken the bottle and he took a swig and raised it in a toast to its naked owner, who stood breathless at the entrance.

We screeched to a halt when we'd turned the corner and I lowered the bike to the ground and ran to check Sal's shoulder.

'Let me see,' I said as Sal winced. His T-shirt had taken the brunt of the rust, and it was the force of the hit between his shoulder blades that seemed the source of the pain. 'There's no blood,' I said, relieved.

'That was epic,' said Daz, shaking his bleached head. 'Shame you dropped one, Sal.'

'He knew who I was,' Sal said, catching his breath.

'What?' I blinked.

'He said I was Paul Mendoza's son.' Sal rolled back his shoulder as if warming up for a fight. 'The bastard recognised me.'

I tried to think how I knew the man's face. 'Shit,' I said. 'He's from the golf club.'

We looked at each other and Sal put his head in his hands.

'What about those tits, though,' said Daz. 'Did you see how close that chair was to the hedge? And two beers . . .' He gave a high-pitched trill. 'He was all set for the afternoon.'

'He's a fucking perv,' said Sal.

'To be fair, we were watching her too,' I said.

'Yeah, but it's not like we planned it. She was, like, seventeen, and what was he – fifty?' He shook his head. 'That ain't right.'

Daz cleared his throat. 'Yeah. Disgusting.'

I felt the dangerous rush of something course through my veins. It comes to me every now and again, this feeling, in the first few seconds after Arsenal lose a cup final, or back at school when I was one of the last picked for PE. It falls somewhere between anger and helplessness, a terrifying knowledge that the sensation is too big. I never know what to do with it.

That day, I listened.

I picked up Dad's bike and began cycling back. As I built up speed, the breeze rushed through my ears like music. Nearing the driveway, the whirr of Sal and Daz's tyres sounded not far behind.

It was only then I picked up the rock. The idea had come to me earlier, but I knew that returning to the scene of a crime with a weapon would count as premeditation, and any punishment upped accordingly. But now, I leant down and chose a large stone from the side of the road, smooth and polished with a pointed end.

I stood in full view of the house. I turned the rock over and over in my hand, as if to channel the energy of the force in my veins into this lump of stone. Bring it to life.

'Do it,' said Sal, behind me. 'Do it, Nick. Do it now.'

I've always been fairly good at throwing. The times when I'd be picked first were during basketball or if something needed dislodging from a tree. Then it would be *Get Nick*. I'm good with my hands too. Dad thought I'd have made a great boxer if I worked on my nerve.

You're too fragile, he said. They know where to hit you and take you down. There are no second chances in the ring. It's do or die.

The rock hit an upstairs window and there followed the expected and satisfying smash.

We didn't wait around to see what happened. I sped off up the road, feeling the wind on my face as Sal and Daz followed behind, whooping and cheering me on.

Late 2018

Six months after we buried Sal, Dad rang me at the office. He never did that.

'Son,' he said. 'I've got lung cancer. Doctor's given me twelve weeks, six months at most.'

'Dad,' I said.

'I'm quite all right in myself. You'd best come over, though, so we can make arrangements. Friday works for me.'

On Friday night, I stood on the doorstep of my childhood home cradling a six-pack. I lifted the heavy brass knocker and let it fall, and the thud reverberated through the empty hallway on the other side. As I waited for the door to open, I noticed one of Mum's terracotta pots by the step. It had been almost thirty years since the baked earth had known geraniums.

When the door opened, a pale and shrunken face looked out and it took me a moment to realise it was Dad.

'You look well,' I said as I stepped inside.

He took the beers without saying anything and gave them a critical look. 'I'm on the whisky. You want a glass?'

'Sure,' I said, slipping off my shoes.

He fixed my drink and took me through to the dining room, where he'd laid out piles of paperwork across the mahogany table. He pulled out a chair and gestured to me to do the same.

'Dad,' I said. 'Could we sit in the lounge?'

'But I've got everything here.'

'This can wait, surely?'

'No time like the present.' He sat down on the other side. 'That's all I have, anyway. Sit.'

I took a gulp of whisky.

'Now, I want a burial, you know that. Here's my list of requirements for the service.' He handed me a crisp piece of white paper with typed bullet points. 'I don't want a wake. No food or photo montage, no crowd of people I've not seen in years pretending that they cared. No hypocrisy, thank you. Just put me in the ground.'

I sighed.

'I've made preliminary enquiries regarding a plot. I want to be as close to your mother as possible, but I've asked to reserve the one alongside your brother in case there's nothing they can do.'

'Dad, I can't do this right now,' I said, standing up. 'I promise I'll read it, but can we just go in there and put the telly on.' I reached out for his glass. 'Here, I'll make us another drink.'

In the lounge, I poured two whiskies from the almost empty bottle on the sideboard. Dad sat in his armchair and I took the sofa across the room. He switched on the news.

There had been an earthquake in Indonesia and we watched footage of collapsed homes and crying children. The scenes of devastation made me think of Anna. She does that sometimes, appears all of a sudden, and then I can't help but think of her for a while.

'One more thing,' said Dad. 'I've written to Arsenal to request they pass the season ticket on to you. It's all paid up to the end of the season, but after that, I'm hoping they'll put it in your name so you can go in my place.'

'I'm not sure you can do that, Dad.'

'Fifty years, I've been standing on those terraces. That's half a century. Besides, I want to leave you something. You are my son, after all.'

Like I said. Nothing for months, and then a grand, sweeping gesture.

Dad refused to go into a hospice.

'What's the point in making myself comfortable? Face facts. This is my home and I'm not leaving it while there's breath in my body.'

He compromised and agreed to a carer, on the sole condition it was a woman. He had strong views on whether it was right for a man to be a nurse, and had no problem expressing an irrational, deep-seated fear of turning homosexual if he allowed a man to wash his body.

Sheila was a no-nonsense woman with grown children, whose own husband had died a few years before. She wore half-moon glasses attached to a pink cord looped around her neck, had a tight perm and took no crap from Dad.

'I had a bath two days ago,' Dad said to her when I visited. It had been a month since his diagnosis and he was spending more time in bed. 'It's not as if I'm working up a sweat. I'll take another at the weekend.'

'No, Paul, you'll take one right now,' she said, rolling up her sleeves. 'You don't mind waiting, do you, Nick-love? No patient of mine has developed bedsores and I'm not about to let that start now. Come on. Up.'

Dad gritted his teeth and threw back the covers. One–nil to Sheila.

The end came quicker than we thought. I began sleeping in my old room, taking the night shift so Sheila could manage the day while I was at work.

He called out my name at two o'clock on the Friday night before Christmas. I stumbled out of bed and into his room to find him sitting up, the cover pulled tight around him. His hands were clasped across his lap and he looked up at me like a boy waiting for his good-night kiss.

'Everything okay?' I said, rubbing my eyes.

'Son, I'd like a whisky.'

'It's the middle of the night.'

'Will you join me?'

I made my way downstairs. The hall was dark apart from the moonlight shining in. It threw patterns of the trees on the high Victorian ceilings, and when I reached the bottom, I looked out at a full moon.

I poured a couple of whiskies from the bottle on the lounge sideboard and returned upstairs, taking care through habit to avoid the floorboards that creak.

I passed him his glass and sat at the end of the bed, holding mine with no desire to taste it. He took a couple of sips and looked about the room.

'Look at these yellow walls.'

The ornate cornicing had taken on a grubby, golden patina from

years of neglect. 'I guess it must be thirty-five years since it was decorated,' I said, remembering Mum with a paintbrush shortly after we
moved in. She had Sal on her hip.

'And the rest. Look at it. Hardly fit for human habitation. I expect
they'll tart it up nicely for the next tenants, though.' He took a sharp
intake of breath. 'Here you go, Paul Mendoza. About to die in a room
that's not even yours.'

I didn't say anything.

'Your mother wanted to paint this room a rich mustard. Said it
would give the walls a sense of grandeur. It was double the cost of a
tin of magnolia, but look at it now. Yellow from dirt. I should have
let her.'

I took a mouthful of drink.

He looked down at his glass and swilled the liquid around. He
stared at it for a while, then threw back his head and drank the lot.

'I should have let her,' he said again, and rested his head against
the wall.

'Do you miss her?' The words just came out.

He opened his eyes and looked straight through me. I turned to see
if someone was behind, but there was just us.

He was silent for several minutes and I finished my drink to fill the
void.

Then he began to speak.

'We went to the Isle of Wight for our honeymoon. A long weekend. Do you remember, Lou? We had tea and scones at Alum Bay.
There were little tables with red-and-white checked tablecloths and I
told you to pretend I'd taken you to Italy, like you'd said you wanted.'

I gripped my glass.

'After that, we went to Blackgang Chine, and you nearly lost it in
the room with the funny mirrors. People were giving us looks and I
had to kiss you to stop you laughing. Then on the ferry home, we had
just enough money to share a cup of tea, and you let me add a sugar
even though you took yours without. That was you. My lovely girl.'

I thought my heart would break through my chest.

Dad ran a hand through his thinning hair and closed his eyes.

'I'm tired now,' he said. 'I want to sleep.'

I made him comfortable and sat there for a moment, looking at the fading form of his body under the cover and the shape of his head on the pillow. I thought about how you never really know a person, that even when you share the same blood, all that connects you are the words you choose to say and the way you touch each other.

I reached out and held his foot through the blanket.

Silence is also a language. You just hope the other person speaks it too.

I woke to the sound of Sheila tapping on my bedroom door. It was still only getting light outside, but from the colours filtering through, it looked like it would be a beautiful day.

She was on the landing wearing her best brave nurse's face, and I knew.

I arranged a funeral for the second time that year. I usually get immense satisfaction from things running like clockwork, but this was tempered by a kind of longing. Grief, perhaps.

Dad's wishes were carried out exactly. There was no wake, a handful of us at the graveside, and no unexpected mourners at the cemetery gates. Stella held my arm the whole time.

Afterwards, we went back to the house and I sat at the kitchen table. Stella made tea and pulled out a chair.

'When's Laura back?'

'End of next month.'

She pursed her lips. 'Did she not want to come home early?'

I burned my lip on the tea. 'She did, but I said not to bother. It's not every day you go to South America on a three-month trip. What can she do, anyway?'

This seemed to be enough for Stella. 'Laura's a nice girl,' she said.

'Yes, she is nice.'

Stella looked around. 'What are we going to do with all this? Bag it up and take it to the tip, I suppose. There's nothing worth keeping.'

The sides were crammed with Tupperware boxes and tins from savoury crackers. The post-war generation seemed to hang on to every little thing, just in case the day would come when ten torches would be useful. The wooden sideboard in the kitchen was filled with similar tat, along with a handful of cheap supermarket cups and plates. As Stella said, there was nothing worth keeping. The best china had all been broken.

'What happened to Mum's things?' I said. 'I've always wondered.'

Stella put a spoon in the sugar pot and stirred it into her tea. 'Well, I boxed everything up and told your dad I'd take it to the charity shop, but he insisted I leave it all. My head wasn't in the best place. Maybe it would be dealt with differently now, leave it all out, perhaps. But it was another time. Nobody talked about things. Did you never ask him where it all went?'

'Sal did once. It didn't end well.'

We drank our tea and after a moment, she said, 'Did your dad ever tell you about Grandpa?'

'Grandpa?'

'Our dad, he never knew his father. We think it might have been his mum's employer – she was in service – or the son, perhaps. There were rumours. But there was a lot of shame about that kind of thing back then. All we know is she was kicked out when it was found she was pregnant with Dad.' Stella poured more tea from the pot into her cup. She added a sugar, paused then added two more. 'He adored his mum. She died of TB when he was ten, and at the wake it was asked of all the relatives who'd take him. None spoke up. He went to an orphanage in the end, but I often think of him sitting in that room with his family, listening to their silence. Poor sod. You just want your family to love you.'

I stared at my cup. 'I never knew any of that.'

'It was our mum who told us, crying, after a bad night when your dad came home after curfew. And who knows what details she left out.'

'Dad used to fight with Grandpa?' I pulled at the loose tufts of skin around my nails.

'When you know love and it's ripped away like that . . . What must that do to a person?' She stared at the tablecloth, her mind lost somewhere forty years ago.

I heard the slow, faithful tick of the clock on the wall.

Stella pushed her cup away. 'What I'm saying is, something like that, it never leaves you.'

I thought of Grandpa in his feathered cap and sheepskin. How he'd tug our cheeks and press a battered fiver into our hands when we left to go home each fortnight. Dad had known a different man.

These footprints we leave stamped on the next generation, the pieces of best china on the floor for someone else to pick up.

Three Days Later

I was back at work the following week. My boss said to take a fortnight's bereavement leave, but I couldn't see the point. I'd only spend it playing video games in my pants, and falling into a pit so low it would only leave me stuck.

Laura was still abroad. She emailed to say their expedition group was about to hike up to Machu Picchu. Rio had been insane. She'd had to wait ages to get a photo that didn't include a stream of social media influencers in the background. I emailed back to say how ironic it was that pilgrimages to these sights were booming, yet the level of crowding made it impossible to experience anything remotely spiritual. We are all just seeing to be seen, I said. She didn't reply.

One morning a few weeks after I'd returned to work, I went outside for my mid-morning break. I'm one of the only smokers in the building these days. There are a handful of others, mainly middle-aged, too along in years to care much about really changing. I guess you get halfway through life and accept the damage has been done.

I knew I should quit. One day. But my vice is also my pleasure, so I take my smokes in the side streets, where I avoid my colleagues passing with their oat-milk lattes and vegan sausage rolls.

On this particular morning, though, I opened the door and walked straight into Anna.

She drew a sharp breath when she saw me. 'What the—'

I put the cigarette to my lips.

'I didn't know you worked here,' she said, looking up at the building behind me. This was surely a lie, it being clearly displayed on every one of my social media profiles.

'What brings you to the city?'

'Oh,' she said, tapping her foot, 'I've a meeting with someone round the corner. A director. They need a set designer for a new show.'

'That's great.' I lit up. 'Sorry for not replying to your message, by the way.'

She shook her head and looked down at her shoes. 'I just wanted you to know I was thinking of you. Your dad was nice to me once.'

I didn't ask her source, but assumed the messages left on my profile had shown up on her own. This is a strange by-product of social media, the broadcasting of news we'd rather forget to people we want to remember.

I blew a plume of smoke into the air above our heads. We smiled at each other.

'So when's quitting time?' she said. 'We could do that drink?'

I thought of the lasagne-for-one in the fridge at home then looked at her face. A face I knew so well yet could never picture when we were apart. What if this was to be the moment everything changed?

I met her in the scruffy little garden behind my building. She sat on a bench under the streetlight, beret on her head, gloved hand around a coffee cup. This is a mistake, I thought. I should just go. I should turn round and head for the station and go home for the night.

But my feet kept taking me to her.

She stood when she saw me approach, and I shuffled to a stop a few feet away. I felt that old, familiar ache stirring deep in my stomach.

She was the first to draw.

'You cut your hair.'

I nodded and felt the sweetness of a fresh cut against my palm. It was worth the cost of a London barber and the indigestion from a rushed lunch. *I get it cut when I feel nervous*, I said once in my bed. *It makes me feel better somehow, cutting my hair.*

'Let's walk and talk,' I said, brushing her fingers as I took the empty cup and dropped it into a bin.

Anna drew her scarf tighter and fell into step beside me. 'I got the gig.'

'I knew you would,' I said, pulling out a smoke.

'Did you have something to do with it then?' she said, laughing.

'I just know that if you want something then you usually seem to get it.'

She gave me a sideways look. 'You hardly know me and yet you always have faith in me.'

I lit my cigarette and held it in the hand furthest away from her. 'I know you,' I said.

We walked to Exmouth Market. The sun had almost set and the breeze carried that familiar wintry scent of burning wood. It was getting closer to the clocks changing and I was looking forward to spring, to my workday being freed from bookends of darkness. Soon the air would smell differently.

'How beautiful,' said Anna, as we crossed the road. She pointed to the festoon lights strung between the terraces.

'We should have come for lunch,' I said. 'They have great street food during the day.'

'Next time,' she said, and we smiled.

She chose a restaurant on the corner and the waiter seated us at a table furthest from the window, but as we began to peel off our layers, she looked past me and panic clouded her face.

'There's someone I know,' she said, grabbing a fistful of my jumper. 'Quick, go.'

We left the menus unopened and the chairs pulled out, and took the long way to the door.

When we turned a safe corner, she laughed and clapped her hands and her face was pink with excitement. 'I'm sorry,' she said, pressing a hand to her mouth. 'I shouldn't care any more, should I? You've just always been my clandestine friend.'

'What are the chances?' I said, shrugging my coat back on. Would it always be this way?

'Wine,' said Anna, looking at me. 'Let's try wine.'

I led us to a small pub away from the main thoroughfare, a place I'd sometimes visited for a colleague's last day. It was small, quiet and comfortingly basic. She chose a table in the corner as I bought our drinks.

Her jumper fell from one shoulder, pillar-box red. Like a traffic light, I thought as I carried the wine and two glasses over. Red for Stop, Nick. Stop. I almost dropped the bottle.

'You're always nice to bar staff,' said Anna as I sat down. She was resting her chin on her hand, watching me. 'I remember that.'

I reached out and took the hand she leant on. She wore two rings and I brought them near for a closer look. I'd already clocked that her left hand was bare and this instantly made my throat begin to itch.

'I have small hands, so finding rings to fit is a nightmare.'

'Show me,' I said, and we went palm to palm like at prayer. Two women at a nearby table threw us glances and I imagined how we must look from their angle. The way we leant towards each other with a respectable distance apart, the finding any excuse to touch each other. They could see us before we could.

I poured the wine and she chinked her glass against mine.

'Wait,' she said. 'A toast.'

'To getting older?'

'Hell, no. To us. All these years later.'

There was a brief silence as we drank and our eyes met. Warmth began creeping up my skin, warmth not from wine but from the glance of the person who sees right through you.

Anna set down her glass. 'Someone said to me recently, *You're young, but you're not young-young.* I wanted to scream.'

'I find it best to avoid mirrors these days. You still look pretty good, though.'

Anna looked down and I swear her face was pink. Feeling bold, I took her hand in mine again and inspected her fingers. 'Still not quit that habit, though.'

Quick as a reflex, she snatched back her hand. 'I spend an obscene amount on skincare and supplements, but yes, I still bite my nails. We control what we can, don't we? Are your lungs still black?'

I slapped the edge of the table. 'Like my heart.'

'I never thought I'd care about getting older,' she said, her finger tracing the top of her glass. 'And I don't, really. But there's so much I want to do and now less time left to do it.'

'I think this means we're grown-ups.'

'God, don't say that,' she said, laughing. 'I thought I'd magically transform into a capable person when I hit my thirties. I'd know exactly which medicine was required for every illness, I'd be prepared in an emergency . . . But I'm thirty-five and still haven't a clue.'

'Listen to us,' I said, shaking my head. 'Talking about the sand of time running out like we're a couple of geriatrics. We're fine.'

Anna rested her chin back on her hand and gave a wry smile. 'I sometimes wonder if that's what draws me to you. The longing for a time before I knew responsibility, before I had to spend an hour on hold to an energy company or wait in line at the post office. Perhaps you're my way back to a time when I had nothing to do but sit on a boy's bed and listen to "Karma Police".'

I smiled. 'I think you remember those days as being easier than they were.'

'Seriously though, are you happy?'

I nodded along to imaginary background music. 'What is happiness anyway, if not just chemicals in your head?'

She frowned. 'You don't really think that. Take your job. Do you love pensions? I thought you wanted to be a writer?'

I drained my glass and went to pour another. 'Don't you ever just fall into things without realising? I seem to make a habit of it.'

We spent the rest of the bottle talking about not very much at all. It was easy to be in her company, and yet there was a tension that kept us taut. We allowed silences to creep in, enjoying their quiet punctuation, while pulling at our sleeves or peeling the wine label. Everything was in balance, and yet everything was in flux.

When the bottle ran dry, we stumbled out into winter, our cheeks flushed with the glory of wine on an empty stomach. As we stood on the pavement and wondered what to do, a cab pulled up in front. The door opened and a man in a tux jumped out and turned to offer a hand. It was a bridal party, tipsy and laughing and whooping the air. The bride smoothed out her white dress and bunched her veil into a ball, then they all hooked arms – the bride, groom, bridesmaid and best man – and ran across the street to a restaurant with candlelit windows and faces pressed up against foggy glass. The door opened to a chorus of screams, and they were swallowed up into the fray.

We smiled at each other in the dark.

On a street corner, we bought a polystyrene cup of warm candied nuts that we shared as we walked to our train. There was a change to the tone of conversation as we looked at passing cars and people instead of each other.

'I watched a programme the other day,' said Anna, 'the one where a celebrity traces their ancestors. You know it? It was so strange, all these stories they discovered of people from centuries ago. People just like us, with hearts and lives and desires. They thought they had forever, but they died like everyone else. And it struck me, sitting there on my sofa – why am I spending an evening watching a show about dead people, when one day I'll be just like them? Why try to pass the time when I hardly have any to begin with?'

'We would probably do things very differently if we thought about death every day.'

'My boy Joe asked yesterday if he'd be alive in the year 3000. I had to tell him no.'

'Obviously.'

She gave a strange sort of laugh. 'See, "no" is the normal answer, but I was told I'd live forever. The answer given to me was "yes". My normal was not like everyone else's.'

An ambulance screeched by and we stepped towards each other in the confusion, Anna brushing my arm.

'You never ask me anything about my life,' she said.

This was true. In all the years since I'd heard she'd got married, I'd never once mentioned her husband, and since the day she emailed to tell me she was pregnant, I'd never once asked after her son.

'I'm never sure how much of your life I can take,' I said.

There came the loudness of someone leaning on a car horn and I wished we'd taken a quieter route.

'But you never wanted what I have,' she said. 'Marriage and kids . . . they were never part of your plan.'

'I'm not good with the marriage thing, but maybe the idea of a kid doesn't scare me like it once did. I would just want to be a good dad if I needed to be.'

'You would be a good dad,' she said, her voice soft.

I stared at the bottom of the cup. 'Thank you.'

'I could never have lived with someone without a ring on my finger. I would have lost half my family.'

'I know that.' I threw the cup in a bin. 'It's why I didn't stop you from leaving me when I should have.'

'But you would never have married me.'

'We both know this.'

She threw up her hands. 'Why don't you just view it as a stupid piece of paper?'

I took a step towards her. 'It doesn't mean I don't think about it with you.'

Long afterwards, when this evening and its subsequent days are over, I keep thinking of a particular moment. When we finished our wine, we paid the bill in cash and picked up our coats. Outside, before the bride's arrival, I helped her into her jacket and wrapped her scarf twice around her neck. Then we stood there for a moment, quite still, looking at each other, and she said, 'I've never seen you in the winter before.'

We sat together on the train back to Ashford. The carriage was almost empty and the windows were black, surrounding us with an image of our own reflection.

When we were almost home, she turned and said, 'You know I've left my religion?'

I looked at the lack of a ring on her finger when she said this. I opened my mouth, but words didn't come.

'Do you know the story of Lot's wife?'

I shook my head.

'Lot was a prophet,' she said, 'told by God to leave his city before it was destroyed. He was commanded to flee to the mountains and not look back. So he ran with his family while the city burned behind them, but Lot's wife looked back and so she became a pillar of salt.'

'Salt?'

'Harsh, right? I've known this story all my life. But when I read it recently, I was struck by how absurd it is. Surely it's only by looking back that we can see how far we've come. How much further we have to go.' She looked through the window at the darkness. 'I feel like I understand her. Stuck in that limbo between your past and your future. Not sure how to let go.'

I watched her chew her lip in that funny way she did.

'You know the worst thing? The poor woman doesn't get a name. She's held up as some kind of example to the world and she doesn't even get a name.' She shook her head. 'I'd always had doubts, but when that twigged, I was done.'

My knee brushed against hers and I glanced down as she said, 'Sometimes it takes something small to see something big.'

'What about your family?' I finally found my voice.

She folded her arms. 'Joe is my family now.'

I could see there was hurt all over her body, wounds she was trying to hide. This is what we do when we try to get through the impossible: we don a suit of armour and go out to war.

'It's only now I see it,' she said, her eyes on my knee, on the part of our bodies that touched.

'What do you see?'

Anna looked up. 'Nothing lasts forever.'

The train began to pull into the station and we stood to leave. As we waited for it to stop, I leant into her a little too close. There were no crowds pressing in or people pushing past. I did it because I wanted to.

'Walk me home?' she said when we'd passed through the barrier and into the cold. I must have looked confused because she smiled and nodded down the road. 'I live in town now.'

'Oh,' I said. 'Sure.'

It felt like hours since a cigarette, and I rooted around in my pocket for my lighter. 'Shit. I think I left my lighter in the pub.'

Anna softly punched my arm. 'So here's your chance to quit.'

'Never say never, but I've bumped into you today and I don't think my heart could take it if I threw in another curveball.'

'Wait, here you go.' Again, she touched my arm. 'I took some matches from the restaurant where I had my meeting.' She pulled a tiny book of matches from her pocket and smiled as I lit up and offered it back to her.

'Keep it,' she said, and closed my hand into a fist. 'You never know when you might need them.'

'Much obliged,' I said, turning away slightly to exhale, and there was a brief silence as our eyes met.

'It's meant to be twenty degrees tomorrow,' she said, slipping on her gloves as we started to walk. 'What is going on with the planet?'

'We act all responsible and say we fear global warming, but we're secretly glad of it too. The heat on our skin.'

We played the game of *Do you remember?* Of corners in car parks, of lifts home from work, of songs playing at the time of a particular kiss. She talked of Sal and of times she remembered. I loved him through her eyes.

'Look, the Mems,' she said as we crossed the road and went through the park gates. The gardens were dark and empty, and the shadow of the war memorial loomed large over the grass. 'It's funny. Count up all those summer days we spent together and it probably wouldn't exceed a month. Right? One month of us hanging out. And yet there are places in this town where I have lived most of my life that I cannot pass without thinking of you.'

I was glad of the darkness, that she couldn't see my face. 'You are and always will be more than a month.'

One afternoon she described in perfect detail – what we did, the clothes we wore, what was said – and however much I tried, I could not recall a single moment of that day. It didn't happen, I said, and she insisted it did. It didn't happen, I said again, because if it had happened like you tell it, I would never have forgotten. Not that. I would never have forgotten that. She smiled. But I remember, she said. I remember the parts you don't.

She lived in the little street that curves around the church in the centre of town. It's the only part of central Ashford that feels like a village, with the higgledy-piggledy period frontage along a cobbled path. In the churchyard, tombstones huddle and lean together, their laps bare and forgotten.

'This is me,' she said, coming to a stop outside a tiny terraced house in the corner. There was a light on upstairs, and I wondered if someone was waiting for her on the other side of the wall.

Opposite her front door was the face of a gravestone, and in the glow of lamplight I could make out the fading letters: *Here lies Mary Stephens. Died aged 48. Loving wife and mother.* The rest were covered in lichen.

'What a welcoming entrance,' I said.

Anna followed my eyes. 'I love it. A useful reminder of where we end up.'

'That's one way of looking at it.'

'I'm too intense for you,' she said.

'True.'

'I'm too intense for most people, but then most people are wimps.'

'Some people don't want intense but it doesn't make them wimps. You shouldn't be so hard on people.'

'Wow, look at that,' she said, rooting around in her bag. 'I touched a nerve.'

'Not my nerve. I'm just working on seeing the world from all perspectives.'

Anna put her key in the door and the latch clicked. 'Still condescending, I see. Bye then. Thanks for walking me home.'

She flinched as I took her arm.

'Hey,' I said. 'Let's not do this. Sorry if I said something wrong. I've not been in the best place lately and my head's pretty tired.'

She softened under my grip. 'Of course.' She smiled in the dark. 'Are we too young for a nightcap?'

I knew I should go.

She pushed open the door and I followed her inside.

278

Can we dine at the banquet of all we should have done / by Anna

I want your hands to cup my face like I'm your final cigarette
Strike a flame and light me up
Watch me burn
Put me to your lips because you cannot help yourself
Savour me

I want you weak

No more apologies
I want a confession
My body as your rosary
Repeat my name
As you trace the biography of my skin
That finger on your left hand
The one that smudged the pen
And moved to the front of class
I choose that one
To be the first in years not to feel like an examination

Can we dine at the banquet of all we should have done in your bed
Can we fill glass goblets with red wine and smash them against
   the wardrobe
Can we shoot and bleed and hardly cook so that it's almost still living
We are rare
I have never eaten game but I have played plenty with you
Wrap the bird in pastry if you like
Or gnaw hunks of meat from the bone
It all ends up the same in our stomachs
The glorious juice on our chins

Too much? I am too much for you. I will go on talking like this of
   how you could never handle me and how this would never have
   worked until you

                          stop my mouth with your tongue

I don't want to tell you I'm sorry
But I want to be on my knees in front of you
I want your ink spread over me
To know if the salt I swallow will season my core
I am desirous of a banquet
I am greedy and yet you are all that

I want / I want

the obvious things:

The weight of you on me
Your eyes on mine
To watch you blush like sunsets
The sight of your bedroom ceiling
The way light spills in through the door
I want to know how you fuck
I want to know how I fuck you
How you look there beneath me
Watching as I put on a show
(Don't let me put on a show)
Reach up and touch me
Speak the words you never said
And after,
When we are tired and sore
I want to know whether you like to be held
Or if you like to do the holding

Can we dine at the banquet of all we should have done
When we had years
That night in your bed

Let us make a toast to what's to come

The door led straight into a tiny front room. I looked around as she switched on some lamps. There were beams I had to duck under, and enough space for a small sofa and an armchair. The furniture looked second-hand and the curtains had clearly come with the house, but there were patterned woven rugs layered over the painted floorboards and lush green houseplants adorning every surface and I knew these were hers. She'd tacked prints of famous paintings to the walls, and around the sofa and on the floor were leaning towers of books. It had a simple, lived-in feel. Loved, even.

'So what's your poison?' Anna said, standing in the middle and turning to me.

I slipped off my shoes and coat. 'Let's go with coffee.'

'I'll give you a tour in a mo,' she called over her shoulder as she went into the tiny kitchen. 'It'll take all of thirty seconds.'

Under the stairs were rows of canvases and pots of brushes and tubes of paint. An easel stood near the kitchen door, a paint-splattered artist's smock draped over a canvas in progress.

I looked over the collection of items on the mantelpiece. There was a small vase of white flowers, a box of matches, a twisted metal sculpture with a hammered pattern, a child's watercolour painting of an alien. I was gleaning precious details of her life by looking at the possessions she chose to display, a knowledge she might not other-wise reveal. I looked closer at a framed picture of her with her son and recognised it from online. He had her face, all cheeks and lips, and the pale-golden hair of his dad. His hand was in hers and they were eating ice creams and laughing.

A large mirror hung on the wall. I could just make out a gloomy outline of myself in the foxed glass.

'Ready?'

I turned and saw her at the foot of the stairs, her hand on the ban-ister. She had her head cocked to one side, as if she'd been studying me while I studied her.

As she walked upstairs, I looked at her leather skirt and imagined running my hands up her legs like I once did. A brief time when I had permission.

She went into the room at the front, the one from where light had shone. A sign saying 'Joe's room' in childish scrawl was taped to the door. The faint scent of fresh paint lingered in the air. The room was simply decorated with a small bed, a chest of drawers and a wall of low shelving crammed with toys. Above the bed was a large poster of a figure in mid-air, diving from a mountain into a lake.

'I like the picture,' I said.

Anna reached out and touched the edge of the print. 'Isn't it funny how we put pictures like these on kids' walls, then when they grow up, we expect them to stay exactly where they are?' She smiled, her mind far away.

'Where is he? Joe.'

'His dad's,' she said, looking down. 'We have joint custody. I hate it. I stayed longer than I should have, because I couldn't bear the thought of letting him go.'

I wanted to ask more. I wanted to know all about this side of her, this new limb that she had grown while we were apart, that was everything to her and utterly foreign to me. But she kept it hidden, like a private part of herself. It's only later that I discover that she was scared to talk of him, scared it would send me running, as if I couldn't handle the idea of her changing from the woman – or girl – I thought she was. I was another little boy that needed looking after, a small pat on the head.

'Come,' she said, leading me out.

A bathroom opened off the poky landing. She held out the door and I glanced inside at a white suite with dated tiles. There were no signs of a man on the shelves or around the sink. No razor in a glass, no newspaper by the loo. Just pots and potions and thirsty-looking plants.

At the back was a room painted a warm, orangey red. Her room. A double bed took up most of the space. There was a wooden stool for a makeshift bedside table, and a narrow wardrobe in the corner alcove. On the windowsill was a clear vase of water in which stood a tree branch with leaves the most vivid shade of red. The room was dark but for the moon and a puddle of light from the landing.

Anna leant against the door frame, her hands behind her back. 'So did you mean it?' she said.

I looked at her, confused.

'What you said, about me being hard on people.' A strand of hair fell in front of her eyes as she looked down at her feet. 'See, I only joke when I call myself intense. You think I am, though.'

I put my hands in my pockets. 'You have a fire and conviction. It's intense, but a good thing.'

She kept her eyes on the floor. 'Why do I get the impression you think that's anything but a good thing?'

I took a step towards her. There were no chairs, and it felt wrong to sit on her bed. The space was tight, and the red walls and ceiling made it feel like the room was closing in. I leant against the open door.

She looked up. 'You need to say something good about me right now.'

'You are one of the most intense and inspiring people I know. Nothing but love from me, honest.'

'This should be a game,' said Anna. 'Saying good things about the other. It would make a change.'

I reached out and tucked the strand behind her ear. 'We aren't here to do anything but help each other. It isn't you versus me.'

'Do you want something good?'

'I'm okay, you don't need to do that.'

'I never said I had to. I want to.'

I closed my fingers around the book of matches in my pocket.

'You make me feel safe,' she said. 'Do you know what I mean? It's rare in a man.'

'If it means something to you, then it's important. That's all I need to know.'

She pulled at a splinter of wood on the door frame. 'You make me feel like everything is okay when I'm around you. I have this weird, knotted feeling in the pit of my stomach, but it's okay. This probably won't make sense, but you feel like home. It's not something I've felt before.'

I looked down at my knuckles. 'That's a lovely thing.'

'But it's not just that. You have always been dangerous for me. Forbidden. I feel both safe and terrified around you, and I can't decide if that makes you completely wrong, or exactly right.'

Her words fucked with my senses. To listen to her was to look in a mirror.

'Do you know what I really loved?' she said. 'When you leant over me on the train. I loved that.'

The inside of my mouth ran dry and I had an urge for cold water, to soothe my throat and clear the way for the words I knew I should speak.

'I'll tell you what I want,' said Anna, her face in the shadows. 'I want your hands in my hair and your mouth on my neck and I want you to make slow love to me like you care and then I want you to pick me up and fuck me hard against the wall and make me know exactly how you feel.' She tore the splinter of wood from the door with her fingertip. 'Is that Nick a figment of my imagination?'

'The one who wants to fuck you against the wall?'

'The one who would do it.'

I couldn't stand it any longer. I stepped forward and put my hands on her waist and she pushed against me in reply. And then my mouth was by her mouth. Her breath was on my breath. The force from her tongue renewed every part of my body.

I kissed the darkness round her shoulders where her hair hung loose. I sat on the edge of the bed and pulled her close, lifting her top and feeling her skin.

'Wait,' said Anna. She was holding my head against her waist and I looked up at her. 'Are you sure?'

I thought of the man I should be and the behaviour expected of him. How my mind should be racked with shame at the thought of touching another woman. But she was not another woman. She was me, and I her, and it was everyone else that was shameful.

I closed my eyes and nodded.

She must have taken my silence for doubt, because 'No,' she said, kissing the top of my head. 'Not like this.'

We were still for a moment.

'Would it be okay if I stayed the night?' I said. 'Call it friends or whatever you like.'

Anna stroked my hair and tilted my face up towards her. 'Friends?' she said, smiling. 'So is that what we are?'

★

We awoke at dawn to the sound of church bells. Sunshine streamed on to the bed in harsh stripes, warming the duvet above our half-naked bodies. We were apart but our feet were touching.

I turned on my side to face her. Her face was the barest I'd seen it.

'You're like a little boy when you sleep.'

'You were watching me?'

She pushed my leg with her toe. 'I've often wondered how it would feel to have you in my bed.'

'To be fair, you already knew.'

Anna smiled. 'Some things you forget. You don't know at the time the memories that will stick around. And this is my bed, remember. It's new to you.'

I reached out and gently rubbed the finger where her ring used to be. 'What happened there?'

She withdrew her hand and slid down the bed, under the covers, out of sight. I followed. The sheet brushed against my ear. The little space we now inhabited was both light and dark with nowhere to hide.

Anna turned to face me, tucking both hands under her cheek. 'People change,' she said after a moment.

'Sometimes.'

'I think they do. And sometimes people change and we don't want them to. We expect them to stay exactly the same, exactly how we know them, because we think our experience of them is who they are. But you never truly know a person.'

'True.'

She looked down. 'If I wear a ring, it doesn't mean ownership, of me or my body. It's a mutual understanding, perhaps. But we only ever belong to ourselves.'

I felt the warmth of the sun through the cover. It felt like both heaven and hell to be in such a confined space with her. 'I guess people have different views on what a ring means. Best be on the same page before you put one on.'

She reached out and stroked the same finger on my hand. 'And yours?'

'You know my shit. Sore subject.'

'I still think it means something.' She turned on to her front, propped up on her elbows. 'To stand in front of everyone and say, *This person. I choose him.* There's a braveness to it.'

'I can see that.'

She rested her head against the pillow and looked at me. 'Who you are at nineteen is a world away from who you are at thirty-five.'

'Was he not on board with the whole leaving-the-flock?' I tried to ignore the familiar scratching in my throat, the craving for my vice.

Anna gave a slight shake of her head. 'I expected it, though. As a woman, there's a script you're meant to follow in the religion. The husband's in charge. He owns your body, makes the decisions, and if the wife doesn't obey then it reflects badly on him.' She bit her lip. 'And he cared a lot about what others thought of him.'

'I can't imagine you sticking to a script, especially that one.'

Her smile faded. 'He was lovely when we met. We got on well, and I thought, *This is a man who will love me and let me be who I am.* But it takes a strong mind to resist conformity, and strong minds are not encouraged. We threw ourselves into playing the roles expected of us, but I knew almost straight away that I could never be what they wanted. I tried. I thought having a baby might do it, make it easier for me to play the part. But it only made it worse.'

'How?'

'I wasn't just responsible for myself any more. I'd brought this brand-new person into the world, and I cared more for him than I did for some spirit in the sky. But even as a mother, you're meant to love God more than your child. I couldn't do that. I couldn't understand the concept of a god who would want me to do that, and the thought of it wouldn't leave me alone. And then there was the example I was setting to Joe . . . I don't want my son growing up to think he has the right to tell his wife who to be. His dad wasn't trying to be cruel, but he'd morphed himself so much into who he thought he should be that I didn't recognise him any more. And I didn't recognise myself.'

'You did the right thing for Joe,' I said, taking her hand.

'Is it strange for you, that I have a son?' Her eyes on mine.

'It's a part of you I know nothing about.' My grip tightened on her hand. 'But I would like to.'

'I don't want to be a fraud any more, Nick. Pretending to be someone I'm not. And I won't be with someone who thinks that I should be. It's a funny way to love.'

My cravings had now doubled in intensity, and all I could think about was punching the pillow and kissing her. She could read minds, because she threw the covers off her bare legs and said, 'You go into the garden for a cig and I'll finally make that coffee.'

It was a small cobbled yard hemmed in on all sides by the crumbling brick walls of other buildings. A red child's bike rested against the side gate and large jungle plants lived in the corners. I imagined her out here in the coming warm evenings with a book, lit by the tungsten glow of the fairy lights draped around the walls. It had obviously been a fairly depressing space, once upon a time, but she'd transformed it. Stretching over from next door were the branches of some kind of Japanese tree, its maple-shaped leaves a fiery shade of red. I recognised them as the same as the branch in her bedroom.

I sat on a garden chair and leant against the wall, enjoying the first hit of the first cigarette.

'Enslaved by your addiction,' she said, appearing at the doorway. Her arms were folded across her chest and her top had slipped from her shoulder.

I exhaled. 'Aren't we all?'

She looked up at the sky and closed her eyes against the sun. 'Can you believe this is February?'

I watched her enjoying the heat. Global warming wasn't something to celebrate, but it had been a long, hard winter.

She stretched out her arms and yawned. 'Milk and sugar?'

'Aren't I sweet enough?'

Anna smiled, a shy smile I'd not seen before, and then she disappeared through the door.

I watched the coffee swirl in a blue-and-white patterned teacup.

'My mum had this china,' I said, and a memory appeared of it in pieces on the floor.

'Mine too,' she said, smiling. 'It's called Willow. There was a box of it in the charity shop. Plates, cups, saucers, all for a tenner. Not sure when I'll use the gravy boat.'

'All those dinner parties you're going to host?'

She made a face. 'Yeah, I can just about make toast.' She sipped her coffee. 'Guess I need to learn now, though. I've reverted back to childhood, figuring things out for myself again.'

I looked down at my cup. A tiny fly floated in the black liquid. 'It must be scary, starting again. Being alone.'

'When are we ever not?' She set her cup down on the side. 'I'm tired of someone always wanting a piece of me. I can't be what everyone wants me to be all the time. It's exhausting, living like that. Isn't it?'

I nodded without really considering the question. I do that sometimes, give the reaction that I think the other person is expecting or wants. Part of me thinks this is one of my good attributes, pleasing others, but it doesn't seem to do me many favours.

'As I get older,' said Anna, 'I feel more and more like an island. We're born alone and we die alone. So much of my life was about moulding myself to someone or something, as if I could escape the reality. But we're always alone.'

'I'm not sure that's a comforting thought.'

'Whether or not it's comforting is irrelevant. You can't base belief on what you'd *like* to be true.'

'Then how do we connect with another person? How does that explain the bond we can feel with someone else?'

She sipped her coffee as she considered the question. 'Perhaps we're all connected deep down at the root. An island is alone above water, but at its very depths where everything is hidden, it's attached to the earth's core.'

'This is becoming quite the philosophical discussion.'

'Too much for you?' she replied with a smile.

'I never imagined you in a house like this, though,' I said, nodding at the Tudor brick walls that threw us in shadow.

'Me neither,' she said, looking up. 'But the rent's cheap and it serves its purpose. What kind of house did you see me in?'

I stroked my beard as I thought about it. 'A gypsy caravan, perhaps.'

She laughed. 'So not a house at all then?'

'No. I guess not.'

'A person's home reveals a lot about them. Who they think they are or who they want to be.'

I looked up at the bedroom window. 'And what do poky windows and rooms reveal about you?'

'I'd love big windows – all that light – but then people would always be looking in. Here, I can hide.' She pushed up her sleeves. 'This is just a springboard to somewhere else.'

I nodded and this time meant it.

Anna put out a hand and almost touched me. 'There's something I'd really love to do, and it'll involve me encouraging you to smoke, so you should say yes.'

I picked the fly out of my coffee and drained the cup. 'This sounds dangerous.'

'Can I paint you?'

'Like one of your French girls?'

She laughed loudly and the tips of my ears began to burn. Nice one, I said to myself.

'Oh God,' she said, putting a hand to her mouth. '*Titanic* is the perfect analogy for us.'

'I always thought we were more BDSM.'

There was a glint in her eye, as if she'd caught me out. 'So he's finally admitting he's into games.'

'I think we all know who'd be the dominant one in this relationship.'

She reached out and took the cup from my hand. 'Watch your lip. Now, I'm painting you and I won't take no for an answer.'

I put my hands out in front as if waiting to be cuffed and she gave me a light slap.

'Shall I put some clothes on?' I said, looking down at my loose boxers and T-shirt.

She shook her head. 'I want you smoking and just like this.'

I waited as she set up her easel and paints. She'd put on jeans and a navy smock that reminded me of the lab coat I used to wear in Chemistry, when we'd mix powders together and blow things up. Her hair was piled on top of her head as if to eliminate every distraction. My top lip began to sweat.

'Back in a sec,' I said, but she was too busy working out the light to hear.

In the bathroom mirror I tried to picture what she'd see when she began to paint, when she had nothing to do but study me. There was a hard gnawing in my stomach, the butterflies an actor feels on opening night.

I should have said no.

As I came out, I looked in on the unmade bed we'd slept in. It fascinated me as a child, the idea that each night, people across the world go to a specific place in their house to put on special clothes and lie horizontal. It's as essential as breathing air, this venturing into the unknown. We cannot exist without it. And when awake, new lives are forged and futures made in the space between the sheets. The bed is a portal to another dimension. We know this, even as children, when we pretend our parents' bed is a boat to distant shores.

The white pillows still bore creases from the weight of our sleeping heads, and I wondered if I'd ever see this bed again.

Downstairs, Anna was standing in the open doorway, her body silhouetted against the bright outside. I couldn't see her face, but I knew she was smiling. 'Ready?' she said. A blank canvas leant against the easel.

'Where shall I go?' Seeing her dressed was a reminder that I was not, and I clasped my hands together in front of me.

She patted the open door. 'I was thinking here. Leaning back so you don't get too stiff. Oh, and lose the shirt. That okay?'

'Do I have a choice?'

'Always.'

I pulled my top over my head and dropped it on the chair. 'Put me where you want me.'

I let her lead me to the door, where she pushed me gently back against the wood. That familiar small 'v' formed between her eyebrows as she concentrated on my body.

'I need my smokes.'

'Don't start yet,' she said, tossing me the pack. 'I'm almost there.'

'How long will it take?' I could feel the top of my head getting warm in the morning sun.

'You got somewhere to be?' she said, brushing something off my arm. 'Because the best things take time.'

I cleared my throat and rubbed my head. 'Tell that to the sun before it turns me lobster pink.'

'Okay, okay,' she said, moving towards the easel. 'Let's start.'

Anna hit a button on a speaker and music began to play. Classical, strings, a passionate violin.

I shook the pack and pulled out a cigarette with my teeth, cupping it with my hand as I lit the end. Feeling her eyes, I looked up and she said, 'God, I love that. How you do that.'

'How I take out a fag?'

'The way you move,' she said, sharpening a pencil. 'You do it every day so you don't see it. But it's all new to me.'

I took a drag. 'I should quit.'

'You really should.'

'But then you won't think I'm beautiful any more,' I said.

'Don't get cocky.'

'Until you've tried a cigarette, you have no idea how wonderful it is.'

'Of course I've tried a cigarette,' she said, striking a match and lighting a stick of incense. 'On your bed, remember? I'm sure I coughed the entire time, and my boy's severely asthmatic. Hence your confinement to the garden.' She took a deep breath and raised her hand behind the canvas. 'Now, quiet. I need to concentrate.'

She sketched for about half an hour. I felt the passing of time through the sun on my face, as it started on my forehead and worked its way down on to my torso. I chain-smoked throughout, turning to exhale away from the house.

Anna muttered the odd thing under her breath, but mainly she worked without speaking. I'd turn to look at her sometimes and she'd be casting furious looks at the canvas and occasionally me. I wondered whether she'd stared at me long enough that I'd become a new person.

'You know I'm due back at work Monday,' I said as I reached into my pocket for the pack and took another fag with my teeth like before. 'Will it be done by then?'

Anna kept her eyes on the canvas. 'Shut it.'

After she'd finished sketching, she tucked the pencil behind her ear and picked up an artist's palette from under the stairs. She stood at the table and looked over the pots and tubes of paint that she'd spread out, and one by one, she squeezed a small amount of paint from her chosen colours on to the palette.

'What's the cost per tube?' I said, nodding at the table.

'Let's just say I choose my subjects very carefully.'

'Maybe I should pay you. Isn't that what people do?'

'I believe prostitution is the oldest job there is, yes.'

I gave an awkward laugh. 'No, I mean a patron. I could be your patron. Like the Medicis.'

She looked at me, impressed. 'I did not take you for an Art History buff, Nicolas Mendoza.'

My face began to burn and I shifted against the door in an effort to divert attention. 'I have many layers, you know.'

'Clearly.' She picked up a palette knife and began to smear some colours together.

'For transparency, I should probably admit I watched a three-minute video on Renaissance art. That's the only fact I remember.'

She turned back to the canvas. 'Well, that'll come in very handy next time you're at a dinner party or trying to pick up a woman. We love that shit.'

I laughed. Anna began to load on colour and her knife made a repetitive scraping sound against the canvas.

'You're the first man I've painted,' she said after a minute, her eyes on her work. 'Apart from a couple of old dudes in a life drawing class, that is. But you're the first man I've known.'

An ant scurried across the flagstone by my feet, its black body a tiny dot. I watched as it went one way then another, reaching the edge and hesitating before crawling into the shadows between the slabs. 'Why me?' I asked.

She stepped back from the canvas, tipped her head to one side and looked from the picture to my body then back again. 'Why have we been like this for nearly twenty years?'

'Like what?'

'Never quite taking hold of each other.'

I closed my eyes against the sun. 'You and I exist outside the lines.'

'I read an old diary recently,' she said, picking up a paintbrush. 'I've always kept one, writing a few pages now and then about my life and what's happening. Things I don't want to forget.'

'I hope I feature prominently,' I said, my eyes still closed.

I opened my eyes a moment later to find Anna looking at me. 'I don't mention you at all,' she said.

'That's nice.' I brushed my hand against the hair on my arm.

'You think that means I didn't care?' She smiled. 'You were too big to write down.'

I nudged my toe into the shadows between the slabs where the ant had gone, pushed hard and felt pain from something hidden in the gap. I could sense it had a hard point, sharp, and I felt a twinge of pleasure as it pricked my skin.

'So who did you record for posterity?'

She arched an eyebrow as she worked the paint. 'Oh, the one I thought was it, and the one I knew wasn't. Every girl has one of those.'

'The broken heart?'

'Did I ever tell you?'

'Lisa did.'

Her brush paused mid-air and she looked confused. 'Wait, what?'

'Lisa. From the cinema? She told me once on a night out. I got an earful about not hurting you. She seemed like a good friend.'

Anna looked at her canvas, her eyes glazing slightly. 'She was,' she said quietly. 'We lost touch when I got married. My fault. But yes, a heart was broken and it was definitely mine. It made me more cautious afterwards. Careful.'

'First loves are strange things.'

'Aren't they? But I'm glad of the experience now. Some people go through life never truly feeling anything.'

I watched the cigarette smoke curl through the air. 'I'm starting to

293

wonder if we even want a happy ending. Most people wouldn't know what to do with it. I think it's closure that we crave.'

'People don't want closure,' said Anna, her eyes on her work. 'Look how they watch ten seasons of the same show. We're drawn to the familiar. We want that rush again and again.'

'Sometimes the pain, though,' I said, shaking my head. 'You can't imagine life without it. Relief from that would be something.'

She stopped painting and looked at me. I saw it out the corner of my eye, her hesitation as she thought of what to say. I counted every beat.

'I've never thought about it like that.'

We didn't speak much for the next hour. She worked at the canvas, dabbing and scraping and looking at me, and I put on a baseball hat of hers to shield my head from the sun. It was navy with a New York Yankees logo embroidered on the front. It made me think of Sal.

Finally, she put down her palette and brush. 'Relax.'

'Finished?' I stretched my arms towards the sky.

'Oh, sweetheart,' she said, laughing. 'You have no idea.'

I pulled on my top and walked round to the front of the canvas. I saw what she meant. There was a pencil sketch of me standing against the door, a line of shadow cutting my body in two. My upper half she'd painted pink, but with added sinews and lines that were red and thin, as if my skin was translucent. She'd drawn the walled yard, the Japanese branches extending upwards, and the walls of surrounding houses jutting in around the top. The only sky was a jagged-shaped star formed from the gaps between the buildings. It loomed over the scene. I glanced up from the canvas and saw that from this angle, that was exactly how it looked. Except she'd painted it red, the sky. Blood red.

'I have to build it up in layers,' she said, gesturing. 'Oil has deeper pigment than acrylic. See how rich the colour is? It lasts much longer and that's why it's expensive, but you have to wait for it to dry before you add more colours. It takes time.'

I didn't reply. My eyes took in every inch of the canvas, finding clues, piecing them together, searching for meaning in every stroke. She had drawn my skin as if she could see right through it, but looking at the picture she'd created, it was Anna being revealed.

I saw her as if for the first time.

'Say something,' she said, chewing a nail. 'Tell me you hate it. Tell me you love it. But give me something.'

'Hate it?' I turned to her. 'Look at this. I've never met anyone like you.'

Anna smiled, relieved. She'd been winding a long strand of hair around her fingers, and she let go as I finished my sentence.

'It'll probably take a month to finish,' she said.

'You don't need me to pose any more?'

'It's fine,' she said. 'I can do it from memory.'

I wiped my clammy palms against my T-shirt and was again aware of my nakedness. 'Do you sometimes wish you could run away from everything?' I said. 'Just for a moment.'

She gave a half-smile and I saw a faint blush appear on her cheek. It was the same shade of pink as my skin on her canvas.

'We never did do Venice,' she said.

From: ANNA
To: NICK
Subject:

You asked about my family.

When I decided to leave, I packed a suitcase and left Joe with a friend while I went to see my parents. I tried to make them see. How I couldn't lie in a bed I'd made when I was twelve, when they let me promise myself to an organisation. This is my life, I said to them. For all I know, I'll never get another. You have made a vow, said my father, and you must keep that vow. Does the vow count if I don't believe it? I replied. And do I honour a marriage vow to a man who no longer exists as he did? To God, he said. You owe your vows to God.

I wish I could believe. It would all be so simple if I could only just believe.

Does God want me to lie? Does he want me to worship with my lips while dying inside? Would they prefer me to be dishonest, just so long as I don't bring embarrassment to their faces?

I left them there. My father at the window with his hands behind his back, my mother crying on the landing as I shut the door.

The punishment for what I've done is total cutting off. They are told not even to say hello to me on the street.

I tried to run from this before and he couldn't take it. I'm not sure if you could either.

And so I begin again.

We spent the weekend together, holed up in her little house. I didn't leave once, except for Sunday morning, when I rose early from her bed and went to the corner shop to buy the paper and a fresh loaf. I took a key to let myself back in, and when she came sleepily downstairs mid-morning, I handed her a cup of fresh coffee and began on the bacon. I found my way around the kitchen just fine. It was like I'd always been there.

When it was ready, I handed her the bacon sandwich and watched her take a bite. Ketchup dropped on to the plate. 'Don't hate me,' she said, and leant forward to whisper, 'but I prefer brown sauce.' I slapped her gently with a tea towel.

The second night I stayed, we lay and kissed in the darkness. An unspoken line was drawn that we didn't cross. We held hands and talked of how our future might be. We used words like *might* and *maybe*, never *shall* or *will*, but we were sketching an idea all the same. Was it serious? Are the words we whisper at night truer than the rest? We'd come close and retreated so often that the rules of engagement were lost to us. Perhaps this was just a stolen weekend, like one summer's afternoon by a lake.

I was in the garden when her son came home on the Sunday. I didn't hear the knock.

'Hello,' I said, as he appeared in the doorway, and bent down to gather up the scattered newspaper. We'd sat in the sunshine and read the supplements, not speaking much except for the reading aloud of random sentences. Now, seeing him there, I felt compelled to clear up the mess I had made in his yard.

Anna appeared behind him and casually draped her arms around his neck. 'Joe,' she said, smiling. 'This is Nick. He's a friend of mine.'

Joe frowned at me with a sideways glance. He looked up at his mum and back at me, chewing his lip just like her. 'Hi,' he said quietly.

'How was your weekend?' I said, putting my hands in my pockets. It had been a long time since I'd spoken to a child.

At this, his bottom lip began to tremble and he spun round and buried himself in his mum's dress. She looked surprised and kneeled down to hold him, waving at me not to worry.

'Joe? What's wrong, sweetheart?'

His shoulders shook as he hugged her. 'I lost Goldie,' he sobbed.

'No! How? Your dad didn't mention it.'

He let her go and rubbed his fists against his wet cheeks. 'At the cinema. Dad told me to leave him in the car but I put him on the chair next to me so he could watch it too. And then when it finished . . .' His eyes filled with tears. 'I forgot he was there.'

'Didn't you go back?'

Joe shook his head and hugged his arms against himself. 'I didn't remember until we got home. Dad said it was too far away. He said I should have left him in the car like he said. He rang the cinema but they couldn't find him.'

Anna threw her arms around him as he began to howl and let him shake against her. 'It's okay, sweetheart,' she whispered in his ear. 'Let it out. Let it all out.'

When his crying had stopped, she pulled back and smoothed his hair. 'Go ride your bike in the sunshine and I'll get you a cake, okay?'

He nodded and went over to the little red bike and climbed on, giving shy glances in my direction. I smiled and turned away, not wanting to embarrass him by noticing his tears. I sat on one of the garden chairs as Anna came back with a teacake that she unwrapped from its foil and gave him. He perched on his bike and bit into the sweetness of marshmallow.

'Who's Goldie?' I said as Anna sat down.

She rested her chin on her hand and stared at Joe. 'A teddy he's had forever,' she said quietly. 'I'll have a heck of a time getting him to sleep tonight.'

I watched her watching her boy. 'You're a good mum,' I said.

She smiled and her cheeks flushed pink. 'I could be better.'

'We could all be better.'

'I think it's so important to let boys cry,' Anna said. 'To let them feel the bad as well as the good. His dad says I'm making him too soft, but thank God. We can't expect them to feel for others when we tell them not to feel for themselves. Why do we think strength means silence?'

Then she looked straight at me.

The Next Day

I left early before her son awoke, slipping down the stairs like a stranger and putting on my coat at the door. Anna stood still, wrapped in her robe, waiting.

'I had a lovely weekend,' she said.

I zipped up my padded coat. 'Me too.'

Her eyes glanced from my face to my hands as I fumbled fingers into gloves. We loaded the silence like a gun. I knew she wanted me to speak.

'Thanks for having me,' I said, leaning in and patting her back.

'Thanks for having you?' she said, laughing and pulling away. 'What on earth is that?'

She was right. The way to end this weekend was not with politeness, but it felt like a strange mood had settled between us and I didn't know how to break it apart. Outside, it had turned cold again so I put up my hood.

'Hey,' she said, stepping forward and taking my hand. 'Don't be a stranger.'

Even in gloves, the feel of her hand in mine sent waves of blood through my body. We looked at each other and saw our futures. She smiled. I kissed the back of her hand.

I didn't contact Anna once in the weeks that followed.

I saw online she'd won a major award for a theatre set she'd designed, but I couldn't bring my finger to like the post. Instead, I read the article again and again until I knew it by heart.

If I saw she was online, I'd quickly come off and ignore it a while. I turned off my *Last seen* so I left no trace. These games we play.

Why did I do this? Why draw so close to her and then recoil like a spring? Why make out I didn't care when I knew in my heart I would break up with my girlfriend?

You tell me.

Please.

I had imaginary conversations with myself on the loo and in the bathroom mirror, and they always ended with everyone happy, like we'd all sat round a table and been rational and had felt exactly the same way. Those conversations are my favourite. If only they happened.

There were a couple of weeks left until Laura returned, and some twisted reasoning in my brain said I should be loyal until then. I didn't trust myself around Anna, and now that I knew my intentions, there was no stopping the force of my feeling. At night, it consumed me.

I focused on other things, as if time would pass more quickly through distraction. I cleaned behind the fridge, cooked meals from fancy recipe books, spent longer at the office, until my boss gave me a back-slap and a raise.

One weekend, I met Daz for a drink. He'd recently split from Gemma, his longest relationship, and his wounds needed tending.

'I know why it didn't work,' he said during the third pint. 'She was out of my league.'

I sat at the picnic table across from him. It was March and chilly, but Daz was a smoker too. We wore beanie hats pulled down over our shaved heads. Daz was working nights laying tarmac on the motorway and he was dressed in his orange overalls, about to head off on shift. The hi-vis stripes down his sleeves shone in the lamplight.

I took a sip of my beer and said, 'More likely it was the women you kept shagging behind her back.'

He shook his head. 'She never knew. I know how to keep birds apart.'

'So you thought she was out of your league, but that didn't stop you screwing around?'

Daz blew a long line of smoke into the air and raised his hands in protest. 'When am I supposed to find the time to change?'

Laura couldn't understand why I was still mates with Daz. 'But he's so, so . . .' Working class? I wanted to say, but she'd wrinkle her nose and go, 'He doesn't seem to care about doing anything with his life.' I'd make some half-arsed defence on his behalf. I didn't admit that I often thought this too, that our continuing friendship was born partly from an ease of familiarity, but also from a shameful desire to be reminded that someone was a bigger fuck-up than myself. I was a bride who deliberately picked an ugly bridesmaid. I was a shit.

'Looks are overrated,' I said, tapping the ashtray.

'It's not just looks. Mate, she was a TV producer. She'd done stuff. Lived abroad, had investments, didn't have to google what something was on a menu. She was legit.'

'Unlike you?' I said, trying to keep the tone light.

'You know what I mean,' said Daz. 'She was one of those girls. Like that Anna you used to mess about with.' He jammed the cigarette into the plastic ashtray. 'I always screw it up.'

Anna messaged a few days before Laura came home:

What gives? We spend an entire weekend together then you disappear off the face of the earth. Friends don't treat friends that way.

I waited an hour to read it then another hour to reply. *I'm sorry*, I typed. *I've been really busy. Nothing to do with you, honest.* I regretted the *honest* as soon as I'd sent it.

Half an hour later, she replied: *After all that stuff we said. I thought we were finally getting somewhere. But once again, you hit the reset button without telling me and we go all the way back to the start.*

There is something in me that enjoys other people making the effort, to show that I am wanted. I guess this is what they call *ghosting*. It's cruel and unkind, but it comes from a good place.

I don't know what you mean, I replied. *I told you my girlfriend was coming back within a month. It's the end of the month.*

I'd be lying if I said I didn't feel a pang of pleasure at typing those words; a light pulse of power. After all, she'd made me wait years. How hard could a few days be?

The blue ticks that showed it was read lit up immediately and I put down my phone.

I got in bed and thought about her for a while.

Then I turned over and went to sleep.

A Sensible Coat / by Anna

I hate the winter for the darkness at four
For the school run downpour
For the cold shoulder I give a 'mum' coat
Like I can resist what I am

But I hate the winter mainly for the moment we go to embrace
after buttoning up our coats
and yours is a wall of blue
keeping the warmth inside you
Not like red October when you hugged me in a car park and as
you let go I said
Wait
So you held me still and I leant my face against your normcore
grey and felt the heat from your body and it was just like

coming home

We let go
But you took my hand
and said
Be safe

I once knew you in summer and it was the sweetest thing
Holding hands in beer gardens and fireworks and travel brochures
and passport renewals
You weren't conventional then

I hate the winter because it covered you back up
Like the ice I scrape from my windscreen
Turned away from the sun
You took the words you said at midnight and hid them under
your hood
I called you out for giving me lines and not following through
with lips
So you put on your gloves and keep touch to yourself

Fending off my punches
But you cannot deny that you gave me your tongue
I read its softness like braille
The flowers are dying
and perhaps they will never come back

God I hate the winter
But there is hope

I've never known you in the spring

A Few Days Later

I met Laura at the station. I'd bought a cheap bunch of red carnations from the supermarket and held them in front of me like a first date. I thought she'd find it funny.

I saw her first. Her face looked pale and tired and comfortingly familiar. As she approached the barrier, she fished in her pocket for the ticket while hunched over from the weight of her hiking pack. When she came through the barrier, she saw me and stopped.

'Oh,' she said. 'I thought I was getting a taxi.'

'Why would you get a taxi?'

She shifted the pack on her back. 'I forgot I'd told you which train I was getting. That's all.'

'Well, here I am. Hi, by the way.' I put my arms out and she leant in. She kept her hands by her sides and I found myself patting her back.

'You look well,' she said, pulling away. 'How have you been?' And then she stepped forward and hugged me again, as if she'd only just remembered the dead dad. This time she put her arms around me and gave a warm squeeze. 'Sorry I wasn't here.'

I kissed the top of her head. 'Let me take your bags.'

I slung the pack over my shoulder and took the holdall she was carrying. There was something nervous and strange in the way she held herself and pulled at her hair, running her fingers over and over the ends.

'Here.' I passed her the cellophane-wrapped flowers. 'I bought you these. As a joke.'

'Oh,' she said, taking them with a confused expression. 'Thanks.'

She turned on the radio as soon as we got in the car, and I gave her a sideways glance as I reversed out of the space.

'Good flight?'

'It was fine,' she said, looking out the window.

I drummed my fingers on the steering wheel as we waited at a red light. 'Glad to be home?'

She was looking at the buildings as if she'd never seen them before. 'Strange how everything looks exactly the same,' she said through the glass.

'I guess not much has changed in three months.'

Laura laughed, a strange, hollow sound. 'I guess not.' She looked through the windscreen at the line of traffic ahead. 'Weird the things you miss, like British number plates.'

And me, obviously, I considered saying.

'I'm making a roast dinner,' I said. 'All the trimmings.'

'Lovely.'

'Everything okay?'

'What?'

I changed gear. 'You seem . . . distant. Just tired, or something on your mind?'

She turned and blinked as if seeing me for the first time. 'Oh, sorry. I got no sleep on the plane, thanks to a kid kicking my seat. My head's just clouded, that's all.' She gave a warm smile and put her hand on my leg.

When we reached the house, I parked in our designated space and went round to the back to grab the bags. I looked at Laura through the car as she stared at our front door. The boot slammed shut and she jumped, then turned to undo her seat belt.

Inside, I dropped the keys in the pot. Laura stood in the hallway and looked around, then put her hands in her pockets and said over her shoulder, 'I'll take a shower.'

I switched on the oven. Upstairs, I heard the sound of the bathroom door shutting and the rattling of the pipes. The cat purred around my legs, and I picked her up and rubbed her stomach.

I was sitting on the edge of the bed when Laura came out, her hair wrapped in a towel. She paused when she saw me, then went to the window and closed the blinds. She stood in front of the mirror and towel-dried her hair without speaking, then undid the one wrapped around her body and draped them over the chair.

I took off my clothes. I reached for her hand but she pushed me back and climbed on top. Then she fucked me with her face towards the ceiling. Slivers of light shone through the edges of the blind, and I watched her body as she arched her back and didn't make a sound.

After it was over, she stood and returned to the bathroom, locking the door behind her. I put my clothes back on and went down to make the dinner.

'So, are you going to tell me anything about your trip, or have you taken a vow of silence?' I pushed away my empty plate and took a sip of red wine, ignoring the inner voice that asked when I was going to change the conversation. I'm doing what's expected of me right now, I replied. Breaking up can wait.

Laura pushed the dregs of a sweet potato around her plate. 'My trip was . . . life-changing,' she said at last. 'You should have come.'

'I'd have had to return a month in, obviously.'

'Oh. Yeah, course.' She blushed.

'And we agreed it would be an amazing thing for you to do on your own. I couldn't have taken that amount of time off work.'

She made a face. 'God forbid you ever ask your boss for a favour. The hours you spend there.'

I cleared my throat. 'They did me a favour a year ago when I looked after Sal, remember? If you mean I don't want to piss off my boss, I guess you're right.'

She dropped her fork on to her plate and covered her face with her hands.

'Nick, I'm pregnant.'

Today I went to the graveyard.

I haven't been since Dad died. Laura said it was a strange way to grieve, how I was going about it, and I'd shrugged and replied inwardly that it was easy for her to say with her ninety-year-old grandparents and her family together each Christmas. People who can't possibly know are always the ones that think they do.

But today I was driving through the village and the main road had been shut. They were diverting people down another road, the one with the graveyard, and it felt wrong to drive by and not acknowledge it. Like passing people you know on the street and avoiding their eye.

I shut the car door and leant against it a while, smoking and watching a gathering of people around an open grave. Their black clothes looked awkward in the sunshine, and their eyes were fixed on the hole where their loved one lay in a wooden box. They took turns to throw in a single red rose – Dad had forbidden such extravagances – then made their way down the path towards me.

I didn't look at their faces out of respect, but I heard their tears and saw the screwed-up tissues in their hands. That's how you do it, I thought. Make it obvious. Wear the pain so they look away.

Dad's grave still looks new. The turned earth has finally settled, but I've yet to sort a gravestone. The one requirement he stipulated was that it be made of granite – long-lasting – and that the inscription be simply his name and the dates on which his life had started and finished. In the end, letters and numbers are all we become.

Bunches of yellow flowers were laid across his grave and the one next to it. Sal's. I knew these were from Stella, who came by every fortnight. Sal's headstone was a plain slab of oak that read: *Salvatore Mendoza, Beloved son & brother, Died 22 April 2018 aged 35 years*. The inscription had come within budget as long as the 'and' was an ampersand. Dad had been pleased at that and jingled the loose change in his pocket like he did when Arsenal won.

I looked at Sal's grave for a while.

One time, drunk on whisky, I told Laura I'd always felt responsible for what happened to Mum. I asked for a lolly, I said. Cause and effect. If I'd stayed quiet, he wouldn't have dropped a box. That's ridiculous, she said, frowning. If anything, Sal's the one. He picked up the gun. I'd just looked at her. I know she meant to be kind.

I found our mother in the corner of the graveyard, over by the ragstone wall. It had been twenty years since I'd stood in that spot.

Stella still looked after it. The grass was free of weeds and the granite headstone still looked shiny and almost new. *Here lies Louise Eve Mendoza*, it read. *Loving wife and mother. Born 4th January 1957, Died 25th September 1991. Always in our hearts*. No expense spared.

The clumps of bright red geraniums Dad had planted still pulse with life.

I was the only person there. I sat cross-legged on the ground so I was level with Mum's name. This is when people talk, I thought. Stella says she talks to each of them as if they were actually there in front of her, telling them about her week and what I was up to. She says it helps keep the memories alive.

'Hi, Mum,' I said to the air. I wanted to swallow the words as soon as I'd said them.

She's not here, I said to myself. That cold lump of stone is not my mum. This grass is not my mum. Whatever is there under the ground is not my mum.

Can you hear me, Mum? I said with every beat of my heart.

Where are you?

'Aren't you going to say anything?' said Laura from behind her hands.

The timer dinged and began its repetitive beep. I walked slowly over and cut the noise, then stood there, looking at the apple pie I'd made for dessert. The top was decorated with lattice strips I'd rolled from fresh pastry.

'How could this have happened?' I said finally.

She was silent for a moment. I heard her take a deep breath and the chair creaked as she leant back. 'I guess there were a couple of days when I was slow taking my pill. Only by a few hours, but perhaps the time zones . . .'

'So how far along is all this?'

She paused. 'A little over three months, maybe.'

'And you've only just found out?'

'Of course I haven't just found out.'

'You knew on your trip? Why didn't you tell me?'

She sighed. 'Why do you think? Look at you. I've just told you in person and it's like someone's died.' She shifted in her seat. 'I mean . . . you're hardly jumping for joy. God, Nick, I've been so nervous.'

I curled my hands and dug the tips of my fingernails into my palms. 'It's a shock. That's all.'

'To be honest, I wasn't sure what I was going to do.'

I picked at the seal around the edge of the oven door and fought an urge to rip it off. 'And have you decided?'

I could sense her looking at me, then, 'What do you want me to do?'

'You know my feelings about kids. I've always been open with you about that, and I thought we were on the same page.' I heard her silence. 'I'm trying to get the idea straight in my head.'

'What do you want me to do?' Laura said again.

'It's your body. I'm not getting involved with that.'

'You were involved with my body the second you came inside of me. You had your pleasure and then left the business of avoiding conception to me to handle, so please don't try to find a loophole.' She folded her arms.

'I'm saying it's your decision. It's your body. Would you rather I ordered you to get rid of it?' I ran a hand over my head and laughed in disbelief. 'What do you women want?'

'How many of us are you trying to please?'

'You know what I mean. I'm trying, Laura. I even made dinner and dessert.'

'Do you want a medal? Praise for not being a moronic bloke? Self-improvement is purely to make yourself look good, then. It's still about ego.'

I groaned into my hands. 'That's not what I'm saying.' I sat opposite her. 'I'll support you no matter what. If you decide not to keep it, I'll be there every step of the way. If you do decide to keep it . . .' I looked at her. 'I'll support you with that too.'

Laura stared at me, her arms still folded. Her eyes were big and sad and searching my face for the answer to an unknown question. Or maybe she'd asked and I hadn't heard.

'If I gave you the choice,' she said, 'what would you have me do?'

'That's an impossible question.'

'Fucking hell!' she screamed, and pushed her plate off the table with such force that it hit the wall and broke in two. 'What does it take to break you? God, Nick. Just tell me how you really feel.' She started shaking as sobs spilled from her mouth.

I pushed back my chair and went to her, holding her in my arms in a kind of brace. I smoothed her hair and tried to calm her crying. 'Laura, please. It's okay. Please stop.'

After a while, her tears began to subside and she relaxed against my hold. I rocked her gently and she clung on to my arm encircling her neck. We stood there for a few minutes, stuck in this rhythm, until finally, she stopped. She gripped my arm and said, 'I decided I want to keep it. The baby. I want the baby.'

Ribbons of smoke began to peel around the corners of the oven and I realised I'd forgotten to take out the pie.

'There we go,' I said, kissing the top of her head.

Life has a way of giving you the answer.

PART FIVE

I try to be better.

I begin to take the later train to work. I'm still at my desk an hour before the rest of the office, and although the train is more crowded, it means I can wake Laura with a cup of tea. This seems right. She has been having waves of sickness, and I feel useless when she has her head down the toilet. I hold back her hair and rub her back. My feelings of inadequacy will only increase with her changing symptoms, and a cup of tea and a later train seems a small and rather pathetic sacrifice.

'When's the scan?' I ask when she returns from the first doctor's appointment.

She turns away to the kitchen counter and riffles through paperwork. 'Hmm? Oh, they'll send a letter.'

'Give me as much notice as possible,' I say, taking an apple from the bowl. 'So I can clear my schedule.'

'Will do,' she says over her shoulder as she walks out.

Laura texts me a few weeks later as I'm heading into a meeting: *Shit, I've just rung the doc and the scan is today! The letter must have got lost in the post. I've got to be at the hospital in an hour. Mum's coming so don't worry.x*

It would take at least an hour to get back, even if I reached the station as a train was about to leave. *That's a shame*, I reply. *Was looking forward to being there.*

As I put down my phone, I realise it's true.

When I walk in, Laura is making dinner. Steak with caramelised onions. My favourite.

'So?'

She doesn't turn from the hob but gives a half-smile over her shoulder. 'Hey. How was work?'

'Fine. Work was fine. How was the scan?'

315

'Good. Everything looks healthy.'

'That's wonderful,' I say, looking around the counter. 'Where are the pictures?'

'Here. I'll send them to you.' She picks up her phone and types in the passcode.

'You don't have actual photos?'

She pauses as she types. 'Oh, I didn't bother. There's a charge – can you believe that? The sonographer did let me take some pictures on my phone, though.'

I frown. 'You didn't want proper pictures of your baby's first scan? That doesn't sound very "you". I'd have thought you'd stick them to the fridge. Get a special magnet with the date on.'

She puts her phone down and turns back to the hob. 'I didn't have any cash on me, okay? Jeez. You've got them now.'

I take my phone out and open the four pictures. They are black-and-white close-ups of an alien-like blob. I can make out the shape of a little nose, a pointy chin, and the grainy shadows of long fingers. Its body is like a football.

I pull out a chair and sit at the table. Laura doesn't turn. 'So when's it due?'

She takes the ketchup from the fridge and squirts two circles on the edges of two plates. 'Early autumn, sometime.'

'They didn't give you an exact date?'

'Mid-September, they said. Probably. Apparently it's measuring quite small for my dates – to be expected, I guess, as we don't know the date of conception – so it may well change at the next scan.'

I nod and don't reply. I look at the pictures some more, and when she brings over the plates, I put the phone in my pocket and look up and smile. 'Thanks for this. Looks great.'

She smiles, a warmer one. 'I wanted to make it up to you. For missing the scan.'

A few weeks later, Daz calls.

'Mate,' he says. 'Gem's seeing someone. Let's go out and get wasted.'

I know Laura would hate me hungover right now, with her

growing stomach and no let-up of sickness, and I know I should explain this to Daz. But of course I don't.

Somewhere new has opened in town and I convince him to try it out. It's one of those hip bars catering to the college crowd with cheap drinks and sourdough pizzas.

I know as soon as we enter that it's not Daz's sort of place. Instead of football on an oversized telly, there is the beat and strings of live music, and a stack of retro board games in place of a fruit machine. There are butcher-block tables and galvanised silver chairs, industrial lights with exposed pipework, and the staff wear checked shirts and denim aprons. Their dishevelled hair is styled with just the right amount of I-don't-give-a-shit grease. This vibe has been doing the rounds in London for a while so I'm used to it, but I can tell by his hesitation that this is all new to Daz.

'What the hell is that on the floor?' he says and we look down. 'Sawdust. It's fucking sawdust.'

I slap his shoulder and nudge him towards the bar. 'Come on,' I say. 'Three-fifty a pint. Think on that.'

We take our drinks round a corner to the table furthest from the band. To the side is an open kitchen, where a chef is rolling dough and tending to a brick pizza oven.

'Bloody hell,' says Daz, sitting down at an old barrel. 'Maybe we should have just gone to The Phoenix.'

'Let's at least appreciate that it's unlikely there'll be any fights here. And we can feel very on-trend.'

'I don't give a rat's arse about being on-trend.' He sniffs. 'Do you reckon they sell pork scratchings?'

I look about at the other tables. 'They're probably in fashion again. I think there's been another generation in between us and them, anyway.'

'Next stop, care home,' says Daz, and he takes a long sip of beer.

'You've seen Gemma, then?'

He sighs. 'Don't really want to talk about it, to be honest.'

We drain our glasses and he leaves to get the next round.

At the nearest table are a group of lads in their early twenties, lean guys who eat right, and bike instead of bus. They are dressed in different shades of blue and grey, and a couple wear Perspex glasses. The topic of discussion is the design of a new building in town and debating whether it is a sentimental pastiche or a juxtaposition of Modernist sensibilities. One is doodling on a napkin. Another says 'post-modern'. Architecture students.

They make me think of Anna.

Daz returns with four pints. He's taken a sip from each so he can carry two glasses in each hand by their rims. 'So we don't have to go back up there again.'

We talk about football for the first pint. Then as we start the next, Daz says, 'So, Pops. Looking forward to D-Day?'

I give a default shrug. 'Sure,' I say, then tap the glass. 'Actually, you know what? I am.'

'The mask slips for a moment.'

I shake my head. 'No, I've been wondering if this is what I need. A spanner in the works, so to speak. Baptism of fire.'

'Are you still going to be talking in riddles when it's here?'

I smile. The pints are kicking in. 'I guess I'll have a new language to learn.'

'Look at us, sitting here,' says Daz, shaking his head. 'Five years ago there'd have been ten of us round this table. Now I'm last man standing.'

'You hold that flag with pride.'

'Nah.' He looks down at his pint. 'It was Gem that didn't want them. I suggested it a few times, but she said I was enough of a kid already.'

I don't know what to say to this. She has a point.

Daz nods at a bearded server wiping down a nearby table. 'Look at that nonce.'

The bloke wears a white sleeveless vest with a shirt tied around his waist and a tea towel slung over his shoulder. Down one arm is an intricately inked sleeve of mountains and wolves and unidentifiable faces, woven through with leaves and tendrils of long branches. He wipes the table with languid strokes, a man used to being watched.

'He's got an Indian chief on his arm,' says Daz in a low voice. 'The guy's as British as they come. What the fuck does he have to do with American Indians?'

318

'I guess a tattoo on your knuckles of a trip you cancelled twice is more original.'

'Well, at least it would have meant something. This is what I don't get about blokes these days. They're so desperate to be real, *authentic*, that it just comes across as fake. There's too much thought put into it.' He swigs his drink. 'Look at them in their lumberjack shirts. Bet the skinny twats have never done a day's graft in their lives.'

I finish the last of my beer. 'When I get back from the gents, how about a final pint at The Phoenix so that you shut the hell up?'

He signals a thumbs-up and I go off in search of the loo. I approach the counter and am about to ask when I look across and see Anna sitting alone at the bar. She is watching the band and her fingers tap along to the music. Of course she would be here, in a bar pitched at the quirkier end of Ashford clientele, and I wonder if my subconscious knew this all along.

It's been sixteen years since I first saw her, but every time is like the first.

She is dressed in a short black dress with her hair pinned so that it falls down her back. She wears fancy earrings and looks far too well dressed for a hipster bar in Ashford.

My voice would never carry above the music so I reach out and touch her shoulder. She turns and her entire face smiles.

'Nick, hey!'

It's the first time we've spoken since those messages after I stayed at hers. Three months, perhaps. In that time, I've imagined her to be angry, so it's disconcerting when she jumps down and plants a friendly kiss on my cheek.

'You look great,' I say without thinking.

'Thanks.' She looks me up and down. 'Would never imagine you in a place like this,' she shouts, cupping the words to shield them from a wailing guitar.

I lean into her ear and notice new piercings around the edge. 'Don't tell me you've come for the music.'

She puts her fingers in her ears and shakes her head. Her ring finger is still bare. There is something on every finger but that one.

'What are you doing here then?' I shout.

Anna looks at me then down at her drink, as if working out what to say. I'm still working out why she's not upset.

She leans in and I catch a hint of her scent. 'Actually, I'm on a date.' Then she smiles at someone behind me, waiting in the wings.

He is tall and slim with glasses and good hair. Handsome. He smiles politely then mouths *Ready?* at Anna, who nods and steps towards him. I watch him take her jacket and hold it open for her. Definitely not a first date.

Now I know why she was so pleased to see me, and I look for a trace of smugness in her expression. She gives a friendly smile, says, 'Good to see you, Nick', and then he puts his arm around her and they walk out.

She could not have timed it better. It felt like being beaten in a cup final in the closing minute of extra time, when there isn't a damn thing you can do but have another drink.

I walk back to the table. 'Let's go,' I say, picking up my coat.

'Phoenix?' says Daz, pushing back his chair.

'You bet.'

A Few Weeks Later

We are hanging wallpaper in the soon-to-be nursery. Or I'm attempting to hang wallpaper while Laura stands in the doorway, telling me what to do.

'I think you're getting it wonky,' she says, cocking her head to one side and narrowing her eyes.

I'm at the top of a stepladder, my arms outstretched against the wall, and I'm dying for a beer. 'Why not tell me how to fix it? I'll do it however you want, just please make up your mind.'

'I think you need to raise the left side by about a millimetre.'

'How much?' My arms feel like they're going to drop off.

'A millimetre.'

'I hope you mean a centimetre, because if you're putting me through this for what is effectively the width of the tip of a pencil, I'll throw the roll out the window.'

'Sorry, yes. A centimetre. Or maybe half.'

'Right.' I bite my lip and raise the left side hardly at all.

'Perfect.' She claps her hands. 'Beer?'

When we bought the house, I went to B&Q and got a drill and a few power tools the sales assistant said I would need. The drill came in reasonably handy when we moved in and transformed the house into the IKEA catalogue, but ever since, it's sat in its case on the shelf in the shed along with the other bits. We just seem to prop pictures now.

I brush the paper on to the wall, taking care to smooth out any bubbles. I enjoy this part, when my arms are free and I can work quickly and methodically. When there is nobody to tell me I'm doing it wrong.

Laura comes back in and hands me a beer, and I sit on the floorboards with my back against the wall and snap the ring-pull. It makes a satisfying *tcht* and then my thirst is quenched.

I feel a surge of pleasure as I look up at my handiwork. One wall done. Paul Mendoza would be proud. 'Where else did you want it?'

Laura points at the alcove. 'There. We'll paint the rest a pale grey. I'm just deciding on the samples.'

I nod at the strips of brightly coloured owls and birds littering the floor. 'You've got another roll, right?'

Laura puts her thumb to her mouth. 'No. Just the one.'

'You're kidding? There's nowhere near enough. I thought you'd said you'd measured it?'

'I did. It's a ten-metre roll and the total wall area comes to just over nine.'

I shake my head, staggered by her stupidity. 'You always need more for wastage. Unless you want the alcove done with tiny remnants that don't match up.'

'Oh. Well, no. Obviously I don't want that.' She shrugs. 'We'll just have to go back and get another roll.'

'Doesn't work like that, Laura. You need to check it's from the same batch or the pattern might sit differently.' I take a smug swig of beer.

She puts one hand on her hip and the other rubs her bump. 'Look at you. One YouTube tutorial and you're an expert.'

I kick at the curling remnants on the floor. 'You'd better go and get another roll now. Take a note of the batch number. I don't want to have to set up again for that tiny section of wall. It'll waste another Saturday.'

'Didn't realise decorating your baby's room was such a chore.'

I take a deep breath. 'It's not a chore. But I'll have to paint it soon, because you said you want the fumes gone by the time it's born just in case they cause asthma, and we still need to order carpet. I work all week, remember? I'd like to manage the time wisely.'

'Can't we go together? Clean yourself up and carry on with it later. We can get lunch in the café upstairs?'

I had already spent countless hours in the baby department at John Lewis, nodding with my hands in my pockets while Laura pointed at cots and debated the differences between the shapes of plastic baby baths. She stood at the soap shelf and unscrewed the cap on every bottle, taking a sniff before thrusting it under my nose. I'd murmur in approval or make a face, then she'd replace the cap and turn over each bottle to study the ingredients, googling the scientific names to check whether any of them meant palm oil, which apparently was very bad.

I finish my beer and shake my head. 'I'd rather not. You go and I'll clean up, ready for round two. Maybe grab some lunch from the drive-thru?'

She gives a slow nod. 'If that's what you want.' Her phone beeps as she walks out and there's the sound of the bathroom door shutting. I hear her phone start to ring and the sound of her voice carries through the crack under the door.

'Hey, babe. How was the trip? . . . I bet . . . It looked amazing. Did you ride on a gondola? . . . Ha, brilliant . . . Eh? . . . Oh my God, that's wonderful! . . . One knee? . . . Perfect . . . Send me a pic of the rock! . . . You must be glowing . . . No, I'm definitely not glowing . . . Sick as a horse . . . Belly getting huge . . . Never mind . . . Listen, hun, I've got to go, but send me that photo, yeah? . . . So happy for you . . . Yep, let's celebrate with the girls next weekend . . . Okay, got to go . . . Byeeee.'

She stays in the bathroom a while, then I hear the toilet flushing and the tap.

I begin to gather the scraps of paper and stuff them into the bin bag. When I turn, Laura is in the doorway, leaning against the frame.

'Kate just rang,' she says. 'Tom proposed while they were in Italy. They're getting married.'

I raise my eyebrows, feigning surprise. 'Good for them.'

She looks out the window and nods. I carry on clearing the floor. I know exactly what's coming and consider climbing into the bin bag and throwing myself out.

'Funny,' she says, her eyes distant. 'I should be jumping for joy when a best mate gets engaged to the love of her life. But all I can think is that they've been together for *two* years. And he's already popped the question. But then, two years is a perfectly reasonable length of time to get to know someone, isn't it?'

I grab the dustpan and brush from the side and start wiping at imaginary dust. 'I guess it means different things to different people.'

'Two years *is* about normal. Not like eight years, though. Eight years should be plenty.'

I straighten my back and sigh. 'It's too hot. I need another beer.'

Laura moves to one side as I walk towards her, and we pass without touching. I jog downstairs and into the kitchen, where I take a beer from the fridge. There is already a six-pack in the door, but I grab a few from the crate on the floor and make room for those too.

I look through the open window into the garden. The sounds of neighbouring children on a trampoline filter through. At the end is the fence panel with the hole that I've still not got round to fixing, despite it dropping into conversation at least once a week.

Laura appears at the door.

'Are we going to talk about the fact you're developing a drinking problem?' she says as I take a long sip.

'It's a heatwave, okay? I'm doing DIY. I think it's allowed.'

'So what's the excuse every evening? Or when you walk in from the train each day and your breath stinks of beer?'

I sigh. She's right. I know she is right. I am getting worse. But I also know that it's not the drinking she's bothered about.

'You're never going to marry me, are you?' She says it quietly and with a tone that betrays what we both know, that she already has the answer.

I turn to face her. She looks at her hands and I remember when someone else asked me this question, once in another life. When I told myself I was sure.

'It doesn't mean for me what it means for you,' I say.

She folds her arms tightly across her chest. 'But in that case, what difference does it make if you sign a piece of paper? We own a house together, we're having a baby. Surely we're committed? Aren't we, Nick?'

'Exactly. So why does it matter if we're married?'

She pulls at the hem of her top. 'It just does, somehow.'

I drain the can. 'I don't expect you to understand. You were very lucky with your 2.4 children upbringing.'

'Please don't make fun of my family.'

'I'm not,' I say. 'It's a beautiful thing, the example you were set.

But it's very different to mine. Listen.' I step forward and take her by the shoulders. 'I'm here, I'm wallpapering the room, I'm in a relationship with you. Why do we need a party to say that out loud?'

She looks up, a spark of hope in her face. 'Is it the actual wedding day? Because we can just go to the registry office, if that's what you want. I don't need a crowd.'

I feel a stab of conscience as I realise I'm about to stamp on her again. But I'm getting tired of repeating myself. She knows what I want, and yet it's like she wants me to hurt her again and again. 'It's not just that.'

Laura throws up her hands in frustration.

'Okay,' I say. 'Let's say you convinced me. Imagine that after years of begging me to ask you, I finally did. Would you really be happy, knowing the only reason I asked you to marry me was so you'd stop going on about it? And would you really want me to do something that I didn't want to do?'

Laura shakes herself free from my hands and looks at me, her eyes moving from one side of my face to the other. I have seen that look before, on her and other people. They are looking for answers and words that I'm not sure I have within myself to give.

Somewhere in another garden, a happy child screams.

A Few Weeks Earlier

I don't know what took me to her door, but five pints of beer and a barrel of hurt pride could change the world.

I'd left Daz after our final drink at The Phoenix. He was at that tricky point of either getting emotional or balling his hands into fists, and I wasn't in a fit state to play wingman to either. I got him into a taxi and gave the driver a twenty.

I stood outside her house in the corner of the square and looked at the church clock. It was after midnight, forty-five minutes since she'd left the bar. Her windows were dark and it seemed like there was nobody home, but perhaps the lights were off for a reason.

I kicked a loose cobble on the ground.

I took out my vape and had a quick drag. I needed soothing and this was the fastest route, a chemical hit straight into the bloodstream.

It had only been a few weeks, but they were no match for the fags. Not just in terms of the buzz. Cigarettes at least have the looks and allure of a glamorous past, a hint at something rebellious and dangerous beneath the skin. James Dean wouldn't have posed with a vape. It felt sad and pathetic, chewing on a piece of plastic. Like an addict with no control.

I did a few circuits round the cobbled square, throwing a sideways glance at her windows when I passed in case I detected movement.

When I was halfway through my fifth lap, a figure stepped out from a side street and I knew instantly it was Anna.

I stumbled and quickened my step. She seemed to pause and throw a halfway glance over her shoulder before picking up her pace, then I realised how it looked, how she thought I was a danger.

This filled me with dread and I heard a drunken *Hey!* issuing from my mouth. At this, she left the path and pushed through the churchyard gate before starting to run. She must have been trying a short cut.

'Hey,' I said, running after her. 'Hey, stop! Anna!'

She looked over her shoulder at the sound of her name, scared. When she saw me, she stopped and steadied herself against the church wall, closing her eyes and catching her breath.

'My God,' she said, her hand on her heart. 'You scared me to death.'

'It's just me,' I said.

'What the hell are you playing at?'

'What the hell am I playing at?' I drew myself up, puffing all the air I could into my lungs. 'What the hell is your boyfriend playing at, allowing you to walk home alone at one in the morning?'

'I'd say you can hardly call him out for being ungentlemanly. Don't you dare shout and run after a lone woman in the dark.'

'So he is your boyfriend?'

She narrowed her eyes. 'Piss off.'

'You are still angry at me then.'

She laughed. 'You don't want me, but you don't want anyone else to have me.'

I swallowed. 'That's not true.'

'Really? Why are you here then?'

'You don't understand.' I shoved my hand into my pocket.

'No, you're wrong.' She straightened herself and smoothed down her dress. 'You sleep in my bed, you tell me you want to be together, that you'll break it off, then you change your mind and are too much of a coward to put it into words. Typed or spoken. Don't worry, I understand perfectly.'

'You think you do, but you don't.'

She threw up her hands in exasperation. 'Maybe what you think I think isn't actually what I think. You realise humans don't have access to each other's heads? That's why they invented language. To tell others what they're thinking. Try it sometime.'

'You know how I feel about you.'

She leant back against the church wall and sighed. 'Two-beer Nick is tender and beautiful and everything I knew he could be. The other is a master in avoidance and speaks in silences, and is a reminder of why this never went anywhere.' Her voice grew quiet and she looked away. 'I always thought that was down to religion, but actually, I left my entire life for someone before you. I would have done it again.'

I felt a tightening around my heart, like being slammed with the back of a shovel.

'It's sort of perfect, actually,' she said, smiling to herself. 'We started in a heatwave, and we ended in one.'

'I'm sorry,' I said.

She looked at me, her face soft. 'That's what's so hard. I know you are. You want to speak the words but don't know how.'

I rubbed my face with my hands. 'You get me in a way that no one else does.'

'But I'm not nineteen any more, Nick. I'm thirty-goddamn-five with a kid. I don't have years to waste.'

'I'm sorry.'

'Yeah, so you said.' She took a deep breath. 'Do you know the maddening thing? That time I asked if you'd ever just pick me up and screw me against the wall – I asked whether you would ever do it, because I knew in my heart you never would. Not unless it came from me first. You have no agency. Life just happens to you.'

'Laura's pregnant.'

I saw a flash of something across her face, shock or pain or maybe revulsion, and she looked down at her feet. 'Oh,' she said.

'I didn't know how to tell you without sounding like a dick. Although you thought that anyway.'

'Congratulations.'

I took a step towards her. The green moss-stained graves took on a strange glow in the orange lamplight. 'Maybe this is more realistic. Life doesn't have happy endings, does it?'

Anna glanced up at the church and smiled. 'I'm starting to realise an end is just the beginning of something else.'

'You know we'd have driven each other crazy.'

She looked at my face and then down at my body, making a careful study of my features. 'You often say that,' she said. 'Is that really what you think?'

I ran a hand across my head and held it there. 'Don't you?'

She thought about this for a moment, and then, 'I think your coolness would have tempered my hot head. I think we are different enough to have stayed our own selves, so that when we came together, it would be electric.'

Above our heads, the church bell gave a dull ring to signal a new hour.

Anna looked at me. 'I think we'd have been magnificent.'

From: ANNA
To: NICK
Subject:

I'm sorry I said you have no agency. I'm sorry I said you had no guts. That you can't do anything unless you're told to, that you'd never be a man to sweep me off my feet.

Forget what I said. Don't change. Ignore my stupid mouth.

I love your gentleness. Yes, you cause pain like everyone, but that's being clumsy. Not knowing where to put your hands.

Let me show you.

I've told you before that you make me feel safe.

But have I told you that one of my strongest memories is when I rang you a year into my marriage. I was on my driveway, locked in my car, him at the window looking out into darkness with disgusted eyes. I'd felt scared during a row and fled the house to call you. No one else could help me at that moment. I wanted your voice. You asked over and over what was wrong, if I was okay, and I just fed silence back to you down the phone, an occasional sob, a fight for breath, my hand clamped on my mouth to stop my heart from spilling the words I'd already said inside. How that night in your bed, when you'd stopped when you didn't have to, how in that moment you forever sealed your fate in my mind as the one who would never hurt me.

There was a time at a service station when a man touched me up as I sat alone in the sunshine, and I ran inside to text you. I hid in a corner and wanted to scream, but my shaking fingers typed a message instead. You won't remember because I never told you. I hid it with a "hey, how are you?" but it was a selfish thing. Because in that moment, I didn't care how you were. I needed your name to light up my screen.

What I also never told you was that on the worst nights, when I lay awake and knew my entire life was a lie, I would let my thoughts drift into you and your face and your hands on my skin and the sound from your throat as I fixed my mouth around you, and then it would be morning. There was no break between my conscious and unconscious thought. You were a calm pill and my entire rest was you.

This is how it is when you make a girl feel safe.

June 2019

A few weeks after our argument, Laura and I go to a party to celebrate Kate and Tom. I had hoped it would be one of those engagements that never led into an actual day, but from the moment the embossed invitation lands on the mat, it ignites a crisp season of silences.

'Not hanging around, are they?' says Laura as she slides the invitation out from the envelope and props it against the toaster. 'But I guess when you know, you know.'

She leaves the room as soon as she's said it.

It takes place at Kate's parents' pub out in the countryside. Laura's friends have impressive jobs in law, medicine or publishing, and Kate's job as a yoga instructor marks her out as the quirky one of the group. She's a good-looking blonde who wears long skirts and winters in Ibiza. She once gave Laura a crystal for her birthday – 'Citrine, darling, for manifesting wealth and abundance' – and her favourite thing is to be agony aunt for their friend set. I can tell she doesn't like me.

We enter the pub and she immediately bounds up and hugs Laura. 'Oh Lols, you sweetheart,' she says, taking the wrapped gift – I have no idea what – and throwing me a dazzling smile. 'Nicky, help yourself to a drink from the bar. The boys are all over there.' She nods in the direction of the other side of the room.

I take my lager and join the boyfriends. When Laura and I first got together, I was struck by the size of her friendship group. There are eight of them in total, all with respective boyfriends who have changed very little over the years. At the time we met, my own mates were pairing off and settling down, swapping pub for park. Laura's world brought with it a ready-made circle of friends to take up the slack.

The lads and I talk about rugby. They are trim and athletic and work in the City, managing something or other in finance. They play squash at weekends, and apart from the odd bit of bragging about their stock performance levels, they are nice enough. Daz would hate them.

'So Nick,' says Tom, putting a hand on my shoulder. 'Laura turned into a witch yet? I hear the hormones are a riot.'

I laugh. 'Yeah, I guess. She's managing okay, though. I just wish there was more I could do.'

'Only benefit I can see is having a designated driver for a while,' says Christian, nudging me and spilling white wine on his designer loafers. 'And I bet the sex is great. Pregnant women are always horny.' Christian works for a pharmaceutical conglomerate and has a habit of sending me hardcore porn videos. I haven't worked out how to ask him to stop.

I smile and shrug.

The conversation moves on to cricket, before tennis and a brief chat about the golf. I know the bare minimum about the latter, a light education gleaned from the sports section for moments like these. I contribute a comment or two, enough to play a part and not blow my cover. Most of the time, I drink my beer.

At about 10 p.m., Anna walks through the door.

The beer I'm drinking goes down the wrong way and then I am coughing and spluttering, and Christian is whacking my back. When I turn, red in the face, she is looking straight at me. I give a sort of wave, and she turns away.

She's on the arm of some bloke. A different one. He is tall and Terminator-like, with a buffness that seeks to be seen. He leads her over to Kate, who gives him a hug and jokily squeezes his bicep. I watch as she turns her attention to Anna, who is clearly being introduced for the first time. Kate chats away and Anna nods politely and says the occasional thing, then Kate waves them towards the bar and heads straight for Laura.

Laura has ignored me so far, taking refuge either on the dance floor or in the corner of a booth. I've thrown the odd glance in her direction and they're never returned. When she reaches Laura, Kate whispers in her ear, and then Laura is standing and looking in Anna's direction, then at me, then back at Anna.

I make an excuse to the lads and take my beer off into an empty function room set up for children and elderly relatives. In here, sofas – those hard leather ones with buttons that push into your back – and armchairs are spread out in a sort of circle, and the music is dulled and distant. The older partygoers have already departed and the children are crowding the dance floor.

I drop down on to a sofa and let out a long breath. This will be my refuge for a moment before slipping outside for a blessed vape. Give the eyeballing a chance to calm down.

I lean my head back and close my eyes. What feels like seconds later, there is a light tapping on my head, and I open my eyes to see an upside-down child staring at me.

'You were sleeping,' she says. Her tone is accusatory.

I keep my head still and move my eyes from side to side. 'So what if I was?'

'You can't sleep at a party. It's the law.'

A drop of snot pauses on the end of her nose and she wipes it against the bottom of her hand with expert skill. She wears a red dress with ribbons in her hair. My knowledge of kids is slim, but I'd guess she's about six.

I sit up. My empty glass is beside me on the sofa and I lean forward to put it on the table. 'You better get back to the grown-up looking after you.'

She huffs and sits down next to me. 'I don't want to go back out there. Grown-ups are boring. They just stand and talk, and they keep pouring their drinks all over my dress.' She smooths her lap.

'Grown-ups *are* boring,' I say, feeling for the vape in my pocket. 'Don't ever become one.'

She cocks her head and looks at me. 'Like Peter Pan?'

'Exactly.'

She thinks about this for a minute. 'But you're a grown-up. So does that mean you're boring too?'

I give a slow nod. 'Exceedingly so.'

She flicks her hair over her shoulder. 'Well, I'm never going to be boring. When I'm a grown-up, I'll stay up as late as I want, have midnight feasts and go on great adventures.'

335

I think about what's going on out there in my absence. If only there was a bar in here.

'Play with me?' she says, bringing out a little bag of plastic figures.

I check my phone. 'You really should be getting back out there.'

'In a minute, I promise.' She unzips the bag and begins taking them out. 'I'll be this one,' she says, holding up what looks like a princess with red hair. 'She has magical powers. She can bring dead people back to life.'

No messages. 'That's a pretty great power to have,' I say, putting my phone back in my pocket.

'Now we need someone for you to be . . .' She riffles through the bag. 'Do you want to be a man?'

'Not really.'

'Yes, go on.' She hands me a plastic figure, a prince with golden hair. 'Be a man.'

I jig him about on my knee. 'What do I do?'

She looks at me, confused. 'Play.'

'Don't tell anyone this, but . . .' I lean in and whisper, 'I've forgotten how.'

'It's easy,' she says, taking out another figure and placing it on the table. 'You just make them talk. Like this. "Now you listen to me,"' she says in an American accent, waving her figure at mine. '"We're going to storm the castle and save the king from the evil witch. Stay close to me and we'll go in together. Stay close now, you hear?"'

'What will we do when we get there?' I say, getting in character. 'We'd better make a plan. There might be booby traps.'

'Boobies?' she says, laughing.

I clear my throat. 'I mean, the witch might have set a trap. And wait, what if the king doesn't want to be saved?'

She looks at me, impressed. 'Oh, he definitely wants to be saved. He just doesn't know it yet. But we'll make him see.'

I raise my eyebrows. 'Ah,' I say. 'We'd better get a move on then.'

A woman sticks her head round the door. She looks drunk and annoyed. 'There you are. Where have you been?'

'In here, playing. I made a friend.'

The woman gives me a suspicious look. 'Well, get your toys and come back out here with the others. Come on, hurry up.'

The girl puts the figures in her bag and zips it shut. 'I have to go,' she says, standing. 'That's my mummy. She gets really angry if I don't do what she says.'

'My dad was like that. That's the good thing about being a grown-up. You can do what you want.'

'You're lucky. I want that more than anything in the world.' She turns and smiles at me, then she runs through the door and is gone.

I go to pick up my glass and realise I'm still holding the plastic figure. I look at it for a moment, feel its moulded face and parts, a designer's idea of how a man should be.

I place it on the table. Its face looks sad.

The beat of an electronic bass throbs against the wall. There is cheering. I pick up my glass and head back out into the crowd.

When I walk out, there is a lull in the music and I hear someone say *Anna*.

I stop.

The voice continues and I recognise it as Laura's. She is standing with Kate and one of Kate's friends whose name I don't know. They stand close together, about four feet away, talking and shaking their heads. I see them through the leaves of a potted palm, behind which I am hiding. This feels both completely ridiculous and the safest option.

The music gets louder and they have to raise their voices to make themselves heard. This makes my accidental eavesdropping easier.

'So who is she?' says the girl with no name.

'Nick's ex,' shouts Kate. 'Laura's boyfriend.'

'Not exactly his ex,' says Laura, her back to me. She has one arm folded across her chest, the other holding a water. 'Apparently they had one crazy hot summer, but they never even slept together. When we met, he called her "the one that got away".'

The girl with no name rolls her eyes. What the fuck does she know.

'I had an ex with one of those,' says Kate. 'They create this myth

337

thing in their heads that's completely detached from reality. You end up wishing they'd actually shagged each other, just so—' I couldn't hear the rest.

'Not helping, Kate,' shouts Laura.

'It can't have been that hot if they never even had sex,' says the girl.

'She was from some weird cult,' says Kate. 'You know those people who knock on your door and say the end of the world is coming? Proper loony.'

'What's she even doing here?' says the girl. I take pleasure in noticing lipstick smeared all over her teeth.

'She's here with Tom's cousin,' says Kate, pouting. 'I didn't even know they were going out. Swear, Lols.' She grips Laura's arm. 'I'd never have let her come otherwise.'

They are quiet for a moment as they stare at the other side of the dance floor at something out of my line of sight. Anna, perhaps. They sip their drinks.

'She's not *that* pretty,' says Kate.

'I think she's weird-looking,' says the girl. 'Her features are wonky. Her forehead's too big. Men are so strange, the women they go for.'

Laura takes a gulp of drink and runs a hand through her hair. 'Are you both fucking blind?'

They look at her and I take a step back.

'Let's get you another drink,' says Kate, putting her arm around Laura.

'A real one?'

Kate gives her a squeeze. 'Not long now,' she says, and leads them towards the bar.

Promise you'll tell no one, she'd said that day at the lake.

I promise.

I lean against the wall in my corner and wait for my heart to quieten. I know what I need, but I can't bring myself to walk across the room so I try a nearby door. It opens into the kitchen, which is dark and quiet, and I walk between the stainless-steel counters and through the fire-exit door to the outside.

And there is Anna, in the little cobbled yard, leaning against the wall with a glass of red wine.

'God,' she says under her breath when she sees me. She gives a strained smile and looks down at her glass.

'Shall I leave you?' I say, turning as if to go back through the door.

She sips her wine and shrugs, not bothering to look at me. Instead, she presses the point of her heel lightly on the ground. 'Do what you like,' she says into her glass.

I hesitate, then straighten my back and put my vape to my lips.

'Look at you,' she says. 'Evolving, are we?'

I take a drag and try to enjoy it. 'Baby steps.'

'Yeah, well, I'm pretty sure the second-hand smoke is still a killer, so if you are going to hang out here, maybe move further away.'

I take a step back. 'You didn't seem to mind me chain-smoking in your garden.'

'People change.'

'Speaking of evolution, that's quite an impressive caveman you've come with. Does he call you Jane?'

Anna laughs, but the tone suggests it's not at my joke. 'How's your pregnant girlfriend?'

I exhale and give a slow nod. 'Still pregnant.'

'So I see. If looks could kill.'

She says this drily, not making eye contact. I have been around this Anna a few times and know how hard it is to break. This meeting is unexpected, but it feels like it might be the last time. I don't want it to end badly.

'It's her best friend's party,' I say. 'She wasn't expecting you.'

'No, well, I wasn't expecting you,' she says, looking at the ground. She clears her throat. 'And I'm used to girls not liking me. I don't know why but it happens a lot. Always has.'

'They're intimidated by you,' I say, leaning against the wall.

She looks at me and laughs. 'Come on.'

'It's true.'

'How the hell am I intimidating?'

I blow vapour in her direction. 'Look at you.'

'Me?' She is several feet away but waves dramatically at the smoke she thinks is killing her.

'You don't see yourself how I see you.'

Anna turns away. 'I don't see why girls would find me intimidating.' She gives a shrug. 'At thirty-five, I really should start calling us women.'

I'm quiet for a moment, watching her, but she keeps her eyes fixed somewhere else. 'Look what you've done with your life,' I say. 'You said to me years ago that you wanted to be a painter, and now you're winning awards. You live life as you want. You're strong. That's intimidating.'

'God, is this going to be like when you called me "intense"? Because this really isn't the time.'

'I'm just giving you something good,' I say. 'I know you like that.'

Anna takes a breath. 'So now you give me something good? Sixteen years and one pregnant girlfriend later.'

'Tarzan's waiting.'

She downs the last of her wine and wipes her mouth against the back of her wrist. 'Yeah, you made that joke,' she says, and pushes herself away from the wall. 'It wasn't funny the first time.'

'I'm just impressed with your range. A few weeks ago it was a skinny intellectual with glasses and now it's a Neanderthal with arms like hunks of meat. Who's it going to be next month?' I'm being a dick, but this already feels like a lost cause so why not die with guns blazing?

Anna looks at me, hurt, and I know I've succeeded. But there's a twinge in my heart, the one I felt sixteen months ago when I served beans on toast to a soon-to-be dead Sal. I think about touching her arm and pulling the words back inside.

She is watching, working me out, and then she gives her shoulders a little shake and starts to walk over.

'Think I'm a slut, do you?'

I shake my head.

'You've listened to too much angry rap.' She sticks out her chin. 'I got married at twenty, so maybe cut me some slack?'

'Sure,' I say.

Anna gives an unconvincing laugh. 'I bet you don't like me when I'm like this. Giving you shit. Well, you say you like strong women – here you go. My strength is more than a turn-on. It stands up for itself. You think it means I don't let things bother me, but I have enough fucked-up pain of my own. And you don't like seeing it, because the second you sense anything that's a challenge, it feels too much like hard work. You only like strength when it suits you.'

'It doesn't matter whether I like you right now or not, does it?'

We are silent for a moment, facing each other like lone rangers waiting for the other to draw. Then a smile begins to curl at the edge of her mouth and I watch her lick her lips. It has a dangerous feel.

'I read once that the worst part of torture is the beginning,' she says. 'When you're full of your own illusions and fears about black and white, and the terror that black may win. Then as torture goes on, it slowly changes your state of mind to a kind of drunk, masochistic giving in. It becomes something you cooperate with.' She leans in a little too close so I can smell the wine on her breath. 'It becomes something you almost like, because you see through it. You no longer fear what it can do.'

I feel the techno beat pumping through the walls.

'You remind me of my first boyfriend, who completely broke my heart and then would fuck me whenever he needed to feel better about himself.'

She is so close, but then she brushes my arm and goes in through the kitchen door.

This is our last goodbye.

Red / by Anna

Red is for alarm bells, for fire engines, for accident & emergency,
    for a shout of watch out, for a bull that will not be tamed
Red is for rage
Red is a plastic-wrapped rose in a club when I was seventeen
Red is the time you stood over me on the train and I never told you
Red is for your eyes on my body
for leaving a café before we've even sat down
Red is the wine I cannot drink because of how it stains my lips and
    how I want it kissed off

Red is the ketchup I ate in your bed

Red is for the child we never had
For the life that bled away
month after month
For the times I cut myself and wanted you to heal me

Red is the sauce I lick off the spoon as I sit on a counter and
    watch you cook
Red are my knees as I push you down to the kitchen floor
We let the sauce burn

Red is for the apple on an ABC
For fruit at the eve of the world
For nails driven through veins
The book of Revelation
Drunk
The cup of Babylon
The mark of the Wild Beast
The fire that is coming just for me

Red is the sound of my name on your mouth, a word you only
    use as warning
Damn my vain attempt to make you bleed and know that you
    are human

Damn red and all its shades
Red is the colour I want

Red is the transfusion I consent to
You taking my wrist and cutting me open and pouring yourself in
I want you inside
Not waiting for permission
Red is for rape / Yes I'm sure
The screw against the wall
The I Do you'll never say

Red is a colour you never wear
Because you can't handle red
or any of its spoils

I will always be an island
.
.
.
but fuck I bleed too

Three Weeks Later

Laura is in the garden when I get home. It's apparently the final day of the heatwave, with storms due in the night, and I'm glad to see the last of the heat.

She is standing on the patio, her hands on her hips and looking into the distance, the horizon obscured by the walls of neighbouring houses. On the table beside her are pots and a half-used bag of compost, with a scattering of dropped soil on the slabs below. The handle of a gardening tool sticks out the top of the earth.

'What are you up to?' I say, and she jumps.

'God, don't sneak up like that.' She turns her body towards me but looks at the ground. 'I'm planting bulbs.'

'You're meant to be on bed-rest,' I say, pretending to disapprove. Laura has been signed off work with extreme morning sickness. Apparently it's rare to continue past the first trimester, but she says the doctor confirmed it's not a sign of anything wrong.

'These are for the autumn.' She rubs her growing belly, accentuated by her striped top. 'They'll appear when the baby comes. I probably should have waited for the weekend, after it's rained. It would have made the soil easier to work with.' I notice patches of fresh earth in the beds.

'So why didn't you?'

'Oh . . .' she starts to say and shrugs. 'There's only so much daytime telly I can take. I needed to do something.'

'You're not one to ignore doctor's orders,' I say. She hasn't looked at me once.

'Hmm,' she says, wiping her forehead with the back of her wrist. She strips off her gloves and drops them on to the table. 'I'm going in for a water. Why don't you start on the beers?' She brushes past.

I ignore her tone and go to the fridge. 'Thanks. I will.' The sound of the ring-pull is a starting pistol in the room.

'Kate and Tom have set a date,' she says, running the tap. 'Twenty-third of December. Christmas wedding.'

'That's nice,' I say, taking a deep swig.

Laura lets the tap run a while and stares out the window. I know this is my cue to not leave the room, because if I walk out now after she's said that, I'll never hear the end of it. And the end of it is exactly what I want.

'I need to ask you something,' she says, her voice distant.

Here we go.

'Do you see us having any more? Babies, I mean.'

I take another gulp and throw up my hands in defeat. 'You want me to decide whether I want more kids before the first is even born? I'm assuming that's a joke.'

Laura fills a glass and shuts off the tap.

'Why did you buy a four-bedroom house with me?' she says. 'What are you planning to fill the rooms with? Apart from the ghosts of ex-girlfriends.'

I drain the can and drop it into the recycling. 'All right, Laura,' I say. 'Enough, please.'

'Don't deny it then.'

'There's nothing to deny.'

She folds her arms and nods. 'I don't even get Drunk Nick.'

'What?' A fear grips my heart.

She turns slowly around. I search for my phone in my pocket and release my breath when I feel its boxy shape against my leg.

'When people get drunk,' she says, 'that's when they talk. What's in their heart. What they can't say sober.' She shakes her head. 'But not you. Nick Mendoza's shutters are always down.'

'I don't know what you're talking about.'

Bullshit. I know my emotions are held hostage by a hot summer in 2003, and long before that, by the scream of a gun being fired and ice lollies melting in the sun. There are other lives existing parallel to this one, their shadows stretching far. How different things could have been if I'd found a way to let them go.

'Sometimes I've thought about getting you blind drunk,' says

Laura, 'then asking whether you ever want to marry me. That's what the girls tell me to do.' She smiles sadly to herself.

'Trick me, you mean.'

'Don't worry, there's no point. You don't even want me when you're drunk.'

I know I should walk over and take her in my arms, lift her chin, tell her she is talking madness. I know this is another cue to do another thing I don't want to do.

I stay right where I am.

'It's a girl,' she says, and my face goes red, as if I'm being accused of something, but then she puts a hand on her stomach and looks down and says, 'The baby, I mean. Girl.'

My jaw begins to ache and I realise I am grinding my teeth. I put my hand to my mouth and knead my fingers into my cheeks and chin, trying to feel something. 'You found out? When?'

'I had a scan today. A private one.'

I debate opening the fridge and taking out another beer. 'So that's both scans I've missed. If you want me to feel part of this, then you really should let me be there. It's my baby too.'

Laura picks up her glass and takes a long gulp of water. She takes a deep breath as she grips the edge of the worktop.

'Actually,' she says, 'it's not your baby.'

The metal fridge door feels cool and refreshing against my forehead. It reminds me of times when I've had a bug or food poisoning, when there is no greater comfort after vomiting than pressing my face against the cold tiles of the bathroom floor.

'I wasn't sure until today,' Laura says. 'The scan showed I'm only sixteen weeks. So there's no doubt in my mind any more.'

'Whose is it?' I can hardly hear my own voice.

'His name's Matt,' she says. 'He was part of my team on the trip. He's Australian, and a surfing instructor, if you can believe it. He plays guitar.' She lists his attributes like she's setting up a date.

I open the fridge a little too forcefully and the glass bottles in the door rattle together. I crack open another can, feel the liquid run down my throat, and I close my eyes and try to enjoy it. She lets me be.

'Are you in love with him?'

Laura looks away. She picks at the edge of a utility bill on the worktop, flicking the paper between her forefinger and thumb. 'I've tried to forget him. You have to believe I really have tried.'

'I know,' I say, and I do.

'I don't know how it happened,' she says, shaking her head. 'I didn't go out there looking for it. It's just a very intense thing, being with someone in a confined place, day and night. You get to know each other on fast-forward. It starts to feel natural sharing every meal together, talking before you go to sleep, and then . . .' She gives a long sigh. 'I'm so sorry.'

'Here,' I say, unzipping my bag, which I'd dropped on the table when I arrived home. I pull out a linen-wrapped notebook with MEMORIES embossed in gold on the front. 'I saw this in a shop today and thought you'd like it. It's for writing down all the "first times", and the funny things kids say and do. I thought we could write it together.'

She takes the notebook and flicks through the pages.

'I wish my mum had had one,' I said.

Laura starts to cry. She hugs the notebook to her chest and puts a hand over her face. There is no noise, just a slight shaking of her shoulders, and I stay right where I am.

'This is what I've been waiting for,' she says, sniffing. She goes to pass it back to me, but I shake my head and she holds it tight. 'I'm not someone to be settled for, Nick. I want to be somebody's everything. I wanted to be yours.'

It's quite a thing to be almost forty years old and hate yourself.

'Does he know?' My voice is calm and steady. Two-beer Nick.

Laura takes a deep breath and nods. 'He says he wants to marry me.'

I raise an eyebrow. 'Fast mover.'

'Not really,' she says, looking at me. 'He just knows what he wants.'

I put my head back and drain the second can. 'That's good,' I say. 'That's really good.'

PART SIX

Christmas 2003

Stella was clearing the table. The turkey carcass sat on the serving platter, its meaty remnants plucked and put in Tupperware for Boxing Day leftovers. All that was left was the hollow hulk of what had once been a living thing.

Sal and I helped clear the final bits. Dad snoozed in front of the soft blare of the telly, left on throughout dinner to act as a buffer against any lulls in conversation. It wasn't so bad that year. Arsenal had so far gone unbeaten all season and words like 'invincible' were bandied around with talk of being crowned champions. Dad had carved the turkey with vigour. He even donned the hat from a cracker he shared with Sal.

In the kitchen, Stella washed up while we dried, the radio crooning out festive tracks. Sal had gone out in town the night before, and Stella was screaming with laughter at a story about a drunken run-in with a lamp post. He described it with typical Sal theatrics; slapstick falling over and sound effects, his blond curls spilling out from under a paper crown.

'Oh, Salvatore,' she said when he'd finished, dabbing her eyes with the edge of her Marigold. 'You are a live one.' She peeled off the gloves, fixed herself a snowball and took it to the lounge for the Queen's speech.

Sal picked up a plate from the rack. 'You going out this week? Thought you might have been there last night.'

I nodded as I hung the gravy boat from a peg on the dresser. 'Tomorrow with Daz. That girl he's seeing is out, so we have to go too.'

Sal took another plate and held it in mid-air as if he'd just remembered something. 'Did you hear Anna got engaged? Lisa told me last night. The wedding's next July.'

I watched the water drip from the plate.

'What happened there? You were together all summer, then boom. Over.'

I slid the paper crown off my head and looked at it. 'Yeah, not sure.'

I could sense Sal's confusion. 'But you were joined at the hip. Something like that can't end without a reason.'

'Isn't that what happens in life? People come and go. Besides, you know the deal with her religion. She's only meant to be with someone who thinks the same as her. Hence the engagement.' I crumpled the party hat and lobbed it into the bin.

Sal rolled his eyes. 'Come on.'

'It's true.'

'Yeah, maybe according to official rules. But if she was really into it, she'd never have given you the time of day in the first place.' He dropped the dried plate on to the stack that lived on the dresser. 'Bit of a twat, really, aren't you?'

'Cheers.'

'You're welcome. Bloody hell, Nick. Any idiot could see you had something there.'

I threw down the tea towel and pulled out a chair. 'We don't all have your gift of the gab, Sal.'

Sal folded his arms. 'You think you get more than one Anna in a lifetime? That you'll feel a connection like that again? I saw you together. Beats me what she saw in your emotionally retarded self, but I'm telling you: it was legit.'

'Yeah, I'm a twat. You made your point and I agree with every word. Hindsight is a beautiful thing.' I leant across to the fridge and took out another beer.

'So what are you going to do about it?'

'What the hell can I do about it? Storm the church and stop the wedding?'

'That'd be a start.'

'Life isn't a movie, Sal. There are rules and ways of doing things, and consequences for ignoring them.'

'Yeah,' he said, rubbing his chin. There was something comical in the contrast between his red paper crown and the rare seriousness of his expression. 'There are rules. But we're not talking about passing exams or choosing a stock portfolio. This is love, you daft prick. And if you're going to attach protocols to that, then . . .' he shook his head, 'you're beyond saving.'

Stella calls a few weeks after Laura leaves. I know she's keeping an eye on me. Everyone thinks they're subtle with their texts and drinks, but they forget I was the one checking in with Dad and Sal. It's hard getting used to being on the other side.

Her voice crackles with patchy reception, but I make out a *How are you, love?*

Laura took a suitcase of clothes and nothing else. Mum will come by for the rest, she'd said, nodding at her things around the bedroom. I carried the case down two flights of stairs and stowed it safely in the boot, then she gave me a pitying hug and drove off in our car.

Now I stand in a sea of boxes. It took two weeks of sofa slouching with a box set and beers, but last night, halfway through the second season, I hit pause on the remote and climbed into the loft to retrieve the boxes we'd kept after moving in. I went from room to room, throwing everything in, not bothering to tape them shut.

'Is the house on the market yet?' says Stella.

'The agent's coming round next week. Just doing a bit of house-keeping first.'

'Listen, I've had a call from your dad's landlord. Something about Paul owning a field behind the house?'

I run a hand back and forth across my head and frown. 'I didn't think Dad owned anything. There was nothing in the will?' Stella had been executor.

'He says it was all done by handshake. You know how your father was. Anyway, he's at the house this afternoon and asked if you'd meet him there at midday.'

I spend an hour hauling boxes out on to the empty drive.

I stack them neatly on top of each other, heavies at the bottom, lighter ones on top, taking care to distribute the weight so the boxes form three tight and even squares of nine. No gaps between edges.

When I'm ready to leave, I lock the door and stand on the drive, enjoying a vape in the sunshine as I survey my morning's work. There is the faintest pounding between my temples from last night's bottle, but the act of purging seems to have tempered any pain. It feels like the first day of a new year.

I take out my phone and type a quick message to Laura's mum: *Hi Sally. The boxes are on the drive for you to collect. The forecast says rain coming. Take care.* I hit send.

As I'd gone round the house, packing up all trace, I began to write 'Laura's things' on each sealed box. After box three, I changed tack. NOT MINE, I wrote instead. I stabbed the black permanent marker against each box and dragged the letters tall to fit the entire side. When I dumped them on the driveway, I ensured the writing faced out.

There is a twitching of net curtains at the house next door and I smile.

Hello, Nick, I say to myself. Nice to meet you.

Someone is standing at Sal's grave. Mathilde. Her hair is dark again.

I decided to take a detour on the way to the house. Something about the clearing out of Laura, of every trace of that life, something about the ritual of that had left a hungry void. I had an urge to see Sal.

I approach with cautious steps, walking on grass instead of making noise on the paving with my shoes. Even here, where I have a legitimate right to be, I am trying not to disturb.

I crush a twig and she turns. Her face is unexpected. It is red and stained with tears, and her hands fly to her cheeks to wipe away the evidence. It hurts to realise how much I understand this woman.

There are no greetings or niceties, no chit-chat or awkward hugs. When I reach the grave, I stand beside her, and we look at the headstone, at what remains of the man we loved. She hugs her arms to her chest.

'I was on my way to Paris,' she says finally. 'My mother is ill. The train stopped at Ashford and I looked out the window at the sign. When the whistle went, I knew. I grabbed my bag. I jumped off.'

'I'm sorry about your mother.'

She sniffs and rubs her nose with the back of her hand.

'How was the . . .' she swallows, 'the funeral. I don't know how to do such things.'

'Shit. It was shit. I wish I could have missed it.'

We are quiet for a moment and listen to the sound of cars passing on the other side of the grey flint wall.

Mathilde slips a hand in her pocket and pulls out a square box, which she opens to reveal a mirror with a crack down one edge. She looks at her torn reflection and attempts to erase the black streaks on her cheeks with the pads of her fingers.

'When I was twelve,' she says, 'I left our apartment door open. Always close the door, my mother said. If you leave it open, Pepé – our little dog – will get out and be lost and we'll never get him back again. One day, I came in from school and forgot to shut the door. I made a drink and looked for Pepé. I couldn't find him. And then I heard screaming and the sound of tyres, and when I went on to the balcony, I looked down and Pepé was lying in the road. A man got out his van and scooped him up and held him like a baby. I couldn't go down there. I sent the maid. I couldn't go down there.' She snaps the mirror shut.

'Was he okay?'

She looks at me, frowning. 'He'd been run over by a truck. A tiny dog.'

I nod and take out my vape. Mathilde follows by lighting a pre-rolled cigarette and we stand in front of Sal's grave, smoking like old friends.

'I don't do regrets,' she says after a while, 'but I sometimes wish I could be softer. You know? Life has always felt to me like a huge act of violence. Someone has to dominate. Blood will be spilled, whether we like it or not. The only choice is whether you are the one bleeding or the one with the knife. With your brother, I was both. Now, I am starting to wonder if there is a different way.'

I do not answer. I smoke and think about Sal. I think of the moments in my life when I have burned and felt on fire, when I have given into the feeling in the moment and not stopped to question the sensation but felt the warmth of it on my skin and known, known, known that it was the whole fucking point of being alive. We will have time to pause when we are six feet under.

'Laura and I broke up.'

I feel Tilly look at me. I feel her knowing smile.

'Well,' she says. 'What are you going to do about it?'

Dad's landlord was a larger-than-life person. When he came round on occasion to inspect the house, Sal and I would hide behind furniture and watch him move from room to room. He didn't really walk, more a case of rocking from leg to leg, pushing himself off a door or a wall to get the momentum going. Sal and I were fascinated by the enormity of his stomach, which prevented him from seeing his own feet. We called him Mr Fats.

I see him standing outside the house as I walk down the driveway, my feet crunching on new gravel. He looks just the same. This familiarity, the echo of a distant memory proved true, hangs heavy in my throat.

My phone beeps and I open a message from Stella. *Nick, I need to see you. Can I come round later when you're back? I'll wait in the car if you're out.*

Sure, I type.

He turns as I approach. 'Aha,' he says, as if pulling me out of a hat. 'Good to see you, m'boy. Now a man, of course, and so like your father.' He has the scarlet nose and warm, crinkling voice of an alcoholic.

I nod, smiling. 'So they say.'

In the hallway, a decorator stands on a tower, rolling brilliant white streaks across the Victorian ceiling. Dustsheets cover the floorboards. I expect they'll tart it up nicely for the next tenants, though, Dad says in my head.

'There's a family moving in next week,' says Mr Fats. 'Two boys, just like you and your brother. Salvatore, isn't it? Is he well?'

The question throws me for a moment, and I put my hands in my pockets and clear my throat. 'Fine. Sal's fine,' I say. 'My aunt said something about a field?'

He waves me into the kitchen, where papers and plans are spread across a decorating table.

The room has been painted white and new kitchen cabinets have been installed. There was no proper kitchen when we moved in. A large range cooker had sat in the corner, seventies brown, and it heated the boiler and the entire house. Dad built makeshift units and fitted a length of worktop he'd found in a skip, and Mum ran up some patchwork curtains on her sewing machine to hang along the front. She said she liked the French cottage look, but of course they had to be washed regularly and that was more work. She didn't mind, she said.

The new units are clearly from the budget range, but at least they have doors. I think of the boys moving in and how they won't be embarrassed to have friends back after school. Not now the kitchen is a kitchen.

'Here,' he says, jabbing a fat finger on a large map. 'This is the one.'

I lean in. I see the rectory on the plan and recognise the field he points at as about a quarter of a mile behind the house. Sal and I used to cut through it sometimes on the way to town. I remember it as about half the size of a football pitch, surrounded by farmland, butting on to a country road with an old slaughterhouse rotting at the far end.

'Your father did extra work for me once,' says Mr Fats, 'and because of the recession, I didn't have money to pay him. We agreed the field instead.'

'How long ago was this?' I say, confused as to why Dad had never mentioned it.

'Not long after you moved in. We never made it official – solicitors cost money, you know – but it was his all the same. Damn fine man, your father. An honest man, like myself. I should think you'd like to get paperwork drawn up now, though. Here.' He pulls a card from his pocket. 'Ring me in the week and we'll make a start. Oh, and you may want to get hold of a van. I seem to recall your father stored a load of junk in the old abattoir. Boxes and bags of things.'

A shiver. 'Actually,' I say, clearing my throat, 'I might go now and take a look.'

*

Outside, I begin walking down the garden towards the fields. The smell of fresh paint fades as I pass Mum's old vegetable patch, now overgrown, and the observatory hidden by a sea of brambles. I walk down the middle of the lawn where Sal and I played football, past the thicket where we made our camps, under canopies of the trees we climbed. I do not look back once, even when I go through the gate and have to half turn to close it behind me.

I will not be a pillar of salt.

It is just as I remember.

A scrubby-looking field, with clumps of long grass that have a flat, lonely presence, as if they never had the chance to grow. Thick, ancient trees straddle the boundaries and throw much of the land in shadow. The Victorian brick slaughterhouse sighs in a far corner, its tiled roof beginning to cave in the face of old age. Fingers of ivy fan out across the crumbling walls to strangle a building made by long-dead builders. Nature always wins.

As I walk round the building, I turn towards the sound of trickling water, and there, edging out from under the fence, is a stream. It twists like a ribbon through the neighbouring field and exists on this side of the rusty iron fence for no more than a few metres before curling back through the boundary. I think how strange to divide the land in this way, but how many deadly wars have been fought over a patch of water, water that is rushing through and can never be contained.

Paul Mendoza would have looked at this field, with its road that means access, and water that means life, and he would have thought this a good spot.

The entrance is overgrown and I pick up a large stick to beat back the brambles. Thorns catch my skin and leave their mark. I suck the blood from the deep ones.

When the path is clear, I push at the splintered wooden door, but it has jammed after years of never being opened. I feel it give a little, and standing back, I take hold of the door frame and kick with all my strength. The door slams against the wall and I step inside.

Sprays of dried blood run across the tiled walls with wild abandon. They have darkened to black.

In the centre of the room is an Aladdin's cave of boxes and trunks, old suitcases and plastic zip-up bags piled on top of each other. Instead of mountains of gold, there are stacks of books, clothes, and cases of music records. A path winds through the middle.

I knew it.

I cover my eyes with my hands so that everything is dark, so there is nothing but the sound of my own breathing. When I open my fingers, as if by magic, the boxes are still there.

She was here all the time.

The first bag I open is filled with her dresses. There are polka dots and flowers, pale stripes and leopard, prints I saw every day. I pull one out and hold it up. It is a white summer dress with red spots, and the creases are yellow from the damp of thirty years of being folded. I remember the sight of it as I hid in her wardrobe with Sal, and how the hem of a skirt would carry her scent. I inhale the fabric, but she is long gone now.

In the middle of the path is an armchair covered in pink mildewed satin that I recognise from her room. Where she would throw her clothes. Next to the chair is the portable record player from my childhood, one of those travel ones that lives in a suitcase. On the turntable is a record covered in thick dust. 'San Francisco (Be Sure to Wear Flowers in Your Hair).' Her favourite.

Beside the chair on the floor is a half-drunk bottle of whisky and old cigarette ends, coated with decades of dust. Those nights when Sal or I would wake crying and nobody would come. Dad's bed would be empty and the car still in the driveway, as if he had vanished into the walls. The next morning, he'd be there filling our bowls with Rice Krispies, and we'd glance at each other and grab a spoon. We never asked where he went, and he never told us.

Like her, he was here all the time.

I wipe the dust from the record, adjust the needle and flick the switch. Nothing. I take my phone from my pocket, search for the song and press play. The sound of music fills the room.

Some boxes are sodden. There are thin gaps in the roof through which water has dripped and destroyed. One box is filled with shoes that I remember lined up on a shelf in her room, and I imagine Stella packing them away, her cheeks wet.

The song ends and I hit repeat.

A couple of the ruined boxes are of books. I make out what I can of the spines. Dickens, Hemingway, Woolf. She loved to read and would always buy me a book for my birthday. I try to prise a couple out, but they are stained with mould and the covers disintegrate at my touch.

I keep searching.

Finally, in a leather bag, I find a jewellery box covered in shells. It was a cheap souvenir she bought on that holiday to the Isle of Wight, when Sal lost Elephant. It's a small box with a fake tortoiseshell lid, and the sides are decorated with pink shells stuck on with clear blobs of glue.

I open the lid and swallow hard.

The box is filled with cheap costume jewellery. I don't want the real stuff, she said once. Too much of a worry. What if it got lost? But in one corner is a little compartment, made for a special something, and inside is the ring I bought for her thirtieth birthday. Silver-plated with a pasted red ruby and diamonds.

I turn it around in my fingers, feeling the smoothness of the metal against my skin. Now I recognise the style as Art Deco, but as a nine-year-old, I had just thought it a nice ring. I'd walked into the Argos store in town – the cash I'd saved from a summer of paper rounds folded neatly in my pocket – written the code number on to the paper slip and handed it to the cashier. I had felt so excited when they called my number and I collected the little box, and then Stella had taken me to Clinton's, where I chose a sheet of wrapping paper covered in tiny red hearts.

I zip the ring into my jacket pocket. I know just what to do with it.

After I've gone through every box, I stand in the middle and look about. The clothes and books are too damaged for a charity shop, and the furniture is thick with mould. I already have the photo albums. There is no sign of any papers or diary, and I know Dad would have taken those.

When the idea comes, I know it's exactly what I should do. I begin dragging the boxes outside to a small clearing away from the building, working quickly and without conscious thought. As I drop each box on the scrubby ground, I am hit by the smell and dust of thirty years of decay.

When the slaughterhouse is clear, I untwist the cap on the whisky bottle and shake what remains over the pile of my mother's belongings.

October 1990

Once when we were kids, Dad took Sal and me on a camping trip in the woods behind our house. This was instead of a holiday. He borrowed a tent from a golf friend and assembled all the required paraphernalia: camping stove, lantern, medical kit, tin kettle, sleeping bags, etc. It was to be a chance to teach us boys survival skills, and we were each given a compass and a penknife along with strict instructions on what we could bring. We were to collect water from a nearby stream, and during the day we would fish for our dinner in the lake that the stream fed into.

'Can I bring my Game Boy?' said Sal as we loaded our rucksacks on our backs. Stella had won a bit on the pools and bought one for his birthday.

'Don't be ridiculous,' said Dad, the enamel cups strapped to his rucksack clattering together.

'I won't play it all the time,' said Sal. 'Just when I'm bored.'

Dad ignored him. 'Here, take this.' He pushed the heavy metal lantern into Sal's skinny arms. 'Drop it and you'll be in trouble.'

Mum's involvement was kept to bringing sausages and bacon each morning for breakfast, as well as fresh milk for Dad's tea. We'd hear her humming as she walked through the woods, then she'd appear through the bracken, swinging a cool bag by her side. Sal would go running to her. She'd unload the food from the bag – the meat had been decanted into a metal tiffin box so Dad wouldn't comment on the jarring sight of plastic – then she'd pick up any empties and turn for home. 'Can't you stay?' Sal would beg. 'Just for breakfast?' She'd glance at Dad, who'd be stoking the fire or studying a map, then she'd kiss Sal's head and say, 'I've got to get back. Things to do. Have fun without me, boys.'

Then she'd be gone and it would just be us three again.

On this trip, Dad taught us to make fire.

We each had to find a softly curved sycamore branch and tie string to each end to make a bow. Then he showed us how to use the penknives to carve a socket and a fireboard to rub against the drill. After five minutes of twisting the bow against the drill, Sal began to complain.

'You have to wait,' Dad said to us both. 'There's no point blaming the fire. It's waiting to happen. It's down to your skill and your technique and you alone. If you've carved it right, if you've got enough friction, it will come. Cause and effect, remember? It just takes time.'

Sal gave up. He walked off to the stream to watch the fish.

After another fifteen minutes twisting the wood, mine began to smoke. 'Look! Look!' I shouted.

'You see,' Dad said. 'What did I tell you?' He slapped my back.

I don't know why Sal wasn't more into it. We both loved *Swiss Family Robinson* at the time, the scenes where they build the tree house and fight pirates. We'd play camps in the garden every day after school and pretend to hunt rabbits for supper. Sal was always the leader.

But that weekend, he sighed and huffed and whined that he was bored. And when he got ill from drinking water from the stream, the only thing to do was pack up early and go home.

Dad and I carried everything. Mum ran out and scooped up Sal when she saw us trudging up the garden, then tucked him in bed and stroked his hair as he puked into a bowl. Dad put the camping gear in the garage and went inside to read the weekend papers.

Nobody remembered that I'd made fire.

I stripped the plastic beads from one of Mum's cheap necklaces and used the twine for the bow. It was a necklace I'd never seen her wear, the kind Madonna used to wrap around her wrists. This felt okay, deliberately destroying something she owned, because I'd never seen her wear it. It was as if she'd never owned it at all.

I carved the tool with the penknife attached to my keys. Dad called it a Swiss Army knife. I suppose penknife does sound small and humble, whereas referencing the military would provide an opening for him to talk about his army days. When he felt part of something greater than us.

The lads once laughed at me for carrying one. Where do you think you are, they said, the bloody Jungle Book? They changed their tune when we found ourselves in a dinghy in the Lake District for Daz's birthday with bottles of beer and no opener. They loved the penknife then.

I've been twisting the bow for half an hour and my arms are in agony now. I hear his voice in my head, telling me to push through the pain; the fire is there and it is me that's not finding it, but my strength is beginning to fade.

For the past twenty-five years, I've had a lighter in my pocket, and this is the day I've needed it most.

Smoker's lungs, Anna had said that day at Dungeness when she'd passed me coughing on the stairs. Serves you right.

Wait, Anna.

I pull the wedge of cards from my tatty leather wallet and flick through until I find the book of matches. Pale grey with a red embossed stuffed cat on the cover. I tap the book against my leg and shake my head.

'Sorry, Dad,' I say aloud. 'Know when to quit.'

I stand in front of the pile of boxes, a crude effigy to my mother, and take out a match.

Do it, says Sal from somewhere inside and I remember when it was a rock in my hand, the day I smashed the window. Do it, Nick. Do it now.

It's a jolt out of the dark when I realise what life is. The mysterious, hidden, sheer beauty of it all. It blindsides me on a Thursday morning when I see an old man crossing the road, or teenagers kissing at a bus stop, or a pair of identical twins. It's the past and future in one. There's a moment of knowledge that passes as quickly as it comes, that I cannot grasp hold of, and for a brief spell, life is intoxicating.

She is not here, in this slaughterhouse, in this heap of dead things, just as she is not in the bottom of a bottle or alone in a graveyard. The answers aren't in the past, even the past of my own creation. I know that now.

I save the record and the jewellery box, and the ring inside my pocket.

Strike.

Flame.

Throw.

Boom.

Date: 15/8/2017

From: ANNA
To: NICK
Subject:

Remember those sunflowers outside your house, the ones you said were planted for your mum? The first time I saw them that July, they stopped me dead. Three glorious faces, golden, as tall as me, stretching up towards the sun. You told me your aunt Stella replants them every spring from the seeds of last year's flower. Life grows from death.

You walked straight by, key in hand, ready to lead upstairs. You saw those flowers so often that you didn't notice them any more. Isn't that funny? That when we are faced with life and beauty every day, we no longer pay any attention. No, funny's not the word. Tragic.

I drove by there this week and the patch of earth was bare. No sun-flowers. And I thought, his aunt Stella didn't plant them this year. Maybe Nick's dad said not to bother. Or perhaps Nick's dad doesn't live there any more. And I felt sad that I had no idea, that I no longer had a hold of the basic knowledge of your life.

This is a random email. Sorry. But I thought of you and how you no longer saw those flowers, and that maybe sometimes we need things to switch off for a while so that our eyes can open again.

The winter has its place.

As promised, Stella is outside the house. The boxes have been taken.

'How are you, love?' she says as I approach. 'Holding up okay?'

I squeeze her arm. 'Tea?'

'Why not?' she says as I unlock the door, but makes no move to take off her jacket. We walk through to the kitchen and she gives a sideways look at the rooms. 'Where is everything?'

'Gone,' I say. 'All gone.' And I look at her and smile.

As I make our tea, I tell her about the field, of the boxes and bags of things, of how I stood in front of the fire and watched it burn and left only when it had softened to ribbons of smoke. She sits quietly and listens, and her eyes fill with tears.

'Oh, Nick,' she says, holding her bag tight and still wearing her jacket.

I stir two sugars into her tea and set the cup down in front of her. She reaches across and adds another sugar.

'I found some letters,' she says, her voice breaking on the final word. 'In a box of your dad's things he kept under the bed. They were tucked into one of your mum's books.' She opens her bag and pulls out two crumpled envelopes and lays them on the table.

One says 'Nick' and the other, 'Sal'. I don't recognise the writing, and then I do and I'm a boy again. It's on the sick note in my pocket to give to the teacher, the self-addressed envelope coming back through the door.

Time seems to stretch as I stare at the letters, and there is a rush of blood to my head like when you get too quickly out of the bath. I reach out and slide the one with my name towards me.

'I haven't read them,' says Stella, a little breathless. 'But I've been wondering about the contents, and I think I should tell you what I know. In case it's that. Maybe you should know anyway.' She looks down at her hands. 'Maybe it would help.'

'What?' I go to open the envelope.

'No,' she says, and her hand shoots across the table to stop me. 'No, not now. That's for you and only you. And so is Sal's.'

'What do you know?' I just want her gone.

She covers her face with her hands for a moment and breathes deeply. 'When you were little, before Sal was born, your dad and mum would have these rows, blazing rows, that didn't end well. I was there once.' She shakes her head. 'Your dad moved out for a while. He couldn't cope with not being the centre of your mum's life any more. My brother always was a selfish man. You know that. And becoming a mother must change a woman. It has to. Giving up your body, giving up your days . . . They expect women to do it all and stay exactly the same.'

I stare at my name on the front of the letter.

'So he lived with a friend for several months, like bachelors, drinking and God knows what else. Your mum – they were living in a flat then, you know, in town – got friendly with someone in the building, some bloke who'd recently moved in. Divorced. He was nice enough, would offer to get things from the shop for your mum or fix a leaking tap. Your mum and him, well, I guess they fell in love.'

I look at her, my mouth open.

Stella sees my expression and rushes on. 'I don't mean Romeo and Juliet, Greek tragedy, run off into the sunset. I mean, your mum was lonely, stuck in that flat with a baby. She knew it would never amount to anything and she'd never properly leave your dad. But we all need some love and attention. That's just human. Then one day, your dad came back unannounced and found them together watching the telly. He went crazy. Started trashing the place. Punching the walls. The fella couldn't take it, he moved out the following week.'

'What about Mum?' I whisper.

She swallows hard. 'Your dad moved back in, and a couple of weeks later, your mum found she was pregnant with Sal.'

'You don't mean . . .' I shake my head. 'No.'

She looks out the window. 'All the while your dad was moved out, he and your mum were still, well, intimate together. She couldn't bring herself to say no to him, if there was a chance he'd come back.'

My insides are churning and I feel like I'm going to be sick. 'Did they ever find out for sure?' I say. 'Take a test?'

'I asked your mum once, but she wouldn't discuss it. I always wondered, though, if that's why she gave him an Italian name. To remove any doubt.' She sips her tea. 'Who knows why we do the things we do?'

Scenes from childhood run through my mind and I can feel the anger between Sal and Dad in the hairs standing up on my arm. The blame. I remember Sal crying in his sleep after it happened, sobbing for someone who never came, and then Dad appears on a French sun lounger, cradling Mum's body and screaming.

I put my head in my hands.

She leans forward. 'I'm telling you this because I'm worried what might be in those letters. I think you can handle it, though. Sal, I'm not sure. He was always the more delicate, deep down.' She pushes Sal's letter towards me. 'We expect our parents to always be what we need them to be. We forget they are human too.'

I pick up the other letter. 'Sal should have known all this,' I say. 'It could have changed something.'

'Perhaps. Or not. We do what we think is best.'

'What about me?' I say, looking at her. 'What do I do?'

Stella stands, puts her bag over her arm and walks round the table. 'I have carried this in my heart for almost forty years,' she says, kissing my head. 'It's time to open up.'

My Nick

Happy third birthday!

I have decided to write you a letter every year from now. Another year older, another year wiser, for both you and me. I cannot believe you are three already. It seems like yesterday I held you in my arms while your dad wheeled us up to the hospital ward. Every bump of that wheelchair was agony, but I didn't care because your tiny hand gripped my finger.

The past year has been a whirlwind. You adore your brother and this makes me so happy to see. I hope you will grow up to be the best of friends. My little Nick, promise you'll always look out for him. I can tell already that you're going to be the strong one. Capable. You give the softest kisses and instead of his name, you call him 'Va-va', which I think is you saying 'brother'. I love that you have your own word for him.

My boy. My heart hurts when I think of how much I love you, and how I want to tell it to you every day. I hope you grow up feeling loved and happy, and I hope you become a man who gives it back. I will do my best to show you how.

I am writing this in the park, as you kick a football and your brother sleeps in his pram. He is starting to stir and now you are hungry, so I will finish up here until next year.

My sweetest boy.
Your mama. X

My little Salvatore,

Happy first birthday!

I get to start at the very beginning with you. Poor Nick won't have a letter for his first two years because I didn't have the idea until now, but never mind. I hope to give you both a stack of envelopes when you become men. The days are going so quickly that these letters can be a sort of diary for us both.

You are my daredevil. You are cheeky and mischievous and always happy. I'm not sure I've ever seen you without a smile – even when you cry, all I do is pull a face and you are laughing through your tears. You love to touch things you shouldn't – the lamp, the plant, anything you can pull over. You turn and give me a smile when I say no, like it's all the more fun when it's forbidden. I fear what this says about Sal the man!

Oh my Sal. You test me like no other. When you climb on to the back of the sofa, or scramble up the rocks in the garden, I want to rescue you quickly before you hurt yourself, but I know I have to let you fall. That's the only way you will learn to get back up again. Don't ever let it beat you.

I think, in a way, you love the feel of the fall.

Embrace life like this. Surrender yourself to the feeling. You can't see these words I am writing in black ink without the white paper beneath it. And so you can never know true happiness without also knowing the pain. You have to have both, my sweet. Find a way to marry the two.

My sunshine boy.
Your mama. X

I start at The Phoenix. It's a Sunday and quiet. I sit at the bar and order a whisky, and the first taste is cold and then hot and prickly as it swills across my tongue. It hits hard in the pit of my stomach. I want the burn.

The next sip I hold in my mouth. The tingle feels like dancing and I have a sudden urge to laugh, loud and uncontrollably. But instead I drain the glass and feel it bloom in the back of my chest.

Drinking alone is pathetic. I consider phoning Daz, but when I finally make out the clock on my phone, I realise he'll be sleeping after his night shift. Besides, he is still cut up about Gemma, and for once, I want the attention.

From there, I stumble round the corner to the place with the saw-dust and craft beer. I think I see someone I know on the way – they give a sort of wave and then look me up and down as they pass me – but it's hard to tell. I make it through the door and at the bar I order straight-up scotch and a margherita pizza. The girl behind the counter gives me a suspicious look, but goes ahead and takes my money.

I buy a bottle of whisky from the off-licence on the way home and tuck it under my arm. I wonder what happens if you drink the whole thing.

In the kitchen, I pour enough dried food into the cat bowl so it overflows, and she pushes against my leg and purrs with love. I unscrew the cap on the bottle and watch the whisky spew into the glass. My mind is still sober enough not to want the neighbours see-ing me drink from the bottle.

When I step out on to the patio for a vape, the smell of jasmine hits me like a punch in the heart.

On my phone, I bring up her number.

I wish I were better for you, I type. *I am tired of the pain.*

The freshly planted pots still stand on the patio table, along with a half-used bag of compost. I pull out a chair and fall into it.

There is a long purr and the cat wanders through the door to join me. She walks in that long, languid way that cats do. I stroke her for a while, making her happy, and then she settles down on a large flagstone that's been soaking up heat. She rolls back and forth, side to side, stretching her limbs and throwing glances to check I am watching. *So I have you*, I think. *You won't leave*. And then I notice for the first time in the sunlight, bold and bright and real, that her black fur is dark brown.

I bring the glass to my mouth and look at the liquid swirling against the side. I look through it, at the base of the glass, at the backwards writing, and I look through that too. I think of life as a maze and how we are trying to find our way through, to a world that's apparently waiting if we go down the right path, but you don't know it's right until you take a wrong turn and then have to feel your way out. You try the next and the next and the next. But what if you know you'll never get out.

Things like this come when I'm looking through the bottom of a glass. The words make perfect sense.

Perhaps that's why she gave him an Italian name. To remove any doubt.

My Nick, promise you'll always look out for him.

He brought the box out because of me.

I have always been responsible.

And then someone is shouting.

They are screaming in my ear.

Something presses cold against my cheek and I turn my head so the other feels it too. A long groan, deep and ravenous, the sound of the monster under the bed. It takes a moment to realise it's me. This must be what happens when you drink yourself into oblivion, a separation of your body from its senses, or at least a near-total drubbing of the connections in between. How wonderful it is not to feel anything.

My body is lifting up and, for a blissful moment, I think I am going to heaven. I try to open my eyes and everything is white. This is it, I say to myself. So it was true after all.

Something hard hits my elbow and chin, more moaning, more

yelling in my ear. There is a strange echo, as if I am encased in something. I half open my eyes but all I see is white.

I hear the rushing of water and remember how I once read about the waters of life extending out of heaven, and it is so real that I feel the spray on my skin. And then the water is harder and colder, and it soaks through my clothes. Instinct kicks in and I thrash my arms and legs and whatever surrounds me is slippery to the touch. It feels comforting against the side of my face.

The voice is still shouting. It has a familiar sound. Wake up, it says, and someone slaps my cheek.

As my sight clears, I realise I am sprawled in the bath with the showerhead pointed straight at my face. The water feels cold. A sobering baptism.

Standing over me is a woman with black hair and an upset face. She has tears in her eyes. Anna. It is Anna. I've never seen her like this before, or at least not over me. I reach out to see if my fingers will pass through her.

She bats my hand away. 'Wake up!'

'I'm awake,' I say, my cheek still stinging from the slap. Feeling is returning to my brain, the synapses limbering up from their slumber. I cover my face with my hands. 'Can you shut the water off?'

'Oh, sorry,' she says and turns the tap.

I wipe the water from my face and lean my head back against the bath, as if I am using it in its proper context, not fully clothed and empty. I look up at Anna, who stands over me, one hand on her hip as she chews a finger on the other. There is something in her expression that I cannot place.

'What the hell are you doing?' she says, gesturing at the state of me.

'Hello to you, too.'

'No,' she says, shaking her head. 'Don't try to be funny. Look at you.'

I sigh. 'I know.'

'There's a half-drunk bottle of whisky on your dining table. Was your plan to drown yourself?'

I try to piece together the day. 'Where did you find me?'

'Here, like this.' She lets her arms fall loose over the edge of the bath and crosses her eyes. I start to laugh, but then she says, 'I thought you were dead, Nick. Dead. Christ.' She covers her eyes as if to erase the memory.

I glance at the empty bathroom shelves. 'It's not been the best month,' I say.

Anna takes her hands away. 'Yeah, I heard.'

We have just enough mutual friends to make this likely, and I nod as if I am okay with the knowledge that she knew and never got in touch. 'How did you get in?'

'You didn't answer the door so I ran round the back. Did you know there's a hole in the back of your fence? It stole a piece of my skin.' She pulls up her top to reveal a thick bloodied scratch on the side of her waist.

I instinctively reach out to touch the wound, and have an urge to kiss better the layers of pink flesh. 'I was meant to fix that years ago.'

Anna presses my fingers against her skin. When she pulls away, her T-shirt falls and I see a red stain on the white cotton where the blood has seeped through.

'How did you know?' I say. 'From my message. How did you know to come?'

She looks down at her hands. 'Sal, remember?'

I feel in my pocket for the ring from the jewellery box. The smoothness of the metal slips over my finger as I pull it out and turn it over in my hand. 'I didn't mean for this to happen,' I say, looking at the ring. 'I was coming to find you, to give you this. It was my mother's. But . . .'

She waits.

'You found me first.'

I repeat the story from Stella then nod at the letters dropped on the floor. She picks them up. Her eyes drink the words written by the first woman I loved. Mum's rushed and inky scrawl has bled through the pages, leaving a light pattern of dashes on the back.

'I've not heard her voice in nearly thirty years,' I say, swallowing. 'I'd forgotten how it sounded.'

Anna stares at the letters. 'This would break me too.'

I draw up my legs and fold my arms across my body. The warmth of the whisky has faded and I suddenly feel very cold. 'Why does everyone leave me?'

Anna is very still. She stares at my feet. I know she is thinking of what to say, of which words will act like a balm. The silence grows heavy between us, and I want to cover my eyes again with my hands, but then she leans down and kisses my forehead. 'That feels very motherly,' she says, and bends lower to kiss next to my mouth. 'Ex-lovers get cheeks.'

Our eyes meet and we stare at each other for a brief moment. 'It's never been the right time for us,' I say, catching her wrist as she holds my face.

Anna strokes my cheek and looks at my mouth. 'When is the right time?' she says. 'I grew up thinking I would never die. Any day, any day now, Armageddon would come and I'd pass through into Paradise. It was like a dream at times, foggy and abstract, but I believed it all the same. I would never die. It must sound so stupid.'

'No,' I say. 'You believe what you're told.'

'But what it does, living like that, it removes any urgency for your own life. You're always living for another world, another life, and it means you never quite take hold of what you have right now.' Anna stops and looks at me. 'We're not so different after all.'

The light outside has faded. The mottled glass on the bathroom window is a pale shade of grey. 'Where do we go from here?' I say.

She climbs into the bath with me, and I move my legs to let her in. We sit at each end, facing each other, except I am soaked through to my skin.

'I know now I'm going to die,' she says from the other end of the tub. 'It feels like I've been given another chance and I don't have years to waste, because nothing lasts forever. This is my time.' She looks at me. 'This is our time.'

'I remember trying to get you to question your life, all those years ago, and now you've found your strength. It's beautiful to see.'

She smiles. 'I was told I'd only find true love within my bubble, that the world would always hurt me. It's not that I now think it won't. It's that I'm ready to risk it.'

I swallow hard. 'What if I loved you, though. What if I think about you in my worst times, and in my best times, and in all the rest of the times too? What if the reason I haven't once cried for my dad and brother is because I'd also be crying for something else, and then I'd hate myself even more? What if all of that?'

She is silent for a moment. She looks at where our legs are touching, where our bodies have no choice but to meet, confined within the cheap acrylic tub. 'You've known the very worst of things,' she says. 'Maybe that can be your superpower. What is there left to fear?'

'What if I never get back up again?'

There is a light drip from the bath tap. Anna puts a finger to the spout and the water trickles over her hand and down her wrist.

'I know you like making everything safe, but they don't call it falling in love for nothing,' she says. 'You have to give up control. Take a leap and see where you land. The past can't hurt us any more, Nick.'

The inevitable pressure of several drams of whisky starts to beat against my skull. 'You know I fucking love you,' I say.

Anna smiles. 'I know. I've just been waiting for you to say it.' She takes the ring. 'Before I put this on,' she says, 'I need to know if we're on the same page.'

I reach out and slide the ring down her finger. It fits. 'Let's jump together.'

She closes her hand around mine.

I crawl to her and put one hand behind her head, burying my fingers in her black hair. I long for its darkness around my face again.

'Wait,' says Anna, taking my hand. 'I don't want to fix you, Nick. I don't want to complete you or us to take ownership of each other. I don't want to wave you off in the morning with a packed lunch, or iron your shirts, or pretend to like your shitty music. I want to be free just to love you, as you are, as I am. And remember it's not just me you'd be taking on. There's also a boy who'll soon be a man.' She touches my lips with her fingers. 'If that's not okay, then go ahead and kiss my cheek and I'll be on my way.'

Anna is so close to me now.

Can people really start again?

I push myself forward

         her lips taste of cherries

Mid-Eighties

It is perhaps my fourth summer.

The air is warm and sweet. I am sitting on the grass, the Victorian rectory looming up on one side. Sal kicks away on a blanket, the wool with the Scottish check that itches my skin when I touch it. Perhaps that is why Sal kicks so hard.

Mum comes through the French doors on to the veranda, holding a tray up high so she doesn't trip. I can see the top of one of the sundae glasses, the ones with the fluted edge that Mum calls 'very precious'. She says this about everything that can break. When she sets the tray down on the ground, I see she's filled the glass with three perfect scoops of ice cream: pink, yellow and brown.

Neapolitan, she calls it. I try to repeat the word and she laughs and sounds it out.

Ne-a-pol-i-t'n.

She smiles when I say it again. Here, she says, and she hands me the silver spoon with the long handle.

I try the yellow first. It tastes like sunshine, and I let it melt on my tongue while Mum tickles Sal. She kisses his toes one by one, then moves up the inside of his bare leg until she gets to his nappy, where she pretends to chomp on his flesh. He is going out of his mind.

I wear a daisy chain on my wrist that Mum made while Sal napped inside. It was my job to gather the best daisies from the lawn, and then she lay on the grass beside me and pierced the stalks with her fingernail before threading them through.

When she finished, she took my wrist and passed it gently through the loop, then went inside to fetch Sal. It is rarely just the two of us any more. I waited and kept my wrist outstretched. I'm going to keep this forever, I said to myself while she was gone. It's precious and I can't let it break.

As I eat the sundae, she sits cross-legged in a thin summer dress and drinks what looks like orange juice from a tumbler. The ice cubes chink against the glass and she closes her eyes after every sip. I ask if I can have some, but she says it's just for grown-ups. I didn't know they made an orange juice just for grown-ups.

Eat up, she says. Dad will be home soon.

My hand flies to my mouth and I wipe my lips with the back of my wrist, hiding the evidence of my good time. I look down at my clothes and the way I am sitting, in case there is anything about me he wouldn't like.

Shall we have some music?

I nod, and she starts to stand but knocks over her glass. She says something then spins round and does the wagging finger. Don't ever say that word, she says. It was naughty of me. Forget it now. And don't for God's sake tell your dad I said it, will you?

I shrug and she goes inside with her empty glass.

Fuck, I say in my head.

Fuck fuck fuck fuck fuck fuck fuck fuuuuuuuuck.

I'll never forget it now.

Mum returns with a full glass and the portable record player. She pops the clasp and lifts the lid, and a moment later, her favourite song starts to play.

She begins to dance.

Look at this! My beautiful family on a beautiful day!

Mum puts a hand to her heart in shock.

Dad has come through the side gate and is leaning against the wall, watching us. His sleeves are rolled up and his cap pushed back on his head, spilling out black curls. He's happy. He's in a good mood.

I clap my hands.

Dad jogs over and kisses Mum's cheek. He throws down his paper and drops to his knees in front of Sal, who is crawling around on the blanket and unsure of the grass. Sal laughs when he sees him, and he leans against Dad's shoulder as he clambers to his feet and pulls his hair. Dad puts on a hurt look and kisses Sal's cheek.

Shall I make you a drink? asks Mum.

It can wait, he says, pulling her close. Come here.

Dad! I say. Do the dinosaur!

Dad smiles as he stands. He walks away a few feet and turns his back to us, kicking off his shoes, getting into character. He throws down his cap and ruffles his own hair. He's quiet, lulling us into a false sense of security, and then he jumps around, his hands and feet out like claws, a contorted face yelling ROOOOOAAAAAR-RRR like an extremely realistic T-Rex.

I scream with delight.

Sal just screams.

Dad picks him up to comfort him, but this just makes it worse.

Let's have the song again, says Mum, moving the needle back to the beginning. She takes Sal from Dad and he buries his face in her hair.

Dad picks daisies from the grass and tucks them behind her ears. You can't dance to this without flowers in your hair, he says, and she looks away and smiles.

Dance with me, Paul.

Dad falls down next to me and props himself up on his elbows. He takes hold of my wrist and raises an eyebrow, but then drops my hand and turns back to Mum.

I look at the daisy chain hanging limply against my skin. I must have crushed it in all the excitement.

Look at your mother, says Dad, loud enough for her to hear. Isn't she something? He gives a perfect wolf whistle.

Mum says nothing but I watch her face turn pink. She kisses Sal's curls and balances him on her hip as she begins to dance. Her bare feet twist on the lawn and she twirls her hand through the air. As the music builds to its crescendo, Mum starts to spin Sal round and I look up to see if he is laughing, but the sun is shining behind them and I can no longer see.

2020

We are here, in the field, with the sun on our faces.

This week we got word that they would be open to the idea of the slaughterhouse being converted. But the walls must remain intact, they said. *We would not be opposed to a sympathetic conversion with an extension of modern architectural merit . . . a merging of old and new.* We'd already said we had no intention of pulling it down.

Anna stands to the side of the building, working out the footprint. She asks me to hold the end of a tape measure while she walks off at varying angles and scribbles numbers on a notepad. I let go of the end and it hisses as it sucks back into the metal case.

Joe is standing where a fire once roared. The patch of ground is grey and parched, thirsting for new life, and he jumps on the cracked white earth. Can this be my room? he says to his mum, and she smiles and looks at me. Please? It will be warm because I think this is where there was a great fire. The greatest fire the world has ever known.

You'll have to ask Nick, she says. It's his house too.

Please, Nick?

I walk over and we high-five. It can be wherever you like, I say. In fact, we'll build the rest of the house around your room. Yours will be the first room we decide on.

His smile. Hers too. I slide my arm around her waist.

Isn't it something when you feel life greater than you ever hoped for rushing through your veins? When love comes looking.

This boy, whose blood is not mine, and his mother, whose is.

Nothing lasts forever. This is not a drill.

Author's Note

To write the character of Anna, I drew partly on my own experience of growing up as a Jehovah's Witness. The religion is not named in the novel – although a Witness will likely recognise the depiction – because it was never my intention for the book to be about dogma. It merely serves as the wedge between two people falling in love.

Saying that, I *was* drawn to the idea of giving shade to a character in a doomsday religion. Most people's idea of Jehovah's Witnesses are of a strange, cloistered group who interrupt Saturday mornings by knocking on doors, or who don't celebrate birthdays and allow their children to die rather than accept certain medical treatment. Witnesses believe they are famous for preaching the good news, but arguably they are known primarily for the more extreme aspects of the religion. When I would tell *worldly people* that I was a Jehovah's Witness, the reaction was usually one of disbelief, as if it were impossible for them to reconcile the reality of regular old me with their preconceived notion of (what they assumed to be) an extremist cult member. This disconnect always fascinated me. In Anna, I wanted to sketch a person who is complicated and made up of flaws and good intentions, just as all people are. Indeed, just as Jehovah's Witnesses are. I wanted to take away the 'weirdness', the idea of them being *the other*. Scratch away the surface of upbringing, world-view and circumstance, and we are all the same underneath.

I mean no disrespect to the religion itself or those of my family who are still in the faith. It can be a wonderful way of life, with a strong sense of community and belonging, but sadly this does depend on its members being content to ignore any doubts, as well as accepting that any love they receive is conditional on remaining in the religion. I was not able to pay that price. The widespread cover-up of child sexual abuse within the organisation – unknown to the majority of its members due to the blanket distrust of anything from the outside world – the inability of its leaders to apologise for their handling of the matter, not to mention the subsequent shunning of victims who inevitably leave due to the ongoing trauma of seeing their abuser escape justice – all these overwhelmed my conscience. However, I respect the feelings and experiences of my family who are still active members of the faith, and I hope they can likewise respect mine.

This is Nick and Anna's story, and Sal's too. As my editor Jill said during our first conversation, it is not just a love story, but a story about love.

There is always room for love.

Acknowledgements

They say it takes a village to raise a child, but it can be equally said of publishing a book.

To my agent Madeleine Milburn, thank you for plucking *Another Life* from the slush pile and seeing its potential. I'm hugely grateful to you and everyone at MMLA, especially Liane-Louise Smith, Georgina Simmonds, Georgia McVeigh, Rachel Yeoh and Anna Hogarty. You are all responsible for me dropping my phone on several occasions.

To Jillian Taylor. From the moment I read your first letter after reading this book, I knew you would be the perfect editor. And you have been. Sharp and precise, encouraging, always cheerful, and a constant champion of Nick, Anna and Sal, not to mention of me as a writer. Thank you. I feel so lucky to have you polishing my words to make them sing.

Thanks to everyone at Penguin Michael Joseph who played a part in bringing this novel to life: Jill, Emma Henderson, Sarah Bance, Lauren Wakefield, Claire Bush, Grace Long, Ellie Hughes and Ella Watkins to name a few. You have fielded my questions without an ounce of impatience.

To my first readers – Sarah Barnett (sister extraordinaire), Ella Berman, Clare McVey, Katie Tether, Greg – thank you for your observant eyes. You all loved different things and identified the (same) parts that needed work. The book is stronger for it.

Thanks to my brother John for his expert knowledge of Manhattan real estate and to Owen Nicholls for double-checking the cinema projection lingo when my own memory failed me. Also thanks to my brother Dan for proof-reading the golf scene. You'd think the sport would be hard-wired into my brain with it being the TV soundtrack to my early years, but thankfully all I retain is our collective love for Seve Ballesteros.

To Mum and Dad, who may hate this book. Thanks for practising a sort of benign neglect that allowed me to spend my childhood wrapped up in movies and books, absorbing story structure and being left to my own devices. My imagination could take flight and this is the result.

To friends and family who stuck by me when I had no choice but to confront my doubts, and to the new friends I have gained. You have no idea how much I appreciate you. (And to those who have edged away . . . Despite the fallout convincing me more each day that I made the right decision, I still have nothing but love for you in my heart. My door is always open.)

Thank you to Mr Smith and Mrs Cowley, my English teachers at Highworth. You read my words aloud in class and made me feel a million bucks. To my other teachers, whose lessons I found dull and rarely handed in homework for, and who used to say I would fail in life . . . Sorry to disappoint you. Your textbooks were the first to meet the bin. Even at fifteen, I was enough of a precocious brat to know life is too short to spend on things that don't bring joy.

Finally, thanks to Greg for your love and friendship, and to Roman, Remy and Val. The unconditional love I feel for you is what led me to unravel my life, and now I am stitching it up in new and brighter colours. This one's for you, boys.

Loved *Another Life*?

You don't have to
wait long for more from
JODIE CHAPMAN

Read on for an
extract from

OH, SISTER

Coming 2023

Half a Heart

Zelda

'Has someone come with you for support today?'

Zelda doesn't hear the question. She is distracted by a shaft of light coming through the window that shines a perfect square on the blue rubber floor. Dust dances in the stale office air.

The nurse looks up from her clipboard. 'Is there someone waiting outside? A friend, a family member?'

'No,' Zelda says, folding her arms. 'That's okay, right? I'm only seven weeks, so thought I could just pop the pill and go.'

The nurse smiles, flicking the biro between her fingers. 'So I'm assuming the answer to the question of whether this is your first termination is "no"?'

She says it kindly, and Zelda wants to laugh. She remembers this woman from the last time, and, when she walked in and saw a familiar face, she felt a twinge of comfort. But the nurse has no memory of her. Zelda wonders how many women with electric-red hair dressed in men's clothes come to the clinic and whether she is really that easy to forget.

'Third time a charm,' says Zelda.

The nurse writes on the clipboard, her face free of judgement. She wears half a heart on a chain around her neck, and Zelda remembers her own, which her friend Leila gave to her at the turn of the millennium, soon after they left school. Zelda wonders who possesses the other half of the nurse's heart. She can hardly remember Leila now.

Outside, there is early-morning traffic, the sound of a truck reversing, people chatting in the street. The trees that line the pavement have yet to bloom, but the buds are there, waiting. Zelda lets the door swing shut and pauses to light a cigarette. She pulls up her jacket collar against the breeze as she leans against a wall to smoke. A nearby radio talks of an impending snowstorm. *The Beast from the East.* Zelda turns her face towards the sun.

The pills are tucked into her pocket to take when she gets home. She hopes she still has enough whisky left to help knock them back. The cramps feel better when the edges are fuzzy, whatever the nurses say.

A passing woman gives her a filthy look. Maybe it's the cigarette, or the abortion-clinic backdrop. Zelda stares the woman out.

The sweet scent of cinnamon hangs in the air as she starts down the street. The reason for her heightened sense of smell does not escape her, and she decides to buy the thickest, flakiest pastry in an attempt to forget that, right now, her body is not entirely her own. She can hardly remember a time when it was.

Zelda is taking a bite when she turns the corner and sees them. She stops. There they are, up ahead, a trolley stand of brochures on the pavement, two women standing nearby with regulation smiles and knee-length skirts. She doesn't recognize them – she usually goes to a clinic in a different town – but they look like all the others. The banner on the trolley screams LIFE WITHOUT END – WHEN?

She starts to choke and steps back around the corner, pressing herself to the wall. She is too dizzy to notice her velvet jacket snagging on the brickwork.

A nearby alley gives shelter. Zelda has an overwhelming urge to be sick, and so she is, all down the side of a bright blue dumpster. Her vomit seeps on to the ground.

'Fuck's sake,' she says to the floor. 'All these years on and you still let them get to you.'

Blank Page

Jen

Jen dashes into the department store to escape the driving rain. Running is beyond her. She forgot to say goodbye to her feet before they disappeared, before new parts of her took over. Her cheeks, her thighs, her chest, her stomach. All blooming with water and life.

She picks up a leaflet to fan her face. Winter is cold inside the store, but sweat still creeps from her pores. She strips her layers as she walks to the back.

She has spent hours here. Wandering between aisles of cots and baths, and clothing that looks miniature. The volume of paraphernalia is overwhelming. Pete nearly gave up after an hour spent trying to collapse the buggy. What clichés we are, Jen had thought as she watched him. He loses his temper with inanimate objects, and I just want someone to massage my feet.

Jen often lingers, waiting for another mum-to-be. She pretends to smell lotions as she studies the women who look and move just like her. How they rest their hand on their stomach. How Breton stripes stretch over skin. She feels a kinship with these women. All her friends have had their babies, and have forgotten the feel of Braxton Hicks, the acidic twinge of midnight heartburn, how it feels to climb into bed with thighs and torso slick with oil. Here, in these aisles, the women are living the same things as her.

She waits a while, and eventually two young women turn down the aisle in her direction, holding hands and stopping every now and again to pick something up. A pot, a picture frame, a pair of nail scissors. Jen tries not to watch. But she cannot look away from their hands, the way their fingers tangle. The sight is equal parts foreign and familiar.

They give her a brief glance as they pass. Blonde and brunette.

Jen tries to get a look at their stomachs, but the blonde wears a loose dress and the brunette's oversized denim jacket is done up. She cannot work out which is the mother, if indeed either is, and she frowns. Make it obvious, she thinks. I want to know. But their stomachs give no clue, and neither do their faces. She cannot tell if their cheeks are fuller than normal, because she doesn't know what their normal is.

Jen follows them as they move out of the aisle. They walk down the middle towards the door, before stopping by Make-up to embrace. The blonde kisses the brunette. It is a goodbye kiss. Anyone can tell. She strokes her girlfriend's cheek, whispers, then walks out. The brunette watches her go, and, after a long moment, she climbs the stairs to the café.

The queue at the till takes forever. Jen taps her feet. She gives her armpits a discreet sniff then steals quick sprays of bottled scent. When she has paid, she finds her feet moving towards the stairs and taking them two at a time. So much for not being able to run. She pauses at the top, fighting for breath, feeling the writhing weight inside.

'Are you okay, dear?' an old lady asks, touching her shoulder.

Jen nods, putting her energy into convincing the woman she is fine. She pulls away with a sweet smile and goes towards the café.

The brunette sits in the corner with a full cup of coffee. She looks out of the window, and Jen stares as she waits in line. The woman is a little younger than her, late twenties perhaps. Dark curls frame her face, and she looks lost as she stares out across the street.

Jen sets down her tray on the adjacent table. Sitting down, she takes out a pen and the baby journal she bought. The brunette looks at her briefly, then sighs and turns away.

Jen takes her time with her herbal tea, stirring the bag in the pot, drawing comfort from the steam. Nothing like a hot drink, she thinks, and is reminded of her mother.

She spills the first sip on her stomach. Her sigh catches the attention of the woman, who looks down at Jen's bump and smiles. 'Oops.'

'You'd think I'd have learnt,' says Jen. 'The number of tops I've ruined. I'm too far away from the cup.'

The woman smiles again but with sadness. She turns away, and in this moment, Jen wants nothing more than to know her story. 'Not long until I can have caffeine again,' Jen says, pointing to the coffee.

The woman gives a polite nod. 'Any day now?'

'Ten weeks. I can't wait to meet him.'

'Congratulations.'

Jen touches her belly in response, and the woman glances at the rhythm of her strokes. She watches Jen's hand for a moment, then her eyes drift up to Jen's face. Oh, Jen thinks. There is a stab of recognition, perhaps even yearning, in the woman's face, and Jen wonders if it's also in her own. All she knows for sure is blushing skin.

'I have to go,' says the brunette, rising.

'But your coffee?' Jen feels a rising panic, not wanting her to leave.

The woman looks down at the untouched cup, as if surprised by its presence. 'Never mind,' she says. 'I didn't want it anyway.'

Jen opens her mouth, but no words come out. Instead, she gulps her tea and watches the woman move away. When she disappears completely, Jen sighs and turns to the first page of the journal. *Final Days of Pregnancy*.

She looks towards the staircase, then down at the blank page.

Newer Model

Isobel

26th March

Took the car for its first MOT. It passed (obviously) but perhaps now is the time to trade it in for a newer model. Spoke to Steven about going to the forecourt at the weekend, but he didn't reply. In strange mood so I made his favourite chicken pie. Tried ordering groceries online, but the red peppers they delivered were green! Never again. Sunny and warm today.

27th March

Toni came for coffee. She didn't comment on the new sofa, even though I saw her eyeing it. Her new haircut is much too short – she looks like a springer spaniel. I'm glad I don't have curly hair, as it always looks so manic. Must be hell for upkeep. Went to the meeting. Cloudy and cool.

28th March

Spoke to Patrick and tried Cassandra, but no answer as usual. More time for her friends than her own mother. The trees we planted still look small and sickly. It must be several years now. Steven says the soil is likely full of rubble left from the original build. I said we should have it excavated and returfed, but he isn't keen. I suppose the lawn itself is fine. Doesn't so much matter what's underneath. Steven took the youngsters from the congregation bowling. More cloud.

29th March

Booked night away for our anniversary in October. Haven't told Steven. Tried a new cookbook that Jude recommended, and the recipe called for ten spices! Honestly, the carrots tasted *foreign*. I wonder if she cooks it for Patrick. He liked his food plain as a child. Can't imagine he's changed that much. Warm today.

30th March

Steven left. Rain.

He just wanted a decent book to read ...

Not too much to ask, is it? It was in 1935 when Allen Lane, Managing Director of Bodley Head Publishers, stood on a platform at Exeter railway station looking for something good to read on his journey back to London. His choice was limited to popular magazines and poor-quality paperbacks – the same choice faced every day by the vast majority of readers, few of whom could afford hardbacks. Lane's disappointment and subsequent anger at the range of books generally available led him to found a company – and change the world.

'We believed in the existence in this country of a vast reading public for intelligent books at a low price, and staked everything on it'
Sir Allen Lane, 1902–1970, founder of Penguin Books

The quality paperback had arrived – and not just in bookshops. Lane was adamant that his Penguins should appear in chain stores and tobacconists, and should cost no more than a packet of cigarettes.

Reading habits (and cigarette prices) have changed since 1935, but Penguin still believes in publishing the best books for everybody to enjoy. We still believe that good design costs no more than bad design, and we still believe that quality books published passionately and responsibly make the world a better place.

So wherever you see the little bird – whether it's on a piece of prize-winning literary fiction or a celebrity autobiography, political tour de force or historical masterpiece, a serial-killer thriller, reference book, world classic or a piece of pure escapism – you can bet that it represents the very best that the genre has to offer.

Whatever you like to read – trust Penguin.